To K̶ı
Kris

# Roper's End

# Kris Beckett

# Roper's End

*Roper's End*
Kris Beckett

Published by Aspect Design, 2024

Designed by Aspect Design
89 Newtown Road, Malvern, Worcs. WR14 1PD
United Kingdom
Tel: 01684 561567
E-mail: allan@aspect-design.net
Website: www.aspect-design.net

ISBN 978-1-916919-08-2

*For my lovely helpful readers,*
*Heather, Jayne and Jo – with thanks.*

# Chapter One

When the bomb exploded, Simon Garraway lost an eye, plus the major part of the left side of his face. His plastered arm hung like a concrete-filled sock beside him in the hospital bed, and his left leg was rendered useless, the foot devoid of skin and missing two toes, owing to the leather of his shoe having been cut away, leaving the toes inside.

After three weeks in an induced coma, Simon managed, with effort, to open his remaining eye, which was attempting to identify the shiny white walls of the room which were not that of his bedroom. The eye opened wider as it stared in astonishment at the strange paraphernalia surrounding his bed – until he was forced to close it again owing to a sudden flash of light, which hurt the back of his head. He was confused. Why was he here and not in his own house? And what were all these contraptions bleeping and blinking and strapped to his bed?

He had his answer when he tried to move, suddenly gasping at the pain which shrieked from his hip all the way down to his foot. And there was something wrong with mouth; it was dry and hot and it hurt. There was a muffled noise from somewhere in his head – an organ, deep and low, playing the same monotonous dirge over and over. Why would there be an organ? He'd never owned an organ. And why, he asked himself, was he unable to shift more than a millimetre without a searing purgatorial assault on every part of his body?

Attempting to focus his eye on the shadowy figure sitting beside the bed, he finally recognised his wife. He then thought better of it and closed it again.

Trying to come to grips with where he was and of what had caused him to be in this stark white room was proving too much for him, having expended all his energy on opening the eye. He decided to think about this some time later. After a while, he tried again with the eye, which winced at the glare of the coruscating beam of light bearing down on him, causing him to squeak out a cry, before realising it to be the sun shining through the ceiling-to-floor windows. That flash of light, however, caused a sudden cold sweat to run through him, forcing into his brain a half-remembered moment – a terrifying moment – a moment which needed serious concentration. What was it that that flash of light disturbed in him? He needed to think. In order to do that, he had to close his eye: one thing at a time . . .

Slowly and painfully, what came back to him in short sharp fragments, one second touching the brink of cognition, the next, fluttering away again into the shadows of his mind, was the smile of that pretty girl – the post-woman. Then what? Yes . . . the package in her hand . . . Then the flash . . . The pieces began gradually to fit together and, what he'd first thought was perhaps a bad dream, was taking on a reality he didn't wish to think about.

But then, it could have been dream – because if *was* real . . .

The face of the postwoman flickered in and out of his memory, and his eye twitched violently at the thought of her – of what may have happened to her. This caused his heartbeat to quicken and he became agitated; he had to ask about her and tell somebody what she had told him. It was vital that he tell somebody – anybody.

Fragmented memories of that morning skipped wildly from brain cell to brain cell, then veered away as quickly as it came. He had to keep reminding himself that this wasn't a dream, and to tell himself how important it was to let somebody know. Otherwise they would think . . . What would they think? Vital though it was, every time he attempted to focus, the fear took hold once more and he felt weak. Opening his mouth to speak to his wife – the doctors – the authorities – to inform them all of what he thought he knew – *knew* he knew – he drew in a breath, then gasped, his a throat a burning torch. At which point, he realised, talking might be more difficult than first thought.

But he had to try . . .

Clutching the air and desperate to speak, he once more opened his mouth and wheezed out a fretful grunt, which was the best he could do, but he had that sodding organ to deal with, which was still getting in the way of his thoughts. Why couldn't it shut up and allow him to think? He had to think in order to voice his fears. A tear of frustration worked its way out of his eye as he took another breath; he then became painfully aware that his inflamed lungs no longer worked the way he required them to. Even if he could get his mouth to work, how would he get sufficient air into his lungs to form the words? Exhausted, he fell back, his chest a living furnace, his blistered innards reminding him of the affects the deadly smoke had wreaked

'Shh,' Marjorie said gently.

Drained by the effort of remembrance, he finally succumbed to his pillows. Constantly in the centre of his brain was the pretty blonde postie smiling back at him, her orange postbag swinging nonchalantly from her shoulder. Why did she keep leaping into his thoughts? What had happened to her? He couldn't remember. *Then he did.*

And the sudden remembrance of her smile as she turned her head, followed by that terrible flash, once more threw him back into his pillows, and he closed his eye and wept for her. But had this actually happened? Had she been real? If so, could she have survived? If it was real, though, it was too terrible to contemplate.

It came to him in flashes: the sudden searing blast; Marjorie's scream; the ambulance; then nothing – until now. There must have been a noise, a roar accompanying the explosion. He couldn't recall that, and wondered why, if he could remember seeing the blast, he couldn't remember hearing it.

So . . . if this wasn't his imagination working overtime, it would explain why he was here, unable to move or speak.

The nurse, standing at his wife's side, watched him fight against the pain of his throat; the determined twitch of his mouth; watched the anger, and the tears of defeat overwhelm him as the realisation struck him that voicing this thing – the thing that was so vital to him – was doomed to failure. She had to concede that he had guts, and she stood, waiting, ready with the hypodermic needle should it prove too much for him to bear.

What eventually emerged from his mouth was a guttural croak which sounded like a rusted creaky gate.

'Ghaaaah . . .' he managed.

'Don't try to talk, darling,' his wife said gently, holding back the tears. 'You're going to be all right.'

'Ah . . . nah . . . gaaah,' he spluttered, crushing her hand, his single undamaged eye blinking in a frenzied effort to get it out of his system.

'Ssh,' she said.

'Gut nah . . . ! Hag . . . hag to . . .'

Looking at him blinking furiously, her hand agonisingly squeezed, Marjorie willed him to go on; could see the desperation in striving to tell her something that was evidently weighting his mind; watched his anxiety to project this matter of obvious importance, and saw the effort causing him to hyperventilate. The nurse took a step closer to the bed. Marjorie suddenly heaved a sob as her husband's strength slowly ebbed away at the strain of exercising his lungs, and as he again sank back, worn down by the effort. To calm him, she gently stroked his hand until he finally released his grip.

'Ssh,' she said again, then watched another tear roll down his face when it finally dawned on him that the reason he couldn't say what he needed to say owed, not only to his damaged lungs, but to the fact that he now possessed only half his tongue.

Drained, he closed his eye. Marjorie imagined he would now go back to sleep, but he suddenly came to once more and opened his mouth wide, his eye staring up at her. He remained staring at her before she felt a deep sigh shudder through his body.

*''Ucking 'ell . . . !'* he whimpered softly, imploring her – anybody – to help him out of this nightmare.

The nurse, having checked the levels of the monitor and, before Simon had time to scream at the pain she could see was about to kick in, thrust the needle into his arm, then held his hand as he fell back into a deep sleep.

# Chapter Two

I was in the garden when I heard the bomb, photographing my new rose bush. Earlier, I'd photographed the remains of my breakfast: the egg-encrusted plate, the salt pot, the coffee jug, the soiled napkin, the cat's wet paw prints – and the biscuit crumbs, which seemed to be everywhere. I've got no one now, so it would be good, when I'm gone, for someone to know how I've lived, and the evidence is all here, inside my camera. I always save everything, marvelling at all the new technology nowadays. It certainly wasn't as easy as this in my day.

In those days, in the depths of the African tundra, Afghanistan, or wherever, one had to get the reels of film back to Fleet Street pretty damn quick, otherwise the situation would have changed – usually for the worse – and the photographs would then be in danger of telling a different story.

But that was a very long time ago.

So, back to the present – and to that dreadful day . . .

After finishing my breakfast, I'd gone outside to photograph the rose bush which was just coming into bud. I'd only clicked the camera once, when I heard the bomb. I live twelve houses down from the Garraways, but I know the sound of a bomb when I hear it.

Everyone shot out of their houses, wondering if an earthquake had erupted and, if not an earthquake, perhaps a couple of those bloody great lorries finally coming to grief; the lorries that constantly streak down this road with scant regard for either speed regulations or for us residents. We villagers were all certain that, in the absence of police presence, something terrible would surely happen one day.

But I knew.

We saw the smoke and flames and ran towards the house – *Oaklands* – the Garraways'. I ran, along with my neighbours, to the end of the drive, then backed away from the heat. We gasped in horror – Alma Larkingstall screaming fit to bust – as we viewed the crater where the drive once was, and at the blood flowing like a small river down the drive. And at all the body parts – some, still attached to scraps of clothing – hanging eerily from the branches of the fire-blackened oaks; the few oaks that had survived the blast, that is. Little old Glenys Pugh, the mad cyclist of Roper's End, was yelling her knickers off and shouting that it was not right – whatever she'd meant by that. Although Glenys was a good friend, I couldn't help calling her a silly old fool; of course it wasn't right – nothing is right about a bomb! Especially in a small nondescript village in Middle England. Valerie Frobisher fainted and had to be dragged away. Personally, I would have thrown a bucket of water over her, but Brian patted her face, then carried her home.

*And the stench . . .* That cordite stench of war one never forgets.

A car – a Mazda – which must have been passing at the time, was slewed across the road, the driver slumped at the wheel, blood pouring from his head. Simon Garraway's Range Rover was on fire and Marjorie's little Clio had caved in, both threatening another inferno, and poor Simon was sprawled face down onto what was left of the lawn, his clothes all but ripped off. And there was Marjorie, cradling Simon's head and screaming for help.

I saw Peter Flynn – the only one with an ounce of common sense – phoning for an ambulance before contacting the police, and remember how Peter's son had run over to throw his coat over Simon then, afterwards, had turned to Marjorie to comfort her.

Of all the dreadful scenes I've captured in war-torn countries, this shocked me to the core. This was not a war-torn country; this was a small village in the heart of England. But because of my experience abroad, I was holding up rather better than this pile of snowflakes in Roper's End who'd probably, before much longer, require industrial amounts of smelling salts. In my profession, if I'd so much as looked as though I was going wobbly and squeamish, that would have been the end of my career.

All my neighbours thought it must have been a gas leak, but I knew better.

I took it all in – and at everybody's reaction – and smiled inwardly. Because I guessed, from their body language, that, despite their horror of Garraway's burning body, they were all doing their sums; the main question in their miniscule brains being: if this was a gas leak, how would it affect them. And should they, from this day, change their domestic fuel? I could see it – could see them wondering – weighing up their options; sensed them contemplating how this incident might effectively lower the price of their houses. Their fear was tangible.

The questions rattling through my brain, however, were: how could this possibly have happened in this small backwater of Portlingshire; and who could have sent this bomb? Because there was no doubt in my mind that that was what it was. Plus . . . what had Simon Garraway done to warrant being blown to smithereens?

Despite everyone's disapprobation, I took a photograph.

* * *

Commodore Theodore Kilpatrick and his wife, Julia, lived next door to Freddie Wingrave – she of the clicking camera – and were fed up with her. One would have imagined that Broad Oaks, their rambling pile set in three quarters of an acre, was far enough from the woman's property to preclude intrusion from the ever-snapping camera.

There happened to be a loose brick in their dividing wall which Theo, as he preferred to call himself, had many times attempted to cement in. But that damned woman, he guessed, must watch him at work each time, then immediately shoot out to loosen the brick before the cement had time to set. He'd resorted to using a quick-setting cement but, even then, she'd always manage to undo his work, and he'd find the cement chippings on his lawn the following morning. He fumed. There she was, continually nosing into their affairs. What annoyed him most was that he could never catch her at it.

Whenever they had visitors and had taken them out to view the dahlias and the clematis-festooned loggia, they'd hear the click of that damned camera. Turning sharply round to look at the wall in order to catch the offender, he would find it intact, the brick having been replaced in an instant. But why *was* she snapping away at them, and at anyone who happened to call at their house? Was she just a nosy old bat, Theo wondered, or was there a purpose behind the nosiness?

She couldn't actually know anything, could she? How could she know anything about him?

He was aware that, having once worked for a national newspaper, Freddie Wingrave had, been assigned to all the countries he'd also had access to. But, having only ever met her in passing, she couldn't possibly have known anything about what he was doing, could she? Anyway, it was doubtful that, in her dotage, she would remember when and how their paths had once – just the once – fleetingly crossed in . . . Ethiopia, wasn't it? But he remembered the contempt he'd felt for her at the time, snapping away at all that poverty and disease he'd been glad to get away from. But there was no way she could possibly know of his own professional life?

So why would she now be taking pictures of him and his guests at every opportunity? She could never have been privy to anything he was doing in Naval Intelligence; would never have been allowed access to that sort of information. How *could* she have had access; how could she have knowledge of his department's covert activities?

But it bothered him nonetheless.

# Chapter Three

Marjorie Garraway felt she'd done well to fight back the tears by her husband's bedside as he'd struggled with his pain. Now that he'd been sedated, her face was wet with them, and the nurse put an arm around her shoulder and led her out of the ward. She'd watched as Simon's head subsided onto the pillow as the drug slowly took hold to send him back into oblivion, and now sobbed uncontrollably.

This was her husband who, only a few days ago was full of life – a confident man, laughing, joking, as was his wont – life and soul of the village; a clever man to boot, who'd dragged himself out of the poverty of his family, determined to make something of his life; a hard-working, successful man, who had eventually risen to earn the mega-bucks he'd deserved . . .

Now, here he was, lying helpless in a hospital bed with a pinging monitor above the headboard, in a limbo of life and death. This was monstrous. Would he ever work again? How would she face life if he never recovered? The thought brought a fresh flood of tears. Still in shock, the full complement of chins wobbling in an effort to control herself, she thought back to that terrible morning when she'd tenderly held his head as he'd lain in the sea of sludge which had once been a lawn, willing him to live; at the blood; at that acrid stench of cordite, coupled with the terrible smell of burnt human flesh . . .

She dragged herself down the corridor to the consultant's office, her head filled with questions. The likelihood of being cut off from a life she had, for so many years, taken for granted, she felt her brain turning to mush as she attempted to gather her thoughts. If Simon pulled through but never worked again, what would the future hold for her? She wondered how she could put a voice to everything she felt without sounding hard and calculating. She told herself to stay calm; that perhaps things were not as bleak as they looked right now. This may well be something that could be fixed – surely? It was a hospital. They would fix him – wouldn't they? They'd make it all right again – wouldn't they? The golf club wouldn't take her membership away – would they?

After being offered a seat in the consultant's office, she was promptly offered a box of tissues. There were so many things she needed to ask this man, the first coming to mind was: would her husband ever again return to his normal self? The consultant smiled sadly and sighed, guessing at what she was really asking: would her husband ever again be able to provide her with a lifestyle to which she'd become accustomed throughout the thirty-odd years of their marriage? He'd seen it all before – the tears – the anxiety – the self-preservation kicking in . . . He couldn't find it within himself to lie. So, although witnessing her distress, he explained to her gently that Simon's life had now been changed for ever and that a full recovery was unlikely.

'But, can't you . . . can't you . . . ? *You're doctors, for God's sake . . .!* Surely there's something you can do . . . ?' she cried.

He sighed and sat back. They were all the same, weren't they? This was a hospital, not a garage. It was not always possible to repair people; to mend them by welding on a new body part to get them back on the road, or paint over a few bumps and scratches to make everything look good. Sighing sympathetically and guessing at the core of fear weighing heavily on her mind, he nevertheless felt obliged to lay his unpalatable cards on the table in an effort to persuade her to be realistic, while simultaneously realising that the woman didn't, at this stage, want realism. Marjorie Garraway wanted normal; a husband back at his job, earning a salary to pay for a lifestyle she couldn't imagine living without. He saw it all in her face. She'd closed her mind to it – was in denial; she wouldn't want to hear what he now had to tell her.

As he sat looking at her puffy red eyes, he pursed his mouth, seeing that Marjorie Garraway, as reality was beginning to hit her, would not cope with a disabled husband. This gross lump sitting at the other side of his desk had probably never done a days' work in her married life. He momentarily closed his eyes and almost felt sorry for her. This was just the beginning for her, and he foresaw her future, even if she couldn't, as one long round of bed-wetting. So, as gently as possible, he advised her that her husband was going to be needing twenty-four-seven care for a very long time, and that it was doubtful he would ever be fit enough to return to his office. It might, therefore, be advisable at this stage – and purely for convenience, he ventured with a comforting smile – to consider moving to a house without stairs.

Marjorie was inconsolable. This was another blow to add to everything else; not only was her husband now rendered useless as a bread-winner, but she'd been landed the burden of having to sell her house. Her beautiful house – this des. res. in an extremely des. Roper's End. How could she move house, she sobbed; she *wouldn't* move house; couldn't bear the thought of moving away from the village she'd come to love and from all the friends she'd made during her time here. And where could she live that was anywhere near as prestigious as Roper's End? And, anyhow, how difficult would it be to sell a house with a history of violence – because a buyer would have to be told . . . ? It was the law.

She walked back up to Simon's ward, but couldn't bring herself to go in, so sat in the corridor and put her head in her hands. She loved her house, her golfing buddies, the ducks on the pond, the glorious and spacious common land where she and Simon had taken many a long leisurely walk of an evening. She loved feeling part of this village and getting involved with everything that went on therein; enjoyed the hustle and bustle of helping with the monthly farmers' market in the village hall, joined the women at the food bank centre, sang in the community choir, and regularly attended the small fifteenth century church in the centre of it all, even if she did struggle at times with the words of the Creed.

Marjorie Garraway would . . . *not* . . . move!

She'd never manage to get a decent property in Roper's End! Owing to its popularity, this precious little gem of a village hadn't had anything for sale for years. From time to time a tacky new-build bungalow down Prince Albert Lane would come onto the market but, even if there were such an opportunity, she would never lower herself to that level. That would be too much of a come-down; she couldn't afford to have folk looking down their noses at her, could she, having for so long looked down her own nose at all the bungalows' occupants when she'd encountered them in the Post Office queue? Then there was a question of a nearby golf course, because how could she live without golf three times a week?

So – no – moving was definitely off the cards.

A sudden unsolicited thought flashed fleetingly through her mind that she would have been better off if he'd died outright; at least then she'd have had the full benefit of the insurance money. She sucked in her breath, immediately castigating herself for thinking such a terrible thing, then uttered a cry of despair and reached for the Kleenex once more. But would he live, or would he die? Having been told of all his devastating injuries, and watching him struggle for breath, it was touch and go, she could see.

*How could this have happened?*
*Who could have sent that bomb to Simon?*
*And why?*

She eventually dried her eyes and walked slowly into the ward to sit once more with her husband and, in the quietness, allowed herself to think. Sitting in the chair by the bed, her limited brain cells were being sent on an impossible mission as they did their best to pull all the strands of thought into something she might conceivably recognise. They couldn't fix him – damn them! She'd grasped that. So they'd have to keep him here in hospital, wouldn't they? Because . . . if they didn't keep him here, the future was unthinkable. The consultant had suggested that she move to a bungalow. Now, it was slowly dawning on her that he wouldn't have said that if they'd been planning to keep him in hospital. He was telling her that she would have to look after Simon herself, and that a bungalow would make more sense.

She stared at the wall. How could she be expected to look after a cripple? She had no training in looking after such people. It was impossible. She'd tell them. This was simply *not* possible. They were obliged to keep him here, where he could be cared for by people who knew what they were doing. Simon had paid National Insurance all his working life and he was, therefore, entitled to be looked after by the state. The cheek of it – foisting all that responsibility upon her shoulders! How dare they?

But, what if . . . ?

What if they insisted on sending him home – *but no, no, they couldn't do that, could they?* Because, if they did, there'd be the cost of health care to consider – and how much of a chunk would that take out of the account – *and for how long?* And how long could she manage all these costs, without Simon's monthly salary? They couldn't send him home in that state . . . surely? But . . . what if they did? How would she manage?

Her life was now in ruins – had been shattered with the sudden blast of that bomb!

She couldn't do this . . .

\* \* \*

The next thing she had to deal with was the appearance of two policemen arriving at the hospital asking to speak to Simon Garraway, following received information of the patient's semi-consciousness. They had questions to ask, they said, but had been turned away – told, quite sharply, that Mr Garraway was too ill to answer questions. In order not to waste police resources, however, they decided that, as they were already here, they may as well interview the patient's wife, to ask her if she knew who was likely to have sent the bomb, and if either she or her husband had enemies. They didn't, however, get very far with that line of enquiry. In her present state of mind, Marjorie was incandescent and pulled herself up to her considerable height. Enemies? The Garraways? As the two young policemen were unarmed, they decided, for their own safety, to back away from this megalith of a woman and come back another day to speak to her husband.

Despite Simon's doctor's attempt to get rid of them, the Chief Constable ordered his officers to stick around the ward in the event that the bomber, having failed to kill Garraway, might well try again. It was a further six weeks before they were allowed in to see him. What they eventually learned from him, however, far from shedding further light on the matter, sent all their theories into a tailspin.

'Mr Garraway – Simon – ' DCI Brett Taylor began gently with what he imagined was his best comforting bedside smile, ' – do you know of anyone who would wish to harm you – anyone likely to send you or your wife a bomb through the post?'

'Wrong . . . houthe,' Simon lisped haltingly to the two officers sitting at his bedside. 'Not . . . meant for . . . for me.'

He'd been waiting to get this out; waiting for someone to listen to him.

'Could you repeat that, please,' Taylor frowned.

'It wath . . . wath thent to the wrong houthe,' Simon said.

'Are you sure? How can you know that?'

*'Wrong houthe!'* Simon growled angrily, staring the police officer down with his one hazel eye, his words shooting out painfully from his damaged mouth and ending in a squeak.

'But . . . as we understand it, the postwoman hadn't reached your house when the bomb detonated. She was only halfway down the drive. How can you be so . . .'

*'No! – no!* She wath . . . wath . . .walking *back!'* Simon rasped, then had to stop once more to get his breath. 'walking . . . away from me. She thaid . . . she thaid . . . she'd mith-read the . . . the addreth.'

'So . . . you spoke to her?'

'Yeth.'

'And you actually *saw* the package?'

'Yeth.'

'Did you handle it?'

'No,' Simon breathed and closed his eyes; he mustn't keep thinking of her . . .

'Did you manage to see the address?' Taylor asked.

'No,' he wheezed sadly. 'Offered . . . offered to take it and deliver it mythelf . . . But . . . she took it . . . And I don't . . . *I don't* . . . remember . . .'

'Can you remember . . . ?'

'What . . . happened . . . to her . . . to . . . to . . . *the girl* . . . ?' Simon demanded suddenly.

'I'm afraid . . . I'm sorry . . .' Taylor began with a frown. 'But, Simon, can you remember . . . ?'

'*Pleathe!*' Simon cried, tears coursing down his cheeks. '*No more – pleathe . . .*'

Until then, he'd held out a faint hope for the postwoman. No one had been brave enough to tell him her fate – hadn't wished to upset him. But, basically he'd known because, if the bomb had done this much damaged to him, she wouldn't have stood a chance. A sob escaped him and he lay back, the pain of this verification of his suspicions suddenly worse than the pain in his pulverized body.

\* \* \*

When he was finally discharged from hospital and was driven home, Simon looked out of the window of the ambulance in confusion, unprepared for the vision confronting him; of the smooth black tarmacked drive leading up to the house – the drive that had once been a dingy unkempt concrete slab badly in need of the pressure-wash he'd never got round to giving it. There was also an unfamiliar car sitting upon it – a pale green *Škoda,* something he would never have chosen had he lived to a hundred – plus a red Ford Mondeo by its side. Where was his Range Rover? And Marjorie's blue Clio?

Staring out of the side window as the driver pulled onto the tarmac, the memory of the postie flooded back once more; the sweet smile; the well-rounded posterior as she strode confidently down the drive; his anxiety as she fell; then the all-consuming blast. And a sob escaped him at the remembrance of the girl he'd never see again, and at the dull realisation of how nothing was as it once was, nor would ever be again.

And his precious *Rover*. Where was that? Probably burnt out and as useless as he was himself . . .

Another shock assailed him as, out of the opposite window, he took in the pale beige paving stones laid across an area where the lawn once was, and he suddenly choked at the sight of the raw-looking fence which now replaced the line of oak trees that had once separated his house from his neighbour. And . . . there was an odd smell he couldn't quite put his finger on, but which turned his stomach as it triggered something he was desperate to forget.

He'd thought that, inside his home, though, everything would once more be familiar. However, entering the house, his spirits dropped further, as he looked in horror at the room which he'd previously known as the dining room, now transformed into a bedroom – his bedroom, he guessed – complete with a hospital-sized metal bed festooned with every contraption he'd thought he would be free of. Standing in the middle of the room, a woman in a white uniform suddenly came to life at his arrival and fussed about him, taking charge of the wheelchair and petting him as though he was a puppy just out of the womb.

'*Oh, God!*' he whispered hoarsely. 'Back to 'ucking hospital then!'

# Chapter Four

The Kilpatricks had arrived in Roper's End around ten years ago from Berkshire, Theodore having put about that he'd retired from 'something in the city', about which he was extremely cagey when probed. Sensing a dead rat under the mat, Freddie Wingrove had made it her business to discover what that 'something' was, although she'd never let on, even to her husband. In her experience, caginess was next to guiltiness, so she'd ask a few people who might know. She still had friends in high enough places who would give her the low-down on Commander Theodore Kilpatrick. But, whatever she'd subsequently discovered, she'd kept to herself; wouldn't do to frighten the horses . . .

For all his bluster, Freddie had gleaned from her sources, that Theo Kilpatrick had been forced to move from his Maidenhead idyll, and that the *something in the city* was a smokescreen. Owing to her own experience in the field, she was not as easily fooled as others in the village. He'd been ousted, and had chosen a quiet little village in the depths of the countryside in order to move away from something unsavoury.

And you couldn't get a quieter nor littler village than Roper's End. Although, if one were avoiding unsavoury, they'd perhaps have been wiser to look elsewhere . . .

\* \* \*

When Freddie's husband, Ben, died of a brain tumour four or five years ago, Theo Kilpatrick began to suspect – to hope even – that Freddie's mental abilities were finally coming off the rails. The signs were all there as far as he could see: the constant loosening of the brick; the ever-clicking camera . . . He'd managed to convince a few of the villagers that this might be the perfect opportunity to contact Social Services – or whomever it was necessary to contact – to suggest they get her removed – or committed. The woman was deranged, he'd argue – probably brought on by loneliness after the death of her husband. He would lay it on thick: it caused him great pain, he would say sadly, as she'd always been such a good neighbour, but he only had her interests at heart . . . He smirked at the thought of her eventual removal to a residential home for the aged or, better still, to a mental institution.

He despised the woman; she'd never behaved in what he'd considered to be normal. There was something not right about her. For a start, she was German. A raging xenophobic, he was wary of foreigners of any kind – in particular, Germans – for a very good reason he was unwilling to disclose. But, apart from her Teutonic origins, he'd had, from the start, considered Freddie Wingrave wildly eccentric. Being a naval man, he didn't do normal eccentricity, let alone the wild variety.

He then reached for his phone, pressed a few digits and alerted the authorities. With a bit of luck and a few Hail Marys, he would finally be free of her interference. He'd have the whole village on his side, because it would be obvious to anyone that the place for Freddie Wingrave was not Roper's End and, most definitely, not next door to the Kilpatricks.

# Chapter Five

The knock that day had roused Simon Garraway as he was gathering up his papers in readiness to jump into his Range Rover and set off for work. A pretty young postwoman stood smiling on the doorstep with a package and he dropped his briefcase on the doorstep and smiled back at her.

'Hello. Where's Reg today?' he asked lightly, giving her the once-over.

She clocked his lust as he undressed her with his eyes.

'Oh, Reg retired last month,' she said, the colour rising to her cheeks. 'In the Algarve right now, lucky devil! I've got his patch now.'

'Mm . . . lucky us!' he grinned. 'Roper's End's overdue a bit of glamour. What's that you've got there – another expensive Amazon purchase my darling wife hasn't told me about?'

'Oh, oh yes. This package is for you, sir . . .' she began, looking again at the label. Though small, the parcel looked rather heavy and, with the postbag on her shoulders, she struggled as she turned it over, almost letting it slip out of her hands. ' . . . Oh! . . . but . . .' she frowned, alarmed.

'What's up?' he asked.

'*Oh!* Oh, I'm so sorry . . .'

'Let's have it then,' he said, confused by her hesitation.

He'd almost got his hands on it but she suddenly pulled it back. He watched as her eyes widened and as she glanced down once more at the address label. Then, flustered, she drew in a breath.

'Oh, oh, I'm so sorry to have disturbed you sir, but . . . This is not for you, after all. I seem to have got the wrong address,' she said, biting her lip, as though afraid of being reported to the authorities.

'Wrong address?' he said.

'Look, I'm really sorry, Mr Garraway,' she repeated. 'I looked at the house name rather than the recipient's name and got in a muddle. It's not your house. I just . . . I'm afraid this is not for you after all. I've only been doing this round for three weeks, and I haven't got used to all the house names – all these Oaks and Woods – I can't get my head round them all. Sorry. I'll just . . .'

'Who's it for? Give it to me, if you like, and I'll drop it by,' he smiled, seeing her discomfort and reaching out for it.

'No – no,' she said, clearly embarrassed. 'It's all right, Mr Garraway – but thank you. I'll deliver it myself. It's on my way round.'

'It looks pretty heavy,' he said, taking the rest of his post from her.

'Yes, it is,' she smiled, 'but I'll manage.'

'I could easily do it, you know – but then, if you're sure . . .'

'Don't worry about me,' she grinned, as she half turned away from him. 'I've delivered heavier things than this!'

'See you tomorrow, then,' he grinned back with a wink.

She gave a little wave to acknowledge the flirt, and strode back down the drive.

He watched her, the smile still playing on his lips, as she shrugged the postbag back onto her shoulders and marched off purposefully, clutching the package. He noted with approval the neatly rounded backside as she shimmied smartly away from him, then sighed at the remembrance of his wife's once-neat backside, bringing to mind the sudden realisation that his life was rapidly slipping away. Apart from Julia, bless her, the chances now of a reasonable sex life with a well-shaped backside was an ever-dwindling possibility, given his age and the fact that he was shackled to the well-endowed Marjorie, whose rump could probably now stop the 417 bus to Bracklea.

He shouldn't complain though, he sighed; Jules would always come up trumps whenever he needed to relieve himself in that regard – though even her backside was getting larger, he'd noticed. Merely thinking about Julia Kilpatrick's backside, though, caused his innards to stir with lust. Keep calm, he told himself. It wouldn't be long now: just a few more weeks before their plan would take flight . . .

But would Julia really have the courage to leave Thicko Theo, a man who'd professed to have been something in Naval Intelligence – God help us! She'd sworn she would – but, then, who knew with Julia? Prising himself away from Mountainous Marjorie, as Julia had so delicately labelled her, wouldn't, however, be too much of a wrench. He'd had quite enough of living with a set of golf irons.

Julia was gorgeous, though, and, in increasing her private income from time to time, he'd had the satisfaction of helping her get her numerous face-lifts, which made her all the more desirable, even if that desire could be seen in the eyes of every other middle-aged man in Roper's End.

Folding his arms and leaning on the frame of the door with these various thoughts rattling through his mind, he kept an appreciative eye on the young woman's rear end, which was now making him somewhat horny. He wondered vaguely what she'd be like in the sack. Judging by the wiggle, he thought she'd be all right. Sighing again, he thought he might ring Julia later – see if she was available this afternoon. They hadn't been to that lovely Cotswold hotel for some time . . .

With thoughts of what they'd termed *The Great Escape* occupying his mind, he continued dreamily to keep his eyes on the young postwoman walking down the drive, the smile still hovering on his lips, as, striding away, she suddenly squinted down at the package to look again at the address. He watched when, halfway down the drive, she turned her head back to look at him – then watched helpless as, thus distracted, her foot caught the loop of the garden hose which Marjorie had carelessly left lying there the day before in her hurry to get indoors in order to view some mindless daytime drivel on television. *Watched,* as the girl attempted to right herself; *watched* as she put out her hand to steady herself and found nothing to clutch onto to prevent her fall; *watched* with concern as she keeled over, and dropped to the ground . . .

His first instinct at seeing her wobble, then keel over, was to save her before she landed on the concrete drive, even though he knew he was far too far away to prevent her from hurting herself. Nevertheless, gallantry took over, and he began to run towards her. But, as she'd thudded to the ground, the bomb had detonated and he'd been thrown back by the ferocity of the blast.

He didn't, however, remember much of this until some time later, and then only in snatches. What he did remember was the scream of his wife as she clattered down the steps. It was that primal scream – and, strangely, not the blast of the bomb – that would haunt him for the rest of his life.

# Chapter Six

I have to say in all honesty that, when the bomb went off, my first thought was that I was glad it wasn't me. How awful is that? It's just that it could have been. The threat of reprisal is something I've had hanging over me for the last six years, thought something I thought I'd managed to come to terms with. When I heard that Simon Garraway had told the police that the bomb was not intended for him, that set off alarm bells which I imagined had stopped ringing so many years down the line.

Naturally, the police had questions to ask: Mr Flynn, we believe you and your son were the first on the scene. What can you tell us? But there was nothing I could tell the police that was of any use. Exercising my mind at the time was: what if that bomb had been meant for me? And what if Janet and the children had been the ones destined to go through what Marjorie Garraway was now going through?

Jeremy and I, as I said, were the first to arrive at Oaklands, and we could barely believe our eyes at Simon lying in that pool of blood, the driveway a heap of rubble and dripping crimson – plus the two cars in flames which, in turn, had set alight the oaks. A scene of devastation I hope never again to witness! I rang the emergency services, while Jeremy ran up to throw his coat over Simon, putting me to shame standing at the end of the drive clutching my mobile. My son – my brave son in total possession of an internal compass I daresay he never suspected he had, which is something he most certainly had not inherited from me – risking his life to help; he must have known of the possibility of the two cars blowing up and of being himself blown to kingdom come. But he didn't hesitate.

Poor bugger though – Simon – and poor Marjorie. We just stood there after he'd been taken away, unable to speak. Then, after we'd followed little Miss Pugh, to make sure she cycled home safely, we slowly walked back home.

They're having to move – inevitably; Marjorie couldn't possibly cope now in a five bedroom house with all those stairs. I noticed their house had a *For Sale* sign on it last time I passed, so they'll be gone soon; probably need a bungalow in order to cope with all Si's injuries.

But the thought has dogged me ever since: it could have been me . . .

* * *

After the baby died, the death threats began popping up with alarming regularity. Janet contacted the police, and they did their best to reassure us that they would keep watch. However, that didn't last long; I suppose they're as overstretched as the rest of us.

In the course of my profession, which is thankfully now coming to an end, I've witnessed countless babies dying of natural causes. Most people, despite their grief, will accept my explanation of how their baby died. However, it's more usual these days to have somebody to blame for the deaths; a small number of people who will not listen to explanations of natural causes, and who accuse the department of malpractice. Causes of death can be complex but, as I begin to explain, I can see their brains ticking over: somebody has to be blamed, and how soon can they contact a lawyer . . . Explaining the causes of death to these people is like explaining trigonometry to a cat, but I try by using language they can understand. However, try as I may, if they don't wish to hear, they don't hear.

Next thing I know is a legal-eagle, flush with the sole intent of suing a nurse or doctor or, in my case, the consultant Paediatrician. *Anybody.* Unable to accept reality and refusing counselling to help with their grief, they decide that, in order to come to terms with the situation, someone else has to be made to suffer. Backbones and upper lips getting flabbier by the day.

Perhaps I'm being harsh.

But, seeking a scapegoat is not the answer. Don't think I'm unsympathetic. I, too, have suffered. *Of course* everyone is devastated after the death of a child, nor would folk be normal if they didn't, but it comes harder to those who, from an early age, have never come anywhere near loss or death. Death, however, is no respecter of persons and, however sad this may be, babies do die. And, believe you me, in my department, each time a baby dies, it hits us all hard.

The baby in question was this couple's first-born. The family was wealthy enough to arm themselves with lawyers, with the clear view of suing the NHS and, in particular, me. The hearing was over six years ago, and the anxiety, which is still very much with me, seemed to rob me of several decades of my life, and replaced many of the dark hairs of my head to a permanent grey. My whole family suffered during that time and, as there was nothing I could do to prevent that, I was out of my mind with worry. It was a pretty terrifying period all round because, if the verdict had gone the wrong way, I knew I would no longer be deemed employable.

However, even though I and my department were eventually

cleared of negligence, the baby's family doggedly refused to accept the verdict, and that was when the threats began in earnest and when the nightmares started all over again. The police eventually cautioned the family and took away their electronic devices for investigation, but came up with nothing specific with which to charge them, even though suspecting that they could possibly have hired others to do their dirty work for them – people who were never traced. So, no one was charged and, for a long time, we continued to live in fear of our lives. I finally decided, for the safety of my family, to move. I managed to get a transfer to Portlingshire Health Trust, and we moved here to Roper's End.

Naturally, this couple were out of their minds with grief, I understood that – who wouldn't? Everyone in the department was crushed by the loss of that child. To say that we do our utmost in such circumstances to prevent the death of a baby, is understating the terrible toll wreaked upon all my staff when we've strained every sinew to keep a baby alive, and then, after all our efforts, for it to die. No one in my department is, or has ever been, unsympathetic to the parents of a dead child.

I ushered them into my office to say how desperately sorry we were, and to explain in layman's terms that their baby had had multiple defects and that it was impossible to save him. But the man was angry and firing on all guns, probing furiously as to how this could have happened.

'Something must have gone wrong, Mr Flynn,' he said bluntly, his small wife quietly weeping at his side.

'Nothing went wrong,' I said gently. 'Please understand that your baby had our full care at all times.'

'Then why did you let him die?'

'Mr Robinson, we didn't *let* him die. I can understand your grief and anger at losing your baby, but we couldn't keep him alive. We had him in the incubator for two weeks and did everything we could for him, but he didn't respond to treatment.'

'When we brought him into this hospital, he had breathing problems. That was all!' Robinson said, thumping my desk angrily. 'The midwife I hired said it was merely bronchial and could have been sorted out quite easily.'

'Unfortunately – *very* unfortunately – it *couldn't* be sorted out,' I said, keeping my calm, 'because his condition was far more serious than we'd first thought. He did have bronchial problems, yes, but you see, there were serious issues which quickly became obvious. And it transpired that those issues – those defects – proved impossible to treat. We did our best – *our very best* – to make your son as comfortable as possible and, at the end, ensured that he died without pain.'

'But why were you not able to treat him? You're the consultant Paediatrician. That's what you're supposed to do! *Why couldn't you do your job?'* he said, forcefully stabbing the desk with his index finger.

'Mr Robinson, let me explain . . .'

'No! I don't want all your flimsy excuses and explanations. Something went badly wrong here – and I intend to find out what!'

'I assure you, nothing went wrong,' I repeated.

'You say he had defects,' he yelled. 'What were these defects, and who caused them?'

'No one *caused* them, Mr Robinson. Please calm down and I will explain,' I said sighing gently, looking at his wife's drawn face. 'These cases happen very rarely – I have only come across four such cases in my professional life – and I have to say that it is disturbing in the extreme. Please,' I said, holding up my hand slightly to prevent the interruption I saw coming, 'allow me to continue and to give you the whole picture. Your son was afflicted, I'm sorry to say, with what is known as Patau's Syndrome. His birth weight was abnormally low, and he had serious problems with the underdevelopment of his nasal passages – hence his breathing problems. He was also born with holoprosencephaly, which is a rare condition where the brain has not divided into two halves. As I said, this is a *very rare* genetic condition, but it happens by chance. It's no one's fault.'

'Rubbish!' Robinson shouted. 'I don't believe a word! You'll say anything to get you and your department off the hook, and you're trying, very cleverly, to blind us with science! Our midwife said that, apart from breathing problems, he was a healthy baby. *He was a healthy child until he came into your hospital!'*

'He was admitted with breathing problems, Mr Robinson, because of his condition. As soon as I saw him I suspected at once that he was suffering from Patau's Syndrome and the x-rays proved me right.'

'He was a fine healthy boy before he came into this hospital!' Robinson insisted. 'The midwife said it was a simple matter to sort out!'

'I think you'll find that she was wrong.'

'Ha!'

'Look, I am truly sorry for what you're both going through right now; I know exactly how you're feeling. My wife and I lost our first child soon after his birth, and it took us a long time to recover from that. I really do understand, Mr and Mrs Robinson, and I am so very sorry for your loss.'

A that point, the baby's mother broke down and wept. I reached out for her hand, but she pulled it away and dabbed her face with a tissue.

'I wonder, perhaps – would it help you both to speak to the nurse who was in charge of your son's treatment? She's an excellent, caring nurse, who will explain and . . .'

'And who will give the same story as you, because you've

obviously had time to collaborate! It's a whitewash – you just cover for each other!' Robinson ranted.

'Mr Robinson, Nurses Grimshaw is . . .'

'Totally incompetent – like you! You should be struck off! You're not fit to be a paediatrician!' he yelled, getting up abruptly from his chair, immediately followed by his small silent wife. 'You're all in it together. *And* the Coroner, who will gratifyingly relieve you all of blame!'

'Look – Mr Robinson – I can assure you,' I said, somewhat nettled by then, as they were sweeping out of the door, 'that *no one in this department* is incompetent!'

'And I can assure you, Mr Flynn, that I will do everything in my power to prove that they are. You have not heard the end of this!'

And, hiring the big guns in an attempt to prove my incompetence, he set out to ruin me – to ensure that I lost my job over the death of his baby.

I didn't blame him for being angry; I remember vividly how I'd felt after Christopher had died at two months – how Janet had felt: angry beyond words – and bitter – and helpless. And I had to carry on working in this department with healthy babies . . .

I did, therefore, feel genuine empathy towards Mr and Mrs Robinson, even though suspecting that, through all the anger and bluster, they were doing their best to cover over the fact that the baby should have been brought in earlier by a midwife who should have known better. However, neither the explanation of their baby's death nor any amount of empathy had cut this particular block of ice, so he and his family decided to destroy me.

So . . . could he still be harbouring that grudge which might have decided him to make it his business to find out where I and my family lived? And to punish us? What if he's discovered our new address? And, what if . . . ? I must try to put a stop to these thoughts for the sake of my sanity but, since that explosion in the Garraways' drive, the nightmares of that court case have returned.

That day . . . that day outside Oaklands, when everyone was screaming like banshees, I felt something inside me wither. Most of my neighbours thought the explosion was a gas leak, even though the house seemed still to be intact, but I knew it wasn't. It wasn't until much later that we were told it had been a bomb. It couldn't, as far as I could see, have been anything else. At the time, I hadn't known what Simon would reveal to the police. So, after I'd called for the ambulance, I stood with the rest of the crowd and felt a tremor of disquiet. The terrible thing is that when we'd all been told that the bomb wasn't destined for Simon, all I could think of – *God forgive me* – was: I'm glad it wasn't me.

Little Miss Pugh just stood there, hanging on to the gate post as though her life depended on it, her face ashen and shaking like a leaf, the poor wee thing. I heard her whispering that it wasn't right; she kept saying it over and over, tears streaming down her face. We all knew it wasn't right – not in Roper's End – but she'd seemed so utterly shattered by it, and just stood, repeating that it wasn't right. Her body was rigid and unyielding as I put my arm around her shoulders. Jeremy and I offered to accompany her home, but she wouldn't have it and, before we'd had time to stop her, she jumped on her bike and was gone. I could see she wasn't herself and worried for her. Knowing she'd very likely take the short-cut down Pig Lane – which is treacherous enough with all those hazardous potholes, without the mental distraction of what she'd just gone through – Jeremy and I discreetly followed her back to her bungalow via the main road, to ensure her safe arrival home.

After that, we went back to look at the poor chap in the Mazda, but he was gone; a nail embedded in his skull, he hadn't stood a chance, poor sod; wrong place at the wrong time.

We left after someone fainted and when somebody else bought up the contents of their stomach – but I can't remember who. All those bloody screaming women got on my nerves, but we all stood there until the emergency services had arrived. We waited until the man in the Mazda had been taken away then, realising there was nothing more we could do, Jeremy and I walked silently home.

Janet, bless her, got the whisky bottle out when we got back. We looked at each other and sighed, knowing how lucky we were – that it could have been us. Because, if the bomb had been delivered to the wrong address, was this the address it was meant for?

* * *

Everybody liked Simon Garraway. He was a real 'cheeky-chappie' and had a smile for everybody – even for po-faced Charlie Ramsden, ex-High Court judge and inveterate snob and his equally snotty wife Penelope who, by all accounts, is the daughter of Lord and Lady Harbershall of Welfringham, no less! God, the airs . . . The String Bean was what Simon called Penelope, ex-model and never letting the world forget it, floating about haughtily in her designer rags, as if anyone in this village could give a monkey's fart what she's wearing. Simon laughed at the pomposity, which riled her, as she obviously considers herself several cuts above the rest of us.

Si was the life and soul of any gathering. He was so quick off the mark – his mark usually being Penelope Ramsden, who would invariably lose her rag and storm out in high dudgeon, much to everyone's delight.

Lovely couple, the Garraways – got on with everybody; been in the village for twenty-odd years, he an international banker, and Marjorie helping out at the local foodbank when she wasn't on the golf course. Pity they never managed to have kids. Could have had mine for tuppence when they were small, little sods! Si, though, didn't need much of an excuse to turn up at our place from time to time to kick a ball around with Jeremy when he was a boy. Unlike me, he would have made a great father. Did his bit in the village, too. Helped out at the foodbank when Marjorie couldn't make it. They loved him.

Now his life is well and truly buggered – Marjorie's too. I see them in the village now and then, she pushing his wheelchair, putting up a show of being her old jolly self, when it wouldn't take an assistant charlady in the Sherlock Holmes Academy of Detection to see that she's totally frazzled; he – still traumatised, with half his face still in bandages – staring into the distance as though still living through the ordeal, poor sod.

Janet pops in quite regularly to see them, and takes Emma and Jeremy when they're around. Sadly, their house is up for sale now, so we won't be seeing them for much longer, it would seem. What an utter waste.

That the parcel containing the bomb was meant for neither Simon Garraway nor his wife is totally believable. Si was an investment banker, for crying out loud. Who would want him dead? And Marjorie? Barely credible, unless she'd made an enemy on Portlingshire Golf Course . . .

No, the bomb was meant for someone else. But who?

# Chapter Seven

Penelope was in London when it happened; some photo-shoot for *Vogue* or similar fashion magazine – I can never remember. I considered it fortunate that she still got work at her age (although she'd kill me for reminding her of it), so I didn't mind getting my own dinner for a few weeks – which mainly – *thankfully* – comprises chips – something she'd never countenance in a month of Sundays.

My wife usually combines her modelling work with looking up family in London – Lord and Lady Harbershall – who she doesn't see as often as she'd like. I don't begrudge her escaping now and then to London, from the cloying tedium of Roper's End, as she puts it, especially if it means a few more shekels landing in the bank vaults on account of her ongoing career and – *more especially* – if it means avoiding all those wretched salads she prepares each day so as not to put extra inches onto her waistline. She does her best to make the salads interesting, bless her – but, after so long without a scrap of animal to chew on, one does get the feeling that one's blood might be turning green with all that lettuce coursing healthily through the veins, the body slowly photosynthesising as it cries out for a proper protein-fuelled meal. So . . . I rather looked forward to that particular assignment, because it left left me six whole weeks of glorious cholesterol-inducing chips, accompanied by great hunks of filet steak. My argument against vegetarianism is that, if God didn't mean us to eat animals, why did He decide, in His wisdom, to make them all out of meat?

I rang to tell her about poor Simon Garraway, but she was in 'make-up' at the time, so the call was cut fairly short.

I got to wondering: who the hell would have wanted to kill Simon Garraway? He was a pain in the arse, I have to say, with all his cutting, unfunny remarks directed at Penny and me – and I'd had serious thoughts myself about cutting his tongue out. Cutting out a tongue, however, even if one would ever have got the chance of pinning him down and threatening him with the bread knife, is a far cry from blowing a fellow up, wouldn't you say? – and is too far fetched for words. He was in banking, it's true, but I've never once had the urge to blow up my bank manager.

It remains a mystery.

That day, I set myself the task of cutting the lawn in front of the house, working up an appetite, and doing my best to take my mind off the piece of steak languishing in the fridge. Sitting on my old mower, forcing myself to concentrate on its drone, I ploughed on. I'd only cut half the grass at the side of the house when I heard the explosion. Good grief – if the noise could penetrate the grind of the old sit-on, it was certainly some blast! Seeing flames streak upwards, I immediately ran down the road. Smoke was billowing up from the front of the Garraways' house; God, the stench!

And Marjorie – poor Marjorie . . . sitting in the middle of all that convulsive mess. Like the rest of us, she must have thought Simon was a goner. Before I'd got my phone out of my pocket, however, I heard Peter Flynn call for an ambulance, so I stood with everyone else until it arrived.

Gas leak – bound to be, I thought. But then I later learned it was a bomb.

It didn't seem credible.

I rang Farleigh Cranshaw – Lord Cranshaw – now High Court judge and still a good friend, even after all these years out of the law courts. If ever I need to know something that's not revealed to the general public, he always comes up with the goods. Cranshaw told me that the police report confirmed that it had, indeed, been a bomb. But the strange thing is that the police had somehow got it into their heads that it hadn't been meant for Garraway. However, they'd had no clue at that stage as to whom it was meant for. Surely not me! I've tried and put away some brutal sods in my time, most threatening vengeance when released, but I shouldn't have thought that, after all this time, anyone would see fit to blow me up – although one never knows these days. Grudges can simmer for years, can't they? – piling up like the contents of a litter tray, then suddenly – boom!

All the same, I wouldn't have thought . . .

* * *

Penelope returned six weeks later when all the fuss had died down and the forensic team had taken away all the gore. She has a weak stomach, so I'm glad she didn't have to witness that.

The Garraways' burnt-out cars had been removed by that time. After that, a fleet of tree surgeons came to give the oaks the once-over in order to ascertain which of them needed to be cut down, and then set to, creating a din that had all the dogs in the village barking; you couldn't hear yourself think once they got to work. Then a pile of huge scruffy workmen arrived in their huge scruffy trucks and stank the village out by filling in, then tarmacking, the Garraways' drive. Then landscape gardeners turned up, took up the rest of the lawn and laid rather smart stone slabs which, I must say, looked quite swish when they'd finished. Finally, we had the fencing chaps to put up with! The village hadn't seen that much activity since the Civil War.

Anyway, by the time Penelope had arrived home, it was all done and dusted.

And now the Garraways' house is up for sale. Marjorie was adamant she wouldn't sell, but I expect common sense has informed her of the necessity to move from that barn of a house. So they'll be off soon. Sad that; although I have to admit feeling something akin to relief when I heard of their impending move; at no longer being compelled to stop for a chat when Marjorie is seen wheeling Simon through the village. Damned awkward trying to hold a conversation with someone sporting only half a tongue. And, because the blast half-deafened him, poor sod, one has to yell fit to bust in order to get through to him.

I briefly called in to see him when he was out of hospital, but it was too much for Penny; she can't stand anything like that. Whenever she sees Marjorie pushing the wheelchair towards her, she dives behind a bush. Poor Pen – she's such a sensitive soul.

I remember some years ago when a bomb, addressed to Barney Silcott, circuit judge, was delivered to the mailing room in chambers, and was diffused safely after a sharp-eyed clerk noticed a wire poking out. Lucky for the staff in the mailing room. That's the thing about the bastards who send these objects of destruction – they have no idea that their deadly packages hardly ever reach the people they're meant to reach; it's usually the poor bloody rank and file who get blown up. *But mailing a bomb to a specific house* – well, that's a different kettle of fish; bound to get the bod it was meant for, what?

Ah well, that's enough thinking for today. I expect Penny and I will stroll over to The Goose after dinner; join the hoi polloi for some meaningless platitudes, as per bloody usual; but then, what else is there to look forward to in this boring repository for the elderly? Pen came back with a new frock she wants to show off.

So – ha – I don't suppose much of her earnings managed to find its way into the bank account, after all. But my wife certainly does her best to brighten this place up – says she sees it as her *raison d'être*, as all the women here tend to resemble *Worzel Gummidge's* wife on speed, walking their dogs through the Common in their ghastly wellies and puffa-gilets; maybe shame them into a pretty frock one day. We've been here for a good ten years, though, and it hasn't worked yet.

* * *

*Charlie!* I go away for six weeks – *six weeks!* – and come back to a husband who, in my absence, had come to resemble an oversized Zeppelin, with a belly like a pregnant minke whale on two spindly legs – plus a month's growth of beard. *Plus* a house smelling like an abattoir, damn it! I can only surmise that, during my absence, he'd bought industrial amounts of chips, then barbecued himself several ghastly steaks to accompany them. I had to open every window in the house to get rid of the smell of meat. He's back on salad now, which he'd better stick to, considering the size of him – like it or not!

Coming back to this crapulous stinking backwater was bad enough. God! How on earth did we land in this dreary neck of the woods? I should never have listened to Charlie. You can almost see the straw falling out of the inmates' hair as they march up and down the Common with their damned dogs; impossible at times to differentiate between dog and owner, but one does possess a modicum of tact.

I have to admit that, when Charlie first suggested moving out of London, it did seem sensible at the time and, after seeing a photograph of the house, I was all for it; getting out of Belgravia, which was slowly being taken over by foreigners; all our lovely neighbours having, one by one, moved to the country. But there's country and *'country'*! I never dreamt we'd land in this blasted vomitory!

I'd never been particularly good at geography, so I Googled Portlingshire and discovered that the county was based somewhere in the West Midlands, a part of the country with which I was not well acquainted. How sweet, I thought; Robin Hood country – although, from memory Sherwood Forest might be that bit on the other side, perhaps the eastern part? I gathered from Google that the area is said to have been Henry the Eighth's hunting ground, which sounded quite interesting. Perhaps the royals still frequent the area. A royal connection is always useful to throw into the conversation at dinner parties.

The architectural beauty of its churches was mentioned – but I skipped most of that – along with its mellow cheeses and the Ranborne Hills, which are said to be of historic significance. Google made the Ranborne Hills sound rather spectacular; so, I thought, perhaps we could fit in a spot of skiing during the winter months, and was eager to give them the once-over. When I saw them, however, I realised I'd been wildly taken in. It's just a string of grey-looking humps resembling a couple of upturned pudding basins, the beige houses surrounding it resembling, from a distance, rows of ageing teeth.

I'd never heard of the blasted place, which is hardly surprising, seeing it is but a mere pimple on the map – though I could never have guessed what a foul, suppurating pimple it would turn out to be once the scab was removed.

I'd had a vague memory from school that this was where Cromwell had finally met his Waterloo (or was that somewhere else? – not the station, surely?), but the rest of the information was rather vague. I'd been about as interested in history as geography. So ... having agreed to view the Ranborne Hills, still full of hope, I was livid to find that there was no snow and no chance of skiing. And this village-y thingy, delightfully called Roper's End, *'set in a countryside awash with fields of buttercups and a pretty duck pond'* was another crashing disappointment; it was out of season for buttercups, and there was just one mangy-looking duck on an algae-ridden pond.

By then, it was too late. We'd sold the London house and were committed.

The worst bit was that, on arrival, I discovered that all the dreary women in this God-forsaken hole belonged to that dreadful Women's Institute effort, which seems to be their sole topic of conversation, apart from their open garden events and that smelly farmers' market in the village hall ... It drives me mad. Even the local watering hole, which we dive into from time to time in an effort to relieve the monotony, is not much to write home about!

I'd never lived in the country – well, not properly. My people have a house in Devon where we'd occasionally take ourselves off for a short while during the hunting season, but it wasn't done to mix with the locals. Christmas in Devon, I remember, had always been fun. But my real home, of course, is London: the galleries; the theatres; Bond Street ... You're lucky to find a decent Marks and Spencer anywhere near this provincial rat-hole.

Charlie told me about the bomb, which I suppose livened the place up a bit. He rang to tell me just as I'd had a call for a photo-shoot, so it was difficult to talk for too long. I got the whole story when I returned which, by then, had been transformed almost into folklore – the horror stories varying from villager to villager, each obviously relishing their memory of the disaster.

I have to say that I'd never liked Simon Garraway; however, I wouldn't have wished that on the man. Can't bear to look at him now, though – turns my stomach.

At the time of the explosion I was well out of it in London, thank the Lord, in order to do a spot of modelling and to take time to visit my people, who have a flat in Eaton Square – which is jolly useful at times. So I missed all the fuss.

# Chapter Eight

Julia and I ran over to the Garraways' place as soon as we heard the bomb. There was no doubt that it was a bomb – I'd heard plenty of bombs in my time – *and* witnessed their destruction.

But here in Roper's End?

According to Peter Flynn, who I spoke to a day or two later, the bomb had been meant for someone else – although, as usual, I was the last to hear of it. Apparently, Simon Garraway had insisted that the postwoman had got the wrong address, though it begs the question of how he could possibly know that. But, if he's right, and it was not meant for him, then who was it addressed to?

This seriously put the wind up me, I can tell you. My career in Naval Intelligence, at Bletchley Park, then at MI5, and then my subsequent posting as Foreign Correspondent for Milward Press, couldn't have done me any favours over the years. I've probably been on somebody's hit list for some time, considering what happened back then . . .

But who would know about my past? Not even Julia knows about that. How would anyone have discovered what happened back then? Who might have talked? And why now, after all this time? If they – whoever they might be – had decided to blow me to smithereens, they'd have had ample opportunity over my years in service. Everyone knew where I was based – it was no secret – so it wouldn't have taken much imagination to have got something planted under my car – or to shoot me in the back. Has someone got hold of Top Secret papers? Has someone ratted? But who? My orders had been to destroy everything. What if the the files hadn't all been destroyed? But, then, perhaps I'm worrying about nothing . . .

I'm glad I'm retired and out of all that business now, though. It was a relief to move here to Roper's End out of potential danger. A necessary move, I have to add – because . . . well . . .

But what if . . . ?

Once I realised I'd have to move, I sold Julia the idea of retiring to the countryside. But then, no sooner had I imagined myself settling quietly into this village, I was head-hunted for a job as foreign correspondent for a national newspaper. Although I'd had to get out of the service pretty sharp-ish, I wasn't really ready to retire, so I jumped at the chance to give the paper the benefit of my experience. The sale of the London flat was put on hold, because, having acquired not a few female admirers, I needed a bolthole in the City for a few days' comfort before returning home. Julia was not terribly happy to be left alone in a strange village with the boys, but needs must and, as no one of any import had been given the new address, I had the peace of mind, even when cavorting in the bedroom of the flat, to know they were all safe in my absence.

Then somehow, over the years, I forgot about the dangers – the threats; never imagined in my wildest nightmares that anyone would take the trouble to track me down and kill me – *here in Roper's End*. Not now . . . Not after all this time . . .

But perhaps nobody actually does want to kill me. Perhaps the bomb was destined or somebody else; I sincerely hope it *was* destined for somebody else. It certainly wasn't meant for Simon Garraway, that's for sure – a nicer chap you could never meet in a lifetime. Always down at The Goose's Head, flashing the cash, which I couldn't help thinking was a tad unusual for a banker.

Simon was the life and soul. No one in their right mind could wish Simon dead.

But that small seed of doubt still lingers; that little twinge of *what if.* What if my orders were countermanded and certain papers had subsequently come to light? And . . . what if some ex-Bletchley Park bod had twigged at what they represented and had decided to act . . . ?

I had a few sleepless nights after the bomb, but then settled down again.

Even so . . .

Julia was completely off her head by that bomb for weeks afterwards. Everybody was shocked and upset at seeing Simon Garraway lying in his garden in his own blood, so I understood that. But, what I didn't understand was how it changed her – much more than I would have imagined – and things haven't really been the same between us. I can't understand it. I looked for her afterwards, only to find that she'd left. I saw her car streak away from the drive, and then inexplicably disappear. I waited for several hours – missing my lunch – until she returned home, barely able to speak. I tried to talk to her, but she yelled at me to leave her alone and, strangely, she hasn't been her old self since; quite snappy and argumentative at times. Not like her at all. Odd. I can't get my head round it; she'd hardly known Simon Garraway. Surely his death couldn't have affected her to that extent. But women! Who the hell understands the workings of their minds?

* * *

What a terrible, devastating thing to have happened to my lovely Simon – blown up, out of the blue. It's only now, after a month of grieving, that I can bring myself to talk about it. But

I'm still sick with regret – and Thicko Theo, needless to say, hasn't got a clue.

Why? That's what I keep asking myself – *why?* How could this have happened? I wake up in the night, still seeing Simon lying there in that bloodbath – apparently dead . . . I still see myself staggering over to the oaks on the roadside, holding on to a trunk for support, then somehow managing to get home to throw up. I drove over to the Ranborne Hills and parked in a lay-by in order to scream. I couldn't have allowed my husband to see my distress, or he might have smelled a rat; though Thicko Theo smelling as much as a field mouse would have been a miracle akin to the parting of the Red Sea. Heaven only knows how he managed to land that top job in Naval Intelligence – I'd have thought you'd have to be in possession of a smidgeon of intelligence to hold down a job in Intelligence.

Along with everyone else, I thought Simon was dead. He was just lying there, torn to shreds, along with all our plans. But he didn't die, did he? – although he might as well be dead, poor love.

After waiting for all that time . . . If only we hadn't left it so late . . . If only we'd both been braver and taken the decision earlier . . . *If only* . . . Just four more weeks – four short weeks – and we would have been free. I sat in the car, numb, watching the dismal sky, and as the rain-swollen clouds rolled menacingly over the Ranborne Hills towards me, threatening a deluge, then drove home to face my useless husband.

Simon loathed his wife and couldn't wait to get out of that house – couldn't stand the size she'd grown. He'd once remarked that, had Marjorie's body been a building, it would be earmarked for demolition. When she'd married him, she'd seen the future paved with golden golf irons. That was her life. However, Marjorie is no longer overweight. Possibly through shock and lack of sleep, she's half her original size, and her clothes hang on her like rags. She walks about in a daze and is beginning to resemble something out a zombie film. For all I loathe her, I've come to feel deeply for her plight as I see her pushing Si around the village, putty-faced and wasted, her eyes glazed over as though still living some terrible nightmare. I watch her each day wheeling him about the village as though on auto-pilot. Up and down . . . up and down . . .

Simon, oh, Simon . . .

He was the best lover – the very best. We had such fun together. He was in pretty good nick for a sixty-year-old. At the beginning, it was a financial arrangement, of course, in order to pay for my nips and tucks; I couldn't have managed without that – couldn't imagine Thicko shelling out sufficient dosh for facelifts and hair extensions. My darling husband didn't even notice when I'd had it all done! But then, as he'd very probably register zero on the Gordon Diagnostic Test, that shouldn't have been much of a surprise.

But then – it just happened – we fell in love; the sort of falling off a cliff kind of love. And that's when we'd decided to run off together – out of Roper's End with all its sodding gossipy philistines; out of this depressing hole, where every boring bloody woman belongs either to the Women's Institute or the church choir, their conversation never varying from their favourite subjects: how their tomato plants are coming along, and how stupendously clever their grandchildren are – reminding everyone of the stupendously clever roots from which they were spawned.

No chance of escaping all this now.

I suppose, in the beginning, I was too young to realise just how thick Theo was; too blinded by his rank. He was fifteen years older than I and divorced, but he was a dashing, handsome commander who turned every head, and I'd been so proud to be on his arm! When I got to live with him, however, I came to realise that, far from the dashing commander he'd presented, Theodore Sebastian Kilpatrick would have been in serious danger commanding a rubber duck in his daily bath. He had, of course, lied to me about being an intrepid sailor, bravely fighting for his country. I didn't know then that he'd never seen warfare – never been in a battle in his life; in fact, had only ever been to sea once. He'd barely been capable of holding down the desk job to which he'd been allocated for practically all of his service life, happily sending all those other poor sods onto the battle field.

I'll never get to the bottom of what he actually did at Bletchley Park, nor MI5, because he maintains that, owing to his signing of the Official Secrets Act, he'd never be able to talk about it – but I would bet my grandmother's teeth that it was something dodgy. Because why did we have to get out of our lovely riverside house in Maidenhead in such a hurry? He'd cobbled up some story about retiring to the peace of the countryside, but I'd known him well enough by then to have seen through that.

And, just as the family was getting settled in Roper's End, he left me to take up some foreign correspondent sinecure that took him abroad for months at a time, leaving me alone with the children. I remember the time when, Richard, my eldest, was taken to hospital with appendicitis. Knowing that Theo was due his leave, I rang his boss at Milward Press to ask if he would let me know the minute he was back in the country. I was informed that he'd actually been back for a week – *back for a week without contacting me, his wife*. I knew then that he was playing fast and loose with some woman or other in London but, by then, I was past caring. As far as I was concerned, she was welcome to him.

It was around that time that I thought I'd have a bit of fun myself; well, why shouldn't I? And it was Simon who saved my sanity. So, right this minute . . . I don't know how I'll cope now he's gone.

I'd made one too many excuses for Theo over those earlier years and had tried desperately to make a go of my marriage. But it was no use. By the time I'd met Simon, the marriage had become like the last paragraph in a crime novel when, imagining you'd just cracked the plot, you discover the goal posts had shifted too far apart to give a damn. I was now, with two children, shackled to a moron who could barely use Velcro without instruction. Thicko Theo doesn't even have the wit to know how much he revolts me, nor how much I'm grieving for my lover . . .

I can't leave him now. What would I do, and where would I go? Until a few weeks ago, I thought I knew. Now . . . everything is so bleak. Why didn't we do a bunk sooner, instead of being so careful? We could now be living our lives together in Italy, with only the future to think about. That's the first thing I think about each day: my future . . .

# Chapter Nine

A clearing house for all the misfits and eccentrics of the evolutionary swamp, the small pretty village of Roper's End, apart from the general store/Post Office, up-market pub-restaurant and enchanting little duck pond, comprises retirees from all manner of strange and/or dodgy professions: a couple of questionable foreigners – Freddie Wingrave being one such – a few misogynists and anti-Semites of doubtful provenance, a self-confessed xenophobic ex-mariner, a paediatrician, a scientist, a retired High Court judge and his aristocratic cat-walk-strutting wife, a few open homophobics, and a number of folk under the illusion that their wife-swapping activities go unnoticed – all charmingly and thinly veiled under the heading of respectability; an outpost for the kind of people one would, with an ounce of sense, avoid like the Plague of Justinian.

Then there was semi-retired Doctor Bracknell, to name but a few.

However, as the philosopher Francis Bacon had once put it, 'There is no excellent beauty that hath not some strangeness in the proportion . . . .'

The ancient village of Roper's End was so named because of its long association with its gallows. History, or folklore, had it that these instruments of death had been lined up on what is now known as the Common when, in the sixteenth century, anyone foolish enough to cling on to their Catholic faith, were deemed witches and, therefore, considered evil enough to be hanged. Villagers in and around Roper's End would not, even now, cross the Common alone at night because, over the centuries, folk had claimed they'd heard the screams of those unfortunate men and women before the rope had ended their lives – when what they'd probably heard was nothing more than a fox calling for a suitable mate. But folklore is slow to loosen its ties, so no one fancied risking it.

Roper's End, snuggled deep within the wide range of the forbidding, but protective, arms of the Ranborne Hills, was situated between Bracklea and the city of Hansfield, whose twelve century cathedral sat within a stone's throw from the river Hanse. The village had once been a densely wooded hunting ground for the young Prince Henry, prior to His Royal Highness's elevation into the much-married eighth king of this nomenclature, as he gleefully speared stags, boar and anything else with four legs that happened to move therein, his manor house having bitten the dust a couple of centuries ago.

Nearly all of the earlier occupants of the well-appointed Georgian and Victorian houses in the village – large draughty piles set well back from the Kings Road (*note no apostrophe*) – had thought it fitting to name all their properties after trees in a bid to continue a connection with royalty, perhaps imagining a visit from the Queen to convey her gratitude at their undying allegiance to her illustrious ancestor. With the death of the Queen, the hope lingers on for her son to do the honours . . . The houses, at the time of building, had been named in reference to the grand oaks that had once graced Henry's playground, even though the thought of him looking from above with euphoric joy at the levelled ground where his once royal manor and precious woodland had stood – demolished to make way for houses, tarmacked roads, a children's play area and the all-important watering hole known as The Goose's Head – was perhaps a speculation too far. So, the names of most of the houses, unaltered since they were first built, could still be seen proudly exhibited on walls and gateposts, reminding everyone of the village's – not to mention its inhabitants' – grandeur, simultaneously confusing folk who occasionally found difficulty in differentiating Westwood from Woodford Grange.

The Common, being a wide expanse of stubby grassland, is a favourite haunt of those who owned dogs, which can be seen on a daily basis sniffing hungrily at each others' orifices while their owners leisurely pass the time of day.

Stretching further down the village is the *lower order* – those occupying Prince Albert Lane and Ranborne Hill Road in the newer raw-brick houses and bungalows, on land purchased some twenty-five years ago by a developer from Gloucestershire, into which poured all the wealthy retired parvenus from various areas of the West Midlands, with their small yappy dogs: they, who having sought and failed to assimilate into a village that has, from the start, made no bones about resenting the intrusion, keep firmly to themselves. These dwellings, having been given names such as Gleneagles or The Nook, are regularly sneered at by owners of the likes of Farnby Oaks, or Woodlands, which at least have history to fall back on. Occupying the grander houses on the much wider, oak-lined, Kings Road, with their thoroughbred Borzois and Dalmations, are the *elite*; those imagining that, as they were here first, regard they alone qualified to claim badges of ownership of the darling little village of Roper's End: after all, they hadn't chosen to live here with riff-raff incomers from Birmingham and didn't know what the world was coming to. So, as the latter are unable to do anything about the former – neighbourliness inevitably losing out to segregation – they do the next best thing: to sniff coolly and regard them as burdens they have to bear.

Roper's End, over the years, had become exceptionally des res, and everyone's idea of the perfect village to which to aspire, having gained popularity with those who had nursed an ambition to show the world that they'd climbed up the ladder of success and had eventually made it into this pretty, covetable village. This was the go-to West Midlands Utopia one graduated to in retirement in order to stick up two fingers to the less well-off and give out the message that they were a force to be reckoned with now that their address included that all-important appendage: Roper's End. The mere mention of the village's name was sufficient to make people sit up and take notice; if you'd made it to Roper's End, folk would be sure to look up to you, no matter how small your house nor how strong the Brummie accent behind the garden gnomes and swank. Estate agents, having, for several years, cottoned on to affluent self-made retirees' naked desire for elevation, ensured, therefore, that even the smallest of the bungalows in the village was marked up accordingly.

However, once ensconced in their hearts' desire, the newcomers of Roper's End very soon discovered how impractical it was to live in a village, whatever the prestige, where the nearest supermarket was the other side of Bracklea. To find a doctor – Alistair Bracknell being out of the question owing to his reputation re children – they'd had to cast their nets further afield, which meant a drive rather than a walk and, with their failing eyesight precluding the former – their cars having been taken away from them in a desire to protect the general road-travelling public – and without a regular bus service, they found themselves stuck. Neither was there a dentist nearer than Leighton-on-Hanse – nor a chemist. The town of Bracklea, to the north, was a good fifteen miles away and Leighton-on-Hanse, to the south, twenty miles. Nor was there anything in the village that one might call useful – anything, that is, apart from The Goose's Head opposite the Post Office and general store, an emporium next to useless when attempting to acquire a relatively simple thing such as a block of cheese which didn't bend double in its shrink-wrapped package, or greetings cards which didn't feature cuddly little bears holding pink balloons. If they'd given the matter a tad more thought, they might have realised earlier that the sweet little duckpond was no substitute for decent infrastructure when in need of either food or care.

So, those who had worked all their lives with a view to spending their retirement years here in picturesque little Roper's End, where they'd spent many a summer break admiring its fragrant tranquillity, quickly began to find this inconvenience untenable. What could they have been thinking, they asked themselves: leaving their comfortable houses and all their close friends, to live in a village that was all mouth and no trousers?

# Chapter Ten

Doctor Alistair Bracknell, he of rambling Mansford Oaks, was considered, by most people in the village, to have had got off rather too lightly after he was accused of the molestation of several children in whose care he'd been entrusted and, although he'd been cleared of this crime and allowed to retain his practice, albeit in a part-time capacity, a certain amount of mud still stuck. His wife Helen and daughter Pamela strutted grandly in their green wellies around the Common with their cream-coloured Labradors as though the heinous crime Bracknell had been charged with was but a mild misdemeanour and viewed as a mere passing phase, like acne.

Pamela Bracknell was the local vet and still living with mummy and daddy, with her horse, Carousel, taken, from time to time, out of its stable and trotted around the village with her atop, her unwashed hair, seriously in need of an oil change flapping over her pallid cheeks as she gazed disdainfully down at villagers in order to remind people of who she was. No one in the village of Roper's End allowed Pamela to touch their pets, as she openly sneered at kittens and pet rabbits and children's treasured hamsters, looking down her considerable nose and snorting her disapproval. Farm animals and dogs were the only animals she considered worth her attention, and she was never happier than when called out by a nearby farmer to stick her arm up some poor cow's arse.

As Alistair's Court case progressed, Helen found herself having to suffer all manner of sneers and threats from villagers whose children had been traumatised by her husband's abuse, the acquittal having cut no ice with them. Whether or not they'd imagined that Helen had colluded in this crime, she couldn't tell. Even so, they gave her the same cold shoulder they gave her husband and she found this grossly unfair, as she was privately on their side. She wondered how, in God's name, her husband had managed to get himself acquitted, the police having long ago seized his laptop and the disgusting pornographic images therein. She'd wept at the jury's verdict, knowing him to be guilty. So did everybody else.

Now, even though faced with living with the loathsome turd, she was determined to take a stance and to hold up her head in the village. She told herself that she couldn't allow this incident to be seen to affect her. However, maintaining this pretence burrowed into her mind, and she took herself off, for longer and longer periods, to wander the Common with her dogs.

Alistair got on her nerves, bellyaching about how badly he'd been treated throughout the trial, as though he'd been as white as fresh snow; the one who'd been hounded and persecuted and dragged through the courts by these morons determined to smear his name. He refused to see that he'd done anything that any other man might have done, and constantly voiced this opinion on the matter, making her sick to think of him sticking his fingers where fingers should not be stuck.

Even Pamela got on her nerves most of the time. If she'd left home, like a normal woman, it might have been easier for her to leave too. But no – Pamela was as well ensconced in the house as the horse in its stable. So she'd have to plough on, pretending to the rest of the village that her life was hunky-dory and that nothing would ever touch her.

However, she woke every morning in a sweat of apprehension as she realised that another day had to be ploughed through; another day of pretence and lies. And she longed for someone – anyone – to talk to and to share her anxieties . . .

# Chapter Eleven

Glenys Pugh, spinster of this parish, lived in a bungalow called Holgarth down a cul de sac off Prince Albert Lane and wasn't as daft as she looked.

Earlier in her life, Glenys had worked at Bletchley Park; she'd just walked in and breezily demanded a job.

'And what makes you think you'd be any good working here, young woman?' six-foot-five twenty-one-stone Major Alfred Smithers barked Yorkshirely.

'Because I want to do my bit to stop the Hun from winning the war!' she snapped, glaring up at him from a height of five-foot-one-and-a-half.

'What can you do then?' he smirked.

*'I don't know!'* she yelled back at him. 'That's for you to decide, isn't it? There's bound to be *something* I can do for my country!'

Major Smithers, finding this encounter with the demanding, shrieky young woman standing in front of him strangely uncomfortable, was finding difficulty in maintaining his level of importance; he accepted that she was offering to do her bit for the war effort – but this tupp'ny-ha'penny little bint? This situation threatened to make him look a right fool if anyone of importance should happen to walk by, so he'd have to find a way of getting rid of her. Major Smithers was more used to bullying than being bullied, and was worried that he'd be held in contempt if a lower rank happened to catch him being yelled at by a slip of a girl he had no clue how to handle. So he thought he'd better keep his lip curled in contempt in order to save face if such an occurrence presented itself.

If he'd allowed himself to be honest – self-awareness, being something of an aberration in a man shrouded in the rules and regulations of the British Army – Smithers would have had to confess that women in general flummoxed him; he couldn't quite get the hang of the way their brains worked. On the one hand, he couldn't help admiring this young miss her wish to take a part in the fight against Hitler; should be all hands to the pump, he supposed. On the other hand, did she imagine she could thwart the enemy single-handed? Hm, well, judging by her sheer effrontery, she might well manage to scare the Germans to hell and back if placed on the front line of battle: 'Mein Gott – der Englishe Boadicea! Ahu ab!'

But women? He'd been put on God's earth to bark orders at men; women, in his view, should be kept well away from wartime activities. Of course, they had their uses in the kitchen and the bedroom but that, in his opinion, is where they should stay. You couldn't have them running around Bletchley, taking over the place, except perhaps for cleaners or tea-ladies and the like. Next thing you knew, they'd be ordering the men around – and where, he asked himself, would that lead? This was a place for men. It was man's work. Anyway, women were notorious gossips. How could you ever trust them with the sort of stuff they'd be privy to in the hallowed grounds of Bletchley Park? He'd heard that the boffins had had a recent intake of female secretaries but, in his considered opinion, that was merely asking for trouble.

Now, confronted with this rabble-rousing, knee-high-to-a-grasshopper flibbertigibbet, demanding to be admitted into a male-dominated stronghold in order to fight the war, he was completely out of his comfort zone. This situation had not been in any manual he'd read, but he couldn't very well be seen to buckle under through inexperience. So, fully discombobulated, he decided to keep up the smirk; you never knew who might suddenly appear to witness the handling of a silly young lass, and the smirk would deflect his incompetence and would show them that, as always, he was man enough to control any situation in which he found himself. He'd imagined at first that the full-on smirk, which had sent shivers down the spines of many a fire-eating desperado, might have warned her off, but she was still there, glaring up at him. Lifting his chin importantly, therefore, he picked up the phone.

Glenys was then passed from department to department professing the same vigorous tenacity as she'd shown to Major Smithers. The powers that be, who were also not used to being told what to do by anyone sporting a skirt, let alone by a pretty pint-sized blonde barely out of school, were so taken aback by her chutzpah and determination to work for the Ministry of Defence that they set her to work as a secretary, which she wasn't cut out for, as she couldn't type.

Having come from a less than privileged background, it took time for Glenys to be accepted in the typing pool set, with their elocution lessons and pearls – but, in time, the hierarchy soon discovered that little Miss Pugh was a fast learner and, over her time there, she worked her way up the ranks, finally graduating to the position of personal assistant to one of the top bods at Bletchley, where she was privy to secrets that were very secret indeed to a great many important people. By then, the powers that be knew they could trust her; Glenys was dedicated to her work and intelligent enough, they'd realised, to know when to keep her mouth shut.

And she had kept her mouth shut – all her life – not once

revealing what she'd known. And, not only had she kept it shut about the secrets entrusted to her, she'd never once revealed to anyone in the village that she'd worked at Bletchley Park for the duration of the war, nor would they have believed her if she'd told them. Every villager, therefore, who'd dismissed this dotty old biddy as ready for a residential home for the insane, assuming she wouldn't have known Mickey Mouse from Donald Duck, would have been astonished at Glenys Pugh's sharpness of mind, and of what she'd contributed to the war effort. Dotty she may appear, and old she most certainly was, but Glenys was still as sharp as a pin. Villagers might well laugh behind their hands and look askance at the tiny white-haired doddery pensioner with one foot in the grave, and write her off as a silly old fart as she cycled round the lanes, putting the fear of God into everyone in her path, but there was absolutely nothing wrong, nor had there ever been, with Miss Pugh's brain cells.

As no one in Roper's End had a Scooby-do as to what secrets this eccentric old woman had been privy to, they'd have been even more intrigued to learn of all the wild and colourful antics she'd got mixed up in in her youth. But when, after her death, her bureau was opened up, the key of which was kept well hidden in a plant pot in a corner of her shed (just in case) – because someone was bound to open it up, were they not? – they – whoever 'they' may be – might discover some quite startling and unexpected activities that this old biddy had got up to in an earlier life. All her life was laid bare in that oak bureau: the wild parties; the dances; the drugs; the alcoholism; the abortion . . . As a girl, having lived a somewhat sheltered life, she'd certainly learned to live dangerously at Bletchley Park.

Now into her nineties and pretty much cured of the bottle, she often wondered about that abortion in her earlier life, and what would have happened had the decision swung the other way and she'd decided to have the baby. She would have loved a child – but, being unmarried, that decision would have cost her her job – and she'd loved her job. Had he lived, her son – she'd always thought of the foetus as a boy – would no doubt have a family of his own now, and she would have grandchildren, and perhaps by now great-grand-children. To this day, she looked at new mothers with a burning envy.

No longer pretty nor blonde, Glenys still took care of her appearance, booking weekly appointments at the hairdresser in Bracklea, her white hair immaculate. Afterwards, she'd troll the charity shops for something new, choosing the most outrageous clothes she could find. Her reasoning was that, if she couldn't do outrageous now, when could she do it? She laughed out loud each time she was sworn at as she rode at top speed down Ranborne Hill Road, taking her feet off the pedals and freewheeling with a 'Wheeeee!'

Careering down Kings Road, summer or winter, dressed for any future meteorological possibilities, Glenys delighted in shooting up two fingers at motorists hooting their horns for her to get out of their way. She was getting more than a tad wobbly now, though, and had nearly come a cropper once or twice on Pig Lane with all its deep unattended potholes. She knew full well the risks she took because, had she fallen off her bike in Pig Lane, she'd never have managed to get up again and her body might not be found for several days, perhaps when old Farmer Partridge, who barely left his homestead, trudged back from The Goose's Head one night half cut.

\* \* \*

The most terrifying thing, however, and the nearest Glenys had come to finally popping her clogs, was when she'd just pedalled past the Garraways' house as the bomb exploded. She hadn't stopped shaking when she'd afterwards realised that a mere two seconds earlier would have done for her what it had done to the poor sod in the Mazda.

She'd immediately screeched to a halt when she heard the blast, jumping off the bike and throwing it into a hedge, then running back to Oaklands on hearing Marjorie Garraway's blood-curdling scream. And there she stood, ashen-faced, aghast at the carnage; at Simon Garraway's shattered bloody body, and his wife running out to hold him; at the impossibility of it all. To steady herself, she held on to the gatepost and stood, oblivious of the toxic fumes; oblivious of anything but the destruction.

No. It couldn't be. This was all wrong!

There was nothing she could do, so she'd stood like a log, staring at Simon sprawled on the ground, not knowing if he was dead or alive, shaking with the thought of her narrow escape. And, after the shock of that, tears streaked her face as she sobbed and grasped the gatepost, rigid with disbelief; at the smell, the flames emanating from the cars, and at all the blood dripping from the blackened trees.

Peter Flynn and his son were the first ones to run up to Oaklands, taking in the destructive scene and immediately calling for an ambulance. Standing bone-cold with her mouth open – mouth too dry for utterance – Glenys suddenly found herself surrounded by practically the whole screaming village. It wasn't known then that the shreds hanging from the trees were the remains of the poor young postwoman, who'd happened to have been carrying the bomb.

The screaming was getting to her; it helped no one, and it

angered her. And she suddenly let out a scream of her own: 'Shut up! For God's sake, shut up everybody!'

After that: silence, as they all stared in disbelief at this strange, mouse-like woman, who they'd hitherto rubbished as being a waste of space, imagining that she'd never have the nerve to say shoo to an ant – this frail ancient hinny who was hardly ever seen without her equally ancient bicycle thrashing her way through the lanes . . . This shrivelled old woman yelling at them to shut their noise – how dare she!.

Peter Flynn came over to her as she stood, shaking, howling with grief, wrapped his arms around her and held her trembling little body. She'd been ashamed of that – of giving vent to her feelings and voicing her horror at the bloodbath. But it had just shot out of her mouth, and was as much of a surprise to her as to the crowd.

Glenys had known Simon Garraway well; he'd been her bank manager in Hansfield before his elevation to the dizzying heights of international banking. She'd been fond of him because he had never treated her like a silly old fool. And now there he was, poor devil, torn apart and lying face down on what had been the rose bed in the middle of the lawn.

An ambulance arrived and took both Simon and Marjorie away, and everyone but she – small frozen quivering Glenys, shocked to the core and unable to take her eyes off the scene of devastation – slowly dispersed. Her breath, having slowed down, she finally allowed herself to let go of the gatepost and blinked up at Peter Flynn, quietly refusing his offer to drive her home. Without another word, she retrieved her bike and, in a trance, made her way home, where she opened up the Famous Grouse and collapsed onto a chair. Though, afterwards, she was unable to recall the journey back.

It was all so wrong . . .

Having eventually been told that Simon Garraway had survived the blast, she called at Oaklands with flowers for Marjorie and to assure her that she would always be there for her if needed.

Many years ago Glenys had witnessed a plane coming down, nose-diving into a farmer's field; heard the terrified screams of the men inside it before it careered into the ground, then that unforgettable sound of the explosion as the aircraft plunged into the corn and burst into flames. Late summer, nineteen forty-three. She would always remember. Prior to the crash, the plane's tail was seen to be alight. So many planes had been damaged but, on landing, the crew crawled out of the wreckage shocked but otherwise unharmed. The pilot of the plane must have been searching for the airfield, a mere two miles away, relieved at managing to get his crew back home in the damaged aircraft – only for it to suddenly swerve downwards and crash into that field of corn. She remembered still that marmoreal chill shooting up her spine; remembered her grief at the thought of all those boys gleefully expecting a cheery homecoming – dented, but alive – only to be killed by a change of wind fanning the flames into an inferno.

She'd also witnessed the survivors of these many crashes, their faces burned out of recognition, and/or limbs removed; witnessed their inner pain as they contemplated their future, perhaps wishing that they, too, had been killed outright, rather than have to face the lifelong indignity of being unable to wipe their own arses . . .

These things were brought to mind each time she subsequently saw Simon Garraway. Would he ever be able to wipe his own arse? And what would that do to him?

She never failed to stop to speak to the Garraways thereafter when coming across them in the village; he barely able to speak, and Marjorie having to fill in for him from time to time when he became incoherent. Glenys would bend down to his level in the wheelchair and speak to him, touching his hand and smiling, encouraging him to talk, even though sensing how tiring it was for him, now that half his tongue had gone. His face was an unspeakable wreck but, whereas almost everyone else, unable to hide their distress, looked down at this hideous half-human, wheeled about the village like something fit only for a freak show, Glenys forced herself to look at him in the eye, as though nothing at all was wrong with his face, and watched him trying to smile his gratitude.

She also saw the effort Marjorie was putting in in order to avoid breaking down, with tears just below the surface.

'You know my number, Marjorie,' she said to her in her gruff, no-nonsense voice. 'Don't hesitate to ring if you need anything.'

# Chapter Twelve

'Oh, God. Don't look now, but the String Bean has just walked in, dressed in stuff designed to cause traffic accidents,' Simon Garraway groaned, the last time we were in The Goose's Head with Peter and Janet Flynn. 'Is that the third or fourth facelift? I've lost count. Just look at those cheekbones; they could cut through steel.'

It was not often Simon groaned – but even when he groaned he was funny. I'll always remember him as comic to my straight guy; quick off the mark, telling joke after outlandish joke at our table in The Goose; it's how I'll always remember him – roaring with laughter. He's not laughing now, poor bugger. Right now, he looks as though he's been put together with bits of other people. I saw him the other day and he looked at me with his one bloodshot eye as though he'd never seen me before and, for once in my life, I didn't know what to say to him.

'Simon – it's Bri. Brian Frobisher . . .' I'd said that first time, and he'd offered something akin to a smile . . .

It was his manic laugh I'll remember; no one laughed like Simon. He'd throw his head back and howl full throttle, like a wolf. If there was one thing guaranteed to make Si groan, however, it was the Ramsdens; couldn't stand the airs – though even *they* couldn't manage to dampen his spirits. And he was hilarious when taking the piss out of Penelope, who'd quite obviously been at the back of the queue when they were handing out the humour awards.

The last time we were in The Goose together was only a few days before the bomb.

'What, no gym today, Pen?' he called out as Penelope sashayed in earlier than usual that day, designer-garbed to the eyeballs. 'Workout bench kaput? Or did you get your barbells in a twist?'

Which wasn't particularly funny in itself, but it gave us all laugh just seeing the woman's nose shooting disdainfully into the air.

'Did you know,' he went on, loud enough for her and, indeed everyone else, to hear, 'that every seven minutes of every day, someone at a gym somewhere in Britain pulls a ham string? Why would they do that? My idea of exercise is buttering a croissant.'

Penelope turned her back on us and walked to the far end of the bar.

'Hey! Listen up everybody – got a brilliant idea!' he yelled. 'Why don't we hold a croissant-buttering marathon . . . ? It could become an Olympic sport. Set Roper's End on the map!'

Penelope opened her bag for her purse, paid for her drink, sniffed elegantly, then swanned to the other side of the pub and sat with her pink gin. You could see what was running through her humourless mind: croissants were fattening; *why would anyone joke about a croissant, or even laugh. It just wasn't funny . . .* She'd probably never touched a croissant in her adult life for fear of getting to like them. And as for butter – perish the thought . . . However, owing to Botox having frozen her forehead, plus numerous face lifts rendering a sort of wind-tunnel effect, even if she had found Simon the teensiest bit funny, she wouldn't have been able to laugh because she might have scalped herself owing to all that facial skin having been nailed to the back of her head.

We watched her, sitting as far away from us as possible, awaiting her husband – he of the rotund belly atop two matchstick legs – whose appearance set Simon off again.

'Here he comes – the squire of Roper's End,' he said in a stage whisper, 'Looks like a human set of bagpipes.'

Charlie strode in, oblivious as to the ridiculous figure he cut in his frayed shorts.

'Just had a round of golf with my friend, Farley,' he announced to the whole pub, with all the considered pomposity at his disposal.

'In those shorts?' Simon laughed.

If looks were a crematorium, Simon, at that point, would have found himself a small pile of ash.

'One has certain standards of dress on the golf course. But, of course, you would know about that, wouldn't you?' he shot out sarcastically. 'I changed into casual clothes as soon as I'd had my shower!'

'Ooh, a shower!' Simon said, deadpan. 'I've always wanted one of those. We've only got the old tin bath at home.'

'Well, at the golf club, we have one, if you would care to visit,' Charlie said with a smirk.

'Wouldn't go near the place – my wife does that for me. Saves me the bother of cosying up to the likes of Derek Farley!' Simon said.

Seeing everyone finding all this banter hilarious had Charlie utterly disconcerted – mind you, we'd had one or two bevvies by then – and in attempting to diffuse Simon's scorn of the golf fraternity, he turned his back and huffed to the seat beside his wife. We all knew that Derek Farley was the Chief Constable of West Midlands Constabulary based at 'Poncingville Hall', as we called it, who, with his wife, was known to visit the Ramsdens on a fairly regular basis. What we found so amusing was that Ramsden was informing us all that he was hand in glove with a *Very Important Personage* in the county.

'I hear that golf, though, is very good for clearing ones' mind of thought!' Simon said, a gleam of devilry dancing in his eyes.

'Yes . . . interesting sport, golf,' he began, lounging back with his pint, and we pricked up our ears for another of his put-downs; you could always tell when a put-down was coming by the cheeky wobble of his dimples. 'Interesting history, that game . . . It apparently started way back in the Dark Ages, when Early Man chanted incantations and furiously beat the ground with sticks in order to placate the gods in order to provide fine weather for the harvest. Anthropologists once thought this to be heretical superstition, but it's now considered a respectable sport for all kinds of important people – you know, like chief constables of police – that kind. *Although*,' he went on with a glint, 'if anyone *was* looking for a connection to Early Man . . .'

Si was a hoot.

He'd often call in on us at Farnby Oaks, when Marjorie occasionally let him off the hook, to have a drink and a chat. He had an eye for the women, though, and I caught him giving Valerie the eye once or twice. But he loved kids – and Poppy and James loved him. He'd wait for them to come home from school, then play with them for the rest of the afternoon. Loved a kickabout with a ball. Where he got the energy from, I'll never know. Pity he never had kids. There was a rumour going round some time ago about him having an affair with Julia Kilpatrick, but I never really believed that – because I'm having an affair with Julia Kilpatrick; though it actually isn't so much an affair as a business arrangement: I need sex and she needs money.

Valerie went off sex as soon as she'd had kids; motherhood was what she was born to do, so the kids served her general purpose in life, and she just wasn't interested in bedroom activities any more. So, well . . . a man has to have some outlet in that respect – and Julia is always worth the money; Julia's fantastic.

Val's always been a bit on the squeamish side – stupid bitch

– so I wasn't really surprised when she fainted at the sight of Si lying in all that blood. The last straw that day was that Wingrave woman, pointing out all those bits of body hanging from the trees, and the severed head lying a mere two yards away from Val's feet. Up to that point, we'd all assumed it was a damaged football. Damn that woman!

Val starts crying at odd times these days, but I can't think why. I can understand that it shook her because she thought – we all thought at the time – that Simon was dead. So, okay – she was shocked and upset like the rest of us. But I didn't think she'd cared that much about what had amounted to an acquaintance – a neighbour she barely saw; she hardly ever came with me to The Goose, so she only saw Simon on the odd occasion when he'd call round to ask for the loan of my power drill or some other tool he was short of, when he'd take the opportunity to see the kids. I don't understand why she would still be taking it all to heart after all this time.

Women are strange. I don't think I'll ever understand them.

* * *

Brian's the biggest fool – and, considering his standing as Head of Bracklea Science Laboratories, an utter cretin. He doesn't realise how completely transparent he is; thinks I don't know about his affair with Julia Kilpatrick and the money he regularly pays her; thinks I'm utterly wet behind the ears. But, you see, I see the statements each month. There again, I didn't have to check the accounts to know about the affair. I just knew. You do, don't you?

In an unusual fit of malice, I once asked him – but just the once – about the cash – amounts of five hundred pounds or so each month that I said I couldn't account for. He blew up at me for even suggesting that he couldn't spend his money as he saw fit, considering I did bugger all to contribute to the financial upkeep of house and family; raged and spat and accused me of interfering with the way he ran his life.

I watched his bluster; just sat there quietly until it burned itself out, then calmly asked how he *did* run his life – and did the so-called running of this life include his family? Before he could answer, I added that I hadn't actually accused him of anything improper – why would he think that? I was just asking... He spat out that I should mind my own damned business. After saying that I thought that this was my business, considering that it was a joint account, he then blustered and became cagey, and I smiled inwardly; could see he was struggling to come up with a suitable lie; almost saw the brain cells torturing themselves while they fought to formulate an answer.

I sighed, and spun it out simply for the pleasure of seeing him squirm, watching while he fumbled his brain for something logical on which to pin a credible story; watched as he finally tried to fob me off with an outright improbable story of him having to buy some new expensive power tools – *if, indeed, it was any of my business!* I almost asked him how many power tools he would need to fuck Julia Kilpatrick. But I feigned acceptance and let it go with a smile. However, he doesn't know that I know exactly what is in that shed of his, and no new power tools have appeared there for a very long time.

I needed to have him believe that I believed him, though – because, although I thoroughly enjoyed making him sweat, there was the small matter of hypocrisy on my part, with Simon Garraway and I having had a fairly good fling together whenever time allowed; and so our lies to each other conveniently coincided. The difference was that I didn't have to pay Simon for the pleasure of his company.

Brian's lovemaking is dire. I'd never enjoyed sex, with him banging away inside me night after night without a thought as to how I felt about it so, as soon as I'd had the children, I tried to get out of it as much as possible, which is probably what drove him away into Julia's arms. When I met Simon, all that pent up frigidity changed. I didn't realise what I was missing until I met Si. He showed me how wonderful sex can be.

I shall miss that – miss him . . .

Brian, of course, never guessed about Si and me, even when we fooled around in front of him – which is hardly surprising, considering the fact that, out of his laboratory, he's a total dim-wit who can only see as far as the end of his flow chart.

So . . . bring on Julia Kilpatrick – she's welcome to him.

# Chapter Thirteen

I haven't told you about Toni, have I? Antonio Vascari.

Toni and I met when we casually eyed each other across the room as we were sitting at nearby tables in a stuffy Hamburg café.

Feeling somewhat relieved to have been offered this German assignment, I relaxed, thinking I might explore the city after drinking my coffee. Germany was a vast change for me – home from home; a country which I'd always considered far more civilised than Britain, and which is a light year away from the harrowing parts of the world I was usually called upon to cover: those sweltering fly-ridden third world countries, where the dead are invariably left to rot among the stink of poverty and decomposition. I was more than happy to be in a country where the dead, more often than not, die in clean hospitals and are generally buried with dignity.

As I sat drinking my coffee that morning, I noticed Toni's eyes on me. After a while, he smiled his traffic-stopping smile and finally walked over and introduced himself in fluent German, asking if he might sit at my table. He was so handsome. I think I fell in love with him at that precise moment. He'd noticed the ever-present camera and asked about it. He seemed to know a great deal about cameras and quizzed me about apertures, asking how good it was at close-ups. At the time, I should have wondered about that; should have suspected an ulterior motive. But I simply answered all his questions, enthralled by his coal-black eyes and that *smile*. I told him about the paper I worked for in Britain, and he expressed interest in what I was doing in Germany. We got to talking about where I was being sent to next. His eyes lit up when I'd told him that my next assignment was Moscow. I suppose I did, at the time, wonder why Moscow had managed to get him so excited; also, what he might be up to. But it was no more than a vague thought. As the conversation rolled on, however, I suspected something dodgy about him. His eyes, however, held me in thrall, so I didn't really mind too much about his dodginess.

It was, therefore, with a surge of great disappointment that I slowly came to realise that it was Moscow – plus the camera – that he was more interested in than me.

When I steered the conversation round to him and what he was doing in Hamburg, he said he was a salesman, but carefully omitted to mention what he actually sold. The conversation then veered cleverly and smoothly back to the camera . . .

I should have twigged earlier, I know. But the slowness in acknowledging his true intentions was largely owing to the fact that I was, by then, falling in love with his gorgeous Italian. It was that smile – that killer smile – that was my undoing. My brain was doing its best to tell me that Toni was lying to me, and that he was more than a salesman, but my heart seriously wanted to believe him. If he wasn't salesman, what was he – and did I care?

We parted that day but then, owing to a series of 'accidental' meetings, we began to see quite a lot of each other. When I got to know him better, I realised that he'd been following me. And that's the first time I began to smell a rat – at least a tenth of a rat to begin with – when his questions became more probing and pointed.

And then I knew.

It became obvious that he was working under cover for some organisation, although for which organisation I never got to discover. I knew then that I had to be careful.

My editor was in the process of sending over a fellow journalist to accompany me to Moscow. Our brief was to interview and photograph a Russian journalist who, in running a hostile article in his newspaper, had subsequently managed to incur the wrath of the establishment and had been charged with corruption. I'd always been sent to assignment alone, but the paper felt it safer for me to have back-up in this particular case; this was Russia, after all, where foreigners roaming around alone were likely to be suspect. Like most right-minded people throughout the rest of the world, we suspected the accused to have been unjustly charged, but we hadn't expected to get very far. Our fears were that (a) we wouldn't be allowed to get within a couple of kilometres of him, or that (b) the man would be long dead before we got there.

However, the English journalist to whom I'd been assigned fell ill as soon as he arrived and was whisked to hospital, so my editor said that there was no way I was going to be allowed into Russia on my own – which was a huge relief. During my career thus far, I'd confronted killers of all descriptions, but the Russians put the fear of God in me.

I voiced my concerns to Toni and immediately saw the cogs whirring as he took in this unexpected news of the hospitalised reporter, divining that, what seemed a setback for me, might afford an opening for him. He was desperate to get into Moscow, I could tell but, until he'd met me, hadn't managed to find a legitimate way in. He became very excited as to all the possibilities this new situation afforded him – then came up with a plan to impersonate my colleague. I was horrified at this and, argued against it, imagining all the dangers if he were to be discovered. But, using every ounce of Italian charm, he eventually persuaded me to wire back to my editor that the journalist had recovered, then began to put into place a plan of action. He knew his power – his charm – and, using every ounce of it, knew, from the beginning, that he couldn't fail.

Having then allowed myself to be manipulated, I knew I'd have to cobble up some story to get my colleague to hand over his papers to me, so that Toni could act as my journalist. It was fortunate that the likeness of the reporter, Roger Blandford, was not a millions miles away from Toni, but Toni would have to grow a bit of a beard for us to get away with it. It wasn't a complete doddle, as it was possible that Blandford would become suspicious. Roger was, by this time, in dreadful pain, though, and I managed to get to him just as he was being wheeled into theatre and, therefore, at his most vulnerable. I was aware of what I was doing; aware that it was dangerous and could cost me my job – but that's how I got Toni into Moscow – just as he knew I would.

It occurred to me then that, lurking behind that gorgeous smile, a devious tactical crocodile might have been at work. I was being used. I wasn't stupid; I knew full well that he was using me but, by then, it didn't unduly bother me. I was not especially fond of reptiles but, if that particular crocodile had dragged me down into the depths of the river and asked if he could eat me from the toes up, I would gladly have invited him to do so, and then prepared him a lemon soufflé for pudding.

Now happily armed with the newly-obtained press pass and with me as his photographer, Toni assumed he would have access to information important enough to pass on to his bosses – whoever they were; I never asked. *But I couldn't help myself.* Just gazing at him took my breath away; I would have done anything for him. You may think this stupid in the extreme but, unless you'd known him, you couldn't possibly understand . . .

Care of my paper, we rented a flat, but I'd lose him for several days on end; he'd disappear, then unexpectedly return to ask if

I'd managed to do what he'd asked me to do. I never knew what he did with this information – nor what he got up to during these absences, but knew better than to ask questions. I always found a way to comply with his wishes, and we worked well as a team.

It was during this time that he attempted to recruit me into his spy ring. One evening, he turned up the radio to full volume, suspecting – quite rightly – that the flat was bugged, then finally took me into his confidence. He admitted that he was a spy, and felt he now trusted me sufficiently to declare his true vocation. I couldn't believe that he was asking me to join him in undercover activity, but reasoned that, with my grasp of languages, I could go down that road if I chose – easily. With my camera, I would be a tremendous asset. But could I go that far? I havered, hedging my bets and wondered what this would entail. I told him that I was fulfilling that rôle already – well, as much as I felt able – and hesitated about getting in deeper. He saw my hesitancy and worked on it – could see that I was tempted at dipping my toe into the deep and dangerous ocean of espionage. At that time, the powers that controlled MI5 had had this mental block that refused to believe that a woman could be capable of such work; and I was almost tempted to prove that I was more than capable.

Almost.

When I was with him, mesmerised by those wonderful eyes, I knew with utter certainty that I could achieve anything. But when alone and clear-headed and allowed to sit down and analyse what it would mean, I sensed that, lurking around those murky unknown corners, were perhaps too many areas of dark grey morality – envisaged too many slabs of unpredictability – of peril. Apart from the risks I would have to take myself, how would this affect my husband? So, despite Toni's crocodile grin beguiling me, I foresaw the life he offered leading to an untenable conflict of conscience, something which I would find difficulty squaring with myself. I might have done it, but I couldn't let go of all the *'what ifs'* . . .

But spying would have come naturally to me – and would have been so exciting. If only I hadn't been married . . . I can't pretend that I didn't think long and hard about the possibilities, though. Thankfully, I came to my senses, and retreated from serious thoughts of espionage before they could take hold. That didn't stop him from trying though and, for all the time I knew him, he did his level best to sway me, sensing that I was on the very tip of the diving board. So, each day, he would throw another fish into the waters of my psyche in his attempt to get me to jump into the deep end.

What was so shameful was that I almost did . . .

But I was under his spell, and I rang my boss and asked to stay in Moscow longer than had been planned. The Russian journalist had been sent to the Gulag long before we'd arrived, but I didn't tell him that. I lied to my editor because Toni needed just few extra days in order to complete his mission. He promised it would be only a few days – then we could get out.

Moscow was suffering an unusually cold winter, and the cold ate into me, but I couldn't refuse him. I lied to my boss, and I lied to my husband, saying that, even if I wanted to come home, the extreme weather had caused the airlines to cancel all flights.

I was already getting myself in deep, playing a dangerous game and, if caught, knew I would land in serious trouble and lose my job; in the worst case scenario, perhaps even finding myself slammed onto a train bound for the Siberian salt mines. But I was helpless against the onslaught of charm and what I later realised was Toni's sheer cunning, drip-feeding me bits of information on a need-to-know basis – never telling the full story. He was so clever at withholding secrets that, to this day, I have no idea who he might have been working for. What I do know, however, is that these activities of his were seriously annoying someone somewhere; annoying them sufficiently to commit murder; that whichever organisation Toni was working for had within it a traitor who'd leaked information to someone who didn't like what he was revealing.

But I should never have fallen for that smile. I was old enough and experienced enough to have resisted his charm. But I didn't resist. I loved him. So . . . I'd gone against everything I'd held dear, and allowed him to accompany me to Moscow. Big mistake.

Once in Moscow, he'd slide off piste every now and then and I'd grow anxious for him. I grew worried about him when I was left alone in the flat for a couple of days, not knowing where he was or what he was up to. I worried about the whole thing; not for myself, but because he was beginning to attract unwanted attention. He'd considered himself invincible – but then, no one is invincible . . . Although this devil-may-care attitude was an obvious cover and one that had worked well for him all his life, this was a dangerous way to behave. But he'd laugh if I so much as mentioned the danger – imagined he could spellbind his way out of any given situation just by exercising his charm and flashing that marvellous smile. I knew – we both knew – that he was being watched . . .

Clever Toni. Beautiful Toni. But a Toni in love, and allowing that love to cloud his judgment . . .

It became obvious to each of us that the secret police had sussed that he wasn't a journalist, and that this was a put-up job. The worry was: who had informed the authorities that he wasn't a journalist? That wasn't the only worry, however: Toni's association with me was steadily enraging his spy master, who had been against this subterfuge from the start. His handler told him to drop me, because I was a danger to him. But he didn't drop me and, in his determination not to let me go, Toni seriously let his guard down.

I was out of my mind when he got killed. His death, of course, having been reported as an unfortunate accident: an articulated-lorry driver 'absent-mindedly' driving on the wrong side of the road and ploughing into his small Mini, crushing it beyond recognition.

But I knew that it had been no accident.

\* \* \*

I remember that day and will remember it until I die. The day I was told.

The sun had at last broken through the clouds and, tiring of being cooped up in our dingy flat, I'd decided to wrap myself up and write up my report in the park. I remember looking up to the sky and feeling the warmth of the sun on my face, willing it to choose my words. Having failed to obtain access to the editor of the Russian newspaper for his comments on the imprisoned journalist, I needed to report back my paper to tell them something – anything – in order to explain my failure to return to Britain. So I sat on the park bench, concentrating on how to concoct a story of sorts in order to justify my staying longer than necessary in Moscow.

Then someone tapped me on the shoulder.

When I was told of Toni's death, everything stopped. My brain, my lungs – everything. My whole body ceased to work, and I felt the life suddenly drain out of me. I didn't weep; I couldn't weep. All I remember of that moment, as I sat absorbing the news, were small insignificant things around me: I know that I was sitting in the park with tall trees swaying, spraying their burden of snow in a freak warmish wind, while a weak sun filtered through their branches; that drips of melting snow were dropping onto my head; that, at that moment, a small icicle landed on my notepad with a light thud. I know that birds were singing too loudly and happily at the sudden warmth, and that I'd wanted to scream for them to stop. My darling Toni was dead. All that energy – all that beauty – smashed to a pulp; murdered by who knew who . . . ?

I couldn't move, and the tears refused to flow; I simply sat on – numb – and watched as, beyond the railings of the park, a tram rattled by. And a little boy played in the snow with his ball.

After being hauled in by the secret police, I was relieved of my camera. They took out the roll of film, then handed the camera back with a smile before my eventual release, the bastards. By then, however, there was nothing more incriminating in the film than photographs of an avenue of trees, so I mentally wished them luck with that.

When I could bear it, I went back to the flat we'd shared and looked through Toni's things to locate his notebook – the precious notebook he'd never let out of his sight. After my grilling by the KGB, I was tired and hungry and, in my fury, I turned the place upside down – but to no avail; it was gone, as was everything else of worth. They – whoever 'they' were – had, in my absence, managed to stage a burglary and, when reported, the authorities noted it all down, attempting with little success to keep straight faces. They then 'promised' to find and punish the perpetrator. Their attitude told me all I needed to know.

If it had been a burglary and if Toni's death had, by some remote chance, been an accident, as it was claimed, how was it that someone saw fit to steal his notebook? I understood the theft of the gold chain and his Patek Philippe wristwatch – but the notebook? How many names could there have been in that notebook, and how useful could that information have been to the authorities? Perhaps there were no names – Toni would have been too careful for that; I knew that he feared what that notebook would reveal if he ever lost it – so everything had been written in code. But then, the Russians have experts to crack codes, don't they? And the code, having been cracked, might well have been sufficient to highlight the whereabouts of several other agents.

That's something I shall never know but, after Toni's murder, and within a very short period of time, there was a clutch of five more unexplained deaths in the USSR – all foreigners; Toni had known them all. The notebook alone, however, couldn't have done that amount of damage. There had to be someone on the inside orchestrating all those deaths.

The rest, as I now sit here with my cat, is a just blur – like looking through a veil; that veil of the past which, though impenetrable, becomes fainter as the years pass. One does not forget the breaking of one's heart; it just becomes less keen. It's the guilt that lingers. And beyond the grief was the certainty that it was my fault – had to be. I had brought Toni into Russia; moreover, I'd known that to be wrong. It was all my fault.

It wasn't until after Toni's murder which, looking back, had a certain inevitability, that I realised what a bloody dangerous life I'd been living then and that, if I'd happened to have been in the car with him I, too, would have been killed. But I knew without doubt that I was at fault, and I couldn't – still can't – forgive myself.

* * *

When I got back to Fleet Street, I was not too surprised to find that no one had heard of these murders but, when I showed them pictorial evidence – evidence I'd managed with difficulty to photograph and smuggle out; photographs of Toni and his mangled car – my editor decided to run a story – a story that smacked of treachery, suggesting that MI5 had in its midst a 'mole'. It caused quite a stir at the time, but then was quietly forgotten and not followed up. I was furious at this sudden lack of interest and stormed in to speak to the editor, asking him why this story had been dropped; him giving some lame excuse about more important news items to be covered; me then accusing him of having been threatened by a higher authority, an accusation he hotly denied. But I would have bet my house he'd been threatened with the closure of his paper if he'd printed anything further on the subject. And so any attempt at a follow-up was swept very conveniently under some dusty, ministerial carpet and stamped on to ensure that it stayed there.

I delved – or tried to – but was warned off – told to drop it, or I'd be off the paper. But, in my fury, I felt I couldn't let them bully me into submission; I had to find the truth. It was the least I could do for Toni. I was angry – angry at their studied insouciance at the death of my lover and of all those other men. So I secretly arranged to have lunch with a member of MI5 to ask if he could put out a few feelers – which, of course, my editor got wind of.

He'd also been informed by Roger Blandford, on his eventual return, of my wheedling his papers out of him in order to allow an unknown Italian to obtain entry into the USSR – and was incandescent with rage.

Ben thought I'd retired from the paper but, because of that subterfuge and the fact that I couldn't let this story go without attempting to discover who was responsible for the deaths of Toni and all those other agents, I was, in fact, fired.

For all these years I've been haunted by Toni's death, the shadows of the past every now and then misting my mind and generating that searing anger once more. It's taken almost a lifetime to attempt to get over that anger – and the guilt. Although I'd vowed to discover the perpetrator of that crime, I doubt now that I ever shall.

Someone was responsible for his death and, until my dying day, I mean to keep on trying.

Everybody thinks I've forgotten, but I haven't.

# Chapter Fourteen

Malodorous, with a hint of a boozy lunch and the odd flutter on the dogs, Alistair Bracknell had the grizzled bearing of a disillusioned ape, and the sort of face which, if featured on the front page of a tabloid newspaper, might blight someone's enjoyment of his breakfast egg, then get hidden from the children.

Having just finished his surgery with the two or three people in the village still brave enough to be on his list, he shambled into the kitchen with a heavy sigh to make a cup of coffee, which he laced liberally with whisky; anything to take away the memory of those boring bloody patients with all their boring bloody ailments.

Plus that recent harrowing court case . . . No one had understood how much that had taken out of him – nor cared, it would seem. He was fully aware that certain people in the village now looked at him differently, still suspecting him of being a paedophile – which, to be fair, he was. Okay, so he liked little children; he couldn't see the harm in that. Why the hell should he feel guilty about it? He hadn't, of course, mentioned that to the judge and jury when pleading his innocence.

He slumped down with his feet up on an adjacent chair and flicked his lighter to ignite the cigarette clamped between his lips then slowly filling his lungs, recalled, quite clearly, his time in Albania, where he was given carte blanche to touch up all the children he liked. No one gave a monkey's about stuff like that and, even if the children had complained, it was more than likely that (a) nobody would have believed in that sort of behaviour of a doctor, and (b) who the hell would have cared anyway; so it would be the children who'd get a clip round the ear for kicking up a fuss. People in this country were such fucking prudes . . .

He didn't know what had suddenly made him think of Albania – except for that damned bomb reminding him of the threat to his own life a few years ago . . .

He'd enjoyed his time in Albania, he recalled as he sipped his coffee; enjoyed learning the language, the quaint customs and joining in with all the local traditions, most of which had happily involved alcohol. This halcyon period in his life occurred just after he'd qualified, and after realising how unlikely it was that he would be taken seriously as a doctor in this country, owing to his having barely scraped through the medical examinations. If he stayed here, he knew he'd never get a decent medical practice to take him on. Apart from that, there was another reason he'd had to get out of the country . . . At medical school, he'd played fast and loose with not a few other women and discovered he'd managed to get a fellow scholar pregnant. There was the problem, however, of having just got himself engaged to Helen. He'd contemplated breaking off the engagement and marrying the girl but this, on serious consideration, would have done him no favours, as she, unlike Helen, had not been the daughter of a prominent aged landowner who, by the look of him, could pop his clogs in the not-too-distant future, leaving her the sole beneficiary of his estate. So, unwilling to admit this predicament to her family, he told them that he'd been asked to do a year's charity work in Albania; thought that taking on medical work overseas would look good on the curriculum vitae in order to stand him in good stead for future medical work in Britain.

So, he'd abandoned the girl, put marriage on hold, then had

then hot-footed to a country which was not too particular about poor qualifications – or rumours of an unsavoury kind – except, he guessed, he probably wouldn't have got away with that twaddle today.

He allowed himself a small smile at the memory and blew out a ring of smoke, remembering those wonderful mountains, the freshwater lakes and all those nubile young nurses sashaying down the wards, the skirts of their uniforms riding up as they bent over to lift a patient out of bed . . . He'd been happy there and might have stayed, but for a couple of unfortunate incidents, the threats afterwards having become too serious to ignore.

There had been that business as to the wrong leg being removed from a pregnant woman during surgery. Owing to the regular surgeon having gone down with some bug and unable to perform the emergency operation that particular day, Alistair had agreed, after a seriously bad hangover, to do it himself. He'd never before practised amputations, nor been trained for it – but hey, what could go wrong? You just cut off the leg, then send the woman home with antibiotics.

The expectant mother was suffering from gangrene in her right leg and was, unsurprisingly, expecting the removal of the right leg. But, in the after-blur of several stiff Moscow Mules, the night before, and to the dismay of the theatre staff who had clocked the stench of him before he'd set foot in the theatre, he'd removed the left leg – and the woman had died shortly after, having in the meantime contracted sepsis from the gangrenous leg. This was shortly followed by the death of her baby which couldn't be saved. No amount of apology nor explanation for the deaths had managed to console the husband and, grieving for his wife and child, he'd threatened Alistair with a knife.

Fortunately, Alistair's interpreter at the time had managed to winkle him out of that one, which had left him free to continue practising his incompetence.

Then there was the bother of getting an underage girl pregnant, and her father gunning for him. Daddy, turning out to be a large angry Albanian, set Alistair on a plan to move on and to leave the family to deal with the situation, imagining the problem to evaporate with his departure. Albania, however, being a relatively small country, the girl's brothers had managed with comparative ease to discover his whereabouts, and had nearly succeeded in killing him. That had been bad, putting him in hospital for two months.

Battered and heavily scarred, he jumped ship and drove south to Scutari, again to another unsuspecting hospital, not having realised how easy it was to track down a foreigner; nor had he given much thought, until hospitalisation, as to how big and dangerous Albanian men were.

Fearing for his life and desperation terrifying his dreams, Alistair found himself, after recovery, able to leave for England and for Helen . . .

\* \* \*

Having returned to Britain, and after a few years of marriage, parenthood and a thriving practice, he'd one day received a letter from the father of the girl in Albania, demanding money for the baby he'd fathered. During those years, he'd conveniently forgotten about the girl; had bathed in the confidence that all that trouble was well and truly behind him. He was well out of that business, he'd thought.

Then the letter.

This shock had knocked him back, and put him in a quandary: he may have forgotten the incident, but they clearly hadn't. What to do . . . ? What had truly disturbed him, though, was that these people had discovered where he lived. So . . . decisions had to be made. Should he alert the police? The letter, he realised, would have had to be explained to the police and, having had dealings in the past with Derek Farley's shower, they'd probably dismiss it out of hand. Should he now come clean and confide in Helen, admitting his past sins, in the hope that she'd help him out of this situation? Or . . . should he stay schtum? Confessing to his wife, he guessed, could result in divorce, so staying schtum might be the better option. Simply thinking of what a meal Helen would make of his infidelity – even though this infidelity had happened long before their marriage – made him squirm. He could lose his practice – and the inheritance: her parents were not yet dead. So he stuffed the letter into the bottom drawer of his desk, which he'd then kept locked.

The child would now be around five years old, he mused; but nothing to do with him. They were playing games with him, weren't they? Trying to scare him. This was simply a mind game, and he was damned if he was going to be bullied by a bunch of Albanian peasants. He pursed his lips defiantly as he re-read the letter. This would be best met with silence; that was the only way of dealing with letters of this nature . . . He would *not* succumb to blackmail; wouldn't be going down that particular road. They could threaten all they liked – he wouldn't pay a penny. They could take a running jump!

When the second letter arrived, it got the same treatment.

A further three letters from Albania subsequently dropped through the post and, though disturbing, these also were 'filed' into his desk drawer. They were just trying it on, he mused. How could they seriously think they could get money out of him? Albania being several hundred miles from the United Kingdom, was far too far away to pose any kind of danger – so they were really no threat at all. How could this be a danger, he smirked? Huh! *Albania* . . .

Any more letters and he would definitely alert the police.

For a while the letters stopped and, after a few months, Alistair heaved a sigh of relief, imagining that they'd eventually tired of demanding money and finally realised that he wasn't playing ball.

It was shortly after this thought, however, that a powerful-looking foreigner walked calmly into his surgery, closed the door, and offered a pleasant smile before putting his hand in the pocket of his jacket and pulling out a hand grenade. Still smiling, he revealed what was in his hand. His smile then changed to a grin at Doctor Bracknell's reaction as he stood before him, holding out the grenade. With the two fingers of the other hand, he lightly grasped the pin. Nothing was said; nothing needed to be said. Bracknell had no choice. His heart thudding with the shock, he knew his time was up and that his past had finally caught up with him.

But the grenade . . . And that smile . . . They would stay with him for some considerable time. Would the next time be a parcel bomb? *That* parcel bomb? Had the bomb that had maimed Simon Garraway come from Albania? He shuddered at the thought and drained his cup, stubbing out the cigarette in the saucer.

Even though he had neither seen nor heard from the Albanians since, he'd never, since that visitation, felt entirely safe; had never been able to slough off the thought of how simple it would be for someone to send him the ultimate punishment.

He finally took the empty cup back out to the kitchen, then called the dogs. Slipping the leads onto their collars, he strode out of the door and headed towards the Common to clear his head.

# Chapter Fifteen

Julia Kilpatrick appeared to be in her element, dressed up in designer togs, ready to show off the garden to impending visitors. She had to look her best; Theo had told her that the people they were expecting were old, invaluable friends – important friends – even though she hadn't recognised their names, nor had any memory of having met them at any point in their married life.

The man, introduced as Marcus Fothergay, and his wife, Antonia, struck her from the start as strange, and she felt an unexplained shiver travel up her spine as she shook their hands. She'd never believed in precognition; she'd known people who'd talked about such things but, until now, had laughed it off. But she'd taken one look at the couple walking into the house, and knew there was something not right about them. She knew better than to show it, of course – ever the perfect hostess – and offered them a welcoming smile. She told herself that the couple were Theo's treasured friends and that she'd have pull herself together, as she watched her husband gushing towards them as though they were royalty. And they might well have been royalty for all the hauteur demonstrated, which alone was enough to raise her hackles. Here they were, striding into her home and behaving as though she was some lowly lackey, there to do their bidding, making it plain that they'd come to see her husband, not her. But, even through her discomfort, she continued to smile and to offer them drinks.

As soon as they'd walked in, she'd known that these people were not old friends; they were too stiff and formal to be old friends. Old friends slapped each other on the back and were delighted to be reunited after having been parted for so long. Old friends recalled the last time they'd met. Old friends shared ancient in-jokes that were amusing only to them. This man, Marcus Fothergay, barely managed to crack a smile, and his wife didn't even bother with the effort of exercising her lips. They took the hand she proffered, looking at her askance as she'd been introduced, and had then dismissed her with their eyes.

For some reason, even though having made a tremendous build-up about how he was looking forward to the Fothergays' visit after such a long absence, Theo was decidedly on edge, and Julia watched his odd behaviour out of the tail of her eye. Theo had always had something to say, even if it was total drivel – which was the norm – ever reminding her of an over-excited puppy. But now he seemed unusually ill at ease as he stood before his 'old friend', a bogus grin plastered onto his face. Julia took all this in, feeling as though she'd just stepped onto the stage of a theatre, cast in a rôle without a script, in a play she'd never heard of. They'd just walked into her house in this rude, off-hand manner and barely looked at her. How dare they? Moreover, having been told the couple were long-lost friends, she'd gone to the trouble of baking a lemon drizzle cake!

Julia was the first to admit that she wasn't a natural-born baker, but she'd been determined to welcome any friend of Theo's with her best effort. She'd followed the recipe to the letter, and her delight at the cake coming out in one piece when she'd upended the tin was unparalleled. In her eyes, this was a culinary masterpiece. Now, however, the thought of this culinary masterpiece going down the throats of this stiff and starchy pair, who couldn't offer her so much as a smile, suddenly made her want to throw it in the bin! She wouldn't have bothered if she'd known. The only up-side to this was the gratification she'd derived from the sheer, unadulterated success of the lemon drizzle cake, which had served to boost her confidence: she'd finally made a cake without that inevitable sag in the middle, so could, henceforth, hold up her head at the next village fête.

Even through her discomfort, therefore, she couldn't help utter joy seeping through at odd times at the thought of that lovely cake turning out onto the rack looking exactly as it had on the photograph in her cookery book. All the cakes she'd previously baked for village events to augment the bell fund, or some other good cause, had always been something of an embarrassment, as they'd never ever turned out looking remotely like the photograph in the cookery book. Nor had they ever sold. The galling thing was, however, that this perfect cake – the only perfectly successful cake she had ever managed to make – rather than being purchased to augment the coffers of some deserving charity – was destined to be eaten by this frosty designer-togged grandiosity now gracing the upper end of her couch.

She would just have to talk her way through this, she sighed; she'd done it before, hadn't she? Played the delighted hostess and blagged her way through whole evenings of excruciating boredom – on best behaviour – even though groaning inwardly and silently willing various parties to leave? Viewing this particular party, perched on sitting room chairs in a manner that suggested that they were as uncomfortable as she, she certainly wished this pair out of her house. But she'd keep up the niceties; to do otherwise, she felt, would be to lower herself to their level.

These people had come for a reason; that much was obvious. This was not a social visit. How could it be with this attitude?

She was less than impressed, therefore, but not entirely

unsurprised, when Theo took the man into his study and closed the door, leaving her to entertain his uppish wife, who had, so far not spoken a word. Watching the woman curl her lip at the sitting room furnishings, then disdainfully refuse the offer of sherry with a slight shake of the head and a regal wave of her gloved hand, Julia had a sudden urge to slap her. However, did the gloved hand perhaps indicate that the woman and her husband were not expecting to stay for afternoon tea, as Theo was expecting?

Please, God . . .

The Fothergays, despite the warmth of late September, had each chosen to wear head-to-toe black, and Julia, having never set eyes upon them before, wondered fleetingly if the pair perhaps represented a firm of undertakers and that the purpose of their visit was to measure up one or both of them for an oak casket – a thought which suddenly made her want to laugh. She knew the clothes to be of exceptional quality – but black? – on a day like this? Even the woman's hair was black – a silky black bob, which, come to think of it, might well have been a wig. Her shoes were undoubtedly Laboutin – with those wonderful scarlet soles – the only colour the woman had allowed herself – and the bag looked freshly purchased from Hermes. Antonia Fothergay oozed a brand of sophistication that unnerved Julia; it was a sophistication to which Julia knew she could never aspire, and which caused her to feel awkward and overdressed in her pale blue silk.

Having looked in her wardrobe that morning for something suitable to wear on what promised to be a fine day, despite a slight coolness in the autumn air, she'd chosen a floaty blue Emilia Wickstead and had teamed it with white Roksanda cigarette pants. Sitting now in Antonia's company, she felt silly, and quite the opposite of sophisticated in the face of the severity of designer black mocking her from the far end of the couch.

The silence stretched out, but she'd felt an urge, as hostess, to fill the gap with pleasantries. Racking her brain cells for a suitable topic of conversation, and perspiring somewhat with the discomfort she felt at the realisation that she'd never, in a month of Sundays, have anything in common with this unapproachable *grande dame,* she prattled on about the dahlias – though she couldn't think why – feeling like an insect stuck onto a strip of flypaper, desperate to please, but simultaneously desperate to escape this snotty-nosed woman with her disapproving down-turned mouth. She may as well have been talking to a pot plant for all the feedback she received for her efforts.

So, rattling onwards with meaningless words pouring from her mouth, her head was steaming with resentment as she recalled, once more, the trouble she'd gone to in baking this perfect cake especially for them. All that mixing and sweating in a hot kitchen, and watching the time, worrying about its outcome. What a waste of time and effort. And for what? A frosty-faced bitch who treated her like some dog turd she'd trodden in.

Friends? What total balls! Did Theo think she was stupid? What the hell were they doing here?

But she carried on the monologue regardless. She talked about the delights of living in Roper's End, even though she was fed up to the back teeth with the village's mediocrity; the church, which was one of the earliest in the country; the effort Theo put into their garden; the book she was currently reading; the dogs – which, she'd noticed, had refused to come into the house for reasons she could only guess at – and was just about at the end of her verbal rope, wondering desperately what more she could possibly dredge up to entertain this woman, when the men finally emerged from the study.

Theo appeared somewhat subdued, then suggested they all stroll out into the garden together. Julia was, by then, a nervous wreck, silently damning Theo for taking so long in the study, leaving her alone to entertain the pot plant; a pot plant which, every now and then, had deigned to offer a queenly smirk. Meandering now through the garden with the guests, she prattled on further with her encyclopaedic knowledge of flowers – although attempting to get through to a couple resembling the *Adams Family* on Valium was more exhausting than she was prepared to admit. She'd seen more pro-active yoghurt.

'And here,' she warbled to two stony faces, 'is my favourite: my gorgeous white climbing rose! *Wedding Cake*, it's called.'

Kilpatrick calmly strode two steps behind her, seemingly more at ease now that the business behind the closed door had been dealt with. He grinned broadly, his hands clasped behind his back, gazing at her proudly. His wife, he thought, looked particularly lovely today in the shimmering silk, the sun turning her hair into a burnished golden swathe as it fell over her shoulders. She looked as pretty as the day he married her, he sighed. Julia still had the ability to turn him on, even after all these years and, business over, he now longed for the visitors to go so that he could take her to bed.

Julia, on the other hand, was having other thoughts and, with every ounce of her being, was willing the couple to sod off, in order to drive over to Alistair Bracknell's house to have nooky with the doctor while his wife was away in the Scottish Highlands, paying her elderly parents the dubious honour of her yearly visitation. She badly needed to top up the secret stash of dosh hidden deep inside her wardrobe, having spent a good deal of it on the *burnished golden swathe* which Theo fondly imagined was natural.

Alistair Bracknell, though not particular fragrant, and a lousy lover, was always very generous with his cash, and she needed as much as she could winkle out of him in order to get her teeth whitened. It was all very well for Thicko Theo to say that she looked good for her age, but what he didn't realise was that it took money to look this good.

So, with the rictus grin still pulling her lips apart as she showed the visitors around the garden, she became aware that she was in danger of running out of things to interest them – not that anything much seemed to interest them – and found herself suddenly at a loss as to what to say next. Throughout, the pair had kept themselves aloof, the man now giving off airs of superiority to rival that of his wife, seemingly bored now that his business with Theo was completed. For all that time, Julia had struggled for words – any words, as long as they filled the void – forcing herself ever onward to utter *something,* however trivial. She'd known, even as it was all oozing out of her mouth like so much warm syrup, that she was behaving ridiculously, but hadn't seemed able to stop herself talking.

But now, seated at last in the arbour, she stopped suddenly and looked at them, then silently offered them cake.

She felt a scream boiling up inside her. She wanted to ask them why they didn't behave like normal people; what gave them the right to view her so contemptuously; *and why, in God's name, had they come . . .* ? She didn't know them – had never met them – and couldn't understand why Theo had invited them, nor why he'd chosen to closet himself in his study with this strange man as soon as he'd walked through the door. She'd made them this lovely cake, and now here they were slowly eating it, with no expression as to how they might be enjoying it; eating as though under sufferance. Forcing herself to offer another slice, then ladling it onto their plates, she silently yelled at them to depart, their presence now causing her to hyperventilate.

She was empty of words and had now decided that enough

was enough. She'd done her bit in the shiny hostess department and was getting sick of the sight of the black-clad unsavoury pair sitting in front of her. Clamping her jaw as Theo and the man chatted about inconsequential matters, she poured out more tea – then allowed her mind to wander.

When she was finally free of them she mused, dreamily munching away at her cake, desperate to take her mind off this unpleasantness – when these two automatons had drunk and eaten their fill and left the premises – she'd motor over to the other side of the village to the Bracknells' house. Brian Frobisher – that tightwad – could wait a while longer; she needed a boob-lift and he wouldn't be much use in the financing of that.

She thought about the money – never stopped thinking about the money. She supposed that her obsession with it owed mainly to the parsimony of her husband, who would hand her wad of cash for groceries when she'd asked for it, imagining that even that small amount would leave a dent in his bank account sufficient to render him penniless. Owing to the 'games' she played with the various men in the village, however, she reckoned she'd now saved almost enough money for the boob-lift and eyebrow extensions; she just needed Bracknell to top up the secret fund with his usual generous handout and get her teeth whitened. She'd book a session with the consultant at HealthIsUs in Barnscote and make the appointment for the boob-lift. She'd wait for a morning when Theo was in The Goose then, on the day, tell him she was going for dental treatment.

After that, she'd be ready for another session with Karen to retouch the highlights in her hair – and then . . .

'*What?*' she said with a start, her mouth full of cake, realising she was being spoken to.

'I was just remarking how delightfully peaceful your garden is,'

Marcus Fothergay managed to say without seemingly moving his lips.

'Oh, sorry. Yes . . .' she sputtered, gulping down the cake and wiping her mouth, startled that the robot had actually addressed her personally – that he'd even realised she was a human being – but that was robots for you! – and breathed a sigh of relief that this man, after all, was turning out to have a voice – a forgivable mistake. At least he hadn't asked for more tea because she'd then have been forced to brew another pot, so that was a relief. 'Thank you. Yes. Well, we work very hard at it.'

She caught a slight smirk on the woman's face as the latter viewed the few crumbs still left on Julia's mouth, but Theo smiled lovingly at her, so she felt she might well have said the right thing at the right time – not that she gave a monkey's fart at that point.

This afternoon had been the most excruciating two and a half hours of Earl Grey, lemon drizzle cake and verbal treacle that she could ever remember, and it had felt like several lifetimes. So she was not predisposed to do anything else in the way of talk.

Then, just as she'd given up hope of ever getting rid of them, the pair finally announced that they had to leave. And she stood, as though in a trance as the black BMW edged its way out of the drive and onto the road, taking its black-clad driver and passenger with it. Then, pulling herself sharply together, she set about fulfilling the plans she'd made earlier..

Thoroughly fed up by now and angry at the waste of a whole afternoon, she felt she had to get the sight of Theo almost genuflecting to the two strangers out of her mind – although, once lodged in her head, she guessed the image would be there for ever. She told him she had to run over to Bracklea for milk.

'Milk?' he said, eaten up with lust and more than ready to do the business. 'I could pop down to the shop for milk later. Why would you have to go to Bracklea for it? Why don't we . . . ?'

'Because Marks and Spencer is in Bracklea,' she explained with a sigh. 'The milk from the village shop is foul!'

'And you're going . . . dressed like that?'

'Yes!' she said, her voice taking on a dangerous edge. *'Yes – I'm going dressed like this!'*

'Yes . . . well, don't be too long, will you?' he wailed to her receding back.

He watched with mounting disappointment as she shot off in her car with a mere wave of the hand, then walked back into the house with a heavy sigh to feed the dogs.

\* \* \*

Freddie had heard this exchange from her seat in the garden and smiled, guessing where Julia Kilpatrick was off to – and it wouldn't be Marks and Spencer; she'd bet her house on it. Who knew who it would be this time? Brian Frobisher, regularly seen slavering over her and buying her drinks in The Goose? Swarthy Tom Farrow, the bit of rough down Ranborne Hill Road? Doctor Bracknell? She would, of course, afterwards stop on the way back to pick up a litre of milk from the village shop. Thicko Theo wouldn't know the difference.

\* \* \*

Freddie had gleaned the epithet – Thicko Theo – from something she'd overheard Julia say to Simon Garraway, with whom she'd been having a serious affair – just as she'd learned about *Mountainous Marjorie*. Spying was fun; she would have made a good spy, she knew. She had perfect hearing and enjoyed knowing things other people didn't know about. It was just that she hadn't gone for it when it was offered.

As she sat, waiting for Julia's return, the drone of a light aircraft caused her to look up into a perfect cerulean feather-strewn sky and she smiled at it; not many planes flew over Roper's End – it was usually helicopters flip-flopping through the clouds, disturbing Squidge's afternoon kip. What if she *had* gone for it, though, she sighed? What if she'd allowed herself to be swayed by Toni's beautiful smile and joined the spy club? Would she still be alive? No, she wouldn't still be alive, because whomever had betrayed Toni and his fellow agents would have dragged her down with them. She'd been lucky to have got out of Moscow when she did. She knew that. Lucky that those iron-grey men had eventually decided, after she'd told them a string lies, to release her. What spy ring? Toni Vascari was just a man she'd met by chance in Germany ... They'd become friends, that was all ... Yes, she admitted she'd smuggled him in under the name of Roger Blandford, but that's because he'd always had an interest in Russia. He was a salesman, wasn't he ...? Perhaps he was touting for business? She'd never asked.

She'd assumed they wouldn't believe her, but had kept up the pretence. She'd told them that the editor of the paper she worked for knew exactly where she was and was waiting for her return, she had the feeling that they'd thought it prudent to get rid of her and her camera and to keep their eyes on her until she left their country. Perhaps they thought that it was better to let her go than to charge her with something they couldn't prove – although that had never seemed to stop them in the past ...

The main thing was that she'd got out unscathed – physically, that is; it was her heart which had stayed behind.

And the guilt ... even after all these years. Was she guilty of not having been sufficiently discreet? She'd never know. What she did know was that, somehow or other, she'd been instrumental in getting him killed. But what would she have done differently?

What could she have done to save him? And would Toni have wanted to be saved? He knew he was treading dangerous waters, keeping his head just above the waterline – knew he was playing a tricksy game, imagining his charm would open any door.

She knew what she should have done: right from the start, and before she'd been so swayed by his charm; she should have refused to sneak him into Moscow. It would undoubtedly have ended their relationship, but at least Toni might still be alive. But, even without her help, he would have found his way into the country, wouldn't he? He loved danger; wouldn't have rested until he'd crossed the border, with or without her camera?

Sighing, she clamped her jaw at the certain knowledge that, had she had to live through that time again, she would do exactly the same. He would smile that electric beam, his coal-black eyes melting her heart, and she'd do it all over again. Even if that truth now hurt, she knew she would be too weak to resist him. Because he'd ask her, as he had all those years ago asked her – and because, the second time around, she'd still refuse to let him go.

The sunshine warming her face, she suddenly and inexplicably felt the prick of tears, then allowed them to roll down – tears that had refused to fall that day in the park, but which had fallen many time since – experiencing that stab of guilt for the umpteenth time; the loss – a far greater loss than that of her husband, she was ashamed to acknowledge; that loss tearing at her heart once more.

Her gorgeous Italian. The love of her life.

She would take all that sorrow and regret to her grave.

As she dabbed at her face and wiped her nose, she remembered those last few minutes she'd spent with Toni, kissing him and watching him stride out of the door with a 'See you later . . .'. How could she have known that that would be the last time she'd see him alive.

She was jolted out of her reverie, however, when the silence of the afternoon was suddenly shattered by the dogs next door as they came barking out into the garden at the sound of Julia's car, sending Squidge flying over the wall and dropping with a thump onto her lap, which sent her glass flying.

'Ach! That's a good Merlot you've just spilled, you silly cat!' she cried impatiently. '*And* broken the glass to boot! Look at that! What am I going to do with you?'

She hobbled back into the kitchen to fill another wineglass, returning to await the sound of Julia's voice. Freddie reckoned she'd been gone for just over half an hour. So it must have been Bracknell. And if she'd been in Alistair Bracknell's bed, the woman wouldn't have wanted to linger in Mansford Oaks for too long.

'There! Milk!' Julia said, her voice still angry after the earlier shambles in the garden.

Freddie grinned at the thought of everyone except Theodore Kilpatrick knowing of his wife's goings-on and sniggered malevolently at his ignorance, the pompous twit. It had never occurred to the stupid man that where she might have been heading, after that flimsy excuse for milk, was anywhere but Marks and Spencer. And that's what made it so delicious. Neither had the man ever wondered how Julia always managed to look so good and dress so immaculately when he never gave her a bean.

How the hell had this numpty once held down an important position in Naval Intelligence – if, indeed, that's all he got up to . . . ?

Yes. What had he got up to?

But still, she'd managed to get a few photographs, hadn't she?

# Chapter Sixteen

Penelope Ramsden in her ivory tower – aka the rambling pile imaginatively called Westwood, being at the west end of the village – had been rather more particular in her choice of lover. Derek Farley, Chief Constable of all he surveyed, had been gagging for it – for her; she'd feel his lustful eyes boring into her on each of his visits; heard each sigh of desire. So she couldn't very well disappoint the poor man. She'd therefore played up to him and flirted like the up-market tart she was, and he'd bitten the bait like a piranha on the tail of a shark. This, however, wasn't intended to be anything more than an outlet for Penelope's flirting abilities. It was nothing serious; there was no point in getting serious if there was nothing to be gained by it. At forty-four, she'd simply had to demonstrate that she could still pull if she wanted to; not that she'd normally have considered anyone worth pulling in this dire county . . .

Penelope was used to men ogling her on the catwalk and photo-shoots, and flirting became second nature to her – but one had to keep that sort of thing up, otherwise one might forget how to do it, which would be disastrous.

Having done the rounds with more than a few male models, she had, in her youth, imagined that she'd fallen in love with Adrian Willetts, an ambitious and well-endowed photographer assigned for a season to *Vogue,* who had almost succeeded in swooping her up into a life of glamour. He was a fantastic lover, she had to admit but, if it hadn't been for the promise of front-coverage and world-wide fame, she mused, she might have moved on to something a tad more lucrative. Plans for the the wedding were being drawn up, even though Adrian Willetts – a common or garden photographer – certainly wasn't what her family had viewed as a suitable match for their only daughter. But she'd craved glamour at any cost, and fame beckoned . . .

Lord and Lady Harbershall's distaste had been voiced and, when being informed of their daughter's insistence on marrying this photographer, had sought to dissuade her, as it clearly upset everything they'd hoped for her. But she was determined to go through with it, even though it threatened to scupper her allowance. She hadn't, however, believed her parents would do such a thing – although this matter of the withdrawal of shekels had been rattling in the back of Penelope's mind for some time: would they, wouldn't they? And, as the nuptials drew ever nearer, this poser had hung over her like the Damoclesian sword. But, to save face and to teach her parents that she could do whatever she liked, she dug her heals in, determined to go ahead – because, with Adrian becoming famous, she would hardly have to worry about money ever again, would she? And she'd stamped her foot and told them that she didn't care about her allowance. She and Adrian were destined to be A-listers, and would be invited everywhere. She was ready for it: the parties; the yachts; the dresses . . .

But then, overnight, everything changed.

At a party at the Dorchester, two weeks before the wedding, she'd met Charlie Ramsden, a barrister, who'd been propping up the bar gazing longingly at her, then had plucked up the courage to ask her for a dance. Naturally, she'd flirted with the middle-aged frump, because that's what she did, her motto being to never pass up a chance to demonstrate one's flirting abilities. But, during the course of the dance, she'd gleaned that the barrister could be earning far more than the photographer could ever earn, and who might, if she played her cards right, provide her with unlimited amounts of dosh.

As far as photography was concerned, there was so much competition out there. All right – Adrian was a super-stud and extremely good in bed, whereas, looking at Charlie, she guessed that he would never come up to that standard. Could she do this? Could she actually cancel the wedding? Charlie had hinted about his prospect of becoming a High Court judge, and it became clear to Penelope that Adrian would have to go. The decision was made – and, in the course of a few short minutes, she'd accepted a dinner date from Charlie Ramsden, and the future with the photographer faded into history. The prospect of this new life now promised by a wealthy barrister, with a house in Chelsea and a flat in the heart of London's elite, was a no-brainer.

Turning up for her in his scarlet MG, flashing the cash and promising to whisk her off to the crock of gold at end of the rainbow was a good ploy, and Charlie won hands down over previous lovers, capturing what was truly in Penelope's shallow little heart: a future that offered unlimited shopping sprees in Harvey Nicks and a lifetime of spending what she'd grown all her life to expect to spend. He was a good deal older than she and far from good looking, she had to admit, but he was well on his way up the ladder of success. She could live with that, she decided – well, until something perhaps more lucrative turned up.

For his part, Charlie had been seriously and unexpectedly flattered by Penelope's full attention and sang praises of gratitude to a God who had made possible the bagging of such a beautiful – not to mention aristocratic – young woman.

Advising her parents of her change of heart and decision to

marry a prospective judge did the trick of ensuring the continuation of dosh landing monthly in Penelope's account – plus getting her name re-entered into the Harbershalls' last will and testament as the sole beneficiary of Welfingham Hall. It wouldn't do for it *all* to be left to the Pony Club.

She would perhaps use Charlie for a while, she'd thought on her wedding day – then, if someone more desirable came along, she would divorce him and pocket her share of his estate, which would set her up until she inherited the Hall. It happened all the time; girls had to protect their interests, didn't they?

Strangely, though it may have turned out, even after all these years, she still found herself married to him, largely because most of the desirable men were now married to beautiful, younger models of their own, damn them!

* * *

Chief Constable Farley was anything but desirable and she had no intention of leaving her husband for him. He had a fairly decent income, no doubt, but that wouldn't come close to what she had become accustomed to. However, he'd indicated that he was available and up for any nooky she was prepared to offer. She'd enjoyed the flirt, but wasn't so sure she'd go as far as the nooky; she'd simply wanted to toy with him for a while in order to get him thoroughly inflamed, and to prove to herself that she was still capable of raising a smidgeon of lust in a man. It was just a bit of fun. But, it wasn't *just a bit of fun* for him. He was serious. She could see that. They all got serious in the end, poor lambs, but she'd always managed to find ways of escape.

But this was somehow different, and the day finally came when Farley declared his passion for her. He couldn't sleep, he said –

couldn't concentrate on his work, because every moment of the day his thoughts were of her. It was so pathetic she practically laughed: here he was, the Chief of Police, practically on his knees, begging to fuck her. He'd even spoken of love, which she took with a very large dose of salt. However, after some thought, she finally decided to give him what he wanted – just the once. Then, as with all her other ex-lovers, she'd dump him.

They'd agreed to meet near Stratford-upon-Avon in a workaday establishment considered far enough from prying eyes to warrant recognition. This tryst, intended to happen only once, somehow became fixed for once every month – and then once every couple of weeks; he couldn't manage longer than that, he'd said. This had been two years ago, and she was now at her wits' ends. She couldn't see what she could do to end it. It was meant to be a lark – a laugh – not to drag on for this length of time. She realised, with a sigh, what a colossal error of judgment this had been; couldn't imagine how stupid she was to have agreed to such a thing.

She'd become aware, after a few months' of dalliance with him, that even fortnightly trysts were not enough for Derek Farley's sexual appetite, and he'd begun to beg for more frequent assignations. But she'd balked at that, largely because Farley wasn't up to much in the bedroom – although, to give him credit, proved a damned sight better than Charlie. In an attempt to keep him at arm's length, she said that meeting more frequently may well become suspect and, as Chief Constable, he wouldn't want a scandal, would he?

The proprietor of the Badgers' Lair, registered delight at seeing his regular customers stroll through the door once more, and welcomed them into his rundown, nondescript hotel with his widest smile, guessing that the couple now walking towards him had chosen this particular establishment because it *was* rundown and nondescript.

'Mr and Mrs Williams! How good to see you again,' he gushed.

He'd clocked that 'Mr Williams' was the chief constable of Portlingshire because his face had been on the front page of the local rag a few weeks' ago, and guessed that (a) the woman on his arm was unlikely to be his wife and, (b) that the room in his small hotel was equally unlikely to be used in the middle of a weekday afternoon for an urgent meeting of police minds – if that was not an oxymoron. But he feigned ignorance, offering his usual professional faux-innocent non-judgemental pleasantries. Trade had fallen off of late, so he couldn't at this point, afford to be too choosy about the clients in his establishment occasionally using it as something little short of a knocking shop. So, each time they walked thorough the door of his hotel, he politely handed over the key to room number thirty-two and sighed with satisfaction as Mr Williams's debit card was tapped through the machine.

He'd viewed with interest the obvious souped-up lust of Mr Williams from the first, likening him to a Harley-Davidson, revving up its engine at the traffic lights, waiting impatiently for green. But, ever the polite smile, he'd watched them both in their vain attempt at nonchalance as they entered the lift together.

Penelope sighed as she gazed idly upon her lover's rather too-groomed appearance; the overpowering aftershave offending her nasal cavities; the ingrained professional within him requiring him to dress for each occasion with care – nothing left to chance: the fringed loafers and Argyll sweaters on the golf course; his old school tie and blazer to attend his club; and now the slacks and casual open-necked shirt, now was deemed appropriate for an illicit sexual encounter in a Stratford-upon-Avon hotel; each sartorial section of his life covered by a well-chosen symbol of respectability, overcoming any idle accusation of a randomness which might serve to clog the wheels of the clockwork machinery that informed his life.

Farley was proving too difficult to shift. He got on her nerves, and she groaned at his constant whinging about wanting more regular sex. He wanted to own her, body and soul, and had made it clear that he would gladly leave his wife for her. The thought made her nauseous. After two years, he'd served his purpose – and some! – but this had now got out of hand, and it was obvious that he hadn't read the memo headed 'Loose Strings', which stated that this was just fun: capricious, mercurial, *rootless . . .* There was no future in it. For heaven's sake, if she was going to leave Charlie, it would have to be with someone a damned sight better than this; someone fitter and with a bit more life in him; someone with a great deal more in the bank; someone not so demonstrably obsequious – and someone who didn't pop a mint in his mouth beforehand to disguise his bad breath.

She remembered the very first time they'd made love. Afterwards he'd asked her, lying on his back fully satisfied with himself, if she'd enjoyed it. What kind of man asks that? He was too fond of himself, and she despised the flagrant self-assurance that Chief Constable Derek Farley was the best lover in town. When he'd asked her if she'd enjoyed the sex, what he was really asking was how she'd enjoyed his performance.

Then there was the usual boring conversation as they lay together afterwards, and she steeled herself once more. It was the whiny pleadings that got to her . . .

'I want us to meet more often, Penny. You know that,' he began.

'Well, that could be difficult,' she sighed softly, anxious to roll off the bed and get dressed, but feeling she should stay a tad longer out of courtesy.

'You know I love you,' he said, stroking her leg. 'Let's just get ourselves divorced and go away together – anywhere!'

'Derek,' she lied convincingly, 'you know I feel the same about you. But I couldn't leave Charlie. With his heart condition, it would kill him.'

'Pen, my love, you're too compassionate – it's what I love about you. But I can't live much longer without you,' he whispered into her ear. 'Please, darling – think about it . . .'

She had thought about it – every time he'd mentioned it – and she was getting sick of hearing it. But she sighed again and turned to him, allowing him to kiss her, then got up and pulled on her knickers, scotching any thoughts he might be having of penetrating her a second time.

After waving goodbye to the proprietor of the Badgers' Lair, she was now more than anxious to get home. She and Farley had arrived in separate cars, so she gave him a quick farewell peck on the cheek, then ran across the tarmac to the nippy little sports car that Charlie had given her last Christmas, leaving the Chief Constable to stride purposefully to his Bentley, which had been given to him by the tax-paying public.

* * *

Charlie finished his round on the links, then walked into the Clubhouse for a drink before heading to The Goose to meet his wife, who had just returned from Stratford.

'Good day shopping?' he asked jovially. 'How much did that cost me?'

'Not a great deal today, my love,' she said. 'Couldn't find a single thing I liked.'

'Ah, well,' he sighed, 'that's the way it goes. What'll you have?'

'I *need* a very large gin and tonic!' she sighed, sinking back into one of The Goose's Head's easy chairs and thinking back to that afternoon's heavy workout, wondering if it had been worth the price of petrol, considering Derek Farley's umpteenth, sick-inducing declaration of love.

It had all turned against her, hadn't it? From the beginning, she'd told herself over and over, that this was all meant merely to be an outlet for her libido and no strings attached. Full stop. She thought she'd made that clear. How would she now extricate herself from thrashing about in that seedy little hotel. She didn't know how much more she could take. She had no intention of leaving her husband; Charlie may be a crashing bore, but he was *her* crashing bore and she'd grown genuinely fond of the old buffer.

She had, many times, wondered at her mental state in starting this fling, when she might have chosen someone who wanted what she wanted: occasional relief from the small agonies of life, allowing escape every now and then from the humdrum life in a village that was the bucolic equivalent of Prozac, peppered as it was with old crocks, screaming children and heavily tattooed teenagers one would quite like to see humanely culled; a village not at present twinned with any other, but which had all the appearance and atmosphere of a shared suicide pact with Chernobyl.

She was still a beautiful woman, she reasoned, in what she told herself was a young girl's body – she'd put every effort into it. It wasn't easy for a forty-something woman to keep her youthful appearance but, each morning, as she viewed herself in the cheval mirror, she found herself criticising what she saw, deciding which bit of her body could next do with a tweak or tuck in order for her to hang on to her steadily eroding youth. Countless men had been drawn to her like pins to a magnet – and, in the past, she'd known she could have had her pick of them. With age now rearing its unsightly head, however, this gift she'd been blessed with – this attraction to the male sex – was getting more difficult to work for her. She felt it, and it hurt. Was that the reasoning behind her fling with Farley? But it was all so difficult now. If she broke it off, it would surely be impossible to remain friends with the Farleys; and then what would Charlie think? What would he suspect? If he suddenly lost his golfing partner, he'd discover the affair, and that would be the end of it.

So . . . how *would* she get out of this? Would she *ever* manage to escape this dreary little hole they called a village? In time, perhaps – but certainly not with this macho-man, totally unburdened by charisma, whose ego could be sliced with a blunt knife.

She missed London, and sighed, as now, in The Goose's Head, with her husband at her side, she slowly sipped her gin: she missed the apartment a mere stone's throw from Wimbledon; Ascot; Henley . . . still treasured the memory of all those glorious hats – hats now languishing unworn in their boxes on top of her wardrobe. And those glorious dresses to flounce round in. Flouncing in Roper's End, however, was a joke. The yokels in this provincial neck of the woods wouldn't know fashion if it jumped up and bit them on the arse. If she did manage to escape this pettifogging little nothingness, she certainly wouldn't want to live anywhere but the Big City – and a pretty little flat in Eaton Square, near her parents, would do very nicely. Perhaps one day. One could dream . . .

# Chapter Seventeen

Freddie Wingrave's house was a complete shambles, the dust on every surface equivalent to the fallout from Pompeii, the vacuum cleaner languishing unloved and virtually unused in the downstairs cubbyhole, cleaning fluid under the sink slowly solidifying over the many years of disuse and floor mops all but disintegrated, their handles now warped and leaning crookedly in the basement, hardly ever again to see the light of day.

She was by now, though, used to her own brand of filth, and would lie on her couch, either reading or sewing amid the threadbare cushions and clutter, promising herself each day that she would do something about it tomorrow.

Stirring cognac into her tea, she gazed idly at the explosion of paper – the Leaning Tower of Portlingshire, as she thought of it – stacked up at the end of the kitchen table. What did one do with old bank statements and cheque stubs, and invoices, she wondered, as it all stared malevolently back at her, daring her to disturb it? Ben used to deal with it all: the parking tickets and credit card statements; the television licence; an ancient angry letter from the electricity company demanding payment; the pile of memorial services sheets from 2002 . . . How did one deal with such things? Having suffered a lifelong allergy to opening anything brown, unopened envelopes inevitably ended up on the kitchen table, but in a separate pile, which was about the extent of Freddie's ability to create a filing system. She guessed that, one day, when it caused a tsunami by sliding sideways onto the floor, she would be forced to tackle each pile in turn, the very thought causing her to add another slug of cognac into her mug.

Books – thousands of them, dusty and falling apart – littered each room in no particular order, she frequently attempting to put her finger on the right tome for information on a particular wild flower or unusual butterfly she'd spotted on her walks around the village. Having eschewed the internet, vowing never to allow it to darken her doorstep, she'd wade through room after room, laboriously trying to locate one of the many reference books in order to find an answer to enlighten her, searching wildly for something she was positive was there somewhere. Sometimes the search would take up a whole afternoon, and then the hunt for the book would be abandoned, along with her need for it because, by then, she'd forgotten why she'd wanted it. There was the odd day when, after a mammoth but unfruitful search, she'd simply given up, her eye having been caught by the spine of an anthology of poetry she'd looked for some years back and hadn't been unable to find.

'Ah, so that's where you were hiding!' she mutter, as though it had been deliberately avoiding her and had then had suddenly popped out to surprise her.

She sighed at it all and told herself that, one fine day she would make the effort to completely blitz the house, with all the unread and unreadable books carted off to Oxfam. And she'd do something about the rest of the dust-encrusted debris which, collected over the years and now rendered useless by the passage of time, was destined for the bin.

Just imagine it: every shelf dusted and every book arranged in alphabetical order of author! The vacuum cleaner might get its yearly outing and very probably have a nervous breakdown as a result; clothes would be washed and ironed, which would help greatly if she could locate the iron, plus the ironing board, both, no doubt buried somewhere deep in the basement; the bathroom would be scrubbed of fifty-odd years of grime; the Amazon Forest that had, many years earlier been called a garden, would be mown neatly into submission, once more resembling civilisation – and that old tree, which no longer bore fruit, might get chopped up to light the fire in the sitting room grate to make the house smell sweetly of apples.

She would, of course, first have to deal with the problem of the sudden infestation of ants that had made the decision to take over the house and were now marching towards the gap under the kitchen door with the precision of the Waffen SS. Squidge, who was very good at decimating the mouse population, was no help there.

All these thoughts of cleaning and tidying, however, suddenly caused Armageddon to strike the back of her head, throwing her back once more onto the couch. If she was really going to tackle this job, she needed a mammoth spur – something to happen, or someone to make the effort for. She couldn't just get up and set to, could she? It could take months.

She forced herself to view the sitting room with a critical eye. She remembered one day, after a gruelling spell in Turkmenistan, bringing home a large Turkish rug. As it now sat on the floor of the sitting room, the rug, which had once been a vibrant terracotta, had, owing to the afternoon sun shining directly into the room, taken on the colour of week-old sick, its lack of colour perhaps owing also to the many years of un-vacuumed cat fur which had embedded itself deep within the fibres.

And Squidge, bless is heart, hadn't helped in the least in alleviating the disorder, his fur settling on everything he lay on, which was a nuisance. But, being without Squidge was unthinkable. Many years ago, she'd allowed herself to be dominated by this once-scrawny little tabby which had casually wandered into the house and which, after a plate of chicken, decided that this was where its heart truly belonged. Feeling helpless against the huge amber eyes staring up at her and the forlorn look the cat had managed to contrive in its effort to be accepted, she eventually gave up putting it out and ended up smiling fondly as it settled on her cushions, emitting not a few thousand fleas.

She walked over to the window and stood, watching as a sudden gust of wind whipped up a shower of leaves – leaves which were almost gone from the branches of the beech, and which were now settling into a heap by the back door, bringing to mind all the leaves of remorse that were still settling by the door of remembrance; still gathering and rustling in the depths: the crumpled rusty leaves of sorrow; of guilt; of loneliness. All those unswept monsters of the past she'd hitherto pushed away into the deep springs of her psyche but which, from time to time, managed to rear up to once more tear her apart.

Ben. Toni – darling Toni . . .

Who had shopped Toni? Who was the rat responsible for the deaths of all those fellow spies? Accidental deaths? She would never believe that. There had to be someone in the know – some excrescence lurking unpunished somewhere – who had done this.

Reaching for a biscuit, she sighed and wondered how life might have panned out for them both? Could they have ever let each other go, and could she have left her husband for him? Gone with him to live in Italy, not knowing if he was already married to a third or fourth wife? Could she have taken that risk to live with a spy; have become a spy herself; been his accomplice? That was something that she couldn't answer now. Couldn't have answered it even then.

She strolled back to the couch, disturbing the cat, which jumped off a cushion and onto the table, shook itself haughtily, then walked off with its tail in the air, aggrieved at being so rudely awoken. She picked up a book; all this dredging up of the past was giving her the jitters. She read a few chapters, then made another drink. A drink might help to settle the brain cells; and another few slugs of cognac wouldn't go amiss, either . . .

Marking the place in the book, she gazed around and sighed at the impossibly shabby kitchen. She should move, she thought. She'd been wondering, for some time now, if she should downsize. This house and vast garden were beyond her. She no longer needed five bedrooms – not that she ever did, except to house all her books. And she no longer needed, nor could cope with, a garden which comprised an apple orchard, a fruit and vegetable patch the size of a field, and several huge swathes of grass and borders which needed the care and attention she could no longer give them. But she'd procrastinated for too long, thoughts of the huge upheaval necessary for such a move sending her brain cells into a nosedive; she was too old now. Anyhow, how could she possibly be expected to pack all this stuff into a smaller house, she asked herself? She might be forced to part with most of it. And how could she think of parting with any small bit of it? All her life was here in this house.

She wandered outside to set up her camera in order to snap a colourful display of beech leaves banked up against the shed. But it was then that she heard the voices: Julia's tinkly laugh as it gushed from over the wall, a laugh Freddie knew the woman was likely to use whenever she was trying to impress someone of importance, and Kilpatrick droning on about the importance of having the right soil in which to grow dahlias. Then, coming into her limited view was a pair of strange looking people, dressed in black on a hot autumn day, looking like huge beetles . . . Aha! The Kilpatricks had visitors . . . But these were visitors Freddie had never seen before. Who were they? Why were they here?

Easing the camera off its tripod, she crept over to the wall and gently loosened the brick. Then she saw them full on, as they were shown around the magnificence that was the Kilpatrick garden, with its manicured lawns, closely clipped box hedging and that ridiculous peanut-shaped pond with water-lilies floating upon the surface. Plus – Kilpatrick's pride and joy – those ghastly garish dahlias filling the borders. The ornate arbour on the far wall, a purple clematis climbing prettily up the iron frame, was now decked out with tables and chairs. Freddie watched through the gap as the party slowly wandered towards it, and then as they sat at the table laid out with delicate china, a teapot and a cake, all of which were set upon a flowered cloth.

My word – if the arbour was being used, the visitors must be very important indeed.

She continued to eye them suspiciously and, when she'd considered they were far enough away not to hear the click of the camera button, she took their photographs. You just never knew . . . She continued to watch them until Squidge strode up and rubbed against her legs, his loud purr threatening to give the game away. So, as she'd now gleaned enough photographic evidence of these people's presence, she replaced the brick.

She then slowly walked back to the house with her cat.

# Chapter Eighteen

I couldn't believe my eyes – or my ears. It was him: Commander Theodore Kilpatrick. Right here in my village, and standing behind me in the Post Office queue. It was the tortured upper class enunciation I heard first, as he complained loudly about how long he'd have to wait to be served. My stomach churned at the sound; it couldn't be, I thought. It had sounded like Kilpatrick – but it couldn't surely be him . . . But then, I told myself, there couldn't possibly be another man with those grating vocal cords, whining on about having to wait his turn, complaining of why he had to hang around – of why he didn't come first; the sharp, demanding impatience in every vowel; the lofty expectation of instant service at the snap of the fingers. That Himalayan-strength ego, I knew, could only belong to him . . .

I turned slowly and saw his face, and my fears were realised. His very presence caused palpitations and I had to leave the shop. I stood outside, holding on to the fence, feeling sick and breathing heavily in order to avoid throwing up. I couldn't move; could barely believe that this man – of all the men in the world – had managed to land in my village. Of all the places he could have chosen: Outer Mongolia – the Mohave Desert – the swamp . . . No, he'd had to come and live in Roper's End, right under my nose.

I forgot about the stamps I needed for my letters and reached for my bike, unsure for the moment of where I was and of how I'd manage to get home.

\* \* \*

That was a number years back now, and I'd happened to mention the sighting to Jenny Peck, my long-standing friend from Bletchley. We'd kept in touch over the years and met each other on a fairly regular basis in *Felton Tea Rooms* in Bracklea. The shock of my encounter with Kilpatrick had affected me to such an extent that I shook as I poured out the tea. She asked what was wrong and, after setting down the teapot, I told her of my concerns. Jenny was the only person I could talk to about Bletchley Park – the only one I could trust. Once I'd mentioned his name, Jenny's face changed colour.

'Kilpatrick?' she breathed. 'Are you sure it was him?'

'It couldn't have been anyone else,' I said.

After assuring her that I was certain beyond doubt, it all came shooting out – like lighting the touchpaper of a Catherine Wheel. She was as horrified as I that he'd landed in Portlingshire and almost breathed fire at the thought of him alive and well and living in such close proximity; indeed, gave the impression of being devastated that he was living at all. She'd worked in Intelligence and had known Kilpatrick well.

'Roper's End?' she said at last. 'So that's where he disappeared to . . .'

'Why? Where did you think he was?' I asked.

'Sewing mail bags perhaps . . . ?' she ventured. 'Except that the bastard was always too slippery to get caught! Bletchley couldn't wait to get rid of him, so that's how we got landed with him in Naval Intelligence.'

I didn't think there was anything she hadn't told me about the past, but I was wrong. And, after what she revealed that day, I decided to delve into Theodore Kilpatrick's murky past – which happened to be far murkier than I could possibly have guessed. My heart raced as Jenny went on, barely believing what she was telling me. She advised me to keep a diary to note his comings and goings, and I took her advice.

I'd always kept diaries when I worked at Bletchley – still have them, locked away in my Davenport – Kilpatrick featuring strongly in their pages, because I'd felt, even then, that he couldn't be trusted. When I left Bletchley Park, I thought that that would be the last I'd see of him and, when I retired, I gave up the diaries altogether. But, after I'd said goodbye to Jenny, I went into Smiths and bought a stack of notebooks – and, from that day in Felton Tea Rooms, have reintroduced the habit. One day, the truth will come out; one day, Kilpatrick will get what he deserves. Because, after I'm gone, these diaries will be found by someone who will do something about that, I feel sure.

At Bletchley I'd just been an oily rag to service the machinery. I'd accepted that and knew my place in the pecking order – we all did. And, in the main, we were treated well and were appreciated by our bosses for the hours we put in, many of us there half the night typing up some urgent report. But we never complained.

Kilpatrick, however, was something else. He'd breeze in, treating the plainer women among the staff as dirt under his feet, and the pretty ones as a potential fuck. The warnings to the more attractive to avoid him like a bad smell were sometimes heeded but, more often, ignored. Rumours of pregnancies practically all led to him, but each time he had a knack of getting himself transferred, thus walking away from the trouble he'd caused.

Even though I was quite a bit older than him, he tried it on with me. But I had my standards and rebuffed him by digging the nib of my pen into his palm after feeling his hand up my skirt. But, as expected, I was subsequently punished. He told my boss that I was revealing secrets, which Gerald, bless him, took with a pinch of salt. Kilpatrick, thereafter, studiously ignored me whenever he crossed my path, which suited me fine.

People like that: they may appear to walk under the same blue sky, along the same stretch of earth, and even speak the same language; they may know how to use the right fork and how to dress in appropriate clothes on any given occasion. They may even appear to be human. But they're not. They have, at some point, been dropped from a distant planet. And, once out of their foul-smelling eggs they assimilate and set about getting themselves humanised, fooling everyone into believing that they belong. But all that suppurating festering disease remains inside them, breaking out every now and then to continue to contaminate the earth with their bile.

As far as I could tell, that day, Kilpatrick hadn't appeared to recognise me in the Post Office, which was hardly surprising, considering my age. Little Glenys Pugh? – he wouldn't even remember my name. As a mere secretary, he'd barely looked at me after that nasty scratch with the pen. I couldn't bear to look at him, nor get near enough to become the unpleasant smell under that beaky, grandiloquent nose. But, even by the merest chance of being recognised by him after all these years, I guess he'd have simply curled his lip and passed me by, treating me with the contempt people like that usually treat a nonentity.

I recall how he'd stride importantly into my boss's office, all gold stripes, and with a face like thunder. Then, after throwing his weight around like a child deprived of its teddy, would complain loudly about the inefficiency of the staff – i.e., me – or whatever else that hadn't met his petulant approval. He'd stride out again for all the world as though he was Admiral of the Fleet. How he'd managed to get into Bletchley or even to reach that elevated position in Naval Intelligence was anybody's guess. Money and connections might have been a something of a hint, though.

Everybody loathed him – and *nobody* trusted him. I think we lowly maggots might have had an atom of respect for his rank but for the fact that he was next to useless. There was no problem, large or small that Commander Theodore Kilpatrick, when he rolled up his sleeves, couldn't foul up. It was like nominating Nero to run the fire brigade. And we all joked that he'd probably modelled his peoples skills on the last few days of Hitler's dog.

There were one or two folk at Bletchley we didn't exactly trust, but we all learned tactful ways in dealing with the silver-tongued serpents with the utmost courtesy, swiftly putting anything of importance out of sight. None of us, however, could bring ourselves to be either tactful or courteous to the stuck up son of a bitch that called itself Commander Theodore Kilpatrick, who was only ever the least bit friendly when he needed to pump information out of someone – usually a new girl who would be offered a session between the sheets if she played the game. But he would promptly ditch the charm when he'd managed to get what he wanted. No one knew precisely how he managed to get his information, or even what he'd done with it – but suspicions abounded

One day, by accident, I happened to see Kilpatrick tucked away at table in the corner of a teashop in a village just outside Oxford, where I'd agreed to meet a chap. The chap in question was late and I found myself alone, sitting opposite Kilpatrick, who had his back to me. But I knew his back as well as I knew his front. Sitting close – rather too close – was a man I didn't recognise. My table being too far away, I couldn't hear their whispered conversation, but their two heads, I remember, almost touched. The encounter struck me as suspicious, but then my chap turned up and I tried to put it out of my mind. But it was that constant whispering which kept me watching. Then, as I took a sip of my tea, I saw an envelope pass between them. It was done so quickly that I couldn't tell who'd passed what to whom. But it wasn't right.

Gerald had been on to Kilpatrick long before that and, when I told him about the encounter in the tea shop, he reported the matter to higher ranks. Those above him duly noted his concerns, but nothing was done. I suspect that the reason Gerald got transferred was as a result of his attempt to reveal the parasitic worm in their midst – the worm who someone had wished to protect. The question was: who was it who'd decided that nothing should be done to take matters further?

It's all in the diaries.

* * *

I stood that day outside the village shop, trembling and trying to get my breath to stop myself from being sick, and unsure as to what to do, but then felt a hand on my arm and a kind voice asking me if I was unwell. It was Brian Frobisher's son, James, and I almost fainted with relief. I think I might have collapsed if he hadn't held on to me. James insisted on walking me back to my bungalow, grabbed the bike and wheeled it beside him, then talked me all the way home, his voice calming me down. Once there, he asked if I would like him to make me a cup of tea. I said a glass of whisky would be more like it, and he poured it out for me – then, at my insistence, made tea for himself. He sat with me for a while, making conversation until the whisky kicked in. Only a young lad he was then – couldn't have been more than twelve . . . I told him hadn't had much to eat that day and felt faint. He then set about making me a sandwich.

Unwilling to sound sexist, I was surprised at this young boy's ability to be so proficient in looking after an old woman. Such a sweet lad, bless him.

I have to hand it to the Frobishers – their children have impeccable manners. If he hadn't introduced himself, I would never have recognised him as that small boy I'd seen Valerie walking up to the primary school each day. He wouldn't have been more than five years old then. I often see him around the village these days. Six-foot-something he is now, and quite unlike his runt of a father. And quite handsome in a funny sort of way. However, I'll never forget his kindness that day.

I've seen people looking askance at James, turning up their noses at all the piercings in various parts of his face; his quirky hair gelled up in spikes; plus all the tattoos, no portion of his body seemingly unmutilated. The folk in this God-forsaken village making snap decisions on others, rather than putting themselves out to see below the surface, should take a good look at themselves; folk with minds the width of ticker tape, imaging, in their lofty, empty little lives, that they're ahead of everyone else in the normality stakes, unaware of what boring little ticks they all are.

I caught sight of him only the other day. He was sporting a ropey old pair of skinnies with rips at the knees, and a T-shirt with some slogan or other scrawled across the chest, topped by a leather biker jacket that had obviously seen better days.

But there's an old saying that you shouldn't judge a book by its cover.

When James left the house, I went to bed. I couldn't sleep, though; each time I closed my eyes, the remembrance of that time at Bletchley ran through my head and wouldn't let me go. How would I cope, I thought, knowing Kilpatrick lived a stone's throw away?

I now stare hard at Commander Theodore Kilpatrick when I see him these days, but he looks through me. I don't live on Kings Road, so I suppose I'm classed slightly lower than plankton.

I so wish he'd got his just deserts, but that type never do, do they? As Jenny had remarked, they just get moved on to do their damage elsewhere.

# Chapter Nineteen

'Do you have to look like that?' Brian Frobisher shot at his son over the breakfast table.

'Like what?' James drawled, leisurely munching his toast, perfectly aware as to what his father was referring.

James enjoyed annoying his conformist father; loved watching him getting steadily hot under the collar, his face reddening with unalloyed distaste at his many piercings and at the state of his clothes, which he'd carefully distressed for full effect – and he hid a smile.

Because he knew something...

Like ... *like that!*' Brian yelled with a wave of his arm. 'Like a sodding vagrant!'

''Cos I like looking like this,' James said calmly, reaching for the marmalade and catching a warning look from his mother.

He knew, however, that the cooler and more laid back he appeared, the more irritated his father would get – and, despite the stiffening of Valerie's jaw, it was fun seeing the old man getting worked up about something he could do nothing about. He knew his father despaired of him for bunking off uni, choosing instead to become a shelf-stacker in the Tesco store in Bracklea. He'd had his allowance angrily chopped and been told that, since he'd been stupid enough not to stay the course at Cambridge, he could damned well earn his own living. This, however, didn't bother James – or, if it did niggle him on the odd occasion, he studiously never allowed himself to show it. Which enraged his father even more, because the withdrawal of funds was meant to be a punishment.

James, since early childhood had held little respect for his father, owing largely to the treatment he'd once meted out to Alfie. But this lack of respect had plummeted further, some weeks ago, when he'd discovered the monthly shenanigans with Julia Kilpatrick. So, what had hitherto been a silent acceptance of his father's incorrigible bullying techniques and sudden bouts of unexplained fury, this betrayal of his mother's trust stirred in him emotions he never knew he had. This sneaky, underhand activity with a neighbour whom his mother considered a friend was beyond the pale, and he now looked at Brian with undisguised loathing.

He'd found out about the affair when his mate, Alfie Wendover, working as a waiter in the Old Dog and Bush in Barnscote, casually mentioned over a pint one evening that he'd served lunch the previous Thursday to James's father and a woman who was not James's mother. It was just a throwaway line for a bit of a giggle; not meant to hurt anyone. Nevertheless, it had caused in James a sudden frisson of unease. A woman who was not his mother? Lunching with his father . . . ?

'Just the once?' James asked, doing is best to keep calm after this bombshell.

'No,' Alfie replied with a grin. 'No, they come in regularly – about once a month. Looks like it might be a business lunch or summink.'

Business lunch? Stay calm now – could be something to do with work . . .

Alfie, remembering Mr Frobisher's profession as a top boffin in some important science laboratory near Hansfield, had assumed these monthly lunches with the lady in question to perhaps be prior to meetings that took place later in the day in the hotel's Conference Room, so hadn't seen fit to mention it before. He imagined that James would come to the same conclusion. At seeing James's discomfort at this disclosure, however, he immediately realised his error at mentioning it, and began to feel uneasy; James was his best friend – he wouldn't hurt him for the world.

That first Thursday, when he'd encountered Mr Frobisher in the Old Dog and Bush, he'd smiled at him, thinking the man might recognise him from the old days – the little scruff off the council estate who'd kicked a ball around with James in the back garden. But there appeared to be no recognition – just the merest eye contact – and he hadn't, at the time, had the courage, nor thought it suitable, to reintroduce himself to someone who'd dismissed him in his childhood as a wholly unsuitable friend for his son. Certainly not in the company of a lady. He had no desire to embarrass the man, so thought it wise simply to serve Mr Frobisher in a business-like manner and, as instructed in his training manual, to raise an eyebrow a tad and dutifully lift up the corners of his mouth. It was at the lifting of the eyebrow that he realised that the customer he was serving hadn't a clue who he was; as far as Brian Frobisher was concerned, Alfie was invisible. As a boy he'd always been invisible to Mr Frobisher, and now he was simply a nondescript waiter taking his order, unworthy of a second glance. A world away from remembering skinny little oiks like Alfie, he seemed to have eyes only for the glamorous woman sitting on the opposite side of the table. Alfie could barely take his eyes off her himself...

When he'd thought about the lack of recognition, Alfie wasn't too surprised – indeed he'd been secretly thrilled. As a result of having to smarten himself up since those earlier days of grabbing any piece of unwashed clothing that happened to be lying around his bedroom, then wondering why his classmates avoided him, he now presented a clean respectable-looking young man, the hotel's regulations having brought about a total transformation. And, overnight, he'd changed; this enforce conformity making him aware of what he had been, and grateful to the hotel management for turning him into a recognisable member of the human race. With his now clean-shaven face, neatly cut hair and sporting a crisp white regulation shirt topped off by the smart black waistcoat, he hardly recognised himself when he viewed his reflection each morning in the hall mirror. So it wasn't hurt Alfie was feeling at not being recognised, but elation at having finally made it into the realms of normality. No more Whiffy Wendover, he grinned at himself, slapping on the aftershave after his shower. He imagined that even his own mother, if she hadn't drunk herself into an early grave, might have had difficulty recognising him.

Now, sitting in The Goose's Head over his pint and feeling James's silence as he sipped his ale, he felt awkward. In an attempt, therefore, to explain away his friend's fears, Alfie ventured a logical explanation: this was just an innocent lunch before a meeting, yeah? No need to get het up, mate! Meetings were held in the Conference Room all the time. Except he wouldn't know about Thursdays, because, by Thursday lunchtime, he'd left the hotel. His only motive for bringing it up, he said, was for James and him to have a bit of fun at little Alfie Wendover, the village waif, having allowed himself to get transmogrified into someone so well dressed as to be unrecognised by James's father. That was all. It was just meant to be a bit of a laugh.

But James wasn't laughing. He was calculating the significance of his father meeting a woman at Alfie's hotel. It was the word 'regular' that rang alarm bells. He knew that his father didn't hold business meetings because he didn't work in the sort of establishment that held business meetings; he was the head of a science laboratory and, if a meeting were to be held within his department to discuss matters relating to work, it would most certainly not require a hotel in which to hold it. A luncheon meeting? Once a month? And with just one woman? In the middle of the week, when he was supposedly toiling over test tubes, or whatever he did at his lab?

His suspicion sufficiently roused, it might be interesting, he thought, to find out more about these luncheon meetings. Who was this woman who was 'not his mother'? A colleague his father took out for a treat? Perhaps it *was* work-related. Could be. Could be expressing his thanks to a member of staff for her hard work. Was this anything to get worked up about?

But 'regular'?

'So . . . what happens after their lunch?' he asked, trying to keep his voice steady. 'Do they leave together or separately?'

'Dunno,' Alfie said. 'Thursday afternoon I'm on the football field, ain't I? Once I've seen off the last of the customers and re-set the tables for dinner, the rest of the day's mine. What goes on after that's nuffink to do wiv me.'

'But, tell me something,' James persisted. ' Is it always the same woman each month?'

'Yeah,' Alfie said dreamily. 'Yeah – she's gorgeous . . .'

Which didn't help in the least.

When James tried to push the point and ask whether Alfie knew if a room had been booked for them on each of those Thursdays, Alfie's insides did a reverse yo-yo, and a small warning light in his brain signalled him to back down; a light that screamed, *'Oh, God, what have I started?'*, as he clocked where this was leading. He took a long gulp of ale and prevaricated, somewhat reluctant to either answer the question put to him, or to take it upon himself to speculate on what was in James's mind. He was silently flailing himself for bringing this matter up; regretting the shooting off of his mouth and causing James the anxiety he could see forming on his friend's brow. And desperately needing to get out of this uncomfortable situation . . .

Racking his brains, he finally explained, as best he could – and hoping that he would be believed – that the booking of rooms was not his department and, if caught nosing through the reservations book, he could lose his job; and he couldn't afford to lose his job, even to help a long-standing mate. Unfortunately for Alfie, he was not a natural liar, and he felt his neck redden as James looked at him. He took another sip of his beer, feeling wretched, and fearing that, if he was not careful, he might well end up being the meat between two disagreeable and perhaps unsavoury slices of bread, so he looked down at the table to cover his embarrassment. He wanted to help; had wanted to ease James's distress, and struggled between either losing a friend or losing the only suitable position the Job Centre had had to offer after six months of searching, his confidence waning with each visit. The hotel paid a pittance, but it was better than nothing. Prying into affairs that did not concern him, he said without looking James in the eye, was more than his job was worth.

He'd picked up the vibes – had known James long enough to know when something caused anxiety. And he watched as his friend became steadily more anxious over what could well be his father playing away. He felt that he, Alfie, was to blame for this anxiety and squirmed at his lack of tact, knowing that there was no backing down now; the words were out of his mouth and could never be put back.

He felt sorry for James – and for James's mother – but was torn: on the one hand, he had no wish to get further involved in what was purely a family matter but, on the other, a sudden picture flashed in his mind of kind, sweet Mrs Frobisher, and of how she'd gone out of her way to rescue him from his gin-soaked, uncaring mother by allowing him to kick a ball around the garden with James after school; how she'd fed him proper food, as opposed to plates of greasy chips, with the tomato sauce slapped unceremoniously onto the table. Then his mind turned to her nasty little husband and his attitude towards him as a child; of how the man had always taken delight in mocking him – treating him as an embarrassment. The memory of that was still raw and, watching Brian Frobisher in his hotel each Thursday with that woman, he saw that nothing much had changed. So . . . if Frobisher *was* found to be cheating on his loving, caring wife, then it would be somewhat satisfying to see the man get his just deserts.

Except . . . it was none of his business.

Sitting on his bar stool in The Goose, he thought about Mrs Frobisher and of how, whenever encountering him these days, she stopped to ask how he was faring now that he was on his own. She still remembered his birthday each year, and a present would always be on the doorstep for him at Christmas: useful things; a pair of warm pyjamas; a woollen jumper . . . He could still taste the sumptuous meals she'd provided to fill out his skinny little body, and recalled all the outings she'd insisted upon him joining, along with the family, despite her husband's sneers and snipes at his appearance. Emptying his glass, and placing it on the bar for a refill, he felt a sudden stab of sorrow for her. He was so tempted to stir things up to make that vile husband of hers squirm.

So, when James pressed him, Alfie found himself agreeing to contact him to inform him of any upcoming luncheon reservations made by his father. It was the least he could do.

James, naturally, had picked up on the lie; Alfie Wendover

couldn't lie himself out a paper bag. But at least he'd coerced – finally; probably owing to the fact that he hated his father as much as he.

\* \* \*

James had to wait just over two weeks for his mobile to ring, during which time his mind had gone into overdrive. It was always a Thursday, Alfie said; the day had stuck in his mind because that was his afternoon off. And it was always a Thursday, wasn't it, when Brian came home and declared he'd had no appetite, or that he couldn't eat the 'rubbish' that his wife had put before him . . . ?

When Alfie finally rang to inform him that a table had been booked in the name of Frobisher at one o'clock the following Thursday, James's nerves were all but shattered. He held his breath after the call, attempting to calm himself, wondering wildly how to play this. He could be treading on dangerous ground, couldn't he? What should he do? Should he act upon this knowledge – could he bring himself to act? – or perhaps let sleeping dogs lie?

Thursday was just four days away and it kept him awake. He didn't want to involve Poppy in all of this, but he needed someone to advise him as to what to do. But there was no one; he was on his own here. What had been a seed of thought, not so long ago in The Goose's Head, had suddenly become reality, and he felt nauseous. How could it be right to spy on his father? And, if he did decide to spy on him, what was he likely to discover? If it turned out to be something innocent which could easily be explained away, that would put him in the wrong – *again*. He could imagine the extent of his father's wrath if he was wrongly accused of having an affair. But what if his instincts were correct and he discovered that he *was* having an affair – what could he, James, have a hope of doing about it?

A decision had to be made but, if he went through with this, might he actually witness the betrayal of his mother? It was this latter that stuck in his craw; did he actually *want* to witness a betrayal? Anyway, was it any business of his? But, yes, it was his business, wasn't it? Because, if – and he thought hard about the fact that he could be terribly wrong about this – *if* his father was doing the dirty on his mother, he would have to support her when she eventually realised the perfidious game he was playing.

His father, according to Alfie, was entertaining a woman to lunch – *and perhaps not just lunch.* He had a right to know who she was. Or did he . . . ? Could he bring himself to act upon this dubious information? Did he actually have the balls to go to the Old Dog and Bush to find out about his father and the woman who was not his wife?

Over those next few days he fought his emotions as they wavered from right to left, and he closed his eyes against the conundrum in an attempt to stop these conflicting thoughts from torturing him and depriving him of his rest. He'd then struggle through the following morning blurry-eyed and fractious through lack of sleep. His line manager at Tesco had snapped, after couple of days, that he'd stacked the baked beans next to the pasta, and what the hell was he thinking about? – the man having no inkling of the conflicting thoughts passing through his shelf-stacker's head. But James couldn't let go of the dilemma, however much he tried, his sole thoughts centring on the decision he had to make, and of what he was likely to discover at Old Dog and Bush. His head didn't feel real.

Thursday morning arrived and, on opening his eyes and aware of the day, he had a clear vision of what he had to do. In order to live with himself, he decided, he had to satisfy himself one way or another; settle this thing once and for all. So, clamping his jaws at having finally made the decision, he showered, dressed and walked down to breakfast. He was doing this for his mother; finding out the truth was the only way, wasn't it? But then, halfway through breakfast and watching her flit jauntily in and out of the kitchen, he havered once more and his heart turned over; if he did actually manage to discover something about his father's activities and it turned out to be bad, he could never tell her, could he? How could he bear to hurt his mother; his sweet mother, who had, all his life, shielded him from the excesses of her husband's violent tempers?

With these thoughts exercising his brain cells, he became resolute. He'd have to make up some excuse to borrow the car – because he had to go through with this – *he really did*. Each time he'd closed his eyes the previous night, he'd imagined his father entertaining a woman; laughing; flirting; taking her to bed . . . But that was all in his head, wasn't it? He had to put a stop to this torment – had to know once and for all. His heart thumping, he'd got up in the night to make himself a drink, tried to sleep, lay awake until light filtered through the curtains, then awoke feeling like shit. Yes – he did have to know. Pulling himself out of bed and walking into the comforting heat of the shower, and after surreptitiously calling the office at Tesco to say that he was sick, he went down ready to lie to his mother. Then, feeling more nervous than he'd ever felt, asked his mother if he could borrow her car.

'What's wrong with the bus today?' she said.

'Got the day off,' he smiled. 'Meeting a girl . . .'

'Mm, thought you looked a bit smart,' Valerie grinned. 'Is that aftershave?'

He felt himself reddening. He hated lying to his mother, but knew she was a soft touch and could never resist that glint of wickedness in his eyes, because in his eyes, she saw her own. So she smilingly handed him the key, begging him not to show off by driving too fast. He then drove the twenty miles to Barnscote, located the Old Dog and Bush, then parked further down from the hotel; his father would immediately recognise the *Volvo* if parked in the car park. Wetting his hands, he combed his fingers through his hair, frowning into in the rear-view mirror, hoping it would all stay put for the duration.

His legs, having been told sternly to behave themselves, strolled through the doors of the hotel all by themselves, leaving the rest of his body wondering what the hell he was doing. Meeting accidentally in the lobby, James and Alfie barely recognised each other – James with gelled-down hair and proper clothes, and Alfie looking like an anorexic penguin – but pretended not to know each other. James found himself a quiet corner of the reception hall and sat, his palms wet with nerves. As he waited, he picked up a newspaper to cover his face, silently thanking his mother for attempting to gel down his instantly recognisable thatch, which seemed to have sprung up again during the drive, damn it. He nervously ran his hand over it again.

Perhaps, he kept telling himself – perhaps there was another Mr Frobisher; perhaps this was a misunderstanding on Alfie's part. Maybe he'd jumped too quickly to conclusions.

Dressed in what his mother had called 'sensible clothes', he sat, ostensibly engrossed in the *Daily Telegraph,* which was large enough for him to hide behind, and waited. Out of the corner of his eye he saw Alfie hovering nervously in the dining area.

Although arriving much earlier than necessary, he jerked every time he heard the door swing open, and sat nervously on the edge of the couch, holding on to a newspaper that seemed to have a life of its own as it twitched and crackled irritably between his fingers. He closed his eyes, pursed his lips and sighed deeply as it suddenly came to him: the realisation that this was all wrong. He couldn't do this; he shouldn't be here. And, when the next client entered and he saw that it was not his father, he found he couldn't stand the strain a second longer. He folded the paper and placed it back on the table. He couldn't – wouldn't – do this. He had to go; get out before his father came through the hotel door.

Having made up his mind to leave, he stood and straightened himself for flight. Just then, a waitress strolled silently by to ask if he would like to order a drink. He was was so startled by the voice that he immediately sat down again, stammering that he was just about to leave, but thank you all the same ... However, his mouth had become dry with anxiety and, as the waitress turned away, he called out to her on a sudden impulse – the request coming out in a croak – that a cup of coffee wouldn't perhaps be a bad idea after all.

Ten minutes later, the girl returned and placed in front of him a full pot of steaming liquid, a jug of hot milk and four strands of sugar, accompanied by a plate of biscuits. He stared. Not having bargained for the expense of being presented with what looked like the whole coffee plantation, he gasped. How much was this going to cost? Jiggling the change in his trouser pocket, he inwardly groaned. He'd thought, when ordering a *cup* of coffee, that he might just about manage a small brew – but there again, this was an up-market hotel, not Caffé Nero, and coffee came in jugs filled to the brim with the stuff. And biscuits? They didn't do that at Caffé Nero. He sighed down at the tray before him, realising too late how inadequate the money in his trouser pocket would be in order to cover the cost of this. *He should have thought ...* Anxiety took over once more. Maybe he could prevail upon Alfie to lend him a tenner until Saturday.

He wrinkled his nose at the coffee, knowing it to be too bitter before it reached his lips. He added more milk before tasting it again but still found it unpalatable; Caffé Nero it most certainly wasn't. He sighed. He'd been a fool to come here. This was a total waste of time, he told himself over and over. Alfie was wrong; it was a misunderstanding ...

But it was not a misunderstanding.

At ten minutes to one, the door of the hotel opened once more and James almost choked on biscuit crumbs as his father walked in. He instantly lifted up the broadsheet to shield himself as he heard Brian's unmistakable voice announcing his arrival. Attempting to curb his nausea, he covertly watched as his father strode confidently through to the restaurant, with Julia Kilpatrick on his arm.

*Bloody hell!* – Julia Kilpatrick? Julia Kilpatrick was his mother's friend; they walked their dogs together on the Common ... He held his breath, then steeled himself to peer over the edge of the paper as the two were led to a table by a now nervously fluttering Alfie, all too aware that he was being watched from the top edge of the *Daily Telegraph*. So ... it was true ... This wasn't a mistake ... The paper gave a sudden crackle as his fingers jerked.

*But Julia Kilpatrick!*

James sat on, ostensibly reading and attempting, from time to time, to reach beneath the paper for his coffee cup: bitter or no, he needed coffee to give him strength. Having thus established the truth, his instincts told him to leave, but he was rigid with shock and couldn't move; but, even if he'd wanted to, he couldn't leave now, could he? One false move and he'd be spotted. Having been stimulated to the eyeballs with the hotel's terrible coffee, he just had to sit it out. He hadn't, however, reckoned on sitting it out for the best part of three quarters of an hour. From time to time, he heard his father bark out an order, using his important voice – the one he used whenever talking to minions, as though waiters and shop assistants, being far beneath the breadline than he, were all deaf. Sitting obliquely from him, James could just see the right-hand sleeve of his father's jacket as he ate his meal, but couldn't risk more than glance from the top edge of the paper. He looked up once to see his father stretch out his hand to touch Julia's arm.

*Yuk!*

The waitress sidled up again to ask if he would like more coffee, and he swallowed nervously and shook his head at her with a smile. She removed the tray from his table, then turned and smiled back at him. This small flirt was, at least, a diversion, which momentarily stopped him from dwelling upon his father's liaison with Julia Kilpatrick, and he watched the girl's backside until it disappeared into the hotel kitchen. She wasn't half bad looking; he'd ask Alfie about her . . .

Despite snaffling all the biscuits, his stomach gave a sudden rumble when plates of delicious food were carried past him, reminding him with a vengeance that he hadn't eaten since breakfast. Glancing at his watch, he realised that he'd wasted the best part of an hour sitting in the same position. He'd never sat for so long in his life. When the wine glasses and pudding bowls had finally been removed from his father's table, he sighed with relief. But then Brian, damn him, ordered coffee, which James secretly hoped was as foul as the pot he'd just sent back to the kitchen. The pair then sat, gazing into each others' eyes, seemingly forever. He wanted desperately to get out of this place; this was not somewhere he'd ever take a girl, even if he could afford it; too stuffy and up itself. Which was just about right for his father.

Finally, a nervous Alfie was summoned, a card swiped and James jerked upright as he realised the pair were finally leaving the restaurant. With a choke of alarm, he watched as his father's arm slid sinuously round Julia's waist as they both strolled towards the lobby.

*Please . . . please . . . not that way! Don't do this . . . Just walk out of the door . . .*

But, oblivious of James's silent plea, they strolled to the reception desk, collected a key from the receptionist then, with Julia on his arm, Brian walked towards the lift and pressed the button. James stared, shocked, as his father's hand slid to Julia's backside and squeezed her buttocks, then, while waiting for the lift to descend, swept her up into his arms and kissed her long and hard before they both entered the lift to take them up to their room.

His father . . .

And Julia Kilpatrick . . .

The same Julia Kilpatrick who lived across the road with that pompous husband of hers and those two noisy Dalmatians. *Nooky with Julia Kilpatrick* – his mother's dog-walking friend! How could she? And his father!

James sat on for a few moments more, winded and feeling strangely numb, then he stood and, without a backward glance, walked out of the hotel. He didn't have to instruct his legs this time because they couldn't carry him away fast enough. Alfie watched him go, feeling his pain, then paid the bill for him. Frowning and concerned as to his friend's state of mind, he watched him stride, whey-faced, out of the door. This was all his fault.

James couldn't remember how he got to the car. In a red haze of anger, he threw himself into the driver's seat, slotted the key into the ignition, then sat back, shaking. He shuddered out a sigh for his mother. He'd discovered the truth. But what good would that do? It would simply serve to kill little bits of him every day: all that knowledge he'd have to keep well and truly under his carefully gelled hair.

During the drive back, his anger returned: he should do something to avenge his mother. He'd fucking well use this. He'd find a way of using these extramarital romps against his double-crossing pig of a father. But he'd calm down first – revenge being

best served cold – and he'd make sure it was delivered when his
father least expected it. He'd be patient – he could do that. The
thought caused him to smile. He'd wait and pick his moment;
and he'd get it right, because this knowledge was pure gold. This
would be the perfect ammunition to fire at his father; revenge
for all his mother had had to put up with, and for all the years of
misery he'd caused him throughout his childhood. This would
be so satisfying. But, for the moment, it would be put into a jar
with the lid screwed on . . .

Perking up at the thought, he was beginning to think he might
enjoy that and how he might drop his father in it on a Thursday
evening, down at The Goose with his mates: 'Not surprising you
left your dinner this evening, Dad. You must be stuffed with that
three course lunch at Barnscote . . . ? So, tell me, how did it all
go with Julia Kilpatrick afterwards? I'm just curious, that's all.
Do condoms come with the last course, or are they served with
the coffee?'

Having pulled himself out of his anger, he suddenly found
himself grinning. Then spent the rest of the drive bending his
fertile mind into planning ever more embarrassing put-downs,
and spending a rather pleasant time over it on the way home.

* * *

After ditching uni, he and Brian had locked horns and had had
more than a few full-on rows about him still living at home – *like
some fucking leech'*, Brian had sneered. These rows tended to boil
over at least once a month when the bank statements dropped
through the letter box. James didn't know what all the fuss was
about; the family was not short of money and he earned his own
wages, which weren't *all* spent in the tattoo parlour and pints

of bitter in The Goose. The first call on James's wage packet was always to his mother for his board, saving the rest of his money for an extra chunk of skin to be pierced. He made sure to pay his way, so that he could never be accused of being a burden on the family bank account, and to prove to his father that he was anything but a leech.

What stuck in Brian's craw and made him seethe, however, was that he could find no fault with his son in any particular aspect of his daily life, so all he had for ammunition to fire at him, from time to time, were the excess of tattoos and metal appendages James was managing to acquire, simultaneously aware that he was helpless in preventing what he viewed as a disgraceful mutilation of the body. Rows about this, plus James's decision to quit university, erupted whenever Brian felt like throwing his weight around but, to his chagrin, was invariably faced with silence and the slowly-curling cigarette smoke emanating from his son's nostrils.

Valerie had cottoned on earlier to the fact that James's refusal to get a degree in science was, in the main, a two-finger salute to his father – and she smiled inwardly as she calmly watched every second of Brian's steamed up screaming fits as they shot through the air, causing his face to turn beetroot and causing barely controlled amusement in her son. She loved him for it; he was now old enough to stand up to the arrogant, pompous tyrant who had blighted his childhood with all his lofty expectations in order to bolster his own standing; the bully who had belittled his friend – at all those barbs about Alfie's background – which had hurt them both. James, it would seem, was growing a backbone and she admired him for standing up to his father.

Brian was now blowing a gasket because James had said that science was boring.

'Well, science is not for everybody, is it?' Valerie said. 'Anyway, shouldn't we be wanting our children to be happy doing what they want – rather than what we might want for them?'

'That's right – stick up for him, *as fucking usual!*' Brian yelled, the spittle of revulsion spraying out of his mouth. 'I just want them to get decent jobs, that's all. And shelf-stacking in a supermarket is not what I call a decent job!'

'Why isn't a decent job?' James asked calmly, leaning back on the armchair, a roll-up between his fingers, guessing that this question, coupled with cool logic, would be certain to unstick his father's brain cells sufficiently to turn his pudgy face into a mottled crimson beach ball. Pure comedy gold!

'Yeah – why isn't it a decent job?' his sister Poppy asked, fully aware that she was fanning the flames.

'Because . . . because . . . *put that fucking cigarette out!*' Brian shrieked.

James obediently stubbed out the cigarette, widening his eyes faux-innocently at his father, his mouth turned up slightly at the corners.

'And take that sodding smirk off your face!'

'What smirk?' James smirked.

'Look, just stop it, you two!' Valerie said sharply. 'That's enough.'

Brian let out a sudden growl, cracking his newspaper and sticking it up in a show of disgust, miffed at not being able to answer the question as to why shelf-stacking was not a proper job. If he'd said out loud that it was for brainless failures who'd never get on in life, he would have had the ethics-versus-snobbery book thrown at him – and James, he knew, was just waiting for that nugget to snarl out of his mouth so that he and Poppy could make a meal of it and stamp on him . . . And he seethed at not being able to say what he thought.

'C'mon, bro,' Poppy said suddenly. 'Let's go down and feed the ducks.'

Once they were out of the house and she'd heard the door slam shut, Valerie rounded on her husband.

'Why don't you leave him alone?' she said. 'Every opportunity you get, you're down his throat! You have to bring up that university stuff every single day, don't you? And why shouldn't he dress as he likes?'

'Because he's a bloody disgrace!' Brian shot back. 'If people see him walking through the village in clothes like that, I'll be a laughing stock . . . !'

'Is that what you're worried about? Your sodding reputation? Can't you ever see beyond yourself? What harm is he doing?'

'He looks bloody ridiculous!'

'Is that all?' she shot out with unaccustomed anger. 'Is that all you care about – fucking appearances?'

*'Don't fucking swear at me!'* he yelled, clamping his jaws and eyeballing her.

'So – you're the only one allowed to swear in this house, are you? This is my house, too!'

'Only because I've worked my arse off to pay for it!' he barked. 'Worked my sodding arse off, and what do I get? A son who bunks off uni and dresses like a tramp – and an ungrateful bitch who's too weak to argue the toss and tell him to get into the real world! Sodding milk sop!'

'*So . . .*' she said, stifling the sob she felt rising into her throat, 'this *bitch* should be grateful for being used as slave to pander to your every need, should she? This *bitch* who's ironed all your shirts for twenty-two years and made all those meals you shove down your gullet?'

*'Fuck off!'*

'No, Brian – not this time!' she said sharply, determined to

stem the wobble in her voice. 'You might have wiped the floor
with me for the last twenty-two years, but I won't let you do it
to our son. Don't you think it's his business to choose how to
conduct his life – to give up something he knows he wouldn't be
happy doing? Don't you think you should be relieved that that's
all he's guilty of; that he's not mugging old ladies, or carrying
a knife down his sock?'

'All? He's probably high on drugs most of the time!' he huffed.

'*You don't know that!*' she snapped.

He pursed his lips and turned away from her, shaking up his
newspaper once more with a crack sharp enough to shut her out.

'James,' she went on, addressing the front page of the *Sunday
Telegraph*, 'is a thoughtful and well-mannered boy. He's our son,
and I'm extremely proud of him. I bumped into Glenys Pugh
yesterday in the village, and she couldn't speak more highly of him.'

'Hmm!'

'Give him some slack, Bri,' she said sighing. 'Leave him alone.
He'll find his own feet in his own time.'

'So, for how long do you anticipate that to be?' he snarled.
'How long does it take to contemplate one's navel? And how
long am I expected to put up with playing boarding house to
him until he gets to lodge somewhere else? He's old enough now
to be out there, finding a proper job – getting his own flat –
sorting his life out, for God's sake! Though, without a degree, I
suspect that that's going to take some time. I can't be expected
to keep open house for those sodding little hangers-on for ever!'

'What? How do you expect me to respond to that?' she spat
out angrily. 'They're our children! *Our* children! How can you
begrudge our children a roof over their heads?'

'Because they're both old enough to stand on their own two
sodding feet!' he snapped.

Valerie walked over and angrily snatched the paper from his hands.

'I'm sick of talking to the fucking *Telegraph*!' she yelled. 'Why can't you look at me when you're talking? Why can we never hold a proper conversation?'

'Well – one, you'd have to be worth looking at, I suppose!' he sneered, startled at her sudden outburst, 'and, two, worth having a decent conversation with!'

'Oh, right! And is Julia Kilpatrick worth looking at?' she said, narrowing her eyes. 'Worth having a decent conversation with?'

'What the fuck are you talking about, you stupid bitch?' he muttered sullenly, snatching back the newspaper and managing to avoid her eyes.

'You! You . . . are something else, Brian Frobisher!' she said, glaring at him, her mouth a thin line of hurt and anger. 'And I'm not quite as stupid as you think!'

'Are you not?' he grinned maliciously. 'Well, I haven't seen much in the way of intelligent life inside that mop of frizzy hair for a good many years.'

'Well maybe that's because you haven't been trying very hard!' she replied to that put-down, a lump now forming in her throat.

Deflated and stung by his words, she finally sat and put her head in her hands. Is that what he thought of her? Was that *all* he thought of her? And was that why he took comfort in Julia's ultra-toned arms? She may not ever have been his intellectual equal; they'd both acknowledged that from the start. But Julia Kilpatrick was hardly the *Brain of Britain* herself, for crying out loud! She may not ever have had the looks and glamour that Julia exuded, but she'd always done her bit for all those years in keeping the family together and doing what was required of her. And she'd never complained; she'd simply kept going, because as a wife and mother that's what you did. She'd always managed to hold up her head and get on with her thankless title of *Chief Cook and Bottle-Washer*: managing the house and the children; relieving him of the task of ferrying the children back and forth to school, to the sports field, to music lessons. And she always ensured that her husband looked pristine for the lofty position he held at his laboratory, then had fed and watered him on his return each day. Running round like a headless chicken for all those years – *for all those fucking years* – for a husband who evidently considered her a *worthless bitch* . . .

This was the first time she'd confronted him about his affair with Julia Kilpatrick, and now sat back, watching him squirm, guessing he'd have to come winging back at her and hit out in order to cover his discombobulation.

Thoroughly drained and sitting morosely on the couch, she wondered if this sudden show of anger had been worth it. She took long breaths in and out to slowly calm herself. Knowing how she'd always avoided confrontation, Brian had always managed to get the better of her so, feeling thus overpowered, she'd always allowed him the last word. Today, however, she'd had enough of him having the last word. Even the worm reared up its little head when it had been trodden in the dirt for long enough, didn't it? What had truly got her goat was Brian's declaration of her uselessness. Useless? That was the ultimate straw, and made her seethe. And there he sat, complacently shielding himself behind his newspaper with a look that wrote her off as a valueless piece of shit. She watched him, with a spark of satisfaction, knowing that this challenge had taken him by surprise. Her heart ached, however, with the thought that, for all these years, she'd been nothing to him but a slave.

She slowly lifted her head to look at him; at the face that retained, even through the bluster, that flush of guilt. Even through his evident discomfort, he'd felt the need to use this accusation as a platform to belittle her, using school-playground bullying tactics; attempting to disguise his guilt by changing the goal-posts and shifting the blame of his infidelity onto her: she was stupid; had let herself go and was no longer desirable.

'And . . . if you think you can get rid of our children before they're ready to fly the nest, you'll have to think again,' she said bitterly. 'I believe that we should look after our children for as long as it takes. Without question!'

'Ever the clucking hen!' he sneered, his lip curling in contempt. 'Or would that be *fucking* hen?

*I'm a mother!*' she threw back at him, seeing red once more. 'And all I see right now is a father thinking that this is all about him. Well, it isn't!'

'You've always been too bloody soft!' he said, cracking his paper open once more.

'And you've always been too bloody selfish!' she snapped back. 'When a couple decide to have children, that's a responsibility for life. It's also a responsibility to remain faithful to one's marriage vows!'

Brian, having had enough of this, slammed his Sunday paper onto the carpet, got up out of his chair and angrily left the room.

'That's right – scamper off down to The Goose as per usual when you can't think of the last word!' she shouted as he strode down the hall. *But do give my love to Julia!*'

\* \* \*

That stung him, but he decided to ignore the jibe. Reaching for his coat, he shrugged it quickly on then marched out of the door, slamming it behind him. So . . . she knew, did she? How had she managed that? And did she really know, or was she guessing? Striding through the door of The Goose's Head, he propped himself up on the bar and ordered a pint, then decided to stay for lunch. He wouldn't be going back home for some time . . .

Dourly mulling over his glass in a corner of the bar while he waited for lunchtime to arrive, he thought, not for the first time, of how he wished he'd never married; marriage was more fucking trouble than it was worth. As it stood, he was saddled with a wife who'd avoided sleeping with him for some years now, a loser of a son who thought he was a better man than he for choosing to work as a piddling store-stacker rather than knuckling down in order to get a degree, and a daughter studying art – of all things – gearing up to being a professional board-carrying demonstrator. How the hell had that happened? They'd each had a damned good education, and he'd once been certain of that education leading to something worthwhile. Why go to all that expense for two worthless sprogs who, afterwards, decide not to get themselves a degree? Money down the drain! And how was he going to hold up his head in the laboratory now that Greg Harrison's son had just qualified with a BSc?

As head of the laboratory, if anyone got the slightest whiff of James stacking shelves in a supermarket, no one would have an ounce of respect for him. What if they bumped into him in Tesco when they were shopping? And how would it look? Head of Department with his son shelf-stacking in Tesco, of all places – not even Marks and Spencer! – when every one of his staff had children of the same age, all at various universities around the country, reading science, and all destined for the Bracklea Laboratory after they'd graduated. And him with a son who had chosen to work in a *supermarket!*

The last straw was when Valerie encouraged that scruffy little Alfie Wendover off the Marchstone Estate into the house, treating him like one of the family; couldn't get enough of the filthy little brat. Feeling sorry for him, and giving him James's cast-offs like some Lady Bountiful. Soft as grease.

Agreeing to have the brats in the first place was his biggest mistake. Life was never the same after that. Life was not what it promised, he thought bitterly. Nothing turned out right, did it? Take marriage . . . *Anybody* . . . ? Marriage was pants! Whoever thought that living with the same woman for twenty-odd years was a good idea? It was unnatural. You'd get less time for murder. A man should be allowed his freedom – allowed a bit of variety. But at the time – all those years ago – he'd argued that he'd married for love, whereas he'd married in order for his wife to continue his mother's job of looking after him.

He hated her – hated his children – hated life in general. As for his wife – she'd never be successful at anything, except as a sodding mother . . .

The realisation that kids were forever, and that sending them back in a parcel to Amazon was not possible, came to him when James was around the age of four, and Poppy not far behind. And then marriage had taken a nosedive.

If it hadn't been for Julia . . .

He ordered another pint, then took it to an empty table in a far corner of the pub to wait it out until lunchtime.

# Chapter Twenty

One night in freezing Moscow:

Woken in the early hours by Toni climbing into bed. Heaven knows where he'd been; I knew better than to ask.

'Aah, you're *stone cold!*' I cried, shivering as he peeled back the bedclothes.

'Yes – I know. It's the reason I came back,' he said, 'in the hope of getting warm.'

'The only reason?'

'What other reason could there be?' he teased.

'I can't imagine. So? Do you have a plan in your search for warmth?'

'Well . . . yes, I do, as a matter of fact – I've been reading up on thermodynamics and you wouldn't believe what I learned.'

'Oh?'

'It's just been discovered, and is quite a revolutionary idea. I gather from the manual that if the woman you love most in all the world puts her arms around you, it flicks an internal switch which sets the therms working.'

'Therms? Good heavens! Very revolutionary, that. Think it will work?'

'Well, it does sound a bit far fetched and experimental, I admit, but the manual was quite clear. And the concept is stunningly simple, don't you think. Want to give it a go?'

'I don't mind.'

After a while: 'Is it working?'

'Oh, yes,' he said. 'I think it might be. But we now have to move on to stage two of the experiment.'

'Which is?'

'Stage two states that, if we put our lips together, it kind of completes the circuit and causes a spark.'

'A spark? Good heavens. Couldn't that be dangerous?'

'I sincerely hope so . . .' he whispered.

We stayed in bed for most of that week, purely because it was the only way to keep warm in one of the worst winters Moscow had seen in recent years, the biting winds coming straight off the Eastern Steppes.

During that period of intense cold, I tried to picture Roper's End as it would have been then; folk shivering in the lowered temperature, sealing the windows, battening down the hatches, resetting the central heating and getting out their winter coats against the cooler weather, the temperature in Russia unimaginable to them. The weather in Britain, by contrast, wouldn't cause a total stoppage, nor prevent anyone going about their business. Folk wouldn't, for example, be faced, halfway down a country road, with a twelve-foot bank of snow, then have to wait for two hours in a freezing car for men to arrive with snowploughs and shovels, then wait another two hours for them to clear it.

While cocooning ourselves between all the blankets we could beg, borrow or buy, I yearned for that mild misty chill everyone would be experiencing, to complain along with everyone else of how cold it had become for the time of the year. They should have been in Moscow that year, at minus forty – then they would have known what cold was!

My conscience pricked, though, because I'd originally planned to be home for Christmas. But there I was, shivering in bed, hugging my lover for warmth. Right then, my head was in a different place and I was dreaming of a life together with Toni; plotting to leave my husband – which was despicable. And, instead of rushing back to him in order to spend Christmas at home, I had, to Ben's dismay, delayed my return – quite deliberately.

As Toni and I lay together in that feather bed in Moscow, I wondered if I would ever return to my husband. But, at the time, that hadn't, I'm ashamed to say, upset me unduly.

* * *

Toni was incorrigible, and I'd never have tamed him: an alcoholic, a drug addict, a nicotine addict, a betting addict, a danger addict – and up for any other addictive element that happened to hover within his sights. Danger for him was a magnet, but it's safe to say that if he himself had been the magnet, danger would have found him – clung onto him, begging to be sucked in. If it was wrong, wicked or promised a challenge, no matter how risky this would seem to a normal human being, Toni would – and did – unhesitatingly jump straight into it. It was why he'd chosen espionage above all those earlier jobs – jobs which had worn him down with boredom. This new life was, without a doubt, meat and drink to him. And it was that which had made him so totally irresistible; his daring; his chutzpah; his unpredictability . . .

I'd look at him each morning as he viewed himself in the shaving mirror, humming softly as he brushed his hair into place – as he smiled at his reflection with that unshakable conviction that no harm would ever dare touch him. He'd thought himself immune to danger because he was convinced that, by using that natural charm and all those flashing glittering teeth, he could do anything, however outrageous, and get away with it. From childhood, he'd learned all the tricks that would get him out of trouble by beaming that wonderful wicked grin at a sister or an aunt. So he was very sure of himself; sure that no one would ever resist this spell-binding magic; sure that his own private stock of fairy-dust would, all this life, ease his path and allow him to do whatever he wanted. It had worked so far – so why wouldn't it always work? And I should know, because I'd fallen for it myself, hadn't I?

He never considered the possibility that, one day, his luck might run out.

But, despite that silky irresistible smile, he was ruthless – utterly ruthless – *and fearless*. And clever. He played a dangerous game. And he knew it. It was, however, one game I was relieved to have declined.

Toni had slipped off the wagon quite early on in his life, owing largely to having married the wrong woman while still too young, then had taken a teaching job that he hadn't been able to handle, or had got fired from, owing to the wheels on the wagon having come adrift more times that he would ever admit. I'll never know – but alcohol and drugs had informed his life for too long and wouldn't let him go, addiction having seriously taken hold. It eventually dawned on him that it might not be the answer to every problem in life, but he couldn't help himself and, after brief attempts to kick the habit, he'd open a bottle – then another bottle . . . or three.

He'd compounded matters by marrying a second time, though was rather hazy on information, when pressed, relating to being divorced from the first wife in order to marry the second . . . Then, when that marriage hadn't worked out, he'd married a couple of times more. I knew it was useless to enquire further on the matter of the possibility, or otherwise, of the various divorces – largely because I didn't think I could cope with the truth. And because, even though my head was telling me to face up to that truth and to accept the reality that, if I'd followed him to Italy, he would have dropped me, like he'd dropped the other women in his life, my heart simply wanted what it could take of him in the here and now.

During the few months I'd known him, there would be a continuous stream of apologies for his sins – short unpredictable periods when he'd vow to give up whatever addiction was threatening to destroy him at the time. He'd never go back to that – he wouldn't. He was adamant: no, he wouldn't touch another drop of alcohol; no, he'd never again inject or snort; no, he'd definitely never again ask me for money to lay another bet. But, like the incurable addict he was, he always went back – back to everything harmful and self-destructive; making the most of every ounce of life, almost as though he knew that his time on earth would be cut short.

And, throughout this time, I veered between believing him and treating it all as fantasy. When he made all these promises: that he'd pay back the money he'd lost in the gambling dens; that he'd never go back to Italy and to his wife – whichever wife that happened to be – I'd do my best to believe words that had been spoken with the utmost conviction, even with that scintilla of doubt scratching its talons at the back of my mind. I knew he was lying and that he'd break every promise he'd made to me, as he'd broken all the others – but I didn't care.

After each of those broken promises, he'd become depressed; depressed at his own weakness and inability to keep his word. Which led to the next period, when he would boast that he hadn't had a drink all day, and wasn't that clever of him . . . There would then follow a period of withdrawal, which would invariably manifest itself in a snappy biting temper. That would then be followed by total inertia; times when he could barely raise in head from the pillow when the realisation hit him that, if he couldn't have what he craved, life was not worth living. During these latter periods, he became a child, begging forgiveness from me, his doting surrogate mother. I learned to recognise the emergence of each stage and to deal with them. I tried, but finally came to realise that these incidences of regret would always be short-lived; as soon as he'd gone through the fire of redemption, and all the contrition and apologies were over and done with – as soon as he'd scourged his back and cleansed his soul – he'd rapidly return to his old charming self, confidently assured of forgiveness and a life of continuous self-indulgence.

How many women had fallen for him? How many women had he made these promises to, charming his way into their hearts? And how many had forgiven him over and over, only to be abandoned by him once they'd healed his wounds? It is hard work trying to tame an alcoholic; a thankless, Sisyphean task. There is a limit as to how many apologies one can take without one's spirit breaking.

In his short life he'd managed to marry at least four women; had been in rehab twice; had lost countless jobs through drunkenness and/or negligence; lost his homes, all his money and all of his wives . . . Not that he appeared to regret any of it. And after being thrown out of his last job and with not a single lira left, he'd walked into one of the most dangerous occupations known to man – that of espionage. He'd grabbed it with both hands; this was pure, diamond-encrusted, hair-raising peril – and he was never so satisfied unless on the edge of disaster, ever certain that he would get on by blagging his way out of any given situation. And by switching on that killer smile . . .

He's with me still: eyes twinkling behind a cloud of cigarette smoke – and that smile – that glorious sexy smile . . .

And the bitterness. That's still with me too.

Bitterness is like an illness which, if you don't address it immediately, slowly eats your innards until there's nothing left. You put off seeing the doctor, imagining the disease to go away of its own accord, and then it grows inside you in unpredictable surges like a cancer and, before you know it, it's incurable.

*  *  *

When I arrived back home, I couldn't speak; the shock, coupled with the grief, had manifested itself in my voice and, when I tried to talk, my throat contracted and nothing came out. I'd been deprived of a future that had seemed certain. And I'd loved as I'd never loved before. Overnight, I had been stripped of all hope; hope that I would ever again know true happiness.

During my previous assignments abroad, something devastating would invariably have managed to get to me and, in the sure and certain knowledge that Ben would wipe away my tears, I would come staggering home and talk through all the hurt and anger with him. My darling gentle husband would then hold me in his arms and allow me time to weep and rage at some injustice or other which had been beyond my control; talk me through my pain while I vented my fury at those in power who'd failed in their duty to protect their people; those fat cats who'd pleaded for funds from rich countries with promises to make a better life for their people, but who had, having received financial aid, immediately turned their backs on those starving people and spent it instead on a life of luxury. I'd seen all that, reported it, then waited in vain for something to be done about it.

I knew I could talk to Ben about whatever was on my mind – that I could say anything to him – get it out of my system; knew I could trust him to be non-judgmental. He would calm me. He understood me – understood my job and my need to do what I had to do. He was so perfect and understanding, and listened patiently to all the terrible things I'd witnessed and had had to photograph.

But, this time, I couldn't talk to him – couldn't talk to anybody. The pain was unbearable and threatened to crush me. I took to my bed and cried myself to sleep. I told myself that I should have investigated that murder – all those murders – further; should have done my utmost to find out who had betrayed that group of agents in Moscow – even though there'd been no way and no hope of ever finding out the truth. If MI5 couldn't manage to dig out the mole in their midst, what chance did I have?

Even though it had not managed to crush me entirely, that terrible period in Moscow left me irreparably scarred – with a damaged heart, a damaged brain and just about half of my senses . . . The thick fog of loss spread its tentacles through my brain and I had to hope that time would heal but, with each passing day, I felt that I was losing the battle.

Because I couldn't tell anyone. How could I admit to my husband that I'd lost the love of my life? But then, I asked myself, how could I continue to live with that secret? I wondered each morning, when I eventually managed to open my eyes, how I could begin to live again. How would I learn to laugh again – to smile, and to go back to the Freddie-before-Moscow? How would I learn to cope with the shame that I'd been on the verge of leaving Ben for a gorgeous, dangerous Italian? I had to go on – I knew that, but those dark slabs of grief wouldn't let me go. I had a loving husband who hadn't a clue as to my perfidy. How could I have done that to him? How could I have considered losing him for a wayward, addictive unknown who would, in all probability, have let me down? How could I continue to live that lie?

Each time I closed my eyes, I saw Toni's lifeless body on that unforgiving slab; the smells in that foul mortuary lingering in my nostrils; the smirks of indifference on the faces of the attendants; all of this keeping me awake night after night. I couldn't get out of my head the state of his mangled car as I watched it being towed away.

Once home and out of danger, I lay sleepless and perspiring in bed, afraid to close my eyes, knowing that, dangerous though it all was, I was prepared to allow myself to be drawn into betraying everything I held dear. I'd been an utter fool, swayed by a beautiful smile.

For weeks, I lay motionless on the bed, unable, each morning, to muster sufficient energy to get up; unable to face a day without Toni. What, I asked myself over and over, was there to get up for? What was the point?

\* \* \*

What was the point of anything when the editor of my paper, after happily publishing that first angry article, subsequently refused my pleadings to pursue the investigation of Toni's and all those other brutal assassinations. I suspected he'd been threatened by some source I can only guess at. I remember his fury, pitched against my own fury, when I argued for something further to be published in order to inform the general public; that it was in the public interest to know what the Russians were capable of. I demanded that this unforgivable crime be investigated. The lives of these men had been thrown to the dogs by some bastard, somewhere, someone who had betrayed them to the USSR. I yelled that was his duty as editor to investigate – to print the photographs I'd smuggled out – to do everything possible to shed light on who had organised their deaths.

You may imagine how yelling at my boss went down, and I was

told, in no uncertain terms, to drop it. Hardly surprising then that I was threatened with dismissal if I dredged this matter up again, or attempted to investigate myself.

But I'd had other ideas, and I came back home furious after that confrontation, and set about planning what I should do. I also needed to assess my position with an editor too lily-livered to look into who or what had perpetrated this crime by refusing to put into print was was clearly under his nose. Looking back, though, maybe I'd been too harsh in blaming him; perhaps someone had threatened him with something more than the closing down of his paper . . .

So, lying in bed, unable to face the world, I couldn't think of a single thing worth struggling up for. Ben, bless his heart, sensed that it was better to leave me to get over this thing that had happened to me – the thing I couldn't talk to him about. He must have wondered why, for once, I couldn't tell him what was wrong with me, but he never asked.

After several weeks of inertia, and with difficulty, I managed to pull myself up and get back to work. I was drained of emotion, but felt had to get back in order to heal myself and show the bastards they hadn't won. I tried and failed in my efforts to discover the truth and so ended up losing my job.

* * *

So . . . now, all I'm left with are the memories of that wonderful time we had together, Toni and I, short though it was – and, as I sit here dozing, with Squidge sleeping on my lap and my mug of tea slowly turning cold, the questions keep multiplying. They're still in my head; all those questions that have haunted me throughout my life: what, for example, had happened to Maria Collini all those years ago? What had she wanted to tell me that couldn't have been said over the phone? Had I led Toni into danger? Was it my fault? Why was it necessary for him to die? What had he discovered that might have damaged them? How had the spy ring become known to the KGB . . . ?

The one question – the one important question – that I ask myself now is who was that bastard who was evil enough to have betrayed Toni and his colleagues?

These are questions I'd give my all to get answered before I die.

# Chapter Twenty-One

Julia had disappeared again. Theo had showered, fiddled about with the internet, and then had come down to a late breakfast dressed only in his towelling robe – but no Julia. He called out for her as he sat at the kitchen table, summoning her to provide his breakfast. But the house was empty. So – *bugger* – no breakfast!

This disappearing act happened around once a month, and always on a Thursday – he was nothing if not observant. She'd just shoot off for half the day without a by-your-leave. There were other times when she'd drive off without telling him where she was going. He'd have to get to the bottom of it; show her who was master of this house.

He sauntered over to the fridge and pulled open the door, sighing irritably, then stood, staring long and hard at the milk. The milk stared back. His eyes travelled to the eggs nestling in the well of the door, and he gazed longingly at them, stroking his chin thoughtfully. He then closed the door on them before he was tempted to do something silly. He was aware of the hazards involved in attempting to cook a plate of eggs and bacon all by himself, the breakfast which his wife had cooked for him practically every morning of their married life, and guessed it would perhaps be safer to make do with cornflakes – which would only require milk. He could do that. A bowl of cornflakes was no breakfast for a man, though, he thought ruefully as he peered back into the fridge, seeking further inspiration for an alternative. He failed, however, to see anything that wouldn't require something he'd have to cook. He'd stick to cornflakes; with luck, it might just succeed in filling a hole until Julia came back to cook him a proper breakfast.

He balked at lifting the frying pan off its hook, eyeing it like a gazelle might eye an approaching tiger, the very sight of it giving him the collywobbles as he remembered past misfortunes with the thing. He still shuddered at the remembrance of once attempting to do a bit of cooking when Julia had popped out, in order to show her that he wasn't the completely useless idiot she'd once levelled at him, then had almost managed to set fire to the kitchen. He'd only left the oil in the pan to heat for a few minutes while he looked at the headlines of the *The Times*; then again, perhaps it had been slightly more than a few minutes, as he'd decided to check the FTS Index and the price of market shares. But then – whoosh! While his back was turned, it had burst into flames and had then set fire to a tea towel he'd carelessly left on the stove. The memory of that stench of burnt fat taking weeks to get out of the kitchen lingered on uncomfortably in his brain, and he turned his back on the frying pan in order to get Julia's fury out of his head.

She'd made him promise never to do such a thing again.

So he reached into the cupboard for a cereal bowl, which didn't seem too difficult, then slapped the bowl onto the kitchen table. He then, with a struggle, managed to open a box of cornflakes. He'd have to complain to these packaging people; packets, these days, were constructed from far too flimsy a cardboard. Shaking them out of the packet, however, seemed a task beyond his scope, and bits of splintered cereal somehow found their way to the floor, which was impossible to rectify, as he'd no idea where he might locate a dustpan and brush. After pouring the milk into the bowl and leaving the bottle on the kitchen table to sour in the heat, he scrunched his way out of the kitchen and into the breakfast room, treading the crumbs from his slippers into the carpet as he went. He then remembered that he would need a spoon.

Sulkily spooning cornflakes into his mouth as he sat at the breakfast table, he felt discombobulated at finding himself alone. She hadn't said she was going out, he thought miserably as he chomped through the few cornflakes that had managed to land in his dish. Would she be shopping? But why would she go shopping on a Thursday morning? There was plenty of food in the freezer because she'd shopped in the Bracklea branch of Marks and Spencer only yesterday. So where could she be?

After finishing his breakfast, he dragged his crumby flip-flops back into the kitchen and placed the cereal bowl into the sink, leaving in his wake pulverised shards of cornflakes trodden carelessly, and now embedded, into the breakfast room carpet. He then sloshed water into the kettle and made himself a mug of tea. Somewhat buoyed up at the success of this feat, he plucked the daily newspaper out its box, picked up his mug, then trundled dolefully into the sitting room, oblivious of all the droplets of milk and the odd slither of cornflakes which had managed to fall into the folds of his robe.

But he couldn't settle. He needed her. He needed his wife in order to be told what to do and when to do it and, despite the comfort blanket of *The Times,* he circled the room, at a loss as to how to fill in the morning without her. She must have left while he was showering, otherwise he would have heard the engine of her car. This was too bad. On these odd Thursdays, she always had a logical explanation of her whereabouts; the library to change her books; a chance meeting with a friend . . . But was that really what she was doing? Why was she so secretive . . . ? It was damned annoying.

He sat down again and turned a page of the newspaper, but it was no good – he was too anxious to read – and he threw the paper onto the floor then frowned moodily before circling the room once more.

Halfway through the afternoon he heard her car pull up in the drive and exhaled loudly. So, she'd deigned to come home after half the day . . . ! He threw up his chin, forcing himself to stay calm, reining in the relief and telling himself firmly to expel any notion he might previously have had to dash out wildly to her car in a show of joy at her homecoming; that would be a dead giveaway. He was in a bad mood, and was it any wonder? He'd not only missed his cooked breakfast, but also his lunch, and he was hungry and crabby. Deciding to display his annoyance at her lack of care in failing to provide his meals, he arranged his face accordingly. These disappearing acts had become too regular, so he'd have to put his foot down. This was his wife, whose job it was to look after him.

He could do this. Hadn't he had men under him in the past? And hadn't they, under his command, done exactly what he'd told them to do? He'd been a commander – was *still* a commander; he could do this. He folded his arms as she walked in – had to be seen as masterful . . .

'Where on earth have you been?' he cried crossly as she came through the door.

'What?' she exclaimed, raising her recently threaded eyebrows. 'I went shopping. What do you think?'

'Why?' he demanded, louder than he'd meant to.

'What do you mean, "why"?'

'You didn't need to shop – we've got plenty of food!' he said sternly. 'You shopped only yesterday!'

'Good grief! What is this – the Spanish Inquisition? Why all the fuss?' she said angrily, dumping several bags onto the kitchen table. 'I bought a new dress for next week's party, if you really have to know!'

'But you've been out all day!'

'I bumped into a friend and we had lunch,' she lied testily. 'So what?'

'Well, *I* haven't had lunch,' he said, throwing out his lip, spoiling for a tantrum.

'Well, more fool you!' she shot back, then folded her arms and glared at him. She'd often thought of him as a reverse Tardis: a three-year-old encased in the body of a mammoth; had, throughout their marriage, thought of herself as having three children, except that the one standing before her now was not presently at university, but whining and whinging under her feet all day. 'I go out for *half a day* and come back to the sodding third degree! You could have gone to The Goose for lunch.'

'Yes, but . . .'

'And *don't* shout at me!' she stormed, looking round at the mess.

'Oh . . . sorry. I was . . . Right . . . Well, I suppose if you bumped into a friend . . .' he huffed, rapidly backing down – then, 'Darling – I'm sorry. I didn't mean to shout.'

'For God's sake, Theo, get a grip. You need a sodding nanny!' she snapped, thinking that a good whack round the ears would perhaps be nearer the mark.

He shuffled his feet, watching her moodily as she viewed the state of the house; bit his lip as she sighed at the crumb laden carpet, the ring from his coffee mug on the side table, at his stained bathrobe – and then back at him.

'Can't you do *anything* without causing cataclysmic meltdown? What have you done? This is a pig sty!' she fumed as she turned from him and marched into the breakfast room to discover what damaged he might have done there.

Realising he'd lost a considerable portion of the vantage ground, he trailed glumly after her, attempting a smile, pleading a small smile from her.

Staring at the kitchen table she sighed again as she picked up the box of cornflakes.

'And why in God's name did you have to open a fresh box of cereal when there is a half-opened box right next to it?'

'Sorry . . . I didn't see it,' he whimpered.

'*Obviously* . . . *!*' she sighed heavily, wrinkling her nose at the carton of rancid milk languishing on the kitchen table, the smell of which he'd seemed totally unaware, but which had had time to permeate the house, and she took it to the sink then poured out its contents.

'Look . . . I was just . . . I was worried.'

'Worried? And that's an excuse for not using your eyes?'

'Why didn't you tell me you were going out?' he said, trying another tack. 'I didn't know where you were . . .'

'Well – now you do!' she snapped. 'And why *would* I tell you each time I go out? I'm your wife, not your mother. And why aren't you dressed? Surely you could have managed that without me! And what's all that stuff dribbling down your bath robe?'

'Oh, er, I expect it's milk,' he said meekly.

She cheerlessly followed the trail of crumbs from the kitchen to the breakfast room, like Hansel and Gretel attempting to find their way out of the woods. Would she, like those children, ever find her way out of this densely forested wood of her marriage, she wondered, momentarily closing her eyes? How much more could she take of this excuse of a marriage which, with each passing day, came to resemble a kindergarten? How much longer would she have to bear this useless piece of humanity? The cleaner wasn't due for another week, so she'd have to get the crumbs up herself.

'When's dinner?' he asked lamely.

'When I'm ready to cook it!' she said, tight-lipped, trying to keep the anger from spilling over into that deep well of fury she felt burning inside her as she strode towards the stairs with her parcels.

'Er.. don't forget we're going out tonight,' he shouted to her receding backside as she ascended.

Getting no reply, he strolled back into the sitting room and picked up his paper again with a sigh of relief, then settled down to read the headlines. She should calm down, he thought as he flicked open the pages of *The Times*. She got angry over the slightest thing these days. There were such things as anger-management courses, he'd read. He'd suggest it at an opportune time . . .

\* \* \*

She should leave him – was on the brink of leaving him – Julia reflected, as she fought back tears before slamming the bedroom door against the sound of his whiny voice. He was seriously getting on her nerves; had been getting on her nerves for more years than she could remember. After his retirement, when he'd come home for good, she should have left – except that the children were still living at home then . . . But now that they'd flown the nest, she realised she could leave him. That was all very well, she sighed, but what would she do, and where would she go? Then Simon came along with this wild idea of eloping, and she thought she'd known what she would do and where she would go. That is, until a few weeks ago; the packed bag now tucked out of sight.

She sat on the bed, more depressed than she could ever remember. Life had once been bearable – before retirement had brought her husband back home full time, damn it! Prior to that, apart from ferrying the children to school, five days of the week had been hers.

And then dawned the day when – oh joy! – Katie left for Durham, followed a year later by Phillipa to Oxford. And, once the girls had left home, she'd had all day to please herself. But then, suddenly, retirement had happened and, once Thicko was back home and mooching less than usefully about the house, acting like a toddler and getting in her way, she'd felt trapped. There he was – too bloody much of him, griping and complaining. He was so sodding needy; couldn't do a thing without her; could barely boil water; followed her around like a stray dog, and was about as useful as two-legged chair. So bloody boring he could have put a glass eye to sleep. What was the point of him?

Until that body blow, Julia's weekly schedule with her lovers had been ticking along like a well-oiled clock; she stuffing the cash away in the far corner of her wardrobe for the times when she felt the need for the odd tweak. How else did one live in this flea-bitten sodding village? This sudden retirement had thrown her into a spin; how would she manage her numerous liaisons now that her husband was threatening to end up here under her feet – *all the time?* It had been bad enough organising matters when he'd deigned to come home at the odd weekend. But, suddenly, here he was – *never to leave* – and scraping every nerve in her body. Although she'd known that her husband would have to retire one day, this sudden announcement had thrown her into a well of deep depression. How could he retire? – he was certainly old enough to retire, but she'd never given it much thought. Her life could now be changed for ever . . .

Furthermore, without consulting her, nor seeing the need to consult her, he'd sold the London flat, because he said it wouldn't be needed again, which deprived her of the occasional bolt-hole when needing to escape to the City. Then, with a mountain of baggage, he'd finally arrived home, expecting a hero's welcome.

She'd be thrilled, he thought; what wife wouldn't welcome her husband's retirement?

After his return, plans had perforce to be readjusted and extra-marital sessions arranged with tactics of which the SAS would have been proud. Her head was her diary and, even though lumbered with the returning 'child' to be looked after, she was determined to carry on enjoying her life and retain her routine with the utmost discretion. She told herself that, if her husband had been a good deal more generous, she wouldn't have had to resort to such measures. Each time she left the house for one of her assignations, therefore, she'd smilingly offer up a creditable excuse, then shoot off in her Jag to the next appointment.

She took pleasure from outwitting her husband; though by that stage in her marriage, she'd learned that to outwit someone totally bereft of wits didn't exactly stretch her reserves of deception. When Simon came up with the idea of eloping she was thrilled.

It had been Simon Garraway who had made her life bearable throughout those frustrating years and, during that time, they'd quietly planned to start a new life together. This had now been blown to pieces by that terrible bomb, taking with it this promised new life. Why had they left it so late? Why had Simon taken so long to get all his financial beans in a row before taking the plunge? Money – yes – but that wasn't important now; they should have been satisfied with what they had and left years ago. They could now be swimming side by side in the Adriatic . . . If only . . .

The Italian farmhouse had been all but renovated, the sea a stone's throw away, the sun glaring down . . . It was a glorious part of the world in which to end their days together. They would have been so happy. It had been the thrill of that glorious future that had kept her sane; hopeful . . . And they'd nearly made it, damn it!

As soon as the children had left home, she and Simon should

have debunked and left Thicko to his own devices. It would have done him good to learn some important survival lessons: that eggs needed their shells removing before frying; that fairies didn't appear to wave their magic little wands to change the bedding; and that the washing machine didn't operate until soap powder was introduced into the appropriate slot, nor did it start until the 'On' button was pressed.

But it was all too late; too late to escape all the yesterdays of a stale boring marriage with a stale boring dim-wit . . . Now what could she do? How would she manage to face life without Simon, and without that wonderful promise of Ravenna?

She closed her eyes and allowed the tears to flow. She'd be forever stuck in this rotten marriage in this equally rotten village, and she couldn't now see her way out of either. Now that Simon Garraway was finished, there was virtually nothing of interest in this zombie-ridden dormitory, where original thought was seen as some new strain of super-bug. Simon had kept her alive – had been her reason for living. Despite the string of all the other paying customers in the village, Simon was 'the one'. And she wept every day for that fractured useless body she'd encountered a only few weeks' ago; that body which had once been so alive.

Her other money-spinners couldn't hold a candle to Simon. She's now have to be satisfied with Alistair Bracknell, and the drooling, slavish Brian Frobisher – and even Tom Farrow when she'd craved a bit of rough from time to time. They were all useful, of course, in their own ham-handed way, filling her private coffer from time to time, but they couldn't hope to compete with Simon Garraway in the bedroom. Simon couldn't be replaced by anyone, because she couldn't love anyone else the way she'd loved him.

Leave it to him, he'd said; he would change their future; she should be patient – it was only a matter of time, and then they would be together for the rest of their lives . . . *A matter of time!* Through her tears she allowed herself a hollow laugh.

He'd been her only escape tunnel. And now there was nothing . . .

She'd had more than enough of this one-sided marriage, where everything had to be so uniformly run, she may as well have been on board ship: breakfast at nine; lunch at one thirty; dinner at seven thirty – Vesuvius erupting at any change therein. So she'd had no compunction about leaving her husband to HMS *Broad Oaks* and a solitary life in Roper's End. Fair weather to all who sail in her . . .

She had to admit that when Simon had first mooted this escape, she'd thought it too good to be true – too risky. They'd find out, wouldn't they – Mountainous Marjorie and Thicko Theo – and put a stop to it? And then what would they do? Was Simon saying he was prepared to leave his wife for her? Didn't men always say that? Was he serious – *truly* serious? Did he really love her? She'd thought about it – dreamt about it. She'd mulled it over every minute of every day; could she really do this? Could she leave her husband and children for him? She'd hesitated. But when the decision had finally been made and become real, it was Simon who'd hesitated; said that he had to be ultra-careful in order to avoid any suspicions the bank might have of his so-called early retirement. They'd be scrutinising everything . . . She hadn't known what he'd meant by that, but had trusted him to know best. Had he arranged matters more speedily, they would now be out of sodding Roper's End for good and buying furniture for their farmhouse in Ravenna – and that bomb would have blown up the person it had been meant to blow up, whoever that might have been . . .

Through her tears, she wondered what Simon thought of her now. Looking at his broken burned body on the drive of his house all those weeks ago and thinking, with everyone else, that he was dead, she'd run away from the Garraways' and had been violently sick, then had taken herself up to the Ranborne Hills – away from the village – away from Thicko Theo – to sob out her grief; grief at losing her lover, and grief at losing the life she might have had.

And she remembered, with shame, the day she'd turned away from his battered face when he'd come back from the hospital, and how she'd cried for him – cried for herself and for all their broken dreams. When she'd finally plucked up the courage to once more view the wreck that was once her darling Simon, she'd had to force herself to stay calm; it would not have done for Marjorie to suspect there had been anything between them. Her love for him had in no way diminished. But the shock, and the realisation that she would never again get the chance to escape – never get the chance to live, together with Simon, in the glorious Italian sun; never again climb into bed at his side with a bottle of champers and make marvellous love – caused everything to stop, and she'd stood rigid and whey-faced, unable to either speak or come to terms with reality. No one could help him now; no one could put him back to the Simon he'd been.

Why him? Why did it have to be him?

Sitting now on the edge of the bed, she had a sudden remembrance of that all-too-short retreat to Ravenna; those two whole weeks together had been magical. After a couple of days revelling in their refurbished farmhouse, they'd walked down to the coast, and Simon had shown her the yacht.

'A yacht,' she'd squealed. 'Is it yours?'

'Of course!' he laughed.

She'd known he was wealthy, but this was the stuff of dreams.

'I'll have to give three months' notice to the bank,' he'd said that day as they'd lain in bed together. 'So . . . only three more months, my darling. Only three short months – and then . . .'

If they pulled it off, they'd laughed, the village hags would love it, wouldn't they? Everyone – apart from Commander Theo Kilpatrick, of course – was aware that she was playing fast and loose with various husbands in Roper's End, each hoping that it wasn't theirs – or perhaps were hoping it was theirs because, at least, nooky with Julia Kilpatrick would get them out from under their feet from time to time now the useless lumps had all but retired. Strangely, however, no one had cottoned on to her relationship with Simon Garraway. So it would come as a total shock when they vanished into the blue together.

They'd talked about it endlessly: just before Christmas it would be; of that future when they would both shake free of their old lives and walk away from those wretched, boring existences they'd both suffered with their respective spouses; free of the banality of Roper's End, this small Portlingshire village with its small Portlingshire people. They would then stride confidently together into this new life – but what a life!

But how fragile and precious is hope . . . Now, the new year would arrive devoid of any hope.

# Chapter Twenty-Two

Marjorie Garraway was beside herself. She'd just closed the door on the fourth couple from the estate agency who'd come to view the house. Each couple had taken one look at the gargoyle in his wheelchair and then had walked, with an air of disbelief, into the hospital-look-alike ex-dining-room with all the trappings of the disabled: the catheter bag hanging from the end of the specialised hospital bed; the hoist designed for getting the invalid up and out of it; the commode; the inflatable cushion complete with pump; the hypodermic needle, and the rows of tablets banked up on the table top, which took on the appearance of a demented pharmacy.

After viewing all the paraphernalia and wrinkling their noses at various unpalatable smells, each couple had walked out of the house, relieved to get away, and Marjorie knew by the looks on their faces that this would be the last she'd see of them. Bugger! Would they ever sell?

And there was Simon, who hadn't helped matters by simply being there, the dribble running down the side of his face and his one eye staring out at them like the Cyclops. Showing them round, she could almost read their minds; could see them wondering if they'd be forced to inherit the gargoyle with the house. After the first and second couple of viewers had looked at him aghast, she'd had vague thoughts of hiding him in the garden shed when the agents had given her the tip-off that other viewers were on their way.

During the first couple of months of Simon being allowed home,

Marjorie had lost a considerable amount of weight. She'd never, even on the golf course, expended as much energy as this, as she'd run up and down the stairs a hundred and one times to get things he needed, and her clothes, now two sizes too large, hung loosely upon her leaner frame. During her marriage, she'd gradually ballooned out, but had never seen the point of losing weight, assured by the complacent but erroneous belief that her husband would always love her the way she was. After several weeks of complying with Simon's needs, she'd climbed out of the shower one morning and stepped onto the bathroom scales, at first imagining them to be on the blink. Then, finding she'd dropped to a size eighteen, she was eager to be first in the queue at Primark.

Simon had become so demanding; became insistent and downright impatient when she got things wrong: could she get the Ian Rankin novel from his bedside table – no, he'd read that – the other one; could she get him some mints to suck – not the Polos – for Pete's sake, didn't she know, by now, that his favourites were Mint Imperials? – the ones he kept in his sock drawer . . . ? And it was always she and not the carer who'd do all the running about. The carer, despite her fat salary, smiling wanly at each of these request then standing by the medicine cabinet counting tablets. So Marjorie had hardly stopped to draw breath.

Whenever she had time to think – which was usually in bed in the dark, just before sleep overtook her after another gruelling day – she realised she hadn't been to the golf club for several months. And it was during these moments that she lay, her fists clenched, begrudging all this time spent at Simon's beck and call. The full-time carer was not enough for him, and he hated the thought of his wife leaving the house with that woman in sole charge. So, foregoing her precious time on the golf links – or, indeed, Primark – Marjorie, with a heavy sigh of frustration, would agree to stay by his side.

Occasionally, to ring the changes, she'd trudge tragically through the village, pushing his wheelchair and trying to look the cheerful dutiful wife, which always ended up taking more out of her than running up and down the stairs. It was the people who were her undoing – all those villagers stopping to talk and she, perforce, having to talk back to them. It upset her to talk. She couldn't avoid them, but their kindness was proving too much to bear. If only they would leave her alone just for one day ... However, plastering onto her face a rictus grin, she pretended to welcome their enquiries as to Simon's health, politely answering their queries while, inside, sickened by constantly having to repeat herself.

She'd had time to ponder about Simon's insistence that the bomb was not destined for him – about how he was so adamant in maintaining that the postwoman had said she'd come to the wrong house. But, in those quiet moments before sleep, she wondered if he was telling the whole truth. Over the years, Simon had revealed his many dealings with dodgy bankers in various parts of the world, and she suspected that some of those individuals might well bear a grudge at being investigated. So it was feasible, wasn't it, for the package containing the bomb to have come from somewhere abroad? Could Simon, either accidentally or on purpose, have uncovered a den of corruption from some top banana in a country not renowned for either diplomacy or forgiveness towards some nosey-parker banker threatening to expose him; perhaps some warlord angry at having his bank balance questioned over the dirty money his dubious customers raked in? Might these people have wanted him out of the way? Might they be capable of making and sending a bomb through the post? Some organisation such as the Mafia?

Once Marjorie had conjured up thoughts of the Mafia, she couldn't let it go, and it gave her nightmares.

How *could* Simon have been so certain that the bomb was not meant for him?

Lack of sleep left her edgy and light-headed and, every now and then, she had the feeling she might be living in another universe – indeed wished she *was* living in another universe. This wasn't real, was it? It was all a bad dream.

*Will someone please tell her it was a bad dream . . .*

After a few weeks of this nursing lark, it occurred to her that she wasn't cut out for this sort of life. She wasn't coping; wasn't trained to cope with illness; was finding it increasingly hard to deal with the harsh reality of having to look after someone day in day out when she hadn't a clue what she was doing. Having been cushioned all her married life by wealth, she'd never imagined there was anything that money couldn't put right. It took her a while for the realisation to set in that this was the one thing that money couldn't buy. *Which was grossly unfair!*

Would it be too heartless to put him into a care home, she wondered? But wait. How would she pay for a care home? And what about the golf club? If she spent all their savings on a care home, how would she afford her annual membership fee?

She wanted out. She wanted her life back.

So, she sighed . . . was this it? How long could she be expected to do this? How long could Simon be expected to live? How long did people like this live? – ten years? – twenty? How much longer would she be able to cope; and how much longer before the kitchen knife sliced the throat of that useless carer?

Each morning, she'd stealthily pick up the daily paper from the mat and sneak into the living room in order to relieve herself from the everlasting care. Then, having barely read the headlines, he'd yell for something. Why couldn't he have died? They should have let him die. It would be all over now, and he would be at peace. But he wasn't at peace! How could he be at peace; how could anyone be at peace with those injuries? And, because he wasn't at peace, neither was she. These terrible thoughts of death that she'd castigated herself for just a few months earlier now reared their heads once more and, the more she tried to suppress them the more they grew into a mushroom cloud that dominated her every thought. She hated herself for it, and knew she shouldn't be wishing away Simon's life – but surely it would have been kinder to have let him die; kinder for him – *and kinder for her* . . .

Why had the medical staff insisted on saving a life that would only ever be half a life; a half life destined to be looked after for ever; the burden of care left for her to shoulder? No one had told her how hard it would be. No one had warned her of the all the difficulties this care would entail. *He wasn't the only one who'd been damaged.* How long would she have to bear it: the hospital bed taking up the whole of her dining room; the once pristine kitchen taken over by the carer forever juggling boxes of pills which littered every surface; the colostomy bag; the smells . . . ? Plus the broken human being occupying that sodding wheelchair she tripped over at least once a day – and that shattered, gargling rag doll that was once her husband . . . *God – how long?*

* * *

Barely able to communicate, Simon suffered excruciating pain which stopped him sleeping but, once asleep, produced punishing nightmares from which he'd sit up in the dark screaming. This would send Marjorie and the carer running down to placate him and bung another needle in his arm. The pain . . . How could he bear this pain a day longer?

And how could he bear, for one day more, Mountainous

Marjorie's obvious pique at the nuisance he'd become, as though
he'd deliberately blown himself up to annoy her. He wasn't stupid;
he still had a brain and that brain, during those times when the
sedation was wearing off, turned to thoughts of relieving himself
of her burden, acutely aware that Marjorie wished the bomb had
killed him. He saw the growing resentment each day in her eyes
– and who could blame her? Death was what he'd wished for
himself ever since he'd regained consciousness. A vet would put an
animal down for less. Anything was better than this fag-end of a
life. He'd been rendered a mere scrap of flesh of no use to anyone.

He supposed he was being unfair to hate his wife so much; it
wasn't her fault, but he had to take his frustration out on somebody
some of the time – well, most of the time. And she'd taken the
brunt of all this, so it was no life for her. He was a burden; a drag.

Marjorie was a pain in the arse, fluttering about nervously every
day. And he'd watch that look in her eyes; the look that wished
him out of the way; the look that said, *how dare you ruin my life
– how dare you keep me off the golf links!* However, how would he
have reacted if had it been the other way round? Would he have
been prepared to ditch all his well-laid plans with Julia to look
after her? Would he hell! He'd have shoved her into a care home
without a second thought, then hot-footed it to Italy, forgetting
the woman had ever existed.

He'd clocked the expressions on the faces of various prospective
buyers when they'd viewed the grotesque spectre he'd become.
One look – that's all it took – and the poor devils couldn't get
out of the door fast enough.

Why had all those medics been so determined to bring back
to life that which had been hanging by a thread? Why couldn't
they have been sensible; have allowed him go quietly to his Maker?
But no – they'd had to stick to their unquenchable, fucking

Hippocratic Oath, to save life at all costs. Surely, even they must have realised what his life would be worth once they'd saved him? Why couldn't they have put themselves in his shoes? Why hadn't they asked themselves what sort of existence they would choose for themselves: death, or being stuck in a fucking wheelchair day after interminable day, being fed a diet of pills to ward off tortuous burning pain, and killing hope by inches. Couldn't they imagine the horror of being dependent upon other people for the rest of their miserable, bed-ridden, lives? And didn't they think of his wife – the person doing the looking after?

And now fucked up, with all those carefully-made plans of escape with Julia Kilpatrick down the pan, he couldn't see any point in prolonging it; wished, with every fibre of his being, to end it. But he couldn't, could he? He wept. Why couldn't they have let him die?

Worse – *far worse, however* – than the constant pain, were the nightmares which kept him from sleeping; nightmares which mainly involved the explosion, but which would sometimes include the bank, and he'd wake in the dead of night in a cold sweat. The bank, as a result of his incapacitation, would, by now, be investigating his software; would have had ample time to rumble him. He'd left it too late – been too cautious. His insistence to safeguard the future had been his downfall. How long would that take? The balloon was bound to go up before long and, as he flailed about, churning up the bed linen, his dreams saw the grey suits – briefcases swinging – steadily tramping towards the house. Just a few more weeks and he would have got away with it – could have covered his tracks. But he was helpless now to prevent it coming out.

Sod it. Just a few weeks – that was all. Just a few more weeks . . . Then – *this!*

His thoughts turned to Julia Kilpatrick. Over these last few weeks he'd thought of little else, and of what might have been if they'd made up their minds to escape some time earlier. But he'd insisted on getting the timing right. Timing! What a laugh! Hot tears coursed down his cheeks once more at the thought of his lover and of the promises he'd made of the new life they would share. Ha! *Well – lookee here!* – a new life is what we've got! Before the affair with Julia, he'd been feeling as though he was a mere half of something – he didn't know quite what – going through the motions of living – working the treadmill all hours, then coming home each night to a set of golf clubs in the hall. But then, suddenly, there was Julia. He'd never felt half of something whenever Julia was by his side. He had, at once, become whole, and with all the wondrous possibilities that this wholeness presented, he knew his life had changed for ever. There would be no stopping him now, even if it meant doing something he'd never dreamt of doing before – that of robbing a bank. But he was determined to do anything it took to keep her, however outlandish.

Julia had always been there to put him back together again. Always Julia – to encourage him and make him feel valued. She'd been such fun over the years. He was hopelessly in love, and couldn't believe that his good fortune had lasted as long as it did; felt blessed by this get-out clause from *Mountainous Marjorie* and Roper's End. So, he'd taken to staying late at the bank each evening, working it all out. His bosses had never given him much credit, nor had ever paid him his full worth, but now it would be pay-back time. After slogging away for them for all these years, it would serve them right.

Now . . . without Julia, he was less than nothing. He wished with every sinew that he was dead. Why go on when there was nothing to look forward to? Why prolong the agony? It would be best all round; for all those people, for instance, who'd he'd thought of as his best buddies; friends who now couldn't think what to say to him; folk who were embarrassed – avoiding him as though he was contagious . . . ?

What would *he* have said to comfort someone half alive?

His boss from the bank had been once but, after realising that he'd never work again, didn't see the point in calling again, he supposed. Couldn't blame him. He was no use to anyone now.

What a bloody existence.

# Chapter Twenty-Three

I remember the day the phone rang – my land line. The phone never rang, so the day in question is easy to recall: the eighth of July, nine years ago. I ran in from the garden, where I was photographing a clutch of daisies which had sprung up in the grass at the front of the house. The shrill ring of the phone was such a stomach-churning moment, and my mind did a flip as to who could possibly be calling me.

When I reached the phone, I stood for a long moment, breathless from the effort of running. I reached out and put my hand on the receiver, feeling the vibration, wracked with nerves. Who in the world knew my number? Not only was I not listed in the directory, no one ever rang, as everyone who might have called to enquire of my health – everyone I'd called my friends – was either dead or dying. There was no one left. I stopped, my hand rigid on the receiver. Then I closed my eyes, picked it up and announced myself.

There was silence – then a whispered croak – a rasp of breath I didn't at first recognise – foreign. The shock at hearing this unexpected voice sent me reeling. I didn't know who the voice belonged to. And yet . . . somehow, I did . . . I frowned, attempting to bat away the sound; perhaps someone had dialled the wrong number . . . Who was this? Some idiot having a laugh? And yet..

I was about to replace the receiver when a foreigner was asking me if I was who I'd said I was; a quiet, breathless voice – almost a whisper – *Italian*. I froze. I opened my mouth to speak but, at that point, my legs threatened to turn to jelly, and I felt the need to sit down in order to take in what I was hearing. Because I knew. I suddenly knew. That voice – the realisation of what I was hearing – turned my blood to ice, sending me back to the last time I'd heard it that day in Moscow. Over fifty years ago. It was as though a sudden gust of wind had blown away those fifty years of my life, and I was instantly transported back to Moscow, to my life with Toni – and to that café . . . Yes, it was in that café . . . As I clutched the phone, it all came back to me, accompanied by all the heartache I'd had to endure during that time. And, on hearing that voice, I thought my heart would break all over again. I thought I'd let go of all that grief and, apart from a dull ache rearing up from time to time, imagined I'd had got it out of my system. I certainly had no wish to be taken back to that time. Except that now . . .

I could simply have replaced the receiver but, despite the core of ice chilling my soul, I held on against all those memories which could serve to undo me, my heart threatening to jump out of my chest. My knees suddenly gave way and I found myself sprawled onto the couch – my comfort zone – where I thought I might cope better. Because, strange though it was and, even after so long a period, I knew who the voice belonged to; a voice that I hadn't heard for decades and had all but forgotten that it and its owner existed: Maria Collini, widow of Ronaldo, one of the doomed agents in Russia, betrayed along with my lover.

I had neither seen nor heard from Maria Collini since that time, and yet a picture of that beautiful oval face framed by glorious coal black hair immediately sprang into my mind. As she'd sat in the café, leisurely smoking a cheroot, the smoke and the sophistication curling up mistily into her large brown eyes, I'd gazed at her in awe. And that voice: a mixture of dark treacle and cream. How I'd wished, at that moment, that I could have been her. I remember the languid pose – and those eyes, and the silky hair draped over one shoulder. She was enveloped in a fashionable cream suit I'd have given a year's salary for. I'd never witnessed such polish – such style – and I stared, inwardly screaming for my fairy godmother to transform me to that level of sophistication.

And, until I heard those smooth Italian vowels whispering to me over the wire that day, I'd filed her – and the rest of it – into the recesses of my mind, along with Toni – along with the crushed Mini – along with the grey men with their letter-box mouths screaming abuse at me . . . Or imagined that I had.

That day, I was taken to a small back-street café to liaise with Maria's husband. Just the once – it could only have been the one meeting, because agents knew how dangerous it would be to acknowledge each other. So I guessed that something of vital importance must have happened for them to have agreed to meet that particular day but, standing there in the café, the rapidity of the Italian language escaping me, I never discovered what it was – anyway, I wasn't supposed to be there.

As I listened to that unmistakable Italian voice over the phone, something, apart from that initial shock, jumped out at me. It was not just the urgency singing through the wire; there was something else – the fear in her voice – and it was that which made me sit up and take notice.

'Are you alone?' she rasped quietly.

'Yes, I'm alone,' I said.

However, apart from worrying about my rusty Italian, the thought burning through my brain as I clutched the receiver was: how, after all these years, had Maria Collini managed to track me down? And why would she be ringing me? I'd hardly known the woman.

'Good. Because I have something to tell you. Something important,' she went on, sotto voce. 'It's private.'

'There's no one here,' I assured her. 'Where are you?'

'In Birmingham, at a conference,' she said.

Birmingham? A conference? My mind was spinning. How could she be in Birmingham? She was in England and calling from a city only fifty miles away, on a Monday afternoon in July. This was surreal. Why had she not seen fit to telephone me over those intervening years? And how did she know where to find me?

My hesitancy seemed to annoy her.

'Listen – I can't talk for long – I think I'm being watched,' she rattled on. 'We must meet!'

Watched? By whom?

'Of course,' I said. 'I would love to meet you again – but where?'

She whispered the name of the hotel where she was staying and where the conference was being held, and I wrote it down.

'*Tomorrow*,' she said breathlessly. 'Can you do that? It has to be soon. I go back the day after.'

Tomorrow. It had sounded like command.

'Yes, I could make tomorrow,' I said.

We set a time and arranged to have lunch together, but then the line suddenly went dead.

As we'd been talking, I'd noticed a strange echo, which had sounded as though I was talking back to myself – as though hearing myself as someone else might hear me. I attempted to shrug off the thoughts that were slowly creeping into my head before they'd had time to manifest themselves into fear, but in vain. Once that smidgeon of thought was there, it wouldn't let me go: *bugs*. But, why would anyone be bugging Maria's room? Why would anyone see fit to do that unless fearful of something she might reveal?

So . . . what *did* she know – what *could* she know? And what was it that would finally be revealed?

I sat, still clutching the phone's receiver, as though it might have answers to all the questions flitting uncomfortably through my head. What could have caused Maria to be so nervous? Could there be still be danger after all these years? And might I be walking into danger by meeting her? The more I thought of it, the more worried I got, and I remembered all those tricks Toni had taught me about bugging. Maria had been fearful of someone listening in, but I suspected that someone, somewhere, had picked up the fact that she was about to spill something vital to a one-time journalist.

The hesitancy in her voice had alerted my suspicions to such a degree that I feared for her. I could only guess that she'd been calling from the hotel room and not from her mobile. And I asked myself why, if she'd been so afraid, hadn't she used her mobile . . . ?

The questions multiplied. Was I being over-cautious? Is that what being caught on the sharp end of espionage did to one? Perhaps I'd learned from Toni to be suspicious about everything? I remember his words: *If everything seems normal, assume that it isn't.* I told myself not to be so stupid; what harm could Maria come to in Britain? This wasn't the USSR, for heaven's sake. She would be safe here, wouldn't she? This, surely, was my imagination running riot. A great deal of water had passed under the bridge since those days; no one behaved like that nowadays. How could Maria be in danger now? Unless . . . unless she'd recently discovered something that had finally shed light on the deaths of those six men . . . Perhaps she'd been as assiduous as I in attempting to track down whomever had been responsible for her husband's death. And perhaps, finally, she'd discovered the identity of the perpetrators, therefore proving to be more successful than I . . . ? Was this what she had to tell me?

I finally put the receiver back onto its cradle and watched it with hooded eyes, wondering how that small instrument could have had the power to cause such disturbance within me. Where had all this had come from? – straight out of a clear blue sky without prior warning – just as I was photographing daisies on the lawn.

Of course I had to go up to Birmingham see her – no question – and the sooner the better. If she was in any kind of danger, I'd have to do something to help.

Why hadn't she contacted me from Italy? But perhaps she was not now living in Italy. Perhaps, unlike me, she hadn't managed to escape back home and was still in Moscow . . . And from Moscow to attend a conference in Birmingham? Had she discovered something only once she'd arrived? Had she seen something? Someone? Had she connected the wires to complete the signal? What did she know?

I wouldn't let her down. I was desperate to know what she knew. But I was never to find out.

* * *

The following day I parked in Hansfield and caught the 9.50 train to Birmingham New Street. I took a newspaper with me but I couldn't read. Maria had asked me to tuck the *Independent* under my arm so she would recognise me, and I sat in the train attempting to read the headlines but, brain cells whirring around elsewhere, I gave up after the first five minutes and scrunched it up on my lap, my mind anxious as to what I might learn from this woman who had suffered the same fate as I.

I couldn't get out of my mind all those questions I'd asked myself, but should have asked her. But they wouldn't get answered until I'd finally met her, so I willed the train to stop messing about by stopping at every station along the route and get me to Birmigham. What I needed to know was: what might Maria have learned afresh about that time in Russia, and how? And why hadn't she simply told me over the phone? What had brought her to this country? Why had this suddenly become so urgent that she'd asked to meet me in person?

In all the years that have passed, I promised myself that, if I ever discovered the name or names of those who had betrayed my lover, I'd have no hesitation in killing him/her. I had no idea how I would go about it – but I'd think of something. Nothing too quick, though . . . So . . . at last, here I was on my way to finding out something that would help me in my search for answers; my last chance to perhaps discover a name . . . a reason . . .

Having allowed plenty of time in the event of hold-ups, the train pulled in half an hour before I was due to meet Maria. I asked for directions to the hotel, strolled across the road then, turning the corner, saw the building straight in front of me. Finding it had been a great deal easier than I'd expected, so I primed myself for a bit of a wait. A large placard at the entrance announced the conference in progress that week, the subject of which concerned the environment. I walked through the swing doors and found myself a seat in the reception area, looked at my watch and, as agreed, unfolded my newspaper with the expectation of Maria appearing within a few minutes.

From the start, however, I'd felt uncomfortable, though there was nothing I could have put my finger on. There was no one about, which I'd thought rather odd for a hotel, being late-morning, but told myself that there was a logical explanation: that the whole place may have booked all its rooms to the people attending the conference and, of course, that was where they all were. But there was something else; something that shouldn't have been so prevalent in an hotel: a frigidity. Behind the reception desk, where one would expect a welcoming smile, a dark-haired woman had glowered at me as I'd entered, her coal black eyes darting over from time to time as I sat waiting, as though keeping her eye on my movements. Apart from that, everything seemed normal.

*If everything seems normal, assume it isn't.*

So I sat on, *Independent* in full view, the time ticking towards the agreed time to meet. I'd reached page six of the paper and, when I again looked at my watch, I realised that twenty minutes had passed. Maria had insisted that I arrive on time, as she said she'd only have a half hour break before the afternoon session. I was on time – twelve-thirty she'd said. However, I allowed a small smile as I remembered Toni once saying that Italians and punctuality should never be mentioned in the same sentence so, at that point I was not unduly worried. Another twenty minutes elapsed before the worry began, the receptionist's frosty face unnerving me and the discomfort I felt was slowly turning from disquiet to fear. I looked anxiously around the reception area for Maria, but no one came to claim me. It occurred to me that the conference was perhaps running over time . . .

After waiting almost an hour, I steeled myself to face the frozen-faced receptionist to explain that I had arranged to meet someone and asked if she would be kind enough to ask the organiser if she could account for Maria's absence. Ten minutes later, a woman in an ultra-smart suit strutted importantly towards me on six-inch heels, pulled her face into a smile, then introduced herself. Before she'd spoken, I'd clocked that she was Russian. When I told her who I'd come to see, she frowned – more than a tad theatrically.

'Collini . . .' she said slowly drawing out the name, cocking her head slightly as though attempting to recall the name.

'Yes. *Maria* Collini,' I said, 'She's a delegate assigned to your conference.'

'I not recognise this name,' the woman said, still smiling. 'Please wait. I go check. Excuse . . .'

She returned with a clipboard onto which was pinned a list of delegates, which she thrust at me with a flourish.

'Is no Maria Collini at this conference. See – no Maria Collini!' she smiled with obvious satisfaction. 'You maybe have wrong hotel. Is another hotel which might be holding conference maybe? But she not here.'

'But she rang me yesterday,' I persisted, every atom of suspicion now spiralling, the dead eyes of the woman staring me down, daring me to contradict her. It would take more than a Russian stare, however, to bully me. 'She rang and asked me to meet her at this particular hotel,' I said firmly. 'I wrote it down as she told me – here,' I said producing the scrap of paper from my bag.

'I am sorry,' the woman said smoothly but coldly, the smile still fixed upon her heavily plastered lips. 'I cannot help you. She must make mistake. Perhaps is wrong day. No Maria Collini here – you see list for yourself!' she said brightly, then turned and marched off, pushing open a door marked *Private – Conference in Progress.*

I stood for a moment, stupefied, then went back to the reception desk. If Maria was staying here, she would have signed the hotel register. The robotic unsmiling receptionist, who had been eyeing me with malevolence from the moment I'd walked in the door, now glared ominously, reversing every fixed, welcoming manner in the venerable history of hotel propriety. She'd been standing within earshot of my conversation – such as it was – with the organiser, her face a triumph of the embalmer's art. As I approached the desk, she looked at me through hooded eyes as though I'd just crawled out of a piece of mouldy cheese and was about to mutate into a bluebottle. I said that I would like to look at the hotel register.

'No,' she sniffed, her downturned mouth announcing the word before it was spoken. 'Is confidential!'

'Listen – if I were a guest booking in at your hotel, I would have to sign my name in the register, thereby having access to all the other names therein!' I said angrily. 'So, why don't we assume that I'm wishing to book a room for the night, eh?'

She stopped suddenly and stared, attempting to take this in, her eyes for a moment betraying her ignorance of how hotels in this country are run; of how the secrecy of the USSR was not applicable here. She then snapped back with towering condescension, one corner of her mouth lifting slightly, 'Register is confidential!'

'Okay,' I smiled back. As anger hadn't worked, I decided to try charm. 'If that is so, perhaps you would be kind enough to look at the register for me, to see if a lady called Maria Collini has registered at this hotel?'

Slightly stunned by my sudden smile, she lifted out the register from a shelf below the counter, placed it out of my vision, then began to turn several pages with a long scarlet nail. Immobile, she stared down at it for so long, I thought she might be waiting for the van from Madame Tussauds to pick her up and return her to their vaults. But then she came to life, and glanced up finally with an impatient sigh and a look of something resembling triumph, her mouth a gash of red.

'No. No Maria Collini!'

She had no need to speak further; the defiant narrowed eyes said it all: 'Get out of this hotel, you insignificant little turd in your cheap English clothes'.

For a long moment I stared back at the unflinching face. But the eyes said all I was required to know; those black disdainful eyes staring back, like two bullet holes in a metal door, telling me, in no uncertain terms to get stuffed.

I saw full well that I wasn't going to get any help from this particular quarter and that, if I didn't leave, it was looking increasingly likely that I would be strong-armed out. So I turned away from the heavily mascaraed eyes, strode out out of the hotel and stepped onto the comforting streets of Birmingham, relieved to be back among the living.

So, I wondered as I marched angrily out of the swing doors: what had happened to the regular staff here? Had they all been locked up in the cellar and replaced by these *Stepford Wives,* with their dark bobbed tresses, a hair barely out of place, looking as though they might have the shelf-life of plutonium? And why was I that lone person in the reception area? The place had had the air of an empty film set, waiting for someone to shout 'Action!'

Thanking the Good Lord for deep-foamed insoles, I prepared myself to trudge round the city in order to satisfy myself that there weren't any other hotels holding conferences that day. After several hours of 'Sorry, madam', I was forced to accept – though not too surprised to learn – that the very hotel Maria had mentioned – the one written on the piece of paper in my handbag – was the only one in the entire city purporting to hold a conference on that particular day.

I never heard from Maria again.

\* \* \*

What had happened to her? Had she been followed? Had she been silenced? If so, by whom? Had that list of delegates pushed under my nose by that Russian woman been prepared in advance in order to flash it in front of someone requiring proof of her existence? Had they known in advance of my impending arrival? The whole thing had had the air of having been staged. But, although staged, it was excruciatingly badly executed, and it didn't fool me. They'd been expecting me because they'd heard our conversation, hadn't they? Did Maria really have something vital to tell me? And had that something managed to reach the ears of the same person who'd committed those crimes in Moscow?

*Those artificial women!* I couldn't get them out of my head: those clockwork wind-up dolls, which had all the appearance of having been manufactured en masse deep in some underground laboratory in Siberia. What were these Russian dolls doing in Birmingham?

Where was Maria? Was she still alive?

What could I have done, standing in the foyer of that hotel? I've asked myself that question every day since. Challenging the woman with the clipboard wouldn't have done me any favours because, if I'd taken the matter to the police, they wouldn't have found a trace of evidence to support my story.

Angry with myself for being so helpless, I trekked through the City, worrying about what had happened to Maria, allowing my imagination to run off the scale. What if, for all that time, she'd been at the hotel – *all the time I was there* – perhaps lying unconscious in a locked bedroom, ready to be bundled back to Russia or, more likely, dumped into the sea en route . . . If they'd known I was meeting her, what if they'd gone to the trouble of printing out a false delegate list to prove their point that she'd never been there? Because, having made that telephone call, Maria had unwittingly sealed her fate. Of that I was certain.

When I returned home, furious at having been fobbed off by those ghastly, complacent women, I dialled 1471, knowing that no one would have phoned me in the interim. I needed to get the telephone number Maria had called from, in order to satisfy myself that the phone was, indeed, from the hotel she'd mentioned, and to contact her again. But I got the unobtainable tone – that long whiny tone telling me exactly nothing.

# Chapter Twenty-Four

Holgarth, Glenys Pugh's two-bedroom bungalow, set at the end of an unnamed track off Prince Albert Lane, was, in contrast to Freddie Wingrave's rambling shambolic house, as neat as a pin. Also, unlike Freddie's house, it didn't smell like a two-week-old fish head. The bungalow was, Glenys had always thought, just the right size, because she could put her hand on most things by simply reaching out from a standing position. The tiny white kitchen was immaculate and a masterclass in efficiency: a wire shelf-larder hooked over the kitchen door, stacked with the necessities – jars of preserved fruit, packets of pasta and cans of dog food; under-sink cupboards hid household equipment – furniture polish, a small vacuum cleaner and a neat fold-up mop; pristine white porcelain was kept upon melamine wall shelves; and a line of pots containing aromatic herbs sat on her window sill. Lack of space necessitated various pans, until she needed to use them, to be hidden from sight by placing them in the oven. The only item she hadn't been able to fit into the kitchen was the fridge-freezer, so she'd had it fitted into a corner of her bedroom, and smiled at it each night as it gently hummed her to sleep.

The furniture in her sitting/dining room had all been bought second-hand over the years and sat on a large blue and cream Turkey rug. She'd chosen everything with care. When, a few decades ago, IKEA flat-pack had become all the rage, she'd taken herself off to auction houses around the county and had seized with glee what had, almost overnight, become known as 'brown' furniture; walnut and coromandel, and glorious flame mahogany – all considered unfashionable, but now within her price range.

Glenys had grown up appreciating the feel and smell of wood. Her father, having worked as a carpenter, had had his own workroom in a shed at the end of the garden and she remembered how his love of wood had embedded and shaped her childhood: the smell of all those wonderful aromatic shavings covering the floor of the shed when she came home from school. She'd learned about dovetailing, chamfering and piecrust edging. Her father taught her all he knew about antique furniture, the sheer beauty of wood and how to look after it. But, at that time, antique furniture, beautiful though it was, was to be admired from afar, and thought to be the prerogative of the well-to-do – therefore, well beyond her reach. In later life, having retained all this knowledge, she'd recognised its value and then had snapped up glorious Georgian and Victorian pieces which were being auctioned at reasonable prices.

Her best piece, gleaming with the wax polish she'd regularly fed it with, was the large Victorian Davenport, which she'd purchased some years ago at a knock-down price, largely because it had been considered too cumbersome for the average home. And it was into this Davenport that she kept all her secrets. It had a key, which she kept hidden in the one place she thought no one would look – because you couldn't be too careful . . .

Glenys vaguely wondered, over her breakfast mug, who would get all this stuff when she snuffed it – which wouldn't be too long now, she imagined. The way the world was going these days, she felt she was ready to go. She didn't understand any of it. She sighed every time she turned the pages of her newspaper, and sucked in her breath each morning as she found herself staring with disbelief at some unfathomable item of news

It was enough to put one off one's toast. She'd really had enough.

Frowning at the vexed question of who she could trust to be privy to her secrets when she died, she sighed and folded her newspaper neatly to the back page to solve the daily crossword, before ambling to the shed to take a key from under a dusty flowerpot in order to open her Davenport. She remembered that she had another entry to add to her diary: earlier that morning at the newsagents, she'd seen Kilpatrick mooching suspiciously around the village and now felt an urge to record the sighting.

Each time she saw Kilpatrick these days, she recalled what Jenny had revealed to her all those years ago and, after that bombshell, she'd watched him, her mouth curling with distaste. After that startling revelation, she'd decided to monitor his every movement. This may, of course, have been unnecessary, but she wasn't prepared to take the risk. If, perhaps, when someone eventually found her diaries, it might help to make some sense of the past.

\* \* \*

There was someone in my garden last night and it frightened me. I'm not easily frightened but, with my house being so isolated, I hardly ever see a soul – so what would anyone be doing here? Apart from the postman and the milkman, no one has the slightest reason to come this far up the lane because there would be nowhere for them to go. I have always been aware of how easy it would be for someone to creep into the back garden through Geoff Partridge's fields. A burglar might get into my house to rob me, but they would never get into the Davenport. That's why I've always kept the key in the shed; no one would think to rummage round in there, and you would have to built like a tank to get into my Davenport without a key!

I didn't imagine it. Neither did the dog. I know I'm getting way beyond my use-by date, and sometimes forget what I'm doing or where I'm going. But I know what I saw – although I couldn't tell who it was because he or she moved out of sight pretty smartly when I opened the window and shouted out at them. There's nothing wrong with my eyes.

I have my suspicions as to whom it might have been – though, if I told the police, I know I wouldn't get very far: doddery old fart thinking she saw something in the garden? – make a note, Sarge – tell her we'll keep an eye . . .

I know what I saw.

I admit I'm hopelessly forgetful these days, constantly struggling for the right word in order to fill in the lights of the crossword, and forever getting things wrong. I yearn for those days when I never forgot a thing – couldn't afford to forget a thing; my job depended upon it. I often wonder where it all went, and why it is that, if I can remember every single moment of every single day I worked at Bletchley – of everything that happened to me then – I can't now remember where I put my pen, even when it's clipped to the front of my shirt? I frequently find myself taken back to the past – especially when I'm dozing off and Snout's asleep on my lap; that past, which is as clear as yesterday . . . And, even though it had been a fearful time in many ways, I long to go back there to put things right.

I remember that period as a hovering cloud of fear, as the news bombarded us again and again of yet another aircraft lost– another ship torpedoed. And, if I had to give a name to the colour of those days, it would be Paynes Grey, because we were continually being bruised with all our losses and had so little to look forward to; it was a time of food rationing and blackouts and air-raid shelters and a fear one could touch; of having nowhere to go when you returned from work faced with your house reduced to a pile of rubble. And that grey turned to black terror at the constant fear of being ruled by Hitler if we didn't win the war.

How did we ever get over that?

I suppose we had to and, bit by bit, we managed to build our houses and mend our lives – physically, that is. The psyche is a tad more difficult to mend; you never forget – ever.

I've never talked about that time; written about it in the diary, of course, but could never bring myself to talk to anyone about personal loss, or the loss my friends endured. You do your damnedest to forget – try to heal your heart and mind, and do the best you can to live in the present. But then, one day, when you least expect it, the past rears up its evil head, looks you in the face and dares you to remember – that past, right now, being Kilpatrick . . . How could I ever forget that face – that voice?

The past is another country – who said that? Whoever it was got it wrong: the past is another universe. Those years were like living on a distant planet, watching the world destroy itself, feeling totally helpless in preventing it from fracturing and sending us all flying off the edge. We were all in a funk, because we didn't know then that we would win the war. It was five years of madness. It had all just seemed endless – hopeless.

And then, one day, the flags flew and everyone partied. It was over. The war, that is; it would never be over for all those who'd survived with their life-altered injuries.

But you would think that, after all that, it would make people kinder, wouldn't you; for subsequent generations to realise what we very nearly lost; what we'd gone through; you would think that they would treasure what was gained for them so that they could live a life of safety? Five years of fear and death and deprivation, suffered for those who came after to live lives free of fear? You'd think they'd humble themselves and appreciate what their parents and grandparents had gone through – to see for themselves all those damaged and broken lives caused by war and to thank their stars that they weren't, nor would ever be, called upon to get involved in such terrible times. But, no – all they can think about now is tearing down the very place that gave them a safe country in which to live, iPading all their friends to join the next demo, and throwing all their privileges into the faces of the very people who'd given their lives to allow them those privileges – we, who'd fought to give them the freedom they now abused. If only we'd known then how insignificant they would consider us, and how futile our efforts were!

It is impossible to forget those dark years. All that subterfuge – all that damage. I can't stop thinking about that.

Neither can I stop thinking about that figure sneaking about in my garden last night. I have no one close – no near neighbours – to watch over me, and Sprout, my Cairn, is barely big enough to protect me. The only thing, I suppose, is to sharpen my kitchen knives and keep them near. I may be small and old, but I like to think I can look after myself.

# Chapter Twenty-Five

The garden of Woodland Grange was festooned with banners for Peter Flynn's sixty-fifth birthday/retirement party, and a beaming Janet, wearing a floaty silk dress, welcomed her guests onto the closely clipped lawn.

In two weeks, the garden had been transformed from a nondescript field into a plot she imagined would rival Hampton Court. The purple clematis now climbing up the folly was fashioned into a work of art, and the pond, overhung with a couple of acers and a pale drooping willow, sported gigantic pink waterlilies, and served as a welcome oasis in the searing heat of the afternoon. Balloons and bunting hanging from the trees gave out an air of festivity not seen in Roper's End for many a year.

Janet was beside herself with joy; her husband had, at last, retired and she could now look forward to having him all to herself. He'd been decidedly peaky of late – which hadn't been helped by the explosion at the Garraways' only a few weeks' ago – and she'd worried for him. She thought he'd put all the business of that baby behind him, but could see that the explosion had served to unnerve him once again.

As she ushered her guests onto the lawn, she kept her eye on her son – six-foot-three Jeremy – evidently in his element at the barbecue – and she smiled; how had he got to be so big? – she was looping his school tie around his little neck only five minutes ago . . . Where did the years go?

She'd argued against his suggestion of a barbecue, wanting something rather grander for Peter's retirement party, but had then relented. Leaving it all in his hands would, she reasoned, give her one less thing to think about, especially when Jeremy had offered to organise and manage it himself. She had, however, gone ahead and hired the catering firm as a back-up in case folk eschewed a badly singed sausage or an overcooked chicken leg for a more civilised crudité or smoked salmon sandwich.

Emma, she saw, was graciously handing round drinks, dressed in a pretty blue frock she'd bought for the occasion, which made a change from the usual skinny jeans and T-shirts she seemed to favour all day and every day. Her fluffy strawberry-blonde hair framed the heart-shaped face, giving her an angelic air; though angelic she most certainly wasn't if caught in a bad mood. Right now, though, she was mingling with folk she'd never before met, topping up their drinks and putting everyone at their ease. Janet stood for a few moments to watch her, marvelling at the transformation.

She mentally ticked each box as the party progressed: the family smiling and happily mixing and introducing each newcomer to someone of interest, before moving on to the next newcomer – *tick*; sun shining relentlessly on the growing crowd milling around the garden – *tick*; muscular grown-up son, fully-aproned up, expertly sharpening up his tools and competently manning the barbecue – *tick*; pretty courteous daughter, effortlessly charming everyone with her infectious laughter – *tick*. The hired staff in their smart black waistcoats, smilingly offering food and topping up drinks, her husband gallantly greeting each guest, feigning surprise as each came through the gate – *tick tick*. And the *Big Surprise* now sneaking quietly into the rear entrance while her husband's back was turned . . . *tick* and *triple tick!* And she grinned in anticipation of the shock on Peter's face when he finally saw them.

Everything was up to speed, which was just as well, seeing as all this planning and preparation had made a largish dent in the bank account. Money, however, was far from her thoughts at that moment; Peter's retirement, despite his plea not to make too much of a fuss, couldn't possibly go by without one huge celebration. She'd waited long enough. And she couldn't have chosen a more perfect day; together with her children, the weather had finally decided, after all the recent rain, to be on its best behaviour.

'Darling, you can't possibly wear that old thing!' she'd laughed, when Peter had brought his old boater out of the potting shed.

'Got to cover the bald patch with something in this heat,' he'd said, as he jammed it on.

'Oh, Dad,' Emma squealed as she came in from the kitchen. 'When does the song and dance act begin? And what's that on the front? A *badge*?'

'You wait, my girl,' he'd grinned back. 'When that sun gets to you this afternoon, you'll wish you had a hat like this! *And* – you may not remember, as you were about three years old – I won this badge. Yes, I was was the proud winner of the knobbly knees competition in some God-awful holiday camp we once went to!'

'Well – you'd better not tell anybody that, or they may want photographic evidence!' she shot back.

Janet watched her husband with a smile as he idly walked over to inspect Jeremy's efforts at the barbecue, checking that everything was in place, attempting to sneak a chicken leg but being told firmly that it was not yet ready to eat. Control of the barbecue had always been his prerogative, and he now felt somewhat aggrieved at being left out of the action as his son took over the show with an expertise he'd never guessed at. Always having been the one to shoo everyone away, telling them to leave him alone until the food was ready, Janet saw with amusement that he was now the one being told off. She could see that he was itching to take over; just to turn over the odd sausage that was about to singe . . .

Just under a hundred guests crowded the half-acre lawn – Janet hadn't known when to stop. And she moved slowly around them, glass in hand, mingling with people she barely knew – people who had worked with her husband at some point in his profession life and who'd remained in touch over the years: doctors, nurses, fellow consultants and old university buddies, all accompanied by wives and husbands, each one expressing pleasure at his retirement, but deeply saddened at losing a paediatrician of Peter's stature. Neighbours, too, had been invited, plus various friends of Emma and Jeremy – and Janet's own friends from the tennis club.

The party now in full swing, Hal Barnet, one of Peter's many friends at the hospital, unexpectedly stood up to hush everyone, then proposed a toast, speaking for some length in his soft but confident Connecticut voice as to the void that Peter was leaving in the hospital, and of how much he would be missed; how his kindness and gentle support would no longer be there to help them all out when they need his invaluable advice. This speech was unforeseen, so all the more surprising, and the emotion in Hal's voice as he croaked to a halt brought tears to Janet's eyes.

Peter stood awkwardly, visibly moved by Hal's speech then, in response, pointed out, to everyone's amusement that, now they all had the internet for support, he'd felt for some time superfluous to requirements and doubted, therefore, that he'd be missed at all. He wished Hal the best of luck in taking over the 'baby shop' and asked everyone to drink to his health. Though this was said in his usual jocular fashion, everyone could see that, relieved as he was to be retiring, leaving a hospital which had been his second home, was hard. He'd thought of his staff as family, and this family now shed a tear or two at the cutting of the umbilical cord as Peter said goodbye to them.

After these two short speeches, the champagne flowed and food was passed round, the elderly managing to find themselves a seat in a more shaded part of the garden, the younger guests queuing at the barbecue, perspiring in the heat and attempting to prevent their heels sinking into the grass whilst balancing plates and flutes.

However, Janet had the *Big Surprise* up her sleeve and quivered with excitement as guests munched on their sausages and sandwiches. She disappeared into the house at an opportune moment, and Peter looked anxiously round for her; he knew she couldn't stand the heat and wondered if she was feeling ill. But then, to everyone's delight, she emerged, followed by a group of musicians, which she guided to a shaded area on a small hillock. The string quartet then serenaded the party with a selection from the shows.

'How on earth did you manage that? This is so . . . I'm lost for words!' Peter spluttered.

'You? Lost for words?' she smiled up at him. 'That's a first!'

'You know, you really are a miracle worker, my love,' Peter grinned at his wife. 'I had no idea . . .'

'Of course you didn't!' she said serenely. 'It's your birthday. You're allowed surprises on your birthday, you know!'

'Thank you,' he said, then kissed her.

'*Ooo,*' the cry went up, and Peter threw a wicked grin at the crowd, then nicked a sausage from the barbecue, licking his fingers with relish.

'Wow, Pete!' Hal grinned. 'You limies sure know how to party!'

'All down to Jan – she's a marvel,' Peter said.

'Yeah – you lucky guy!'

The laughter in the garden grew louder as people took full

advantage of the Moet, and folk queued up at the barbecue to collect their steak buns which, for all Janet's foreboding, proved to be an enormous draw, the sandwiches largely neglected and sadly curling in the heat.

It was then into this happy, celebratory throng that a stranger walked. No one noticed him at first, but those who did merely glanced over their champagne flutes, assumed he was a latecomer, then carried on as before. But the stranger had a mission, and spied his prey standing by the barbecue, talking to his son. He then strode purposefully up to Peter Flynn's back and waited until he turned to face him.

Peter, sensing a presence behind him, swivelled round with a smile, expecting to offer a hungry guest a chicken leg. Instead, he found himself faced with someone who, in those few seconds of recognition, caused a streak of sweat to suddenly course down his face. He froze, the chicken leg jammed into his hand, and drew in his breath at the sight of this uninvited guest, the smile, in his confusion, threatening to abandon his face. But, ever the genial host, he forced himself to retain the somewhat rictus grin and said, 'Mr Robinson, how delightful to see you again.'

'So – this is where you live?' Robinson smirked, glaring at the host malignantly. 'Nice place. I discovered it the other day.'

'Good, good,' Peter said, skilfully disguising his discomfort. His heart racing and feeling anything but good, he simultaneously wondered how Robinson had discovered his address and thought wildly how strange it was to be standing in his own garden faced with a man he'd wished never to see again. The grin still stuck to his mouth as though Superglued, he managed to say jovially, 'Now, Mr Robinson – come and have a drink.'

Guests, sensing unease, rubber-necked and raised their brows. Janet stood, staring at the man's effect on her husband, judging the right moment to intervene. She took a tentative step forward, but Peter warned her off with a look. So she stood rigid with anxiety, hoping the man would take his drink and then leave. Who was he, and why had he come?

Peter whisked a glass off a passing tray and proffered it towards his uninvited guest with what he considered his best welcoming beam – a beam which he hoped would hide the panic he was experiencing at being accosted by the man who'd once wanted to harm him for 'killing' his baby. As he held out the glass to Robinson, his back stiffened. A trickle of ice slid down his spine as he realised the damage this man could do. But he kept up the jollity in the hope that Robinson would soften his stance and join the party – a hope that was fading fast. Stiff with the effort of faux cheer, and with his anxious wife and son hovering at the tail of his eye, he continued to keep up the beaming smile – a smile which was becoming more difficult to maintain as the seconds rolled by. And, as he watched the grim features of the man standing before him, fear for his family shot through him.

Robinson suddenly took a step closer, glared into his face then, to Peter's utter shock, with one swipe, knocked the glass out of his hand. Peter's immediate reaction was to step away from the snarling face, but his sandal caught the edge of the barbecue's stand and he staggered back. This sudden jolt tipped his boater over one eye and, in his effort to push it back whilst steadying himself, he threw out his hand, which landed squarely onto the glowing furnace behind him, causing him to yell out in pain. He stood, breathing heavily, clutching his burned hand, staring at Robinson's growing smirk.

The glass splintering onto the barbecue, was sufficient to cause every head to turn, the party-goers drawing in their breath at the stranger's behaviour. The shattered glass, followed by Peter's sudden yelp of pain, caused Hal to immediately rush over. At this sudden cry from his father, Jeremy ran swiftly from behind the barbecue, armed with a towel to wrap around the burnt hand and – Janet saw with alarm – the barbecue prong. Then, towering over Robinson and brandishing the prong, Jeremy stared the man down, challenging him with a glare to try something. Janet and Emma watched in silent horror at the scene unfolding before them, wondering who this stranger was and why he had arrived, unannounced, at their party; moreover, wondering what Jeremy would do to him with the prong should he lay a finger on his father.

This turbulence caused all conversation to stop and all laughter to cease. Jaws stopped mid-munch. In the silence, bees buzzed and leaves tinkled in a gentle breeze. The church clock was heard chiming five, the vibration of the bells travelling through the graveyard, through the oaks on the Common, then carrying across Bob Spraignton's orchards until they reached the ears of the guests at Woodford Grange, suddenly causing the synchronising of watches and reminding guests of all those jobs crying out to be done at home: dogs needing walks, grass to be mown, cats to be fed . . .

*'I don't drink that rubbish!'* Robinson spat out as the glass lay shattered at Peter's feet.

Hesitating sufficiently to make his point, he then lifted his chin in a gesture of disgust and turned on his heels, marching back towards the gate.

The string quartet, at the first sign of trouble, ceased playing and hastily put their instruments back into their cases. And, after the musicians' disappearance, the shock was tangible. Guests began talking nervously again but found their appetites waning. They'd all strained their ears in an attempt to understand the situation, but even the ones who had not heard the kerfuffel were visibly disturbed by the changed atmosphere.

On hearing this rumble of discomfort emanating from his friends and colleagues, Peter held out his undamaged hand and, in an attempt to restore the situation shouted, 'It's all right – it's all right. I just burnt my hand. No harm done.'

However, that announcement came just a tad too late. Already, he knew with a sinking heart, that the party was over, and that no words, however soothing, would counter-balance the damage. Once the man had been seen to leave, each of the guests eyed each other warily, as though pleading to be let out, silently asking if it would it be considered rude to abandon ship. Endeavouring, therefore, to swill down the last dregs from their glasses, they made their decision. It would be in everyone's interest to leave, they told themselves. The Flynns' neighbours in particular. Having witnessed that day at Oaklands, and seeing Simon Garraway's half-charred body lying on the driveway, neighbours were particularly panic-stricken at the uncomfortable thought that this stranger could well have been the sender of the bomb. And they'd asked themselves who might be next. So they shuffled their feet awkwardly before making their excuses to return to the safety of their homes.

Hal, watching Robinson walk off, said, 'Who the hell was that?'

'No one – it's okay – really it is. Leave it,' Peter said quietly and then yelling, 'It's okay everyone. Please – just enjoy yourselves. I burnt my hand, that's all!'

But he saw, with mounting sorrow, as he smarted at the pain in his hand, that folk were already leaving.

'Did he hit you?' Hal asked with a frown.

'No – I just . . . I just stupidly put my hand on the barbecue. That's all.'

'But he caused that,' Hal said. 'I saw him threaten you.'

'Yes . . . well . . .' Peter said, 'it was still my fault.'

The family, now thoroughly upset, watched with alarm at

their disappearing guests, the mood having significantly altered, and sighed with disappointment as, one by one, each of them left, with only half the food eaten. Janet was distraught; all that planning, all that work – and all it took to destroy everything was a rotten little man to charge in and upset everyone, ruining what should have been a wonderful day for her husband. Emma took her arm and led her into the house, where they sat together in silent disbelief.

Hal stayed behind to look at Peter's hand.

'It was him, wasn't it?' he said softly.

Peter sighed. 'Yes,' he said.

'What did he want?'

'I suppose . . .' he said with a sigh, 'to tell me he knows where I live.'

'You should get the police involved,' Hal said. 'He may not have hit you, but I saw the way he looked at you.'

'No, really . . .'

'Come on. You have to do this for your family, Pete. It scared the shit out of me – so imagine what it's done to them. And the danger they could be in now.'

'Okay – point taken,' Peter said, his hand now bandaged.

The two sat on the covered swing together while Peter recovered from the shock of having his birthday bash infiltrated by this dreadful blast from the past, and watched in something akin to a trance as Janet, Emma and Jeremy silently cleared everything away. He could see the fear in their every move as they'd steadily twigged who the stranger was; the anxiety mingling with the disappointment of the ruined party and of all that wasted food.

Robinson hadn't threatened him outright, but the threat had been there nonetheless.

In the intervening years – the years after the court case, when

Peter had been afraid of losing his job and terrified for the future of his family – the years when the nightmares were so bad they'd caused him to cry out in the middle of the night and had shaken him for the rest of the day – he'd largely forgotten about the man. He'd deliberately pushed out of his mind someone who wouldn't accept the death of a baby boy who could never have lived, no matter how much love and attention the National Health Service, nor anyone else, might have lavished upon him; a man who had seen fit to use him as an emotional punchbag. Surprisingly, Peter wouldn't, before today, have been able to pick the man out in a crowd. He did, though, remember every detail of his poor little wife as she'd sat tearful and trembling beside her husband that day in his office.

What would Robinson do now – now that he'd tracked down where he lived? He recalled, with distaste, the way the man had looked at him, and shuddered. It was the same scowl he'd had to suffer sitting behind his desk all those years ago. Robinson, for all his wealth, was a rough diamond who maybe had connections – connections to people who would be willing to carry out orders if paid well enough. He hadn't arrived by accident; he'd driven the sixty-odd miles from his home in Solihull simply to inform him that the issue of the dead baby had not been forgotten, nor ever would be. So why – after all this time? What might he be planning?

Was it now time to leave Roper's End?

The Flynns had thought they were safe here, moving far away from their home in Birmingham to quietly tuck themselves into this small village. But nowhere was safe, was it? Nowhere was safe from people like that. And what if they moved? Would it make a difference? Peter balked at being bullied – at causing him to even think about moving house. He'd be a coward to succumb to threats, he reasoned. On the other hand, he had his family to think about . . .

He'd imagined – or perhaps it had been mere wishful thinking – that, in moving to Roper's End, the danger would go away; imagined he'd now be free to enjoy his retirement unperturbed in this quiet little village that was just a dot on the map. But that particular dream had been shattered that very afternoon. Instead of the sunlit path of retirement stretching joyfully ahead, with all the cares of his job left behind, this would now stick in his gut – every day – wondering what he could do to shield his family from harm.

Hal was right – he should contact the police. But then, what would he say to them? That a man had walked into his garden, smashed a glass and looked at him in a funny way? That was hardly what the police would term a threat.

\* \* \*

With Hal now gone, Peter flopped down on the sitting room couch and sighed. He would keep his promise and contact the police – but not right now.

The party, by rights – *his* party – should still be in full swing. But, thanks to that crazy loon, Robinson, everyone had felt unsafe. One or two of his hospital staff had stayed to help clear up, he noticed with gratitude, but the rest had taken fright and run. He didn't blame them; he might well have done the same. His head now resting back on the couch, he acknowledged Robinson's timing with a wry smile – reluctantly congratulating him on choosing the perfect day to embarrass the whole family and to send all his friends packing. He closed his eyes and, with a shudder, re-lived that scene in his office all those years ago and wondered where this débâcle would now lead.

Janet left the children and the helpers to cope with the

disposal of food and disappeared to change out of her finery and, having done so, sat on the bed and sighed. What a bloody awful thing to have happened. She'd guessed who he was. She hadn't attended Court on the day of the inquest into the death of that baby, but was sure that the man in her garden was the same man who had wanted to bring her husband to his knees. And now he'd discovered the one thing they thought would keep them safe: their address.

In trying to understand how someone, after all these years, refused to come to terms with the death of a child – a child who would never have thrived and who was destined for a short life owing to his terrible disabilities – she couldn't shake off a deep empathy for the man at not being able to let this go. She'd felt all that herself at the death of Christopher. That wasn't simply grief, but anger and despair. Robinson had wanted the child mended, and hadn't understood the severity of the problem. She understood that pit of misery he was in, even after so long; the damage he wished to inflict on someone – anyone – in order to deflect the damage of his own heart.

After Christopher's death, both she and Peter decided that the only way to deal with their loss was to throw themselves into their work; which was a coping mechanism that seemed inbuilt – their DNA. But grief hits people in different ways and even after suffering the party's car crash, she sighed for Mr Robinson and wished him peace.

Pulling herself out of this reverie, she walked down to join her husband, leaving her capable children and their helpers to do the donkey-work of litter-picking and clearing the decks. She sat by him on the couch and took his hand.

'What a blow!' she said softly, clamping her jaws to prevent a threatening tear; she hardly ever cried but, today – while watching her husband's forlorn face – she could have shed tears to fill a bucket. This had been so awful for him.

'Mm,' he murmured dully, his mind elsewhere.

Emma walked in with a tray of tea, which she laid onto the small table in front of her parents, then left to join Jeremy, who was conscientiously bagging up uncooked sausages by the barbecue.

'Will we have to move, do you think – now that he's discovered our address?' Janet asked when Emma had left the room.

'Perhaps,' he said. 'For your sake, not mine. There's no knowing what kind of people we're dealing with. We have to ask ourselves if the children are safe, don't we? If he found us, he could discover where each of them are working.'

'Why *has* it taken him so long to find us?' she said, almost to herself.

'Who knows,' he sighed.

Janet was silent for a long moment, then let out a shuddering sigh as the thought hit her.

'Do you suppose . . .' she began, 'do you think . . . that the bomb was sent by him?'

'I'm trying not to,' he said.

# Chapter Twenty-Six

The *For Sale* signs were going up all over Roper's End.

'Stupid buggers,' Freddie Wingrave huffed after watching the board being knocked into the Sandersons' garden, then went in to feed her cat.

Then there was the Flynns' house up for sale. Gossip was rife: who was that stranger everybody was wittering on about – the man who'd barged into Peter Flynn's party – and what did he want? And why would that incident cause the Flynns to be moving? It could only mean one thing, couldn't it? And that thing would be the bomb! Peter Flynn must have been spooked by something pretty dire to want to leave, folk chattered among themselves, from the congregation of the church, down to the WI and beyond. *So . . . who was that stranger?*

People living on Kings Road clammed up and had been reluctant to share gossip with what they considered the lower orders of the village, viewing them, erroneously, as the only sector in Roper's End partial to a bit of muck-raking. The lower order, on the other hand, aggrieved at knowing it would never get invited to a party thrown by any of the professional bods on Kings Road, was ever eager to muck-rake its toffee-nosed inhabitants. And, what they didn't know – because no one would tell them – they flagrantly made up.

Irene Farrow had only heard part of the story and, at first light on Monday morning, anxious to hear more, was down at the Post

Office – fount of all unverified news, unconfirmed reports and stop-press sensations – with a parcel. The parcel could have waited a few more days, but this was a good enough excuse to dip her nose into something she'd been left out of. And for Irene Farrow to be left out of a juicy piece of gossip was the nearest thing to heresy. She needed to get the low-down on this so that she could pass the information on to Enid Briggs next door, who would, in turn, ensure that the news travelled round the village faster than a greased bullet.

Irene had been no particular friend of the Flynns and had only nodded to them in passing. She'd had little expectation, therefore, of being invited to parties at their house – which hadn't in any way stopped her being aggrieved at not being invited. The little she'd heard of this post-apocalyptic event had set the cogs whirring, and she was determined to get to the bottom of it.

'What's going on up Kings Road?' she smiled at Postmaster Dan Prince, not wishing to dive straight in to what she was desperate to learn; she wouldn't wish anyone to think she was a gossip. 'All those houses up for sale . . . ?'

'Search me,' Dan muttered from behind the counter. 'Like the *Relief of sodding Mafeking*. Do you want this First or Second Class?'

'Second,' she said. 'Why's everybody selling up? Are they all scared out of their wits because of the bomb? Bit stupid, isn't it? After all, nobody's likely to come back with a bomb a second time, are they?'

'Depends, doan it?' Dan's wife Betty piped up from behind the greeting cards stand.

'On what?'

'On 'oo the bomb was reelly meant for.'

'So . . . who do *you* think it was meant for?'

''Oo knows,' Betty Prince said darkly.

Dan, behind the counter, closed his eyes and shuddered as the two women set off on one of their character demolitions which, he knew from experience, could go on for hours, and he needed to close at five. Why did women do that? Nobody was safe, were they? And, despite Irene Farrow's mock-innocent enquiry, he could tell that, as she'd gleaned a small but vital component of a rumour, this was a tree she needed to shake until all the coconuts dropped off.

'So, what do *you* know?' Irene asked, her eyes shining in anticipation.

'Well . . . after Sat'day . . .' Betty said ominously.

'So – what about Saturday? What was that all about?' Irene said, collecting her change from the Postmaster. 'What happened last Saturday? I heard something had happened but nobody seems to know anything?'

'Yeah –well, it were at the Flynns' garden party, were'n it?' Betty drawled, rearranging the cards on the stand.

'*What* was at the Flynn's garden party?' Irene asked, irritably, knowing how Betty Prince loved to spin things out, her eyes glinting with merriment at seeing her audience gagging for any scurrilous snippet of gossip that village folk, from time to time, dropped into her shop, assured of its absolute of secrecy.

'Peter Flynn's retirement party,' Betty said. 'Din you know about that? Din you see all them balloons out their 'ouse?'

'No, I didn't,' Irene said. 'So what happened?'

'Walked the dog up there Sat'day mornin' – great big balloons outside. I thought, 'ello, what's goin' on 'ere . . .'

'So – *what happened!*' Irene squeaked, the suspense causing her to hyperventilate.

'This big bloke, innit? Walked straight into the garden, unannounced, and said summat to Peter Flynn, summat about knowin' where 'e lives.'

'And . . . ? What. Is that all?'

'Oooh, no,' Betty said, carefully patting the cards into place, enjoying centre stage. 'There were some sor' of argiment an' Peter wen all white, by all accounts. The man chucked 'is glass onto the concrete an' stomped off. Then everybody got the wind up and scarpered after that.'

'So what happened after that?'

'Dunno,' Betty said. 'Your guess is as good as mine.'

'I had no idea they were throwing a party,' Irene sniffed.

'No. Well, only the Kings Road lot would get invited to that, wun they,' Betty grinned, watching the corners of Irene's downturned mouth.

'Who was this chap, anyway?'

'Nobody knows,' Betty said. 'Tried to get to the bottom of it, but nobody knows 'oo 'e were.'

'And that's why they're selling up?'

'Can't think of no other reason,' Betty said, grunting at her creaky knees as she stood.

'Good grief! Do you think Peter Flynn could have been the one the bomb was meant for . . . ?'

'Well . . . I dunno – but it makes yer think, doan it?' Betty said, wandering round to the other side of the counter. 'Certainly made all 'is guests think, by all accounts. Suppose that chap could be 'oo sent the bomb – could be the reason why the Flynns are movin' outa Roper's End.'

'It's unbelievable!' Irene said frowning. 'What on earth could Peter Flynn have done to deserve being blown up?'

'Anybody's guess, innit?' Betty said.

'Sodding shame!' Irene said. 'For Kings Road, they're quite nice people, I've always thought. On the other hand, we don't want a repeat of what happened to the Garraways.'

'No, we don't. But it could 'appen when yer think about it. That post girl – poor little Sarah Beddows, lovely girl, God rest 'er soul . . .' Betty said sadly. ''Er mum's in a right state – wen to see 'er last Thursday. 'Ow would you ever get over summat like that?'

'What I heard was that the post girl got the wrong address,' Irene said.

'Yeah, that's what they sez . . . Got the wrong address when she delivered it to the Garraways. But that bomb could 'ave bin for anybody down there, cun it?'

'Yes . . . But the Flynns?'

'You never know, do you?' Dan said, leaning on the Post Office counter, hoping to break up the sortilege in order to get Irene Farrow out of the door and back on to her broomstick. 'You never can tell. Could just as well be the Flynns as anybody else.'

'So, it's not just the Garraways selling up then?' Irene said. 'You'd expect them to be leaving. But the Sandersons next door have now got a sale board out as well – which I suppose, come to think of it, isn't totally surprising, Helena having that heart murmur. And now it's the Flynns . . . I couldn't believe it when I walked down Kings Road with the dog earlier and saw them sticking up a sale board outside their house!'

'Well, when word gets round about the bombing in Roper's End, who'll want to buy anything down the Kings Road?' Dan said. 'So, I don't suppose anybody'll be moving for a while will they, 'cos they're not likely to be selling any time soon, like.'

'But the *Flynns* . . .' Irene repeated with feeling, picking up her shopping bag. 'I've always like the Flynns – such a nice family. My Oliver went to school with Jeremy – lovely lad. They'll really be missed in this village.'

She then straightened herself from the Post Office counter she'd been leaning on, picked up her shopping bag, then gave a small shrug as she smiled and said gaily, 'Well, I suppose the good news is we don't live anywhere near that posh lot up the Kings Road, thank the Lord, so we're never likely to get bombed, are we? Every cloud . . .'

\* \* \*

Charlie Ramsden was enjoying his solitude on the Tuesday following the party, which allowed him thinking time without his wife demanding his attention at every turn. He was tending his prize-winning cactuses, his mind more or less along the same lines – *wrong address* – and had been pondering over it for some time. The gate-crasher at the Flynns' garden party the previous Saturday had forced him into recalling that dreadful crater in the Garraways' drive a couple of months ago, and caused him to ponder further. This, he knew, had got Penelope antsy again, but the drama queen would likely get antsy over any little thing to bolster her argument for moving back to London. He'd have to put his foot down there, he thought with a sigh. Although, come to think of it, he might have to use both feet.

Although unnerved by the bomb, Charlie was not exactly afraid; he was upset more at the thought of losing neighbours he'd come to know and to have the odd pint with: Peter Flynn and Rodney Sanderson. Shame about Garraway, though, but he never had liked the chap.

As these thought ran through his head, he absently stroked the spines of his beloved *Opuntia*. Then hearing Penelope's car screeching up the drive and churning up the gravel as she came to an abrupt halt, he heaved a sigh at the foreshortening of this precious uneventful afternoon. The car would be requiring its MOT in a few weeks' time, but he couldn't see it passing, the way she thrashed it each day. He closed his eyes momentarily at the opening and slamming of the car door then, again, at the opening and slamming of the front door. And he sighed again at the sudden loss of this oasis of peace. The very sound of the splintered gravel had told him all he wished to know about the mood she was in.

'Good day?' he ventured optimistically as she swept past him. 'Huh!' was all the reply he received.

Her mood, foul and fulsome after having suffered the usual unsatisfactory stint in the bedroom of the hotel in Stratford, and she'd meditated fiercely, en route, upon the onslaught she'd rain upon her husband when she arrived home, imagining that, after Saturday's débâcle at the Flynns', she now held the upper hand. Penelope was ready to do battle – because she imagined she now had a watertight excuse to finally end this pettifogging little life here in Roper's End, once and for all, and to put an end to this wet-sponge once-a-fortnight lover with whom she'd allowed herself to get involved. She was livid that she'd let things get as far as this, and seriously had to end it – and the only thing she could do to end it was to move away. Now, thank the Lord, she had the perfect peg with which to pin her argument.

She'd built herself up, therefore, into a crescendo of rage and had arrived home with all guns firing. She'd had her fill of the Chief Constable after today's desultory workout, and she'd make damned sure that, this time, she got what she wanted – what she'd been wanting for some considerable time: to move back to London in order to get out of this predicament with a man she now loathed, and this insignificant blot-on-the-landscape hell-hole that called itself a village – and the sooner the better. She was sick of these sessions in Stratford – sick of that malodorous, stomach-churning hotel. She wasn't put on this earth for such things!

So, on the drive home, she'd planned her strategy: not only

was there the business of the bomb a couple of months ago at the Garraways', she had the satisfaction of now throwing into her rationale the upset at the Flynns' party – which she intended to milk dry. She'd be adamant, she told herself – dominant – throw everything she had at it: the worry; the fear; the danger . . . After her failure to argue her case after the bomb, Charlie wouldn't stand a chance against her argument now.

She strode back from the kitchen carrying two mugs of tea, slapping one down on the table for her husband. Charlie looked up sharply at her sour-puss face, moved the mug two feet away from his cactus, and prepared himself for an ear-bashing.

'We have to move!' she launched without preamble, her mouth a streak of red against the taut skin of her face.

'Why?' he asked, frowning at the tone.

'*Why?*' she shrieked. 'We *have* to – can't you see that? We can't be too careful, Charlie. You *have* to see that. That terrible episode on Saturday really *frightened* me!' she cried out theatrically, giving her well-practised *Blitz Krieg* act full rein as she stood glaring at him with her cold grey eyes, a tear a mere tantrum's throw away. 'After that scare, we'd be stupid to stay here. We have to go back to London now!'

*Blitz Krieg,* however, cut little ice with Charlie, who had been assailed too many times by that volcanic outbreak from the woman he'd live with for the last twenty-two years. It was all so predictable: the sulky pout and self-righteous hauteur of her aristocratic parentage which, she imagined, gave her the unconscionable right to be heard, demanding her every whim to be satisfied, while simultaneously stamping her foot – all in the key of F minor. Never having been denied her own way from birth, he could almost hear the click of her fingers in order to summon a lackey, or a scream for nanny . . . The tone never varied, nor did it, after all these years, move him sufficiently to withdraw his attention from his treasured *Opuntia,* which he thought was looking its loveliest at that moment. These temper tantrums may once have worked with her parents – and, indeed, had once worked with him – but Charlie had now had enough of them; had become inured of their violence after too many toys-out-of-the-pram explosions throughout their marriage. Plus it had all sounded too well rehearsed to his practised ears.

He clamped his jaws against the tirade, refusing to be bullied. He'd learned the hard way, whilst on the bench, how to detect and to deal with bullies, and wished now that he'd recognised this streak of tyranny in his wife a tad earlier, and had applied his hard-earned knowledge from the start of their marriage. But, at the beginning, he'd been afraid of losing her, blinded as he was by love, and he'd showered her with everything she'd asked for: stables to house the two Arabs in Buckinghamshire; the flat in Belgrave Square; the yacht on the south coast . . . She'd almost bled him dry, but he'd gone along with it all and proudly showed her off to all his envious friends. Until Penelope, he'd never had much luck with women, and hadn't bargained on bagging such a beauty at his advanced age – so was drunk with desire.

Only later did he clock that his bank balance was perhaps of more interest to her than he would ever be and, fully sobered up after several hefty withdrawals of the account prompting the necessity of selling his Chelsea house, he sighed, recalling the day when her eyes had lit up at her first sight of his scarlet MG glinting in the sunshine outside the Dorchester. He'd thought she'd fallen for him, but knew now that he wouldn't have stood a chance if it hadn't been for the MG. Nor had he suspected how hard it would be coping with her aristocratic temperament. He had, at first, quickly and avidly become her lackey, fearing her vitriol, and feeling that he would lose her to all those drooling men ready to take over if she were to drop him – which, unbeknown to him, she'd had every intention of doing.

But, he mused now, if bullies only realised how much damage they did to themselves by displaying these strong-arm tactics, high-horsing and sabre-rattling portentously in an attempt to crash their way through any quarrel that didn't meet their immediate demands. Whereas, if they were canny enough to try a more reasoned, moderate approach, they would learn that this latter strategy would be far more likely to get them listened to, honey catching more wasps than vinegar. And if Penelope, bully in chief, had had a smidgeon of intelligence, she would have twigged the importance of that by now; that, if she'd produced sounder arguments in a calmer and more subtle manner, she might have stood a better chance of winning him over.

As it was, his hackles rose immediately at her high-handed attitude and at the sharpness of her voice, and he lifted his eyebrows sufficiently to tell her that this was not working. He turned his back on the livid jutted cheekbones, then turned his attention to his second best cactus, making a show of concentration on its sharp prickles, which were far less prickly than his wife in her present mood.

But on she went, regardless.

He'd been expecting Penelope to use the incident at the Flynns' party to make another attempt to move back to London but, for the moment, put up a convincing show of serenity, which seemed to enrage her to the point of hysteria. Unmoved, and with an inward smirk, he picked up his mug, drank from it, then made a point of placing the mug as far away from his darling plants as possible.

He'd divined that this business at the Flynns' couldn't have come at a better time for his wife; that she would see this as her last throw of the dice for getting out of Roper's End. She'd been working up to it for some time, constantly complaining of the monotony of all those 'leaden, tedious yokels'. But, now on full explosive dudgeon, he watched with half an eye as she hyped herself up in order to squeeze every last pip from her demands to leave this village, and continued to smile as he listened to her rantings, taking each point and logging it into his brain for later use. His eyebrows, having failed to alert her to the fact that she was wasting her time, he decided to let her blether on. And, if oblivious to the eyebrows, he'd let her imagine that he was taking it all in then, when she'd got it all out of her system, would allow her to enjoy the benefit of his legal brain, stamping down, one by one, each demand she displayed with a logic to which she would have no answer, and then tell her why the idea of moving out of Roper's End was out of the question.

As far as Penelope was concerned, the Flynns' party was the *point d'appui* – the spur – that drove her onwards, the irascibility in her penetrating screech rising by the second, as she battled on, unaware of either his indifference or her own inability to convince the solid brick wall that was her husband. Charlie listened in silence to her struggle; at her search for an appropriately damning phrase to make her point, in her determination to stick the feverish little stiletto of intellect into his rather larger brain, his continued indifference sending her apoplexy ever skyward. Charlie had often thought she'd have stood a better chance at gaining a more comprehensive grasp of vocabulary had she attended the state school at which he'd once been educated, rather than at that highfalutin establishment she'd been sent to; the sorts of expensive highfalutin establishments folk of a certain breed insisted on parking their offspring, imagining they would come out of these sausage factories with qualifications that would send them on to lead the country. If Penelope was a typical example of that private education, then God help the country . . . He'd often thought of public schools as being secretly funded by psychotherapists to breed new clients. He himself been given a stonking education at Harrow Grammar before going up to Oxford, and would be eternally grateful to it.

He continued to watch Penelope from the tail of his eye, bemused at her lack of expertise in what she assumed were clever put-downs. If he'd been attempting a put-down of his own, he mused, he'd have made a damned sight better job of it without the use of the dragon-fire that was now shooting from her mouth. He half-smiled in sympathy at her pathetic efforts at dredging up all the smart, sophisticated devices she'd learned from her parents, now trotted out parrot-fashion, seemingly stretching every brain cell to its limits; argument which might have been more effective if she'd ever read a book.

During her last attempt to escape what she considered to be the piddling little village of Roper's End – the bomb at the Garraways' – she'd used every means her feeble brain would allow, but it hadn't been enough, and so she'd bided her time. Now, however, she had something more substantial to bite on, and she would, without a doubt, gnaw on that bone until all the meat was chewed off. He saw it all . . .

She stood, hands on hips, as Charlie reached for the watering can and mildly dribbled water into the pots, awaiting his response to what she saw as a perfectly logical argument.

'*Are you listening to me?*' she bellowed.

'Mmm,' he said absently, concentrating on the cactuses' soil distribution, his glasses slipping down his nose.

Penelope imagined that her prepared argument was flawless and that she'd delivered it impeccably. She'd had to make a meal of it;

couldn't let him win this time. Charlie, with his legal brain, had thought himself to be the only one who could put up reasonable argument, hadn't he? But she would show him! She'd convince him of her 'fears' – and smirked at her foresight in choosing to attend drama classes with Miss Carter at an earlier stage of her life – drama, which had stood her in good stead over the years: the histrionics; the pathos; the tearful sigh . . . thus proving to have been worth every penny. She couldn't have him guessing that she hadn't been the least bit scared, could she? – she'd been made of tougher stuff than that – so she would need to throw up every ounce of drama into the mix. And, having demonstrated this abject 'fear', and of the seriousness of this heinous threat of danger to his darling wife, Charlie would surely see how upsetting this was and of how imperative it was to move back to London; and, like the perfect White Knight he was, he would be worried for her safety and accede to her demands, then whisk her away to her heart's desire – *surely* . . . She couldn't fail, could she?

So . . . this argument for leaving Roper's End, she'd decided upon on her drive back from Stratford, would be used to full Thespian effect, and she practised her tone and her expression in the driving mirror, notwithstanding the fact that she'd just shot a traffic light. Penelope imagined that the onslaught of her tongue would result in her *Get-Out-of-Jail* card – or, more succinctly, her *Get-Out-of-the-Affair-With-Chief-Constable-Derek-Farley* card – so she knew she had to pull out all the stops to thoroughly convince her husband that she was terrified. She would nag away at him until she got her way – and the effort of remembering her lines would be worth it, he totally unaware of her deception, she laughing all the way to the Big City. She'd always managed to get her way, by hook or by crook – crook if necessary – and was quietly assured of the introduction of menace to do the trick.

A ploy which didn't, in the least, fool him.

But she ploughed on, unabashed at his indifference, firing on all cylinders as Charlie patiently waited for her to finish. He kept up his inward smile, knowing that, when she eventually realised that all this hot air wasn't working for her, her next step would be to wheedle – then, perhaps, resort to weeping. She'd tried those tricks once too often, and he had his own way of dealing with it. And, even before she'd walked in the door to blast him with her tongue, he'd known that the interloper at the Flynns' party would be the catalyst, and used to full effect.

He knew nothing of her affair with the Chief Constable, nor of the real need to rid herself of what was becoming an embarrassment, so had little idea of her desperation – except that it had to be something other than simply wishing to remove herself, he'd divined. She'd got herself entangled in something she needed to get out of, he guessed – perhaps a man – but then, he mused with a shrug, decided he'd rather not know. However, he would play it cool for the nonce and let her rant until the steam ran out.

But Penelope had made her decision. Derek would be devastated to lose her, poor lamb – but one had to think of the future, and, when she'd had her way, it would be a future that didn't include Derek Farley. She was anxious to pick up where she'd left off with the Earl of Mortingale, who had a house in Chelsea and, moreover, a castle in Scotland. The only problem was that he still had a wife.

'Go back to London? You must be joking! *That is out of the question!*' Charlie fumed at last, when she'd finally finished her diatribe.

Penelope ground her teeth in exasperation at this, realised suddenly that all the effort she'd put into the screeching and stamping of feet had had no effect upon her husband – then decided on Plan B. She stopped in mid-screech, racking her brains as to her next tactic. *Blitz Krieg* had clearly not worked for her, so she would have to follow up with her version of *Lamentations*. It was the only other option and it had always worked, because Charlie couldn't stand tears. But tears it would be. That would surely do the trick . . .

'But, *Charlie* . . .' she cried out beseechingly, having recently seen Helena Bonham-Carter strut her stuff at The National.

Charlie, however, wasn't having any of it. They'd had this discussion many times before and, at each attempt to dislodge him from a village of which he'd grown fond, he'd put his foot down. He was settled here, away from the frenzy and pressure of London and of everything that reminded him of the Inns of Court; plus the seething mobs in the City and the difficulties of scrabbling for parking spaces. They were well out of it; couldn't she see that? So tears were not going to work this time.

'But, *Charlie*,' she whimpered soulfully, 'it's the only thing to do – don't you see?'

'Are you mad?' he snapped. 'Do you know how much property prices have shot up in London since we left? We wouldn't stand a hope of getting anything anywhere near decent now – and certainly not in Belgravia – except perhaps a second-hand rabbit hutch! And, if property prices drop here in Roper's End – owing to that wretched bomb – we'd get a pittance for this place.'

'But Charlie . . . *Darling* . . .' she wheedled, 'I'd settle for a rabbit hutch – *anywhere* – you must see that it makes sense to move out of this village.'

Perhaps if she'd tried Plan B before her snappy demands, it might, he thought, have touched his heart. But *Lamentations* had come directly after *Blitz Krieg*, barely stopping for breath, and the speed at which this had taken place had arrived far too late to touch any part of his heart.

'It makes no sense whatever to move,' he said sharply. 'We're far better off here in the peace and quiet of the countryside.'

'Peace? With the threat of another bomb?' she lobbed back at him, a tearful croak now on the agenda, *thank you, Helena.* 'You're the one who's mad! Can't you see how dangerous this is?'

'Read my lips, Pen. I. Am. Not. Shifting!' he said, turning to her, his mouth set.

The firmness of his mouth should have warned her that the matter was closed, but on she went . . .

*'But think of the potential danger!'* she howled, a tear now dropping from her eye. 'Don't you care enough about me to shield me from this danger? *Your wife?'*

No man worth his salt could fail to defend that heartfelt plea – inclusive of tear – could he? No honourable man would stand there, preferring to care for his cactuses, allowing his wife to face all the threats of danger this village posed?

However, this final step – this pathos worthy of a West End theatre – in the blink of an eye jumping from this tearful *Lamentations* to full-blown emotional blackmail got Charlie's goat, and he sighed heavily at this introduction of Plan C, the previous two boxes of tricks having been thwarted by cool logic. He'd thought he'd known her well enough; thought he was *au fait* with all her devious little wiles to get her own way. But this accusation of marital negligence slipping so easily off her tongue, aiming barbed arrows of discontent at her husband's seeming lack of care and protection, made him see red.

'There *is* no danger!' he snapped, carelessly catching his finger on the sharp needle of his cactus as he turned to face her. *'Ouch!'* he howled. 'Get me a plaster, would you?'

'Well, both the Sandersons and the Flynns obviously think there is!' she wailed, coming out of the downstairs bathroom with the First Aid box.

'Danger possibly to the Sandersons and the Flynns – though I would doubt that – *but no danger to us*. How could you imagine this to be a danger to us?'

'Well, they're not stupid. They can see the danger, even you can't. And they're getting out before property prices fall!' she snarled, back to *Blitz Kreig* once more, having realised that nothing else had worked as well as she'd hoped. 'Which they will before long – you mark my words!'

'Well, my darling, as I have no intention of selling this house, that information is immaterial to your argument, isn't it?' he snapped back.

Penelope sniffed at this, unable to recognise that she'd lost ground some time ago but, having run out of both words and steam to counter his obstinacy, she sighed heavily. She then suddenly decided that her only recourse to his indifference was to sob loudly in order to show him what a careless, insouciant bastard he was – and she reached for a tissue to dab at her eyes. She was incensed; was not used to being faced with questions for which she had no answers. Charlie ignored this false show of frustration, took the plaster from her then turned back to his cactus.

'How can you not see how *frightened* I am by all this?' she wailed.

'Because what I see, my dear, is you using every effort to manipulate me. And it won't work. And, just for the record, the people in this village are not stupid, as you seem to suggest. I like them, and I *refuse* to be manipulated by you into moving from Roper's End!' he said shortly. 'Pull yourself together, Pen – and get yourself a sense-of-proportion transplant! You're behaving like a toddler!'

'But you don't understand! I have no friends here of my ilk. And there's nothing to do here . . . and they're all so bloody *boring!*' she shrieked, stamping her foot.

He'd wondered when the foot might get stamped.

'Boring? Nothing to do? How can you say that? With all the activities sitting up and begging in this village? There are so many things you could do – so many activities you could join: there's the book club, yoga classes, walking club, quiz nights, the Women's Institute, the farmers' market – you could even get involved in the church,' he said, counting them off on his fingers. 'Just make friends here, and you might find that you're wrong about them . . .'

'Don't make me laugh!' she snarled. 'If you imagine for one minute that I'd wish to join *anything* of that nature with the rest of the rabble round here, you must be as stupid as them!'

'When you say "of that nature", what you really mean is that you imagine yourself to be too high and mighty to join anything that doesn't view you as an earth-shattering super-power!'

'How dare you say that to me!' she shrieked, stamping her foot a second time. 'I just don't get on with the yokels here – I have nothing in common with them!'

'You could *try*, Pen!' he said, sighing heavily. 'You've never tried. That's your problem.'

Penelope, unused to being thwarted, let out a sudden scream, which momentarily jarred Charlie's senses sufficiently to prevent him from properly applying his plaster – a plaster with which his wife had not seen fit to help him. This screaming ruse was one she'd invariably used as a child to get what she wanted and it had, in the past, always worked; had put the wind up Nanny, afraid news should get to her parents of child abuse.

Charlie turned abruptly, the blood now dripping from his throbbing finger onto the carpet, his mood at that moment threatening to turn a similar shade of red.

'Look Penelope,' he said, sharper than she'd ever heard him, mainly owing to his pain, 'you can stop all this fucking nonsense! We are staying here – *and that's final!*'

# Chapter Twenty-Seven

On the Sunday morning after the party, Jeremy Flynn boxed up a fair amount of left-over food, walked down the track off Prince Albert Lane and knocked on Glenys Pugh's door. He'd thought of Glenys first because he'd guessed – although he couldn't be sure – that she struggled financially; it was just an impression he got from the difference in her weight to the weight of her dog. They were all the same, these old ladies . . . It never failed to trouble him at how well animals were fed in comparison to the emaciation of their owners; he'd seen it more often than he liked in his practice in Manchester.

He was fond of Glenys. And she'd was fond of him. He loved her neat little house smelling of lavender, and her small chubby Cairn – so this had been a good excuse to call upon her.

Jeremy knew that very other body in Roper's End, as they cursed her flying past them on that rusty old bike of hers, thought that this skeletal, miniscule Glenys Pugh had to be soft in the head and, therefore, not worth bothering about. But Glenys was the diametric opposite of soft in the head, he'd discovered, when she'd revealed to him things about her past she'd never disclosed to anyone else.

Having once promised herself that she'd keep quiet about working at Bletchley Park, she'd finally opened up to Jeremy Flynn on the odd occasions he'd visited, because she knew he could be trusted; knew, somehow, that he was perhaps the only person in

Roper's End who would believe her. She couldn't think of any other bod in this village – male or female – who would either take her seriously or would be capable of keeping their mouths shut if they had taken her seriously. So, she'd decided, after getting to know him better, that it would be safe to open up to this likeable young man and to regale him with the rackety life she'd and all her friends had led all those years ago. She'd let everybody else in this small-minded apology of a village think what the hell they liked about her.

Jeremy had revelled in those stories, and laughed out loud at the thought of this small shrivelled old lady having, in her youth, led this life of debauchery; a life that might well be considered shocking even today, let alone during the nineteen forties.

He'd guessed, early on in their acquaintance that there had been much more to this small ancient body than met the unpractised eye. Glenys, he discovered, was quietly possessed of a brain far sharper than many of the so-called intelligentsia in Roper's End; he'd come to see that in the wicked sparkle of her bright blue eyes, and had egged her on into delving further, until they'd both ended up squealing with laughter. He didn't pry about her work because he knew that that was something she could never reveal; he'd simply let her take her time to tell him things she *could* talk about.

Jeremy had first encountered Glenys when she'd helped him up after he'd fallen off his bicycle on the Common. He'd been trying out the bike for the very first time after it had been given to him by his parents on his twelfth birthday. His father had offered to accompany him on its maiden run, but he'd thought himself grown-up enough to ride it on his own – then, having fallen off it, he'd felt sick at the thought of going home and admitting to his father that he'd overturned the bike on its very first outing, imagining a wigging and all the 'stupid boy' swipes he'd have to face. He'd badly grazed his knee, which his father would state was his own fault. So there wouldn't be much sympathy there. And a tear jerked from his eye at the pain from the torn skin, which he could see was bleeding quite badly. The only thing for which he was thankful was that none of his mates were around to witness the crash – or the tear . . .

Glenys, taking her puppy for his daily run, spotted him and ran to his aid. She brought out a clean handkerchief to stop the bleeding, then took him home with her and patched him up. Together they'd scoured her shed for a suitable shade of red paint, then had painstakingly painted out the scratch on the bicycle, an activity which she knew would serve to take his mind off his sore knee. All the while, she talked to him in her gruff no-nonsense voice – the voice that had always put people off from holding a prolonged conversation with her – about all the naughty things she'd done as a child and had hidden from her parents. Then she looked up at him and grinned, her eyes glinting with merriment – and he instantly knew he had a friend upon whom he could rely; someone who wouldn't blab to his parents.

That day she'd made him laugh and they'd bonded, so he'd called on her to thank her for her kindness then, afterwards, visited Holgarth on a fairly regular basis, revealing things he wouldn't have dared tell his parents.

Glenys had faithfully followed his rise from boyhood to manhood and rejoiced in his every success – at the glowing school reports and at his prowess on the sports field, through to his gaining a place at university and then on to medical school – and she'd shared Janet's and Peter's joy, feeling as proud of him as they during the ceremony of his doctorate.

Jeremy loved Glenys's compact little house and, each time he came home from his Manchester practice, made sure to visit her, always with a gift. She was still, even in her ninety-second year, bright and witty – and very down to earth; which was why he preferred her company to the snobs on Kings Road, whose children were turning out, for the most part, to be as bad as their parents. Jeremy's only mate in the village was James Frobisher, who he'd always join, along with Alfie Wendover, for a pint in The Goose. He was okay was James; always skint, on account of his parsimonious father, but unfailingly good company.

Much later, Glenys, after feeling she'd known Jeremy long enough, and aware that he was now a doctor of medicine, felt strong enough to tell him about the decision she'd made, when in her early twenties, to abort her baby, and he'd held her hand and watched a tear fall as she relived the day she'd emerged from the clinic childless. There having been no stress counsellors in those days she, like many thousands of others, had had to carry the burden of regret alone. He felt that she still carried that burden of loss, and held her frail little body as she'd wept out her story.

Because of the spareness of her small body, Jeremy had often suspected that, like many of his patients, Glenys wasn't feeding herself particularly well, so, on the Sunday following the party, he trudged up the lane with several cartons and packets of left-overs, even though the thought had occurred to him that Sprout might be the greater beneficiary of this gift. He was pleased, however, to see that, though frail, she was looking well. She was thrilled to see him; on the biscuit, as ever, and eyes shining with curiosity.

'What's all this nonsense about people on Kings Road selling up, then?' she asked brusquely as he carefully laid out all his offerings.

'Ah, well . . .' he hedged carefully, aware of venturing into something which was still a rather touchy subject at home: his own parents' discussions of their intentions to move. 'I think it's quite sad . . .' he said.

'I think *mysterious* would be a better word,' she frowned.

'Yes, well . . .'

'Strange, though, don't you think? What do you make of it, young Jeremy?'

'Yes. Strange, as you say . . .' Jeremy said, his concentration on the goodies box hiding his discomfort as he carefully laid it onto various plates.

He was afraid this subject might come up; aware also that he would have to bat it away before he was cajoled into revealing something that he felt shouldn't be aired, but then became slightly uncomfortable at the suspicion that he'd eventually be goaded into spilling the beans: she had her methods . . .

He wasn't wrong.

'But what do you think prompted it?' Glenys insisted.

'I . . . really can't say,' he said, offering a smile that said, '*Can we drop this?*'

'Why – is it a state secret?'

'No . . . but . . . I don't think I should be talking about it,' he said.

'What on earth to you mean? Come on, Jeremy – what do you know? You can tell me, can't you?' she squealed. 'You know you can trust *me* not to blab! So what's the dope? Is it juicy?'

He sighed. The incident at the garden party still stung him each time he had that flashback of his father's discomfort and the subsequent retreat of all the guests, and he hadn't wanted to talk to anyone about all the complications involved. But . . . Glenys wasn't anyone, was she and . . . yes, he decided, he'd have to tell her, wouldn't he? Besides, her gander was up now, and she wouldn't be satisfied until she'd heard it all. She herself held a great many secrets herself in that tiny head of hers, he knew, so she she was not likely to divulge the low-down of this particular matter to all and sundry, was she?

Seeing him hesitate, she said lightly, '"'There's both meat and music here,' quoth the dog as he ate the piper's bag"!'

He laughed at that, then sighed, 'It's Dad . . .'

She took a sandwich from the plate he proffered, flicked out a linen napkin, then started to munch.

'Ooh, smoked salmon – haven't had this for years! What about Dad?' she said, looking up at him, lips coated with crumbs.

'We held a retirement party for him yesterday and, in the middle of it, he was visited by an individual from the past.'

'And . . . ?'

Glenys waited, narrowing her eyes a tad, then having eaten the sandwich, chomped her way through a delicate little crab and cucumber crescent, afterwards picking up a chicken and asparagus roll, before looking up for an answer. As she ate, she kept her eyes on him, watching him covertly as he struggled with something which had obviously had a serious effect upon him. She munched slowly until he was ready, guessing at the difficulty he was having at keeping his emotions in check. Interruption would be foolhardy she knew, so she waited . . . She'd got to the sausage rolls before he spoke.

Jeremy then told her about the man who had ruined his father's birthday party and revealed to her what had happened all those years ago – that the man's baby son had died and that he'd blamed his father for the baby's death – and she bit into a second sausage roll, listening patiently.

'And your father was cleared of this supposed crime, you say?' she murmured, dabbing her mouth with the napkin.

'Yes. Totally exonerated. But the man wouldn't accept the verdict; he was convinced that it was all a whitewash and adamant that Dad was guilty of killing his baby. The outcome of the inquiry was cut and dried; there was no argument to suggest foul play the man was accusing Dad of. The baby had been born with a deformity so severe that he would never have lived. The facts were all there. He should have accepted that. I don't know how people can be so blinkered,' he finished.

Glenys placed the half-eaten sausage roll on her plate and sighed. Then she turned and looked at him, and he saw the change in her face as she began to speak, and as she twisted two diamond rings on her fingers, something he'd noticed she did whenever she spoke of the past.

'There was a woman I worked with at Bletchley. Lucy Barrington. Her husband was a fighter-pilot, and he was shot down in a dog-fight – like two of the men I knew well . . .' she said softly, her eyes moist with remembrance at the death of the two men she'd loved. 'We'd all lost somebody but, in those days, you just had to get on with it. But Lucy wouldn't accept her husband's death and, every evening, she'd stubbornly stand on the hillside overlooking the airstrip, watching for his plane to land, convinced that he would come back; convinced that they'd got it wrong; that he couldn't possibly be dead.'

She stopped and sighed again at the remembrance before resuming, recalling how she herself had felt at the news of each of her fiances' deaths.

'Every evening, we walked up the hill and talked her down,' she went on. 'It went on for months. We tried to reason with her – tried to tell her that he was never coming back – but nothing worked. The poor girl eventually committed suicide. She simply couldn't face the fact that her husband could be dead – refused to accept it. Then, when the truth finally hit her, she couldn't cope.'

Jeremy watched her struggle and sighed, then said quietly, 'Poor woman.'

'Yes – poor woman. There were a great many of us who lost whole

families and loved ones in that war – and there's only so much the
brain can take. The brain is a delicate organ – unfathomable,' she
said with a frown. 'We're all wired differently you know, Jeremy.
It might well be that this man's son was the long-awaited child.
Maybe the rest of his family comprised girls, and he'd had hopes
of a son taking over his business, or playing for England at Lords.
Who knows what goes on in the minds of others . . . ?'

'Yes,' Jeremy said with a sigh. 'Who knows?'

Recovering from her recollections, Glenys bit again into the
sausage roll and chewed slowly, sneaking a look his reaction.

'But that man,' Jeremy said, 'came yesterday purely to tell Dad
that he was aware of where he lived. A veiled threat, you might say.
He's still out for revenge.'

'Ah – *revenge!*' she said with a half-smile. 'Yes. "Revenge triumphs
over death; love slights it; honour aspireth to it; grief flieth to it."
Bacon.'

Jeremy blinked; it was a sausage roll she was just finishing. He
didn't think he'd brought anything containing bacon. Then it hit him.

'So, anyway . . .' he said sadly, 'to keep us all safe from whatever this
man was threatening, Mum and Dad decided it was time to move.'

'Where to?' she asked.

'I don't know,' Jeremy said, shaking his head.

'Because, wherever they go, this man will find them. If he's
determined enough, he'll track them down – and he will find them.
They can't run away from this, you know. They have to sit it out.'

Jeremy closed his eyes at this.

'Do your parents think the bomb which was delivered to Simon
Garraway was meant for your father?' she asked.

'I don't know what they think,' Jeremy said. 'But I suppose it
could have been, couldn't it?'

'Unlikely!' Glenys said briskly, carefully wiping her fingers on her napkin then reaching for the strawberry tart. 'He'd be far more likely to have come to put the frighteners on. I shouldn't imagine it's any more than that. Some people feel they have to do that . . . Tell them not to leave, Jeremy.'

'I'll do my best,' he said, watching with amusement at the line of cream on her top lip. 'Not that they're likely to take any notice of me. But you sound so sure. How can you be so sure he's not out to get us?'

'I've had dealings with a great many people in my time,' she said enigmatically. 'And, in my experience, most of this revenge business is bluster – probably to save face. I would say that it's fairly obvious that he feels it his duty to visit your house to threaten your father, just for effect – just for the satisfaction of seeing the fear in his eyes.'

'You think that's all it is?'

'I'm sure of it,' she said. 'In fact I would bet my house on it.'

'My parents, you know . . .' he began with a frown that, to Glenys, took him straight back to that twelve-year-old boy with the grazed knee, and she suddenly had an urge to wrap her arms around him. 'They've been shaken badly by this . . . this intrusion. They're good people. Why should this have happened to them? Dad's worked all his life and done a damned good job. And now that he's retired for a bit of peace – this! He's a good man.'

'Mm. It's not the meek who inherit the earth, you know,' she said softly. 'It's all those bastards who strut about thinking they *own* the sodding earth.'

'So, what happens to the meek then?' Jeremy asked.

'Oh, they get kicked in the teeth!' she said.

She watched as he suddenly sat back and shrieked with laughter, then smiled the same smile she'd produced that day he'd fallen off his bike. When she'd opened the door to him, he'd been twitchy and had appeared as worried as that twelve-year-old boy had been all those years ago, and her heart went out to him, just as it had then.

'You know, Jeremy, after the court case, the police will be aware of this man,' she said softly, touching his arm. 'They'll have had him in their sights for all that time, you can be sure. Tell your father to contact them to keep an eye out. But tell them *not to move*. That would be so sad. And it would undoubtedly give great satisfaction to this man to know that he'd frightened your parents enough to decamp because, if they move, he would feel it his duty to track them down once more, ad infinitum, ensuring they'd never feel safe. Whereas, if they stay, he's a spent force. Trust me.'

Jeremy left Glenys Pugh's house lighter in spirit than when he'd arrived. She'd seemed so certain of everything, which had set his mind at rest. Was that old age talking, or did she know something no one else knew? He'd certainly take her advice and do his best to advise his parents to stay in Roper's End, a village he knew they loved. Whether they listened to him was another matter.

Glenys walked with him to the door and smiled.

'Thank you so much for all those barbecued sausages, young Jeremy,' she called after him before he reached the gate. 'Sprout and I will really enjoy our supper tonight. I might even open a bottle of something to go with them!'

# Chapter Twenty-Eight

The two people Brian Frobisher noticed first as he walked into The Goose's Head were his son James and Alfie Wendover sitting side by side over a pint of ale. Brian caught his breath as he immediately recognised the waiter at the Old Dog and Bush. That face – of course! How could he not have spotted that spike of red hair atop the terrier snout? But then, he'd had his mind on other things, hadn't he . . .

As he hovered on the threshold, wondering whether to do a quick about turn, several thoughts crashed though his head simultaneously: (1) how blind he'd been, for two whole years, not to have clocked that little toe-rag behind the black silk waistcoat . . . (2) could said little toe-rag have blabbed to James about his monthly trysts with Julia? . . . (3) if he *had* blabbed, was James now aware of his liaisons with Julia Kilpatrick? . . . (4) and if James *was* aware, what would he be likely to do with that information? . . . (5) would it be possible to discover if he knew and to bribe him not to tell his mother? . . . (6) no, it would not be possible to bribe James not to tell his mother . . . (7) should he get out of The Goose now before they saw him . . .. ?

Julia and he had been careless, hadn't they? Alfie Wendover aside, frequenting the same hotel for their two year affair had been a mistake; they were bound to have been seen at some point by some nosey bint – he saw that now. He remembered his embarrassment, about a year ago, as Philip Forrester, one

of his mature students, had walked into the restaurant with
an airy greeting, and he'd been so taken aback that, in order to
regain his composure, had introduced Julia as his sister. He also
recalled the lust in the man's eyes as he gave her the once-over
then, to compound matters, Forrester had sidled up to him the
next day, asking for her telephone number. He should have done
something about it then. Well, he'd have to do something about
it now, wouldn't he? They'd thought they were safe, hadn't they?
How could they ever have thought that Barnscote, being a mere
twenty-odd miles from the village, was safe?

The biggest threat, he realised, trying to make himself less
obvious by sliding across to the bar, was Valerie. If James got
wind of this and informed his mother, she'd be sure to make a
meal of it. And the next thing would be Commander Theodore
Kilpatrick thundering round to knock six bells out of him. And
Theo Kilpatrick, though a good bit older than he, was a damned
sight larger and could do a lot of damage if he put his mind to it.

With this predicament rattling his brain, and glancing carefully
around the room, he moved stealthily over to order a drink,
imagining he'd managed to avoid the eyes of the youths, who
were deep in conversation over their beers. He positioned himself
behind a large artificial pot plant on the far side of the bar, then
ordered a lager, keeping his eyes on the pair through the plastic
fronds. When the new licensee of The Goose's Head had introduced
all this tacky artificial foliage into the bar area in his attempt to
gentrify the place – presumably so that he'd never have the trouble
of watering live plants – Brian, along with the rest of the locals,
had laughed out loud, sneering at the lowering of standards. But
keeping his head low behind the greenery, albeit plastic, Brian now
silently thanked the new owner of The Goose for his good sense.

Looking out onto the two drinkers enjoying their pints, he

narrowed his eyes at Alfie Wendover. If he had recognised him, he and Julia would have immediately walked out of The Old Dog and Bush; though, even then, he acknowledged glumly, it would have been too late. But he'd been too occupied with lust, hadn't he, to notice anything but Julia? How could he have foreseen that rat-bag, of all people – if Alfie Wendover could actually be thought of as a *people* – waiting at their table? The last time he'd seen the little tyke, he hadn't been able to get away fast enough from the smell. Even now, as he watched him through the plastic and out of his waiter's uniform, he stuck out like a carbuncle on the toe of a skunk, and probably still smelled as bad.

As he sat on, his lager steadily warming, Brian kept a wary eye on the two young men at the other side of the pub, curling his lip at the pair in their T-shirts, flaunting all their tattoos and metal appendages. He could barely hide his contempt; and sneered at his son for having kept in touch with the pock-marked little pimple after all these years. So . . . now working as a waiter, was he? He supposed that that was inevitable, there being no chance of an uneducated lout such as Alfie Wendover ever gracing the halls of a university. He wondered if the management of the Old Dog and Bush any idea of the uncivilised ghetto from which the boy had emerged: that pig pen of a council estate, where one wouldn't dare park one's car for fear of the removal of its tyres? Did they realise that the dirty little waif, to whom they'd given carte blanche to swan in and out of their respectable hotel, waiting on their respectable clients, had come from the Barnspole Council Estate – *Land of the Untouchables*, as he'd once heard it called? He hoped their training manual had included instructions on how to take a bath.

James should, by rights, be knocking around with like-minded friends from university – making friends from *good homes,* networking *people of influence* – instead of slumming it with a scrag end off the Barnspole Estate.

He was ashamed of him – ashamed to own him.

After the second lager, he told himself that there was an outside chance that Alfie hadn't recognised him in the Old Dog and Bush after all; that maybe he should relax and think positively. After all, Alfie would have forgotten him after all those years, wouldn't he? He'd had very little to do with him, deliberately avoiding the little horror. Alfie, having been Valerie's pet charity, he'd distanced himself; had no wish to join all that philanthropic clap-trap about 'giving the boy a chance'. A chance? What chance would anybody from the Barnspole Estate have, the whole community resembling savages one avoided like the Black Death?

* * *

At some point in Alfie's childhood, Valerie Frobisher, who had been a governor at his school, had become aware of his alcoholic mother's neglect of the boy, and seen it her duty to do her best to lift him out of the squalor of his miserable home life, even if only for a few hours in the day, Alfie's mother ever glad to see the back of him so that she could get back to the gin bottle. Inviting him into her home, she knew that James could be trusted not to ridicule the boy. She hadn't, however, accounted for a husband who had sneered openly at Alfie's appearance, something which had inevitably caused friction between them.

Alfie had liked nothing better than to spend time at Farnby Oaks, comparing this large airy house with its vast half-acre of lawn to his own mean little end of terrace in Marchstone, his small patch of yard ending at the brick wall of the bicycle factory. James gradually became his best buddy, and Mrs Frobisher was always on hand to dole out a square meal and home-made lemonade. Pity about Mr Frobisher, but he reckoned that two out of three wasn't bad . . .

To Alfie, Farnby Oaks seemed like heaven. Unlike his own house, it was clean, free of alcohol, and always smelled of fresh food. He'd arrive at the Frobishers' with shoes which flapped as he walked, and dressed – or half-dressed – in clothes so tight, one could see beneath the flimsy T-shirts the outline of his ribs in his thin little body. As James grew larger, she suggested that Alfie become the recipient of his cast-offs. She thought he might feel insulted, but Alfie was thrilled at the idea, because he could now hold up his head among all those school mates who'd laughed at his ragged appearance.

Alfie never forgot Mrs Frobisher's kindness, but had made sure to avoid contact with her husband. Which he had succeeded in doing until his appearance at the Old Dog and Bush.

* * *

As Brian finished his third pint, he looked blearily over at the two youths chatting and joking with each other. They hadn't so much as looked in his direction, so he was pretty sure he hadn't been seen. His head, now nicely fuzzed, owing to the comfort of the lager, he reasoned that nothing could actually have been said because, if James had known about his affair with Julia, he would have told his mother and, as Valerie's attitude hadn't in any way changed towards him, he was pretty confident that he was safe. If James *had* known, all hell would have broken loose by now, wouldn't it? And Theo Kilpatrick would have come down on him like the proverbial. But Theo Kilpatrick had no idea, had he . . . ? So, Alfie must have kept quiet and – ha – he'd

got away with it, hadn't he? Armed with fresh optimism, he
ordered another pint.

However, as the intake of alcohol swilled around his head, his
mind took a turn towards a more realistic zone. He and Julia had
to change the venue for their trysts. First thing tomorrow, he'd
ring The Old Dog and Bush and cancel next month's reservation
then, afterwards, he'd be more vigilant. He'd have to do something,
because he couldn't lose Julia – *God, he couldn't lose her* – even
though she was bleeding him dry.

The two boys, he noticed as he prepared to leave, still had
their heads together, laughing at each others' jokes. He stood,
wobbled slightly then, for safety's sake, decided to leave the pub
by the back entrance.

'Was that your Dad?' Alfie said.

'Yeah,' James grinned, taking another sip of his ale.

\* \* \*

Brian walked unsteadily back to his house, knowing that his wife
would already be in dressing gown and slippers, ready for bed,
though he wouldn't be going to bed at ten thirty because he'd have
to give his bladder time to disgorge four pints of liquid. Managing
to stay upright, he steadied himself sufficiently to be guided by
the Sandersons' hedge but, as he reached the Garraways, there was
nothing to hold on to, and he cursed Marjorie Garraway for being
selfish enough to have rendered the garden open-plan. He'd have
to stagger the distance to Molton-Fry's stunted conifers.

However, he'd barely left the Molton-Fry property, when both
his face and the confidence he'd previously felt at getting out of
The Goose unnoticed, suddenly dropped like a stone. Striding
purposely towards him on the opposite side of the road was Theo

Kilpatrick and, as he came closer, the alcohol in Brian's stomach threatened to evacuate. He thought desperately of ways to avoid the man, but with four pints of lager fudging his brain, found it difficult to figure a way out. His spine turning to jelly, he managed to dredge up a weak nod in Kilpatrick's direction and hoped he might be allowed to sidle past him. But a mere nod was insufficient, and he watched, panic turning to fear, as Kilpatrick crossed the road and made a beeline for him.

'Ah, Brian!' Kilpatrick yelled brusquely, striding across road, his mouth an ominous thin line. 'A word!'

'Oh?' Brian stammered at the ex-Naval commander, as the man suddenly towered over him.

*'What's all this nonsense then?'* Kilpatrick said abruptly.

'Nonsense?'

'All these rumours flying around!'

'I . . . I . . . really don't know what you mean . . .'

He knew, didn't he? How could he have known? Julia assured him that Thicko Theo hadn't a clue about their affair. But he must somehow have got wind of it – *must have.* Village gossips at work! How stupid to have imagined that they'd get away with it for so long. Kilpatrick was bound to find out about his wife's affair with him– and now . . . now . . . He held his breath and stared goggle-eyed at the man, a trickle of sweat coursing down his back. How would he explain his way out of this? What could he do? He could try pleading ignorance; laugh as convincingly as possible with four pints sloshing around his innards, then deny any passing thoughts of finding Julia the least bit attractive, let alone conducting an affair with her. Ha, ha – what on earth would give you that idea? But would he be believed? And how the hell would he come out of this unscathed – alive even? Just looking at the bulk now crowding his space caused his face to twitch and his knees threaten to buckle as he braced himself in anticipation of the pounding he was certain would arrive at any time now. He stepped back, attempting to distance himself, stiffening his arms to protect himself against the anticipated blows.

Kilpatrick, glaring at him in the fast-dwindling light, appeared to be getting more worked up as the seconds ticked by. Brian took another step back as Kilpatrick moved in closer, then felt the scrape of a conifer as his spine told him there was nothing more to step back into. This was the end of the line, he knew, and his breathing became audible in the autumn air. He wondered fleetingly what sort of figure he would present to Valerie when he arrived home with split lips, blacked eyes and cracked ribs – if, indeed, he managed to get home at all and was not left lying in a heap in the gutter.

Kilpatrick stepped ever nearer.

'All these bloody houses suddenly up for sale!' he growled. 'What's all that about? Eh?'

Brian, suddenly and amazingly finding himself in the clear, stared open-mouthed at the man, unable to speak, his vocal cords having been immobilised owing to the deprivation of saliva. Kilpatrick didn't know. *Oh, thank you God! – he didn't know! Of course* he didn't know. He wouldn't have had a clue about him relieving his sexual needs with the man's wife in that small bedroom in the Old Dog and Bush every few weeks, would he? This was why he was labelled Thicko Theo by all those who knew him.

*He didn't know!* Breath in . . . breath out . . . and . . . relax.

At last, finding himself able to breath normally again, he shook his head slowly from side to side to give the impression of ignorance, and in order to relieve it of thoughts of potential damage, grateful to have kept the liquor in his stomach and surreptitiously wiping his sweaty palms on the legs of his trousers.

'Oh . . . Oh . . . You mean the Flynns? Well . . .' Brian said, clearing his throat in an attempt to disguise the fear that had taken control of his speech. 'You were at the party too, weren't you? Who knows what that row was about?'

'Who indeed!' Kilpatrick sighed darkly. 'And who knows who that stranger was, gate-crashing the party, then striding off again with that satisfied smirk on his face? Have you figured it out yet?'

'Well, no. Have you?'

'Not yet,' Kilpatrick said importantly. 'But, with my training, that shouldn't take a great deal of effort. But it seemed to have put the fear of God into everybody within spitting distance – and, the next thing, they're selling up!'

'Are they . . . ?'

'Yes. And even Julia is bellyaching about moving . . .' Kilpatrick said.

*Julia? J* . . . Is she?' Brian squeaked, feeling the breath sucked out of him once more; was Julia really planning to move away? 'But – surely . . .'

'Yes, I know!' Kilpatrick said with a sudden bark of laughter. 'Collywobbles. Women, eh! Same with the Ramsden woman. Everybody wanting to move out of Roper's End all of a sudden! Have to wait and see how things develop, though, won't we, eh?' he went on, suddenly narrowing his eyes at Brian.

'Develop? What . . . do you mean . . . *develop* . . . ?'

Brian's stomach churned once more at what might be viewed as a veiled threat. Perhaps, after all, Theo wasn't as thick as he looked . . .

'Well. Been mulling it over with Charlie Ramsden. Have to wait to see if house prices fall in the immediate future, then decide if it's better to stick it out for them to rise again after everybody's forgotten about the bomb. Have to wait it out, won't we?'

'Oh. Yes. See what you mean. See how things . . . ha . . . *develop* . . .'

Yes. Theo was definitely as thick as he looked.

'Can't rush into these things, can we?'

'No. No, of course we can't,' Brian said, finally managing to peal his back off the conifer. 'But I sincerely hope you two won't move away, you know,' he added weakly. 'Val's very fond of Julia. Well, we're both very fond of . . . of you both.'

Kilpatrick seemed to give him another quizzical look, then sighed.

'Don't worry – I'll talk her out of it, silly goose! Women, eh?' he repeated with a laugh, sticking out an elbow at Brian's arm, sharing this private joke between them. 'Can you make them out? '

'Never been able to myself,' Brian breathed huskily, essaying a small laugh of his own. 'Biggest mystery in life!'

'Too true! Too true!' Theo said before slapping Brian manfully on the shoulder and striding off towards The Goose for a pint before closing time.

Brian, winded by the encounter, stood for a while, going over it, doing his best to breath once more and thanking heaven and all the stars for this reprieve. This took time. It took time, too, for his stomach to settle and his bladder to advise him that now might be a good time to seek out a lavatory.

# Chapter Twenty-Nine

The mail lay on the mat. Marjorie, on her way from the kitchen to the hospital room with two mugs of tea in her hands, hadn't heard the postman walking up the path. She frowned at it, then walked into Simon's room to hand him his tea, before returning to pick up the mail, scrutinising it for bills, or for anything looking suspicious.

The first was the electricity bill, so that was safe, or so she thought until she opened it and saw size of the bill; how could they possibly have used all that electricity in one month? It was outrageous; she'd ring them later and give them an earful. The second letter she recognised as being from her sister, the handwriting unmistakable. The third, addressed to Simon, was franked by the bank. Ah, yes – that would be information about his salary entitlements – the one she'd been waiting for. They'd taken their time! She sat in the comfort of the living room before slitting open the envelope, her anticipation being information as to the length of time the bank was prepared to allow Simon full payment before half-payment kicked in. And perhaps they might have worked out all the bonuses he was entitled to. Surely, the bank would take into consideration Simon's dedication over all those years and extend the period of payment?

On opening up the letter, she discovered that it was not the one she'd been expecting; moreover, this had nothing do with his salary. It was just a curt note from the bank's head office, which

asked – demanded, in fact – that Simon attend its offices in order
to discuss, at his earliest convenience, a matter of grave importance.
   'How ridiculous!' she huffed. 'As if he could travel all the
way to London to attend a meeting about his salary! And *grave
importance*? What on earth did that mean? And are they stupid?
They must know how disabled Simon is and how impossible it
would be for him to get to London. How could they expect his
attendance at their office? And why did they have to see him face
to face when it was a simple matter of pension details? Why not
put all the relevant information in a letter?'
   Puffed up with indignation, she picked up the phone and rang
the number on the letter head, demanding to speak to the signatory.
   'May I ask who's calling?' a frosty voice asked.
   'Marjorie Garraway, wife of Simon,' she snapped back irritably.
   Without preamble, she was put on hold, and there was a ten
second wait before a plummy voice asked if he could be of assistance.
   'You most certainly can!' she barked. 'I received a letter today,
asking for my husband to attend your offices. Are you the person
who signed the letter?'
   'Yes, I am,' the voice said.
   'May I ask what this is about?'
   'I'm afraid I cannot discuss this with you over the telephone, Mrs
Garraway,' the man said smoothly, 'as this is highly confidential.'
   'Highly confidential?' Marjorie echoed. 'Nothing is confidential
between my husband and I – and you will have to go through me,
young man, if you want to get anywhere. Anything to do with
his pension is my affair!'
   'Mrs Garraway, have you no idea what this is about?' the man
asked.
   'It's about his *pension,* isn't it?' she snapped. 'What else could
it be about?'

'Look – I'm sorry, Mrs Garraway,' the man said, 'but, if you know nothing of this matter, I'm afraid I am not the person to enlighten you.'

'*What?* What are you talking about? *"This matter"?* What are you talking about?'

'This is something we have to speak to Simon in person about. It is not something that can be discussed over the telephone.'

'What? Are you telling me that you're unable to divulge details to me – his wife! – on the simple matter of his salary payments? You're a bank, not MI5! And you must know that Simon can't possibly travel to London!' she said, rancour shooting out of her mouth; *she would tell them; they had Marjorie Garraway to deal with here.* 'Simon is severely disabled, and is unable to travel!' she yelled.

'Ah,' the man said. 'Yes . . . I'm sorry about that. Bit of a glitch on our part. The letter, I have to admit, could have been worded a little differently . . .'

'And with a little more compassion . . . ! ' Marjorie interrupted.

'Yes, I agree, Mrs Garraway. And I apologise profusely for our lack of tact. So . . . taking into consideration Simon's disability, we'll have to try another way of meeting him, won't we? But it is imperative that we speak to him.'

'But, if this is about his salary, you can just as easily speak to me,' she said, her voice rising further.

'No, Mrs Garraway, this is not about Simon's salary,' he said, 'and is something which, I'm sorry to say, I cannot discuss with you.'

'But why would you need to speak to him if not about his salary?' she asked.

She could feel his discomfort even from that distance.

'The matter, as I mentioned earlier, is highly confidential . . .' the man said.

'But . . .'

'And, if Simon can't come to us, we shall have to come to him.'

'But what is it about?' she squealed indignantly. 'I have a right to know!'

She heard the heavy sigh before the slight pause.

'Please, Mrs Garraway,' he said. 'Leave this with us, and we'll be in touch. I'm afraid I cannot discuss this further.'

As she ended the call, she frowned, then flopped into a chair to think about this odd conversation. What was happening? Why was everything so confidential? If they were about to tell him they were not paying up after all, why were they insisting on seeing him in person? And, if that's what they were about, they hadn't reckoned on her! She'd get their lawyer and fight this. Simon was entitled to at least six months' salary on full pay; she knew his rights. They wouldn't get away with this . . .

The call, two days' later, was from head office, informing her that their investigators would be arriving the following day at eleven-thirty. There were no ifs or buts; they would be there.

Investigators? What investigators? Marjorie couldn't get her head round this. What was there to investigate? It was cut and dried; they were bound by law to pay a full salary for six months – were they not aware of that? On high dudgeon, she stormed into Simon's room to discuss the matter with him, telling him that they would fight tooth and nail for his salary, and she would be telling those shysters from bank a thing or two when arrived and send them away with a flea in their ears. If they thought they were getting away with this, they were very much mistaken because *they'd have Marjorie Garraway to deal with!*

Staying silent throughout this diatribe, Simon kept up the pretence with a poker face. He'd heard the telephone conversations with the bank – did she think he was totally deaf? And he knew perfectly well what to expect from these visitors when they arrived; he was prepared for them, but he wasn't letting on to her. Let her remain in ignorance – at least until tomorrow . . .

He clamped his jaws at what he would have to face, but couldn't help a wry smile at Marjorie's reaction when she discovered the truth. She would never forgive him for this – but then, he wasn't expecting forgiveness – didn't need forgiveness. He was past caring about his wife's feelings. He was thinking bitterly about the lost opportunity to leg it to Italy with his lover. All that planning and preparation; the house; the yacht – and their lives . . . just waiting for them in Ravenna – waiting to be lived in . . . to be loved in . . .

And he would have got away with it – had been hair's breadth from getting away with it. Two months ago, and unbeknown to his wife, he'd given notice to the bank and was just four weeks away from happiness. Why couldn't he have survived for four more weeks, he'd asked himself over and over? If he'd been given the chance to work out his notice, and hadn't been rendered useless by that bloody bomb, he'd have had time to manipulate the figures sufficiently for them not to suspect his duplicity until Julia and he were swimming in the Adriatic. Just four short weeks and they would have made it . . .

He had no conscience. They'd owed him. And it had been worth the risk. All he'd ever wanted was to please his darling Julia. He loved her and had wanted to spend what was left of his life with her. Now in his sixties, and having suffered forty years of banking, then coming home to golfing stories and village tittle-tattle, he reckoned he deserved a slice of happiness this late in life. Now there was nothing. No escape – no Julia – nothing . . .

The money had been put to good use. Between them, they'd renovated the run-down farmhouse in Ravenna, and he'd bought the yacht. The rest of the cash he'd stuffed into the Italian bank must have built up to a tidy sum, and earned a good deal of interest by now. He'd had to cater for their future; couldn't allow for the well to dry up. They'd never have caught him. It would have taken years for the bank to track him down and get him back to Britain to face the music, by which time, he and Julia would have had the time of their lives.

Just four short weeks . . .

* * *

The following morning Marjorie, ready to do battle, opened the door to two dark-suited individuals, flashing their identity badges and asking to speak to her husband – in private.

'You will do no such thing!' she stormed. 'This matter concerns us both and I insist on being with him at all times.'

Being relieved of their coats, one of the men said, 'And what matter do you think this is, Mrs Garraway?'

'His salary and pension, of course,' she said. 'If you think for one single minute that you can get away with taking that away from him . . .'

'This has nothing to do with either Simon's salary or his pension,' the other man said, smiling gently. 'This is a far more serious matter. And we must speak to him alone before we speak to you.'

'And *then* perhaps we'll get to the bottom of this nonsense!' she fumed.

She strutted angrily to the hospital room and announced their arrival, then allowed herself to be shut out. Walking into the sitting room, she flopped into a chair and picked up the paper to read the day's headlines, keeping half an eye on the dividing door, beyond which only muffled voices could be heard. The carer was in the kitchen and could be heard preparing a meal, and Marjorie wondered if it might be best to get her out of the way.

The men emerged half an hour later and asked her to come into the room.

'Connie,' she called out to the carer, 'I'm right out of stamps, dear. Would you mind popping down to the Post Office?'

After hearing the front door close, she walked into the room and looked from her husband to the two men, then back again.

'I think you will need to sit down, Mrs Garraway,' the taller one said, pulling out a chair.

'Why? What's going on?' she frowned, then looked across at her husband.

'I've been a bit naughty, Marjorie,' Simon said, though he didn't seem too unhappy about it.

Drawing in her breath and feeling herself suddenly go cold, she said, 'What have you done?'

Was he telling her that he'd gambled it all away? All his pension? That there was nothing left?

After what seemed an eternity, the taller of the men said, 'Your husband owes the bank rather a lot of money, I'm afraid.'

'Owes *you*?' she said indignantly, ignoring the fear creeping into her heart. 'What are you talking about? I think you'll find that the bank owes *him* a lot of money! His bonus for a start!'

The man pursed his lips and said, 'Mrs Garraway, I'm sorry to be the one to break this to you, but it has just come to light that your husband has been embezzling the bank – has been doing so for some time.'

Marjorie opened her mouth, then closed it. She swallowed and felt an icy shiver pass through her. She looked at Simon, who looked utterly unperturbed; in fact, looked rather pleased with himself.

Still staring at her husband, she whispered, 'How much?'

'Four and a half million,' the man said, then dropped his head, embarrassed at having to watch the change in her, as the chins were set a-quiver with shock.

Marjorie, apart from the oscillating chins, looked to be turned to rock, and the ice she'd felt earlier suddenly turned into a full-blown glacier, her breath breaking out in short sharp bursts, and she felt numb as she sat staring at her husband.

'*Four . . . and a . . .half . . . ?*'

She needed air and, whey-faced, she half stood before realising she could no longer move. A gentle hand took her arm and guided her back to a sitting position, where she continued to stare at Simon in disbelief.

'*Four . . . and a . . . half . . . ?*' she whispered, almost to herself.

She felt weightless; felt that she was hearing all these words from afar. This was not real. *Someone tell her this wasn't real . . .* An orchestra was pounding away in her head, the timpani doing its best to blot out the rest of their words, and she wanted it to go on bashing away in order to burn out of her brain what it was not fully able to take in. Because what they were saying couldn't be right – four and half million pounds? This wasn't true – couldn't possibly be true. She closed her eyes, convinced that, when she opened them again, everything would be back to normal . . . It would be . . . it had to be . . .

'I can imagine how shocked you must be Mrs Garraway,' the man went on softly. 'Nevertheless, it is my duty, as a representative of the bank, to have to tell you that we have no alternative but to take possession of your house.'

She blinked. '*What?*' she whispered.

'Also the house in Italy . . .'

'*House in* . . . what the hell are you talking about? What house in Italy?'

'And the yacht . . .'

'*Yacht* . . . . *?*' she breathed feebly.

'And your bank accounts – here and in Rome.'

'But we don't have a bank account in Rome – or a house in Italy – or a . . . What in God's name are you talking about?' Marjorie screamed, suddenly finding her lungs, her anger, her humiliation at these men telling her what couldn't possibly be true. She stood over them, her whole body fired up for action. '*How dare you! How dare you* . . . come into this house and accuse . . . ?'

She stopped, a sudden sob tearing at her words, tears streaking her cheeks as their words became truth – a truth which had to be faced. She was drained by it – ashamed – embarrassed, a pulse of nausea now rising in her throat as she attempted to grasp the breadth of it; of losing everything . . . *everything* . . . How could this be happening?

And she flopped down again, staring at Simon's lopsided supercilious grin.

'*We . . . don't . . . have . . .*' she repeated in what came out as a whimper, then put her head in her hands and sobbed at the reality.

The man took her hand and said, 'I'm sorry . . .'

Marjorie looked up at him with glazed eyes and blinked, suddenly coming out her reverie. No, it wasn't a dream. And, yes, this was real.

'*Sorry?*' she screamed at him through her tears. '*You're sorry?*'

'We can't let this go, Mrs Garraway,' the man said, holding on to her hand. 'I know this is hard, but the bank has to be reimbursed.'

Her colour now completely drained, she looked up at him, as a child might look to its nanny for some form of guidance.

'But . . . if . . . if you take everything, where does that leave me?' she sobbed quietly.

'Do you have relatives to go to?' he asked.

'Relatives?' she said, blowing her nose. *'Relatives?* I can hardly go cap in hand to . . .'

The players of the orchestra had now packed up, leaving her brain to face up to what it knew it had to face. She again looked at her husband, sitting smugly in his wheelchair as though having just been told his horse had won the Grand National. He looked back at her, his features showing neither sorrow nor shame over this theft and, as she watched him, her mouth open and her heart threatening to implode, her hand itched to smash the smirk from his face.

'You . . . *you* . . .' she breathed, her mouth quivering, but was unable to go on.

Simon continued to flash his challenging, unblinking eye, his mouth mocking her. He watched implacably as she struggled to take it all in; fought to understand. Let her suffer, the eye said – let her know what it feels like to be stuck in this fucking wheelchair, reliant on strangers to wipe my arse. And . . . wait 'til she hears about Julia – ha – that'll be fun.

'Why?' she managed to whisper hoarsely. 'Why?'

*'Why?'* he laughed at her stricken face. 'Why not? Did you think I'd want to spend the rest of my life with you, you boring lump of lard? Why wouldn't I want to get as far away from you as possible?'

'Why, Simon . . . what have I done?'

'Done? Take a look in the mirror! Look at you – you're a fucking mess! Who, in their right mind, *wouldn't* want to get away from you, having suffered thirty years of your monotonous whining? Who would want to live with a fat soulless slob who could bore the barnacles off the QE2?' he sneered. 'Who wouldn't want to live in Italy with a beautiful woman . . . ?'

The men looked down at their shoes, their minds working as one.

'A few more weeks and I would have been out of this hell-hole. *But ha, bloody ha!* Look at me now! Stuck in this fucking house with you all day and every day. Ask yourself – what's my life worth now?'

The men shifted, looked at each other, then prepared to leave, clipping their briefcases closed and standing awkwardly.

'But all that money!' she cried. *'Four and a half million!* How could you do that?'

The eye stared her down; at her delirium; the shock ravaging her face. He loathed her: at the way she behaved; the way she laughed; the way she held her cutlery; at the cheap polyester skirts she wore that rode up whenever she bent over, showing her oversized backside in her oversized knickers.

'Because I could,' he said.

Marjorie stood, breathing heavily and looked at him, then at the men, as though in a trance, then said, 'How long? How long have we got? I mean, how long before you take the house?'

'The end of the month,' the man said, unable to meet her eyes.

'But then . . . we'll be homeless . . .'

'I'm so sorry,' he said, reaching for his coat, stiff with embarrassment.

Marjorie watched as they climbed into their car then closed the door on them. She stood, recovering from the bombshell. Then, somewhat recovered, she stormed into the room to face her husband.

*'You fucking bastard!'* she screamed. 'You . . . you lousy lying rat! How could you do this to me? What's going to happen to me now?'

'You?' he snarled. 'Why should I care about you? This marriage has always been about you, hasn't it! You and your fucking religion – *golf!* I'm sick of the sight of you! I don't give a flying fart about what'll happen to you – let's get that cleared out of the way. Get yourself back to fucking Grantham and get yourself a fucking job, that's my advice. Do a fucking day's work for once in your life!'

'I . . . I thought I knew you!' she cried, dropping down onto the chair.

'Have you ever tried?' he snarled. 'Have you ever tried to know me? All you've ever been interested in was my pay packet.'

'That's not true!'

'I've slogged my guts out for you,' he said. 'And you've never once asked how I've felt. All those years of tying myself in knots for that sodding bank – all those years of travelling the world – all those ghastly people – negotiating – putting myself in danger. And for you. And you've taken it all for granted, never once cared about what I was going through to keep you in sodding golfing irons!'

'You're despicable! And what was all that about Italy? And a yacht?' she screamed. 'Is that where you were planning to go? Italy?'

'You bet!' he smirked. 'One more month and we would have been out of here!'

'We?'

'Julia Kilpatrick and me!'

'*Julia Kilpatrick?* That whore?' she yelled. 'You planned to run off to Italy with Julia Kilpatrick?'

'Yeah,' he said quietly, almost to himself.

She opened her mouth to yell something back, but was suddenly cut short by the front door suddenly opening with a click, followed the carer, her eyebrows raised at Marjorie's stricken face as she dumped herself back down onto the chair, the tears once again streaming down her cheeks.

# Chapter Thirty

Freddie opened the door to find a woman standing before her.

'Hello,' the woman smiled. 'Mrs Wingrave? I'm Anthea, the area health visitor. Would you mind if I come in to talk to you for a few minutes?'

'If you like,' she replied.

Health visitor? She wasn't ill – Freddie was never ill. Why would a health visitor be calling on her, she wondered as she held open the door? And what would she wish to talk to her about? As she led the woman down the hall, she caught her short intake of breath as she took everything in: the peeling paint; the scuffed walls; the wonky bannister rail. And watched with amusement as the smile gradually left the woman's lips; watched as she wrinkled her nose prior to a sneeze, picking her way down the threadbare carpet and through into the unrelieved murk of the hell-hole Freddie called her sitting room.

'Do take a seat,' Freddie said in her sharp Germanic voice, which sounded to Anthea's ears like an ancient coffee-grinder on the blink.

Anthea looked nervously round for a chair that didn't resemble an exploded mattress, then perched on the edge of the least hairy of the three being offered.

'Tea?' Freddie asked.

'Er, no . . . thank you,' the woman said with a small shudder, then offered Freddie another smile which barely touched her eyes.

Freddie felt sorry for the woman in her cheap clothes, and could imagine the pittance health visitors might be earning for the thankless task of visiting old ladies who had no need of visits from nosy-parkers. However, as the woman seemed fairly untroubled by intelligence, the pity stopped there. The large bag, which Anthea had carried on her shoulder, was now placed on the floor beside her as she sat gingerly, gazing nervously round the room. Delving into the bag, she brought out a clipboard.

'What can I do for you?' Freddie asked brusquely, plonking herself onto the threadbare couch.

'Well . . .' Anthea began, offering another weak smile. 'It has come to our ears that you might not be coping too well on your own these days . . .'

Freddie snorted at that. What did she mean by '*our* ears'? Whose ears was she talking about? Was she perhaps suggesting that she was more than one individual with multiple ears?

'*What?*' Freddie said, staring the woman down. 'Not coping? I've been on my own for forty-odd years and have coped very well for all that time, thank you. So how have all your ears picked up that particular message?'

The health visitor pursed her lips then offered another wan smile in an attempt to keep her cool. At the many conferences she'd attended, the main point hammered home was: *keep your cool – old people can be bolshy.* This was true. She'd dealt with a great many bolshy old biddies in the course of what she'd termed as her career, but Freddie Wingrave, she was quickly realising, was someone to be reckoned with: this, for sure, was not your average bolshy old biddy. She'd also picked up that, even though happily living in a damp hovel overlaid with varying shades of mould – mould which could be seen on practically every surface, weakly yelling '*help me*', and in a sty a pig would turn up its snout at – the woman herself seemed sharp enough to cut through steel and as far as she could tell, was in rude health.

However, even though intimidated by Freddie Wingrave's brusque manner, she decided to ignore that sharpness and plough on, relying on automatic pilot for guidance.

'My department was recently contacted by someone concerned about you . . .' she began, 'so I thought I'd just pop along . . .'

'Concerned? Who's concerned? And why should they be concerned? What does anyone know about me?' Freddie asked, her brow furrowed.

'Well . . . it would seem . . .'

'Ha! *The Kilpatricks.* It's the Kilpatricks isn't it?' Freddie shot.

'I'm really not at liberty to say,' Anthea smiled diffidently.

'You don't *have* to say!' Freddie interrupted. 'I've had more than my fill of that pair.'

'Ah, So you don't get on with your neighbours?' Anthea said ultra-carefully, clicking her pen into life to record this on the clipboard.

'You could say that!'

'Do you mean you've had words?' the woman asked.

'Not exactly,' Freddie said, 'seeing as we never speak!'

'So . . . how do you communicate with your neighbours, would you say?'

'Well, as I've never mastered the art of semaphore and don't possess a Morse coding machine, we *don't* communicate.'

There was a short silence during which the woman hastily scribbled something down.

'It's just that your neighbours appeared to be worried for you, Mrs Wingrave,' Anthea said, looking up again.

'Oh yes? When did that pair ever worry about anybody but themselves? And why would they be worried about me? What is there to be worried about. They don't even know me. What have they told you?'

'Well . . . not a great deal,' Anthea lied softly, having been given the low-down by Social Services. 'It's just been suggested that you might fare better in a smaller, more manageable, home.. ?'

'Has it indeed? How *very* kind!'

'Well, you know, this is a very large house. I would imagine that it's rather difficult to maintain – especially as you're getting on in years.'

'*That,* my dear, is for me to worry about, don't you think?' Freddie snorted. 'I shall move when I'm ready to move. I will *not* be dictated to by a load of busy-bodies!'

'Look, Mrs Wingrave,' Anthea began, 'I'm sure that these people have your best interests at heart.'

'Ha! You really think so?' Freddie spluttered. 'You don't know these people. This is most definitely in *their* best interests. They'd do anything to get me out of here.'

'Why is that, do you think?' Anthea asked, the pen on alert.

'Because they've never liked me. Because they're snobs!' Freddie said.

There was more scribbling onto the clipboard, before Anthea looked up again.

'You know,' she said gently, 'residential homes are very popular with the elderly these days. And they're really pleasant places to live. You'd have plenty of company and, more importantly, they offer care at the touch of a button.'

'Really?' Freddie grunted, her hooded eyes warning the woman that she was on a sticky wicket here.

She was seeing this interview as the equivalence of a parental imperative to eat ones greens, and she was well past that stage.

She knew perfectly well what was good for her, thank you very much, and that didn't include plenty of company. She was getting thoroughly fed up with this woman, who was proving to be about as stimulating as decaffeinated coffee.

'So . . . just think about it, mm? Think about the future,' Anthea ventured with a smile. 'This is a very large house for one person. How many bedrooms? Five? Just think – you'd never again have to worry about the roof tiles, would you – or the upkeep of the garden . . . ?'

'But I *need* five bedrooms. I need room for my books, if it's any business of anyone but mine!' Freddie shot out.

She then slumped back into her chair and let out a heavy sigh, willing the woman to go away and leave her alone.

'Look – I know you mean well, Angela . . .' she said at last.

'*Anthea* . . .'

'Yes, sorry. But, well the truth is, Anthea, that Theodore Kilpatrick would give his eye teeth to get rid of me. He's used every other method he can think of, and your department is being seen as the last resort . . .'

'Why do suppose that is?' Anthea asked, leaning forward.

'Because I'm old and doddery and I don't fit into their idea of how someone like me should live.'

'Is that all?' Anthea said knowingly.

She sighed. Anthea had been told that Freddie Wingrave had been accused of interference and had been caught taking photographs of the Kilpatricks' property and of the visitors they'd regularly entertained. But that information had been given in confidence. But she wasn't winning, was she? She'd come across her fair share of obstreperous old women in her time, but Freddie Wingrave took the biscuit. She decided, therefore, that she'd quit while she was ahead.

But Freddie was clearly not letting her get away that easily. She narrowed her eyes at the raised eyebrows and glared at the woman.

'What do mean – all?' she snapped.

Anthea sniffed. She had a job to do and was determined to do it. 'Well . . . I . . .' she began nervously, then stopped.

In an attempt to ignore the prickle in her eyes as they'd suddenly begun watering, she blinked and looked down at the clipboard, carefully arranging her thoughts as to how to couch words which would not incur wrath in this awkward woman's breast. But she got no further, because her voice cracked as her throat began to contract. She then watched, aghast, as Squidge strolled lazily in from the garden.

'Oh!' she croaked, staring wildly at the cat, diving into her bag for a tissue.

'Something wrong?' Freddie asked sharply.

'It's just . . . the cat,' Anthea wheezed. 'I'm afraid . . . I'm allergic to cats.'

'Ah, well, there's not a lot I can do about that,' Freddie said shortly.

Anthea sneezed, and was suddenly desperate to get out of this house. While talking to the Wingrave woman, she'd been wondering what it was that had caused her unease, assuming that it was dust she was breathing into her lungs. As she sat, she'd wondered vaguely if she'd manage to come out of Freddie Wingrave's house without contracting some form of disease. But it was the cat.

'I . . . really will have to go now, Mrs Wingrave. Perhaps . . . perhaps we could discuss this further at a later date,' she snuffled, picking up her bag and standing.

'I don't think so,' Freddie said firmly, 'seeing as there's nothing to discuss.'

She stood, then walked with the health visitor to the door.

Once back in the fresh air, Anthea said gently, her smile returning, 'You know, Mrs Wingrave, we can help if you feel you can't cope. We could arrange to get a cleaner for you – a gardener perhaps. You only have to ask, and it wouldn't cost much. We're here to help if you need us.'

Freddie continued to glare at the woman.

'Here,' Anthea said, handing her a card. 'That's the number of our office. Do give us a call if you need us.'

'Thank you, Angela,' Freddie said, 'but I'm quite capable of looking after myself.'

Freddie waited on the doorstep with hooded eyes, seeing the woman off the premises and making sure she backed out of the drive without hitting the gatepost, mouthing, without moving her lips, an old Arabic curse: 'May the fleas of a thousand camels infect your armpits'.

Anthea walked unsteadily towards her car. Halfway down the drive, she'd wondered how many cat fleas she might have picked up whilst sitting on that dreadful chair, when, before she'd opened the door of her car, she heard Freddie shout after her, 'And tell that interfering fucker next door to keep his nose out of my business!'

If Theo Kilpatrick hadn't heard that, he was probably in need of the Audiology Department.

# Chapter Thirty-One

I knew that face.

I was freewheeling slowly down the slight incline of Kings Road, daydreaming a bit. I was not in any particular hurry and my thoughts were on which ready meal to take out of my freezer for dinner. The soft early autumn breeze was on my face and in my hair, and I sighed at all those beautiful trees lining the road, enjoying the colours turning to rust, the leaves falling around my shoulders and into the hedges. When, suddenly, a BMW shot out of the Kilpatricks' drive. It slowed as it passed me, then vroomed up the road. But, in that split second, I'd clocked the driver's face.

Everything seemed to happen in slow-motion as I stared at him, and a shiver of recognition ran through me as I skidded to a halt. As I eyed him, every thought I'd had about dinner evaporated. It was him in the driver's seat – it *was* him – I would swear to it – a woman at his side. Each with dark hair and dressed in dark clothes, unsmiling and looking like two black adhesive strips in their shiny black car.

It all flooded back in a flash and, even after all that time, I immediately knew who he was. And I froze, the shock momentarily taking my breath away. That man – all those years ago – passing an envelope to Commander Kilpatrick. Or it might have been the other way round; either way, it had been done in a surreptitious manner sufficient to alert my sense of decency. And, as I stood, watching the car disappear into Ranborne Hill Road, I was, in an instant, taken back to that moment when, waiting for my boyfriend in that small café near Oxford, I witnessed it.

There was no doubt in my mind that it was him; that long horsey jawline; no mistaking a face resembling a gravedigger's shovel, his features having been burned into my brain as though stamped with a branding iron, as was Kilpatrick's. Though a good deal older, his face hadn't change much, and I had an uneasy feeling that the rest of him hadn't changed, either. Because asked myself: why was he visiting Kilpatrick? Why were they still in touch? What were they up to? How was it that they were still buddies after all these years? And, what, after all these years, could they be cooking up? So . . . here they both were – comrades-in-arms touching base. Why? What was his business here? He's certainly risen up in the world with his posh BMW. But then, scum always rises to the top, doesn't it?

My antennae stood to attention as I looked at him and, in that split second, I felt the blood drain from my face as he stared back at me, his eyes narrowing. Was there the likelihood of him recognising me? The thought disturbed me. He would have known that I'd seen something I shouldn't and, like me, perhaps never forgot a face . . .

My blood ran cold.

Once a traitor, always a traitor. But, after all these years, what would be the motive for this re-acquaintance, because a traitor always has a motive, be it money, pride or, more likely in Kilpatrick's case, self-importance. It wouldn't surprise me if the man got himself polished every night.

Kilpatrick . . . I keep thinking about him in his ivory tower on Kings Road and everything I know about him; the manic narcissist with a brain the equivalent of vegetation and the sort of presence that jams lavatories . . . And there he sits, the fool, picking his teeth, the pride of Naval Intelligence, oblivious of his wife's shenanigans with half the men in the village, while brewing up some shady scheme with his old buddy, who looks as disreputable today as he did then. What scheme could they possibly be bending their minds to now? How to get rid of some nosy old woman who might have seen something she shouldn't?

It was after this encounter when, a couple of nights later, I got the visitation in my garden and, as I don't believe in coincidences, I guessed there would have to be a connection; you learn to smell it, like a dead rat before you find the corpse. I'd love to have caught the bastard.

For all his stupidity, though, there doesn't appear to be much wrong with Kilpatrick's memory. Which is what worries me.

But it's all there in my diary: all the sightings; all those snide Kilpatrick remarks supposedly out of my hearing; all those hateful looks . . . *And* that black BMW driving down the road. *Moreover* . . . what I was preparing to do about it . . . If anything should happen to me, someone will be sure to know everything I know.

\* \* \*

The trouble, right now, is there's no one left to tell; no one in whom I can confide. Who would believe me? I can't go to the police; they've already got me down as a crazy old bat. I can almost hear their laughter . . . Jeremy Flynn might understand, but he's gone back to Manchester. And I have so much to tell.

It was fortunate that a few months before the bomb the Wingrave woman had walked into the Felton Tearooms in Bracklea as I was eating a buttered teacake, and asked if I minded if she sat at my table. We'd shared the odd pleasantry at times, she seeming to be the only occupant of Kings Road who wasn't entirely up herself. But that day . . . It was as though the gods had answered my prayer. Because her joining me for tea led, eventually, to the tying of a few loose ends.

As we'd chatted, and it came out that I'd worked at Bletchley Park, her eyes lit up. She wanted to know everything about my time there, and I wanted to know every detail about her career – so we rattled on until lunchtime. She drove me back to the village, shoving my bike in the boot of her car, and we agreed to meet again.

I'd never imagined the woman to be so interesting; nor ever imagined she'd be interested in me. She'd always seemed so confident; a bit aloof, but sophisticated and worldly wise. I knew she'd worked as a reporter in a great many parts of the world with her camera. Much to our surprise, however, we discovered that, after all these years of living so closely together, we had more in common than either of us realised.

I couldn't, at that point, tell her about the man in the BMW; couldn't bring myself to voice my fears. You don't tell anyone anything in wartime, and that's something that never leaves you; that inner dread that you might accidentally blab to the wrong person some piece of information that, however trivial it may seem at the time, could ultimately be used against you. So, even though I warmed to her, I felt I didn't know her well enough to pour out my fears, thinking that she, too, might laugh at me. I don't really have a friend in the village, so it's good to talk to someone with a brain; someone who doesn't regard me as an utter cretin.

He or she was out there again last night and Sprout barked, though I should say that his bark is very much worse than his bite. I should be grateful for any small thing, I suppose; the throaty ruff might give a prowler the impression of a larger, more dangerous, dog.

* * *

The figure is hooded and dressed head to foot in black, so there's no guessing as to whom it might be. No guessing, either, as to why I'm being watched. I used not to bother drawing the curtains because I'm not overlooked by neighbours, but I've now taken to pulling them across the window earlier each night, and to sharpening my filleting knife. And I sit with the poker by my side. It's unnerving.

# Chapter Thirty-Two

Valerie Frobisher switched off the radio after the weather forecast: high blustery winds. Sounded as though they were introducing *Today in Parliament.*

She sighed and picked up the paper, which held proper news – or so she thought, but then found herself turning each page to avoid dubious pandemic statistics, wars in various parts of the world and demonstrators blocking roads. Television news, which was not much better, spent ten minutes of precious air time each night on sport so she turned to a Robert Harris novel she had not read before.

Dinner was then served, the three – Valerie, James and Poppy – silently chewing their T-bone steaks and then demolishing the dish of apple crumble, were glumly aware of Brian's empty chair and his place mat untouched by plate. It was Thursday evening and Valerie, having grown used to her husband's absence on the third Thursday of each month, hadn't thought it worthwhile setting out cutlery for him. Brian would have already eaten, wouldn't he? She knew where he was likely to have been and with whom – *as did James* – and the fact that he wouldn't now be hungry for his evening meal had failed any longer to surprise her. Having ravished Julia Kilpatrick, he'd now be propping up the bar at The Goose nursing a Carlsberg.

James worried for his mother; saw the strain that living with a bully for all those years had taken out of her. From childhood, he'd witnessed how she stiffen each time she heard Brian's key turn in the lock, and how she'd dash to the kitchen, eager to get his food, forestalling the lashing of his tongue if, by chance, it wasn't ready and waiting for him; watched her as she'd always done her best to please him. Except that nothing she ever did pleased him, nor was anything likely to. She'd recently lost weight, and the creases in her thin little face seemed to deepen by the day, her once blonde hair now streaked with grey. She had always prided herself on her appearance, but seemed now to have relinquished all that. To James, though, she was still his beautiful mother, and his heart went out to her as she toyed with her meal.

She'd lost her spark of late. She'd always been at her happiest when surrounded by children, ever funny and bright when either he or Poppy were down at heart, chivvying them up, and encouraging little Alfie to come out of his shell to tell a joke or two. These days, though, she looked as though the stuffing had been removed. She'd always been the one to shield the pair of them – he and Poppy – against their father's vicious barbs. And, when, last summer, James's girlfriend ditched him for Craig Turnbull, Valerie had done her best to comfort his broken heart, and had eventually and inevitably managed to make him laugh at a time when he thought he might never laugh again. During that same period, Poppy had failed her French A-Level for the second time, which had had Brian spitting feathers at her so-called stupidity, and he'd yelled, reducing her to tears. But Mum had swooped her up and taken her to a nail bar.

After the meal, he and Poppy went into the kitchen to wash up, leaving Valerie to her crossword. James had hesitated about revealing to his sister their father's infidelity, wondering whether to let the sleeping, lying, treacherous dog lie. As Poppy washed up, he reached for a tea towel, thinking morosely that she ought to know; that now might be as good a time as any.

Poppy spoke first.

In whispered tones, she asked, 'What do you think's up with Mum these days?'

James sighed. 'Dunno. Could be she's going through the change.'

Dangerous waters . . . He wasn't ready to tell her just yet; perhaps later when he felt a bit stronger . . .

'Nah, she's well over that,' Poppy said, the worldly-wise eighteen-year-old that she was. 'They're so frosty with each other these days, I was wondering if they're getting divorced.'

'Wouldn't surprise me,' he said. 'Don't seem too happy these days – either of them.'

'So . . . where do you think Dad is? Where does he go when he's not here?'

He hovered. Should he tell her now? But he'd hovered a few seconds too long.

'You know something, don't you?' she said, rinsing a plate and stacking it in the rack for him to dry, then staring up at him with her large hazel eyes.

'Yeah . . .' he said.

'Well, come on then!' she shot.

Still he hesitated as he carefully dried the plate.

'Dad's . . . er, well, he's having an affair,' he whispered.

'What? How do you know?' she breathed.

'Saw them together.'

'Saw who?'

'Dad – and Julia Kilpatrick,' he said.

'*What?*'

'Sshhh.'

'Mrs Kilpatrick?' she echoed, the dishcloth sliding from her hands into the water as she took this in.

She stared out of the window for a moment, then turned to look at him.

'How can you be sure?' she said suspiciously, narrowing her eyes. 'Are you making this up?'

'No, I'm not making it up,' he said softly, then sighed. 'I wish it wasn't true, but it is.'

Poppy looked him aghast.

'But *Mrs Kilpatrick* . . . She's Mum's best friend,' she said sadly. 'How could she?'

'Yeah, well . . .' he frowned, recalling the sight of the pair pressing the button for the lift while simultaneously pressing each others' buttons as they kissed passionately before the lift answered their call – a sight he fervently wished he could un-see.

'How long have you known?' she asked, attempting to read his thoughts.

'A few weeks,' he said.

'So . . .' she challenged, 'how could you have seen them? Where were they when you saw them?'

She didn't believe him – didn't want to believe him.

'They were in the Old Dog and Bush in Barnscote,' he sighed.

'Oh, right. So what were *you* doing in the Old Dog and Bush?'

'Alfie,' he said, shuffling uncomfortably. 'He works there. It was Alfie told me.'

'Alfie? Never had Alfie down as a sneak!' Poppy said with feeling.

'It wasn't like that,' James said. 'Alfie's not a sneak. He just happened to mention that he served them lunch once a month on a Thursday. So, I . . . just . . . went there to see if was true.'

'*You . . . you . . . what?*'

'I had to, Pops. I had to find out.'

Poppy sighed, and pulled the plug of the sink, miserably watching the water drain away.

'So it's really true?' she pouted. 'Do you think Mum knows?'

'She might,' he said. 'I don't see how she couldn't have guessed. It could be the reason she's so unhappy.'

Poppy wiped her hands on a towel, frowning.

'Look, Jimbo, are you absolutely sure about this? Because, if this is true, he's a rat,' she said decisively, her voice rising. 'He should be called out. This isn't right!'

'Yes – I'm sure. But just calm down,' James said. 'I'll deal with it. Don't go spilling the beans – you could do more damage than you bargained for.'

They hadn't notice Valerie standing at the kitchen door.

'Who's a rat? Spilling the beans on what?' she smiled.

They both froze, then turned guiltily. 'Oh, er, it's um, Gary Henshaw,' James stuttered, trying to avoid looking at Poppy. 'He's tried on with a few girls at Poppy's college. I said I'd deal with it.'

'Shouldn't you have reported it?' she said to Poppy.

'I think a cracked rib might be a better idea,' James managed to smile before Poppy had time to draw breath. 'I can deal with him!'

Valerie grinned.

'You be careful – you might get a cracked rib yourself, you silly sausage,' she said. 'How about making coffee for your aged mother?'

\* \* \*

Rows in families often start with just one small thing, and it was, therefore, one small thing which brought matters to a head in the Frobisher household when Brian walked through the door after work a few weeks after James had discovered his father's affair. He was late, but not overly late that evening, and he hung up his coat in the hall, grunted his usual greeting and sniffed the air for signs of dinner. It was Friday, so his excuse for lateness being an excess of paperwork at the laboratory was accepted. The family kept out of his way when the black dog was evident, having learned the hard way that alluding to extra work at the lab could cause a bad mood to fester for an entire weekend.

Apart from his waspish tongue, nothing that evening seemed out of the ordinary, Brian slinging down his briefcase for someone else to pick up, growling like a bear at being starved of sustenance, and enquiring loudly as to what the hell was happening in the kitchen to remedy that state. The usual stuff.

It was after a small but cutting remark – nothing out of the way, considering Brian's mood swings and a growing tendency to curl his lip as he barked out orders to a family he'd always assumed he could easily cow with a lift of the brows – that James felt his hackles rise. Valerie, appeared from the kitchen with a covered dish, which she placed on the table, Poppy following with steaming vegetables. Brian, having been doled out a portion of food, sat staring down at his plate with distaste, then suddenly turned up his nose and slammed down his cutlery.

'Fish again!' he said, glaring at Valerie with snarl. 'Can't you think of anything more original than sodding fish?'

'I thought you liked fish,' she said.

'But two bloody days in a row?' he snarled. 'God! I give you enough housekeeping to get decent food on the table.'

'But it is decent food, dad – and it's different fish,' Poppy said. 'This is haddock. Yesterday we had cod. What's wrong with that?'

'Who asked you? Fucking little know-it-all!' he snapped, glowering at his daughter, ignoring the hurt in her eyes.

Valerie opened her mouth to say something, but then decided against it. Instead, she reached over to touch Poppy's hand, while glaring at her husband, her breath held and lips clamped, attempting to avoid a full-on scene in front of the children.

'And what's this?' he said, lifting his wine glass.

'Wine,' James said, deadpan.

'I mean *what is it?*' he yelled.

'White,' James ventured once more, receiving a kick from Poppy from under the table.

'The sodding label, dick-head!' Brian glared, grabbing the bottle. 'The provenance!'

'Oh, the *provenance* . . .' James smiled. 'That'd be Tesco.'

Another kick from Poppy.

Brian picked up the bottle and turned it round to see the label 'Ha, *Chardonnay*! I might have known!'

'Something wrong with Chardonnay?' James asked.

'Yes, there is something wrong with Chardonnay – it's piss! I'm not staying in this sodding house to eat sodding fish! Nor am I drinking Tesco's fucking Chardonnay!' he yelled, getting up from his chair. 'I'm off to The Goose, where I know I'll get a decent meal!'

'The Goose?' James said, his eyebrows raised, arm carelessly resting on the back of the dining chair, looking up at his father with a grin; no one got away with calling his sister a fucking little know-it-all. Neither, for that matter, did anyone call Tesco's Chardonnay piss. 'Bit of a comedown, The Goose, don't you think? Why not try the Old Dog and Bush at Barnscote. I'm told the food is excellent there.'

Keeping eye contact, he watched as his father stopped in his tracks, the muscles either side of his face shooting out as he turned and glared at his son, his hand out ready to slap him around the ears – which he held back as his six-foot two son stood up to defend himself against such an occurrence. Poppy and her mother sat rigid in their seats, their hearts thumping with anxiety as the flush from Brian's face crept alarmingly into his neck.

They all knew that, ordinarily, even the slightest thing would set him off: an article in the paper he disagreed with; a strike; a change of government. In this particular case, the change of mood happened to be when his son alluded to his shenanigans in the Old Dog and Bush.

Both children, throughout their childhood, had feared their father's upsurge of wrath, the most memorable occasion of that wrath being day when James had chosen to drop out of university, and when Brian had screamed such foul-mouthed abuse at him that James had imagined his father to be destined for either a mental institution or hired as a stand-up comedian.

But tonight was different, because James had grown considerably since that time, and not merely physically. And, having just mentioned something which had all the makings of a total shortage of his father's brain, he felt more than capable of saving the man's trip to The Goose's Head by kicking the little runt down the road himself. He stood, towering above him, challenging Brian to deny the accusation, noting with satisfaction his clenched jaw, coupled with colour of his cheeks. And he smiled.

'And why do you think I should wish to go the Old Dog and Bush?' he snapped back indignantly, but rather less sure of himself now.

'You tell me,' James smiled down at the curled lip his father threw in his direction as the droplets of realisation dawned upon him that James was no longer afraid of him. Brian fumed, suddenly bereft of his lashing tail and flames of fire; the swingeing fury which, in the past, had stood him in good stead. And, as James gazed coolly at the mounting guilt flaring up, he saw with satisfaction that he'd struck the very vein of salt in which to rub his father's nose, and enjoyed every moment of his discomfort, deciding to go one step further. 'You seem to enjoy the lunch they serve in that hotel every month, so why would you keep going back if it wasn't so good?'

'What the hell are you talking about?' Brian snarled belligerently, taking a step forward, then regretting the move.

Without flinching at the threat of the clenched fist nearing his face, James said, 'And, when you're in the company of a beautiful woman, it must make the food all the more enjoyable. So . . . win, win . . .'

'You don't know what you're talking about, you fucking little moron – and neither do I!'

'Don't you?' James shrugged, maintaining eye contact.

'You bloody little sneak!' Brain suddenly spat out. 'Have you been following me? How *dare* you sneak up on me, you fucking little . . . little . . .'

'Sneak?' James supplied with a grin.

Valerie opened her mouth, but thought better than to speak at this juncture.

'Sorry Mum,' James said. 'But I think you have every right to know . . .'

'How about "sorry Dad"?' Brian shouted at him. 'You think you know it all, don't you, you clever fucking dick? Spying on me? You little ingrate! After all the money I've spent on you, you fucking little turd – after all I've done for you . . .'

'Done for me?' James laughed. 'Done? By "done", you mean, perhaps, the writing of all those cheques for those rotten little public schools you made me go to? God, that must have taken it out of you – all that writers' cramp you must have suffered, Dad. My heart goes out! All that shelling out to educate me for a career that would make you look good? Thinking that signing your name on something that represented money would release you from any other responsibility? When have you ever actually noticed me, Dad – or noticed either of us? When have you ever taken the time to play with us as children? We were always shoved into the background – always coming second to your mates down at The Goose. You coming home from work, wolfing your food, then swanning down the road to grab your pint glass of ale without a second's thought for either us or Mum. Couldn't get away from us fast enough. We never actually figured in your life, did we? *Ever.* So . . . now you think we should give a fuck about you?'

'*How dare* you speak to me like that, you fucking piece of shit? You don't know what you're talking about, you sneaky little toad!' Brian raged. 'Get out of my sight!'

'Ha. All these years of taking second place to your selfish little life; Poppy and me being barely tolerated and Mum taking all the flak for your foul moods – and . . . I don't what I'm talking about?'

'It's all right, James,' Valerie said coolly, deciding at last to speak. 'There's no need for all this. Calm down, darling. I've known for years about the affair with Julia Kilpatrick.'

'What affair?' Brian snarled at her. 'What do you know? You don't know anything about anything, you stupid bitch!'

He glared at her, a slash of loathing momentarily passing over his mouth, then strode towards her, his hand ready to hit out. James leapt sideways and stood between him and his mother, staring him into submission. As he was at least six inches taller than his father, and as Brian, he knew, was a total coward, the latter suddenly decided to dismiss his wife with a sneer. He then turned suddenly and strode out of the dining room and down the corridor for his coat in his anxiety to shoot out of the house and march down to The Goose's Head. He had not, however, reckoned with his wife, who stood watching him as he reached the door.

'Did just call me a stupid bitch?' she shouted down to him. '*And don't walk away from me, Brian Frobisher!* Every time something unpalatable crops up – something you can't face up to – you walk away. Well, hear this before you swan off down to your favourite watering hole! This bitch you're married to isn't stupid enough not to have figured out what those monthly withdrawals were for, because you're too damned lazy to do the accounts yourself. So what did you suppose this *stupid bitch* would make of all those items of cash withdrawn once a month? And which *stupid bitch* gets fobbed off by your pathetic lying about buying gardening tools? Yes, Brian – I've known. And do you think I care?'

Brian stood rigid. His wife had never spoken to him like this.

'And do you imagine, for one minute,' she went on, 'that Julia Kilpatrick would look at a shrivelled-up little toad like you if you weren't paying her a king's ransom to get her face fixed for the umpteenth time? You fool! If you ran out of money, she'd drop you like a piece of molten rock!'

Shaking with pent-up rage, she stood firm and, for the first time in her married life, faced him down. But she wasn't finished: before the door finally closed on him, she shouted, 'If you walk out of this house, Brian Frobisher, you leave for good!' not quite believing her own voice as it uttered words she'd practised in her head for so many years. 'If you go out of that door, you needn't bother coming back.'

'Ha, that's what you think!' Brian snapped. 'This is my house.'

'You might think differently when I change the locks and consult my solicitor,' she said calmly, almost smiling.

'You're not getting this fucking house!' he yelled.

'I think you'll find that I am,' she said. 'I have two children in my care. As long as they live here, you'll never turn me out of this house.'

Brian, his face now the colour of cooked beetroot, turned abruptly, grabbed his overcoat and left, slamming the door behind him. Valerie, whey-faced, turned and slowly made her way back to the dining room, then flopped down at the table.

James's heart did a flip. He hadn't foreseen this. Watching her now, he felt empty. *She'd known . . .* All this time, she'd known. He could tell by the set of her mouth that she'd made a life-changing decision; that nothing could possibly mend that contretemps. He'd stood like a stone as she'd lashed out with a raging fire he'd never before seen, nor ever suspected had been there inside her; a fire which must have been simmering for all those years of neglect and mental abuse; a fury which could never now be put back in its cage. Tears pricked his eyes, and he longed to take her in his arms and hold her, but he hesitated to disturb the state of calm occupying her as she'd stood, impassive, staring at the door as it closed.

Valerie smiled suddenly, because she'd known that the affair with Julia Kilpatrick would have come to an abrupt halt if Simon Garraway hadn't been blown up. And, with a stab of satisfaction she'd also known that her fool of a husband hadn't had a clue about Julia's impending flight with Garraway. Brian had had no idea what the woman had been planning with Simon, nor what she'd wanted his money for. Did he think that all her nips and tucks were for his benefit? He'd thought he was the only one, the idiot.

She became aware of James and Poppy anxiously watching her and sighed heavily. She'd ended it. No more worrying about what Brian was up to when out of her sight; no more snide remarks about the constant migraines sending her to bed in a darkened room. And no more biting shards of malice towards the children. She was sick of being a victim – of all them having been victims. Standing there facing him at the door, and with her children at her side, she'd felt herself grow strong.

Both James and Poppy were left white and speechless, appetite forgotten, the breath having been shocked out of them. James, having instigated the row, now sat, feeling numb, and watched as his mother suddenly came to life; walking back to the table to stare at her plate of congealed food. He put his head in his hands.

He felt bad. He should have left things as they were. He thought he was being clever, didn't he? But now look . . .

'Well!' Valerie breathed at last, before getting out of her chair and walking up the stairs to her bedroom, 'That's settled that.'

Which left James and Poppy staring at each other in disbelief.

# Chapter Thirty-Three

Jeremy Flynn had done a good job in persuading his parents not to leave Roper's End, and Glenys was pleased when the sale board was taken down, although saddened to see that the Garraways had left.

That was so sudden – the Garraways' departure. No one had seen anyone looking remotely like a buyer for Oaklands – and, if Alma Larkingstall, she of the twitching curtain, had known anything, it would have been all over the village like a rash. Yet the removal van had appeared one day without any warning, and then . . . in a puff of smoke, they were gone. Glenys noticed their absence as she rode past the house on her bicycle, and felt a deep sadness at having missed the opportunity to say goodbye.

She'd gleaned, from hushed tones at the Post Office counter, that the Garraways had had to leave in rather a hurry. Word had somehow reached the ears of certain people – namely Dan and Betty Prince – that Simon Garraway's bank had foreclosed on the house, which could account for the absence of viewers in recent weeks. What Glenys heard in the Post Office, however, she usually overdosed on large pinches of salt. It could be true – or not – depending on what one was prepared to believe from the lips of gossipy villagers who'd little else to occupy their minds.

Something evidently was up, though, because Marjorie hadn't told anyone they were leaving, which had the whole village delirious with excitement, opening up a yawning gulf for something fresh to chew upon. And chew they did. When no more meat was left on the bone, however, Glenys had no doubt they would find another knuckle to gnaw upon in order to make someone else's life a misery. And as the once-juicy goings-on of Doctor Bracknell's misdeeds was now beginning to dissipate, it was imperative to have someone else to shred to bits.

They'd always know, hadn't they, they muttered, that Garraway was a wrong-un? Furthermore, if Garraway had owed money to someone dodgy, might that bomb have been sent to *Oaklands* by a creditor – very probably a gangster – wanting the return of his money? There was also, care of Alma Larkingstall, that business of the silver Mercedes turning up a few weeks ago with two dark-suited strangers emerging with black leather briefcases. Who knew what that was all about, and what might have been tucked away in those briefcases? And it made you wonder, didn't it – because you didn't see many silver Mercedes's in Roper's End . . . ? Alma had said that they were not your average viewer and she'd thought it very odd. And, as the oddness of this sighting was too good to keep to herself, Hester Molton-Fry was the first to be apprised of these suspicions. They'd immediately put their heads together before deciding to let everybody know how weird it all looked, then added to the mix that, as the men had been dressed in black, might they have been members of the Mafia?

Once the idea that the Mafia might be involved, and the news via the Garraways' neighbours had spread, it gave every villager the vapours. The Mafia in Ropers End? Could it now be considered dangerous to live in Roper's End? But they might have known: the Mafia all had flash cars like Mercedes, didn't they – so could this be true? They'd all watched films about the criminal underworld and chopped off horses' heads, so were unshakable in their conviction of what might happen if they didn't keep their eyes open. But Garraway! Who would have thought that

Garraway would be caught up in the criminal underworld? And here, right under their noses! All this time being hoodwinked by that dreadful man, who'd said that the bomb had been sent to the wrong address! Well, you if you believed that . . . ! But it was all coming out now, wasn't it?

And so, this single sighting of an unidentified car containing unidentified men in suits with briefcases put the whole village on high alert . . . Though what they would have done in the face of Mafia thugs, was anybody's guess.

Connie Gilchrist, Simon's one-time carer, had put in her two-twopenn'orth by letting it be known that Simon had now been taken into a residential care home, which didn't surprise her one bit. So, yes, she concurred, happy to fan the flames – those men could well have been gangsters; she'd watched the pair of them getting into their car as she'd walked back from the Post Office, and they'd looked very dodgy. And, to be perfectly honest, she wouldn't have put it past Garraway to have been a drug dealer; all that hopping off around the world! He could have smuggled no end of stuff in and out of the country – and now they'd caught up with him.

*Drug dealing . . . ?* Good grief! That threw up a whole new bone to pick, didn't it?

Gathered in the Post Office, the villagers of Roper's End, having for all these years considered Simon Garraway a good neighbour and all round good egg, lapping up his company in The Goose's Head as he'd kept them entertained, now viewed him as the Antichrist for whom hell was too good. There was no getting away from it: as far as they could gather, Simon Garraway was not only a drug dealer embroiled with gangsters, but had got himself on the wrong side of of the Mafia. And right here in this village!

Glenys wondered which febrile mind had managed to dredge up

these various gobbets of misinformation and then, with jet-propelled speed, twist them into the blood-letting character assassination of someone they'd once viewed as a pillar of the community. Could there be a hot-line to and from some poisonous Tartarean inferno she wasn't privy to? Something in the ether shooting out malignant messages to the chosen few in Roper's End? Standing in the Post Office queue, she inwardly groaned. She had better things to do to occupy her mind and, as she closed the door of the Post Office, her thoughts immediately turned from all those silly gossipers to her own agenda and what she had to do before it was too late. She was working steadily towards her goal, and smiled as she cycled home, thinking about how everything, eventually, would be explained to these ridiculous people. Then they'd have a great deal more to think about than the Mafia . . .

On the way home, she braked suddenly and dismounted, then stood, frowning. She'd gone to the Post Office specifically to buy a birthday card for Jenny and just then, with a heavy sigh, and in the middle of Ranborne Hill Road, remembered that Jenny had died the previous month.

* * *

Sprout went wild again last night. I looked out but couldn't see a soul. I felt it, though. You learn that.

I'm pretty cut off from the village down this lane; there isn't even a lamp post. Maybe I should have thought of all that before I bought the place. But that was way back, when I was still young and working at Bletchley. One never imagines, when young, that one will get old and frail. What I needed then, more than anything, was a place of my own, far away from that madhouse, and Roper's End seemed an ideal place in which to escape during those precious weekends. And the bungalow, I'd thought, would be ideal for when I eventually retired. I'd kill now for near neighbours.

But that seems an eternity ago. When I saw the bungalow advertised in this remote cul de sac down Prince Albert Lane, I jumped at it. Roper's End was a relatively cheap area back then – before it got prettified into Disneyland, and before all the Birmingham-ites had discovered it – so I bought it. At Bletchley I'd dreamt of all the things I would do once I'd retired, then over the years, gradually got the place to my liking and filled it with beautiful furniture.

No one, comes up this lane because it doesn't lead to anywhere of particular interest – just a field of sheep belonging to Gerald Partridge, who trudges up every now and then and, after he's fed the sheep, usually calls in for coffee.

I've never found the folk here particularly friendly because they hate newcomers. And, even though I've lived here for the last fifty years, I'm still regarded as a newcomer by the likes of Hester Molton-Fry. Being a fish out of water, however, has never bothered me unduly, although I know it bothers folk in the newish bungalows on Prince Albert Lane. The 'elite' on Kings Road have always considered me a pestilence, and to the the 'non-elite' in Prince Albert Lane I am lower than algae. No one, therefore, has seen fit to talk to me.

Until now. Now, of course, they want to know if I've heard anything. Unlike the rest of the villagers, I'd occasionally drop in on the Garraways to take Simon a small treat to cheer him up. So they think I must be privy to their lives. But the Garraways never revealed anything about their lives and, even if they had, the village wouldn't get a squeak out of me.

I've grown old here – grown old without realising it. You don't feel old age scraping its claws across the back of your neck until one day it arrives without much of a warning. You perhaps find that cycling uphill is a tad more difficult than in the past, and that bending to tend the roses unexpectedly causes you to wince. But it doesn't really hit you until you wake up one morning and it's there – old age – staring you in the face from the bathroom mirror: the deep crevasses drawing down the mouth; the neck hanging limply in fleshy strands; the lush once-blonde hair reduced to paltry slivers of silver. And it's then you're forced into the realisation that each day – having always been taken for granted – is a benefice to be treasured. I was ninety-two last month, so I feel I've done well and thank God for it, but I know there isn't much time left.

But here's so much still to do, and I wonder if I'll have the time to complete everything . . .

I sometimes dig out the photograph album and look at my young self in disbelief; there I am in a pretty frock, my yellow hair flowing over my shoulders, grinning at the camera. I was quite pretty when I was young. I had lots of men at Bletchley Park swarming round me, flirting with a vengeance – not that I didn't do my share of flirting back . . . And I could have had any one of them if I'd chosen. It was just unfortunate that I'd happened to pick the two men who were destined to get themselves killed.

But for Kilpatrick, I would look upon that time as idyllic – apart, that is, from the cold, and the steady rattle of the pipes as they struggled each morning to pump heat into rooms whose windows in their rotting frames would send it straight back out again. But it was Kilpatrick who was the one blot I remember most vividly on an otherwise happy time. Each time I look at the man now, it takes me back there.

Of all the girls he'd had, Julia was by far the most beautiful. Still is. She could have had anybody. Still does, by all accounts. She must have been very young and innocent when they married. Must be pushing fifty now, bless her, but she still looks gorgeous. And not only gorgeous, but very kind, once taking me to hospital for tests, hanging about for several hours for me in an uncomfortable waiting area – and thereafter occasionally popping me to the dentist and to the vet with Sprout. One of the few down Kings Road who gives me the time of day.

I hear all sorts of stories about her from village gossips, folk obviously jealous about how many men she sleeps with. But, good for her. If I were Julia Kilpatrick, living for all those wretched years with Neanderthal Man, I would be tempted to do the same.

*Homo Neanderthalis,* I read the other day, had recently been discovered to have been rather more intelligent, and not quite as primitive as everyone had previously thought. He's not, however, as extinct as everyone had previously thought.

I must get on. That intruder . . . It pulled me up sharp, making me realise how little time I have.

# Chapter Thirty-Four

It was the milkman who discovered Glenys Pugh's body. He told me later that her curtains were still drawn when he called, and there were the two pints of milk on the doorstep he'd left the day before. He said she always left a note if she happened to be away; but to leave milk souring in the heat all day was not at all like Miss Pugh. There was no sound, even from the dog, which always barked at the jangling of glass bottles, so he knew something was not right. He'd known little Miss Pugh for over twenty years, ever since he was a lad – had had many a cheerful conversation at the doorstep – and he knew her to be an early riser. So . . . he'd asked himself, why would the curtains still be drawn at seven-fifteen? Worried, he'd knocked and called out. That alone would have set her dog barking – but there was silence.

When the police arrived they found the door unlocked, so they walked in to find Glenys lying lifeless with her dead Cairn beside her. She'd been killed around midnight – strangled, Sprout having been knifed, lying beside her in a pool of blood on the Turkey carpet she'd loved so dearly.

My name was in her address book, so they called me. In the absence of a relative, I was asked to identify her body, and I have to say that, although I rarely weep, tears ran down my face as I looked at her – my only friend in this unfriendly place.

No one had seen anything. Farmer Partridge, when approached, said that she'd been complaining lately that she was unnerved by strangers prowling around at night. But no one else came forward with anything useful. Forensics discovered nothing (don't ask me how I know that . . . ): no fingerprints; no tell-tale clues, and the police were saying that this had the hallmarks of a professional job – a premeditated murder rather than a straightforward burglary. Without witnesses, however, they had nothing to go on. It was the premeditated murder of a ninety-two-year-old woman they couldn't understand. And what I couldn't understand. Why would anyone assassinate a harmless old woman like Glenys Pugh? *And Sprout!* That was beyond heartless.

There was no sign of a forced entry; she'd either opened the door to her killer or he'd forced the door once she'd opened it. Had she known him? I know that she would never open her door, even during the day, until she was sure that the voice on the other side was one she recognised. Glenys always went to bed straight after the ten-o'clock news, so someone had awoken her and brought her to the door. But then, why would she have opened it? They must have frightened her into it – perhaps told her they were the police? – some sort of emergency? For whatever reason, she'd opened her door and let in her killer, who had then simply walked out again under cover of darkness.

I told the police the little I knew – that she'd been watched and had several times heard intruders late at night, and they said precisely what I thought they'd say: that, if she'd reported the incidents at the time, they would have taken the matter seriously. Glenys, of course, would have hooted at the emptiness of those words; that reporting a prowler would have achieved precisely nothing. She had never before been taken seriously by the police, nor would have expected them to take her seriously this time

I drove home from the mortuary, shaken. I, who had witnessed so many dead bodies in third world countries during my career, thought I would be capable of coping with this. It had been my job to photograph dead bodies and, though I'd felt deeply about all those atrocities, I'd never let my feelings get the better of me. I'd bottled up my emotions until arriving home to unleash them on my husband. Being called to identify Glenys Pugh, however, was entirely different. This was my friend, and I wept for her – for the ending a close friendship I'd never imagined would happen in this snotty village – and the tears wouldn't stop. Even though I'd known Glenys for only a few short months, this loss was immense.

Who was the prowler she'd been so afraid of? To call it coincidence would be naïve in the extreme; this was everything to do with the prowler, wasn't it? Who was the man in the BMW she'd mentioned in her diary? She'd clearly been shaken by the sighting of that man emerging from the Kilpatricks, but couldn't tell me why. Could that man have been her killer? But why would he, or anyone else, kill her? That question wouldn't let me go. What had she done? Why would someone want her out of the way? Was she about to expose something significant? If this had something to do with her time at Bletchley Park, why wait until now to murder her? It haunted me . . .

I remember, with clarity, that day in Felton Tea Rooms earlier in the year, when I'd happened to mention my assignment in Russia in the 'sixties. She'd smiled as I'd prattled on about how I'd smuggled a man into Moscow, and of how I'd fallen in love with him. Then I mentioned his name, and her eyes immediately widened. She'd stiffened and held in her breath when I told her about Toni Vascari, and of what had happened to him. The sudden change in her was momentary, and perhaps something that many may not have picked up on: that sudden spark at the mention of Toni's name. Then, after she'd lifted her teacup and swallowed, she seemed to return to normal. At the time, I suspected that she'd known something vital – something she couldn't tell me. Even though I was desperate for any little crumb of information about that time, I was aware that I couldn't ask her – which was frustrating. We'd only just met, so how could she know if I was trustworthy? We drank our tea and managed to change the subject, but I could see throughout that her mind was elsewhere.

I found myself mesmerised by those sharp blue eyes, and so, when I'd come to know her better, I went on to tell her everything about that time, watching her face alter from a passing interest to deep concern, her jaw stiffening with something resembling recognition as I went on to the end – to Toni's death. Behind those gimlet eyes, however, there was something . . . something unfathomable.

During morning coffee one day, I told her of the strange telephone call I'd received from Maria Collini and my subsequent journey to the hotel in Birmingham, where everyone had denied her existence. When I'd finished, she picked up the coffee pot and poured out another cup, and I saw the slight tremor of her hand. She eyed me over her cup as she lifted it from the saucer, then smiled again. There was something in the way she'd looked at me, a whole universe of knowledge behind those eyes, and I sensed that what I had just revealed answered a question to which she'd been awaiting for some time. What that was, I couldn't imagine.

Not until much later.

* * *

There was a mere sprinkling of folk at her funeral. The Flynn's attended with their two children. Plus Simon Garraway who, I was told, had insisted on attending, and who was wheeled into the church by by a nurse from the care home he'd been taken to a few weeks' earlier. One or two others were there: neighbours, including Valerie Frobisher, accompanied by her children, James and Poppy. And, of course, Irene Farrow, who wouldn't, for all the world, have allowed a wake to pass her by. Farmer Partridge who, I believe, had had a soft spot for her, also turned up. The rest of the villagers, never having bothered themselves to get to know Glenys Pugh – those who had mistaken her for a baggage of unsound mind and imagined her to be as cranky as her ancient bicycle – had either preferred to stay away or hadn't even been notified of her death.

Aware that she'd lived alone, not many folk in Roper's End had ever gone out of their way to enquire as to her needs, nor even put themselves out to get to know her – all, perhaps, afraid of catching an independence of spirit, like a nasty case of herpes, fearful that their measly existences might be punctured by a free-minded soul lifting them beyond the bounds of their fettered brain cells.

I could think of a few people in this village who I'd have been glad to see the back of, but Glenys Pugh had not been one of them.

*  *  *

If the shock of her murder had been bad, a bigger shock awaited me. A few months after her death, I received a letter from a firm of solicitors inviting me attend its offices.

The morning I received it, I'd put the unopened envelope to one side on the kitchen table, as I hadn't been able to find my spectacles. Later in the day, I picked it up and frowned down at the franking on the envelope – Warbeck and Roberts – I'd never heard of them. Then, glasses on, I took the letter to the window:

> Dear Mrs Wingrave, we write on behalf of Miss Glenys Iris Pugh,
> deceased, and should be grateful if you would be kind enough to attend

these offices on the third of February at 10.00am for the reading of Miss Pugh's last will and testament.

I didn't respond for some time, having made up my mind to ring with an excuse; trouble with my back; foul weather; forecasters warning against floods.. But the letter sat on the kitchen table, staring at me, willing me to do something about it. Then, the day before the appointment, Squidge knocked over a cup tea and, in mopping it up, I noticed that a few spots had caught a corner of the envelope, forcing me to pick it up and wipe it. It was a nudge, forcing me to do something, and I knew that I could no longer put off visiting the solicitor. I took the letter out and read it for a third time, wondering again why these people would wish me to attend their offices. A passing thought had earlier flashed through my mind of the Wedgwood vase I'd once admired, and of the possibility that Glenys might have wished me to have it. But . . . fifteen miles to Hansfield in the driving rain for a vase . . . ?

Despite the rain, however, I knew I'd have to go.

The deluge the following morning was Biblical, smashing angrily against the kitchen window, reinforced by a full-blooded wind, and I stood watching the poor birches at the end of the garden as they bent double with the force. The sky was a sullen black cap straddling as far as the eye could see, setting out its intention not to let up until it had emptied its entire payload over Portlingshire. It matched my mood, and I had a mind to cry off the meeting in Hansfield. I hated driving in the rain. Besides, my raincoat had seen better days and my ancient boots leaked.

I ran out to the car, but was soaked before I'd managed to open the door. I sat shivering in my wet clothes for a moment or two, wondering, yet again, if I should ring the solicitors' office and make the weather my excuse for non-attendance, but then had second thoughts, turned the ignition key and set off.

Parking in the city had its usual difficulties and, even though I have a sturdy umbrella, I managed to get another soaking as I trekked round the streets of the city attempting to locate the office. Then, having arrived at the reception area of Warbeck and Roberts, I sat in my damp clothes, trying to put out of my mind the discomfort of the trickle of water slowly seeping through my boots. I was then called in to Mr Roberts's office, chilled to the bone, my one thought being of the hot bath I would run as soon as I got home. I sat as the man riffled through his papers, getting everything in order, fully expecting others to join me: relatives perhaps . . . old friends she'd known at Bletchley . . . But no one else came; just me, sitting there smelling like a wet dog.

Mr Roberts, a solicitor to his fingertips, with the few wisps of grey hair gracing his otherwise shiny bald head, droned on about this being the last will and testament of Glenys Iris Pugh of . . . whatever . . . And, numbed by the cold, I was just nodding off – until he said something that made me sit up and blink – something that could not possibly be true. It appeared that the content of the will was quite straightforward because, he smiled, Glenys Pugh had left her entire estate to me. I sat, speechless. He rang his secretary to send up a tray of tea, then talked me through the will once more. Before leaving, and in a trance, I took from him the keys to her bungalow, Mr Roberts smiling benignly at my inability to focus as the reality smashed into my utterly befogged brain: *Glenys Pugh had left everything to me.* My breath came out in jerks, and I had the feeling that I was either in the middle of a dream or looking through the wrong end of a telescope. I couldn't take it in; it was all so unreal: that she had chosen to leave everything solely to me. I asked myself over and over the question as to why – why would she do this? And I walked out of the solicitor's office on legs which felt like slabs of jelly.

As to the question of why, however, it didn't take me long to find out.

I drove home from that Hansfield office, my head whirring, barely noticing the wet clothes clinging to my icy body. Then, lying in my bath, wondered how I would find the strength to face entering Glenys's bungalow, knowing that neither she nor Sprout would be there to welcome me. I had the keys, but decided to leave it until my heart had settled and until I felt able to accept that I now owned a bungalow. I had to keep reminding myself of that: it was my bungalow – I owned it

I waited until the rain had had its fun then, one morning, when the sun had decided to show its face, walked up the lane to open the door of Holgarth, preparing myself to face its emptiness, the keys jangling in my hand. The air, having been trapped inside the bungalow for so long, struck stale and chill as I opened the door, and the silence almost undid me: the missing whoop of welcome and the smell of freshly baked biscuits . . . Blood – I guessed Sprout's blood – had now congealed to brown on the Turkey carpet, which I strongly suspected would be impossible to remove. I opened the windows to let in fresh air, watered the few sagging herbs which hadn't died, then sat in her favourite chair, thinking about her. Why couldn't she share her secrets; why hadn't she answered all those questions I needed answers to? During our many conversations, I'd had the feeling that Glenys had known all along for whom the bomb had been destined but, when I'd alluded to it, she'd seen fit to change the subject. She'd been careful, even in her cups, and the copious glasses of wine we managed to put away never once loosened her tongue. I admired that. Care had been her watchword – something she'd never been able to relinquish. Had she been afraid that what had *seemed* to be an innocent friendship might turn out to be something else? *If everything seems normal, assume that it isn't . . .*

Something had happened at Bletchley – that much was clear. And that something had to be Moscow. Did she know who had killed Toni? And did this have anything to do with the bomb? Mulling it over, I couldn't immediately see a connection, although I knew that there had to be a connection. Had she left me to work it out?

I wandered round the bungalow, mug in hand, wondering what she was telling me. Had she left all this to me in order for me to find out something significant – something she could never have told me to my face? I sighed at this, then strolled around – although the property was so small, there wasn't much to see. Everything seemed in order. Except . . . that the door of the second bedroom was locked. Why keep the door of a room locked when she was the only occupant of the bungalow? Even for an ex-Bletchley Parker, wasn't that taking things a tad too far? What was in there? I tried one of the keys, but neither fitted. There had to be a key somewhere . . .

With a sudden flash of remembrance, it kicked in that Glenys had mentioned the keys she'd kept in her garden shed. Keys: *plural . . .* This had been such a flippant remark that I'd viewed it, at the time, as unimportant. She'd said that, if someone ever tried to get into her bureau to find her diaries, they'd have a job finding the keys, because they were tucked away in the shed. I hadn't thought a great deal about that until now.

Why hadn't she wanted anyone to read her diaries? What could be in them that might be so incendiary? This was what it was all about, wasn't it? She was telling me to find the diaries because reading them would tell me all I needed to know. My heart suddenly raced. *The key to the Davenport was in the shed!*

And, if that key was there, would the key to the locked room also be in there?

I opened up the shed and hunted around until I finally upended a pot and discovered a small key – but this was not a door key. She'd said *keys,* so there had to be at least one other, didn't there? On picking up several more pots, there it was – a door key, which I pocketed. The smaller one would fit the bureau, I guessed so I walked back into the house to open the large oak Davenport. I can't think why I hadn't noticed before, but I saw with alarm that the bureau had been damaged; someone had attempted to prise open the flap with something sharp, like a screwdriver, which they'd wedged under the sides of the slope, splintering the wood. The Davenport, however, remained closed. Was this why Glenys had been killed? For the contents of this bureau?

I put the key in the lock and opened it up, then stared at its contents, aghast at all the documents crammed into it – mountains of them. Here they all were – Glenys's diaries, all dated and in order, each one filled with pages revealing her neat handwriting. The first was dated 1951. This was where it all began. Her suspicions, even then were obvious: every snippet of information set down in minute detail. I couldn't even begin to make a start. I'd have to go through the lot, I realised, before I'd get any of the answers to my questions, and sighed at the task. So I decided to leave them for when I had a tad more stamina.

I drew in a sudden breath as something stopped me in my tracks. I'd just flicked through a few of the more recent pages, and what jumped out at me raised the hairs on the back of my neck, as my own words screamed back at me. Glenys had recorded every word I'd said to her regarding the Russia assignment. She must have kept it all in her head, and then come back home to write it all down. She hadn't missed a thing. Why would she have done this? Why had it been so important to her to record, almost word for word, our conversation about nineteen-sixties Russia? My heart pounded as I realised that this had been an attempt to tie up loose ends. How many loose ends were there, though? What did she know of that betrayal in Moscow? She'd obviously known something – and it was in death that she'd wanted me to grasp how vital it all was. She'd trusted me – *and me alone* – to trawl through her diaries to discover for myself something that she hadn't been able to tell me. Stunned, I pushed it back in the Davenport and locked it. There was dinner to prepare, the cat to be fed . . . This was for another day.

But I had to open the door to that bedroom – so, the next day, I stood staring at it. It stared back, as though challenging me – daring me – to open it. If Glenys had kept it locked, what might she have been hiding? I sat in her chair and reached for the whisky bottle; I needed fortification before tackling what I might find in that room. Would it answer my questions, and would I be ready for it? A prickle of sweat ran down my spine at the thought of knowing. After all these years . . . knowing . . .

I opened the door.

If the diaries had made my heart stop, there are no words to describe my feelings as I stepped into that room and switched on the light. There were trestles around every wall; trestles which revealed something so obvious that I felt numb, my whole body turning to ice. Words had never failed me before but, of all the languages I'd mastered during the course of my career, no language – *nothing* – was adequate to do justice to the situation, because nothing would ever go near explaining how I felt as I stared at everything laid out on those tables. I simply stood, rigid, as my disorganised brain attempted to take in what my eyes were trying to tell me.

In my head, I heard her laughter.

I took in a deep breath, trying to get my head round it all, and walked to a corner desk, plonking down heavily on an office chair. Above the desk were two cork-boards – one on each wall – covered with photographs; photographs from which I was unable to tear my eyes – the whisky doing little to relieve the shock as I stared at all the faces smiling back at me. I let out a sudden cry of grief, then let the tears fall, as Toni Vascari grinned out; Toni, along with his five comrades, smiling his killer smile – happy and carefree. The photographs of all these men, smiling cheekily at the camera, were pinned side by side; men united in death. And they told me what Glenys knew I was waiting to see.

She, too, had had a camera, for the second board was plastered with photographs of Commander Theodore Kilpatrick, all edged in thick black ink: dozens of them; small, large, in focus and out of focus, in uniform and out of uniform; pictures of him from a young man through to more recent ones in old age. And it was then that I grasped the significance of the locked door, and why all these photographs had been hidden from sight; Kilpatrick had to be the man who had betrayed my lover and had had him killed. Glenys had known that. This was why she'd been so distraught when the bomb she'd sent him had torn Simon Garraway to bits. This was why she'd broken down and whispered that it wasn't right. It all fell into place, and I felt the colour drain from my face.

*Kilpatrick . . .*

Glenys had talked about smelling evil, and I'd smelled it, though not knowing precisely why. And I'd felt strongly enough about the man to take photographs of my own – photographs which I would subsequently add to the cork-board: Kilpatrick tending his garden; Kilpatrick showing off his dahlias; Kilpatrick entertaining his dubious friends. And perhaps the police might be interested, too, in the photographs of the dodgy-looking man being entertained with his equally dodgy-looking wife last September – the same couple Glenys may have seen emerging from Kilpatrick's drive – the man who could well be her killer.

When I'd finally unscrambled my brain to accept it all, I closed my eyes and sat back. For so many years, Glenys Pugh, like me, had been investigating this crime, but she knew she stood as little chance as I of proving anything concrete. She'd latched on to any small crumb and, when I'd spilled the beans about my time in Russia, my story had added to the ammunition already in her possession. And this, I suspect, was when she'd decided to take matters into her own hands. She'd been on the edge of discovery for all those years, and I had told her something which consolidated all her suspicions. And someone, somewhere had got wind of that something – something which would be damaging – and decided she'd be better off dead.

I'd, at first, been so shocked by the discovery of all those photographs that I hadn't fully taken in the contents of the tables. I knew I'd seen it, but my small brain can only take in one thing at a time, and I hadn't been able to tear my eyes away from Toni's laughing face. As I slowly swivelled the chair to face the table's contents, I felt my blood freeze.

The trestles were littered with bomb-making kit. I recognised this stuff from way back in the field: a set of pliers, a soldering iron, a bundle of wire, a tin box, several jars of liquid and one or two boxes of nails. Glenys, I realised, had been half way to making a bomb – a second bomb. I turned back to look, once more, at Toni's smiling face, then silently thanked the woman who had felt the need to avenge his death.

The components lay on the tables, ready to complete a device sufficient to do damage – a great deal of damage. I looked down at it all. Taken one by one, there was nothing out of the way, each item seemingly innocuous – most of it obtainable from a high street chemist or a hardware store. No one would have been suspicious of an old lady buying a box of nails . . . Having infiltrated the houses of bandits where this sort of thing was commonplace, I'd gleaned enough to know that each element on this table would be sufficient to blow someone to kingdom come.

I walked slowly back to the sitting room in a trance, then reached again for the Famous Grouse and to sit in her chair to think. I walked over to the Davenport to rummage through its innards, lifting out diary after diary in order to discover how she could have discovered Kilpatrick's culpability. And there it was: the passing of information to a man in a café. Someone had known. And someone had wanted it kept quiet.

Then I saw the files. Behind the rows of diaries was a pile of files; old and torn and dusty, and all dated; dozens of them, each bearing a single name: *Kilpatrick*. She must have stolen them and, it wasn't until I'd opened them up that I realise why. I took it all out and spread it onto the dining table and, as I read each one, I felt sick – then hot with fury. *The bastard! The putrid, stinking, plague-ridden bastard!* How was it that the contents of these files had not been sufficient to use against this monster? Why was he not rotting in prison? Who else had seen them? Who had been shielding him? *The bastard – the dirty rotten bastard . . .*

I screamed, tears burning my face. I couldn't bring myself to read further, but neither could I put them back; I had to read them. Glenys had left them here for me to read, and, odious as this was, I owed it to her to give weight to what I knew I had to do, even though, at that point, I wasn't quite sure what that was. My eyes were sore, but the full picture slowly emerged as each piece of the jigsaw fitted together. It was all making sense. I hadn't been wrong about the man, nor had I been suffering from delusions of his persecution of me and his pathetic attempt to convince the authorities of my encroaching dementia.

Back in the room, I picked up a list of bomb-making instructions. It was set out like the ingredients for a cake, each item concise: everything needed to construct an instrument of death – along with illustrations; you couldn't go wrong . . . In this room was the whole works. She'd thought she'd got the bastard – then it was delivered to the wrong address . . . The guilt must have torn her to shreds. Her words still rang in my ears: *It isn't right – it isn't right* . . . No, it wasn't right: that bomb should have landed on Commander Theodore Kilpatrick's doorstep, shouldn't it? But that wasn't your fault, my dear friend.

Glenys's concerns about what she saw that day in the café so long ago had been whitewashed – that much was obvious. In her day, women were not listened to; were thought to be too emotional, or hysterical, or feather-headed. She'd been relatively low in the pecking order and, despite having been privy to eye-watering secrets, a mere personal assistant, poking her nose into something she didn't understand, she would never have been listened to. What could she have proved?

And so, Commander Theodore Kilpatrick had risen up the ranks.

Glenys had all but forgotten about it. Until that day in the village Post Office, when she'd heard Kilpatrick's stentorian voice demanding attention – which is when the diaries had restarted.

I was getting down the Famous Grouse at a fairly alarming rate, but had to get back to the diaries and to read everything from beginning to end. Her frustration screamed from the page: who could she turn to? – who could she trust after her boss had vanished . . . ? She was out on a limb and helpless. I felt her frustration and was furious at all the evidence she'd presented – to no avail.

The darkness slowly crept into the house each night and, thoroughly absorbed, I forgot to eat. On the fifth day, as daylight seeped through the edges of the curtains, I drew them back and sunlight flooded the room. A blackbird, perched in an ash at the end of the garden, was singing its heart out. I felt a sudden surge of energy and smiled. I listened to the bird for a few moments longer then, rubbing the back of my aching neck and strolling into the bathroom to wash my face, I made a decision. Wandering into the kitchen to make myself a cup of tea, I formed the outline of a plan, but needed several spoonsful of sugar to set my brain into gear.

Having reached the end of the diaries, I found myself chilled to the bone by the last entry. And it was this which set me on my journey: a quotation from Virgil's *Aeneid*:

> Even when I am gone, I shall pursue you with dark fires. And when cold death / tears my soul from my body, wherever you are my spirit will be there too.

I walked back into the bedroom, reached for my spectacles, then picked up the bomb-making instructions. It wasn't, I discovered, terribly difficult to make a bomb – not nearly as difficult as one might have thought. And half of it had already been constructed – just lying there, waiting to be completed.

Could I do it? Answer: yes.

Yes, Glenys. I will do this for you, my dear friend. And I shall do it for Toni. Kilpatrick deserves to die: in passing information to the Russians, it was obvious to both of us that he'd been instrumental in murdering my lover and all his comrades – and who knew how many more . . . It's been a long time coming, but we will each of us get our revenge. I looked up at the six men in the photograph and smiled. All those young lives snuffed out while the guilty still strut about unharmed. *'Even when I am gone, I shall pursue you with dark fires . . .'*

I locked up carefully then strolled slowly back home as a golden sun was rising above the trees. The air was alive with birdsong, just as my brain was alive with possibilities. Those instructions will still be there tomorrow. There's no immediate hurry. Some day soon, I shall begin the task of finishing what Glenys hadn't had time to complete.

These thoughts kept me happily occupied as I prepared the cat's breakfast and hummed along to a Bach cantata on Classic FM. Some time soon, I thought dreamily, I will call at Broad Oaks and deliver the package myself.

Because, this time, the bomb will most certainly go to the correct address and be opened by the very person Glenys had in mind.